Julian Lees was born and raised in Hong Kong. After attending Cambridge University he worked for ten years as a stockbroker with UBS and Société Générale. Since then he has written two novels: *A Winter Beauty* and *The Fan Tan Players*. Both novels have been translated into German and published by Random House Germany with a third set for release in 2011. *The Fan Tan Players* has also been published in Polish by Proszynski Publishers. Julian currently lives in Malaysia with his wife, Ming, his three young children, Augustus, Amber, and Aisha and his constant canine companion Boobert.

THE FAN TAN PLAYERS

Julian Lees

SANDSTONEPRESS
HIGHLAND | SCOTLAND

First published in Great Britain and Ireland 2010
Sandstone Press Ltd
PO Box 5725
One High Street
Dingwall
Ross-shire
IV15 9WJ

www.sandstonepress.com

First published by Blanvalet Verlag, an imprint of
Verlagsgruppe Random House GmbH,
Germany, in 2008 as DAS LIED DER STERNE.

Commissioning Editor: Robert Davidson

The publisher acknowledges subsidy from the Scottish Arts Council
towards publication of this volume.

ISBN-13: 978-1-905207- 49-7
ISBN-epub: 978-1-905207-50-3

Cover design by
Typeset in Linotype Palatino by Iolaire Typesetting, Newtonmore.
Printed and bound by J F Print, Yeovil, Somerset

CONTENTS

Dedication:

To Gus, Mui-mui and Bay-mui

Acknowledgements:

A number of publications helped me with the historical and sociological aspects of this book. Of the many works I consulted, I would like to acknowledge my debt to George Wright-Nooth's 'Prisoner of the Turnip Heads' and Philip Snow's 'The Fall of Hong Kong: Britain, China and the Japanese Occupation'.

I am deeply grateful to my agent Kate Hordern for her undying encouragement, inspiration and support.

To my parents, John and Sandra, for always being there for me. To Ming, my wonderful wife, for her understanding. To my three cheeky children, Gus, Amber and Aisha, for their love and laughter. And to Boobert for putting a smile on my face every morning.

I would also like to thank Matt (Roland) Cross for planting the seeds of this story and to my old friend Johnnie Hardy for the many happy hours we've spent together on the banks of the Helmsdale River.

PART ONE

Spring 1928

1

Quasimodo Sunday was a spiteful day. With little to dull its power from the Luzon Strait to the Canton coast, the tropical storm roared off the South China Sea and hurtled across the Praya Grande. Whooshing across the face of the sheltered harbour, it flashed silver spears of lighting from keyholes in the sky. Marl white sheets of rain, like iron wires, cracked along the ground, drawing a net over the earth. Gutters overflowed and trenches grew fat with broken timber and shards of glass. Everything smelled of dank soil and up-rooted trees. At noon, the solid mass of thunderheads had crowded the mouth of the bay, bedimming the shrine of the Sea Goddess, A Ma. By the time the temple stores shut, the *pracas* were a wilderness.

When the sky boomed as it did during that spring day in 1928, the mail steamers from the Macao and Canton Steamboat Company remained in the typhoon shelters at the end of wharves; they bobbed their long, lean hulls to the crash of the waves with no other sound to be heard along the Avenida da Republica apart from the rain and thunder. Had it not been for the occasional hoot from a foghorn or the ringing of the storm warning bell in the Chapel of Our Lady Guia, few would have stirred from their preoccupations at all. But then, later that night, the pigs started wailing, and they kept wailing for hours. Not because the greystone walls of the *Matadouro da Macao* were collapsing nor because the abattoir roof was being dismembered by the wind. They squealed with terror because their pens were being overrun

3

by invaders. Blood-eyed troops armed with sword-blade teeth. Rats. Great long files of them that broke like waves on a shoreline. They scrambled from darkened holes, out of the sewers and nullahs. The floodwaters had forced them out. There were thousands of them. And they blew through the streets like a hot firewind.

At the heart of the seafront, the restaurant in the Hotel Riviera, famous for its frescoed ceilings and spicy African Chicken, was overcome with panic. Pandemonium broke out. Voices clashed, bellboys feinted, elderly Macanese ladies shrieked with fright. Shouts of *"Aiyaa!"* and *"Gow Meng!"* reverberated from the top floor suites all the way down to the basement cellars. Some guests, gambling over a game of fan tan, raced about helter-skelter, open-mouthed with animal fear in their eyes. Others leapt onto settees, lifting their flapper dresses, baring their white thighs and tearing at their feather boas. The rats had come crashing through the verandah doors just as the coolie boys were laying strips of towelling into the shutter frames. They sprang from the brass hatstands, onto the art-deco dining tables, atop of Edwardian chiffoniers – knocking down boaters and cloche bonnets, smashing Baccarat crystal, up-ending plates of curried crab and bowls of *brandada de bacalhau*. They scuttled into the *chambres privees*, in and out of giant Vuitton steamer trunks, up jazz suit trouser legs and down silk jacquard curtains. They tore at the lemon enamel hairbrushes, at the sterling silver vanity bottles, at the alabaster rouge pots and dressing table jars. Then, like leaping fish, they were gone, hurling themselves off the balconies into the main street below.

Shortly before nine o'clock at night, the rats reached St Lazaris Church. By ten o'clock, the rat-pack had overrun the north of the city.

In the poorer parts of town, near the Kun Lam Temple, the rodents shot from under the shadows of the shanty huts, darting into homes, up cocklofts, hiding behind wardrobes and under workbenches. They carried the stink of rotted meat and faeces; weeks-old piss matted to the hairs on their spines. Clawed toes, brown as rust, scraped against doors; long-nailed hands dug into soft, barren walls. The vibrations of their feet passed over houses. *Click, clack, click.* Upon rooftops, onto drain pipes. *Click, clack, click.* The rats scurried up the cheekbones of buildings, pressed their snouts under shophouse floors, dangled from telegraph lines. Dogs barked, roosters crowed, women, young and old, screamed. An hour later, Macao, the tiny, dilapidated Portuguese colony, just about connected to the southern tip of the Chinese mainland, thirty-four miles west of Hong Kong, was overwhelmed; the grand old lady of the China coast had been stormed: the grey horde poured in.

By the Largo da Sien there was frantic activity on the cobbled square. It was nearing midnight and a band of wild-eyed rat catchers, covered in oilcloths, directed their dogs with calls and clicks of their tongues. "Hai! Hai!" they shouted as the mongrels went speeding into the darkness, yelping and growling in the distance. The men had set almost fifty baited traps in isolated places; rectangular boxes, three feet deep and about a foot wide made of wood and wire net. They'd filled them with sour bean curd. Each trap had numerous openings on the sides with the wire inverted so that when a rat entered it was impossible for it to escape. The ratters were in the process of setting down more when a bonfire roared to life in the centre of the square. A boy, no more than twelve, stood with his back to the wind, tossing the cages of squealing vermin into the dome of fire, pulling the cages out moments later with an elongated hook. Soon the air, thick with the stink of roasted meat, mingled with the dogs' whinnying and the ratters' shouts. Every fifteen minutes two men dragged a sled loaded with wire cages into the square – a hundred or so rats each time. The process went on through the night.

For a further seven hours the rat catchers carried out their

5

macabre work, until daybreak came and the people of the besieged city began to emerge from their homes to acknowledge the wreckage. All along the *praya* they witnessed the detritus from the storm: telegraph poles bowing their heads, stripped trees with toothpick arms, their branches like broken ribs, metal roofs bent and distended, folded in on themselves, beaches strewn with graveyards of candle-white fish, the short slapping sounds of the surf regurgitating gurgling carcasses of belly-bulging cows, the thousands and thousands of sandflies, the ash-mountains of dead rodents. Everything smelled of wet, mouldy earth and burned animal hair.

Behind the city the storm sewers continued to flush surplus rainwater through 30-inch underground pipes, draining all manner of debris into the catch basin that ran through to the sea. It was here that a pale hand emerged. Creeping, sliding, it edged forward like a stiff-limbed crab through the surf. Fingertips wrinkled and waterlogged, the hand tumbled about, twisting with the violent artificial tidal flow. On occasion it recoiled as the heavy wrist-rope caught on some scrap, only to surge forward again once the tangling was freed.

A moment later a pale-elbowed arm appeared, followed by a head. The waxen, beardless face was stiffly cocked to the left shoulder. Lips, ground shut from contractions, were blue, refusing to open; the throat, swollen like a yellow marrow, was choked with a string of rosary beads. The stubble on the back of the corpse's neck, where a razor had pruned the hair, swayed like tiny weeds, almost fluffy. There was a shard of broken glass imbedded in the flesh of the neck and the bottle-green skin of the sinewy chest was covered in cuts: dog-toothed scars where rats had gnawed through the muscled pectorals.

The water surged again, forcing the rest of the torso through the mouth of the pipe. The body tumbled. Teeth rattled as the head wrested from left shoulder to right.

Eventually, the legs materialized, followed by the knees, chewed and glazed with brushstrokes of pink. A foot flopped out, white as milk; no shoe attached, no flesh, no tendons. Just stark bone.

2

Nearby, looking through the teeming rain, from a spray of light in a basement, a tiny face came to a window and stayed there, looking out through the smoggy glass. The Slavic eyes, blue like the colour of the sea, stared into the darkness like mesmerized buttons. A wicker hoarding belonging to Sun Wing Fotografia was being blown across the sky. It was an advertisement display showing a folding camera with rack-and-pinion focusing, and for a time the tear-bright eyes watched it fly over the ruined facade of the old cathedral, over the labyrinth of passageways that made up the heart of the old city. In the manner of a giant bird it glided and curled across the stuccoed houses with the balustraded balconies, making shadows across the Edwardian-style parlours recently wired for electric light, then fanned out its tail and pitched forward over the Rua Central, descending in a slow tight circle towards the harbour.

The monsoon raindrops tapped on the glass. The young woman remained in front of the window and blanched only fleetingly when something silhouetted and grey pressed past the window only to cut crookedly up a drainpipe. She smoothed her dark hair over her ears and touched the tight skin along her jaw; the pane was black enough to reveal her reflection. The window showed a girl in her late twenties; her face slender, beautiful, slightly frowning. She had eyes so blue they could have been cut from the sky. Exertion had added colour to her cheeks and brought a fullness to her lips. She rubbed the back of her shoulders and dipped her head, revealing an elegant expanse of neck and a shingle haircut that gave her a bob at the front and very short hair at the back. Big and doleful, her eyes returned to the puddles of water that had collected on the floor and with a towel she began mopping up the mess. The water felt cool on her bare toes; she fastened the hem of her low-hipped skirt above the knees – an outfit she usually wore when practising the Charleston in her room – and mouthed the lyrics to a popular American song, removing a ring from her right hand. This was not her normal idea of a Monday morning, but it was something that had to be done.

Against the near wall was a rosewood washstand with a copper basin. The girl turned up her sleeves and got to work. On her left was a zinc bucket. Bits of dirt floated in it. She wrung out the towel and shoved it under the window frame where the wet pools were forming. She was dabbing dry the tiny cracks in the casement when she heard footsteps on the landing. Instinctively her fingers sought the ancient scar-tissue that ran along the flesh of her right arm and she began to roll down the sleeves of her blouse.

Another young woman appeared in the doorway of the linen room at the top of the steps. Her hair was also bobbed, and she wore a loose cotton dress that went straight up and down. In her hand she carried a copy of *Diario de Lisboa* and a moving-picture magazine. She sported rayon stockings with back-seams and her beige shoes were low heeled with a closed toe. The waistline of her dress was dropped to below the hips, giving her a tomboyish look that was made even more masculine by a flattening brassiere. She would have resembled a man almost entirely had her eyebrows not been plucked and pencilled with thin arches. The wood creaked under her weight as she made her way down the stairs. Having negotiated the slippery floor, she immediately busied herself with work, sorting through a basket of pillowcases, sheets and bolsters. She had a little rouge on her bow-shaped lips and, as the fashion of the time dictated, her lower lip was left unpainted, which made her oily Mediterranean skin appear even oilier.

"Covered in mould!" said the girl with the arched brows. She tossed her magazines to the floor, throwing open pages that revealed images of the newly designed Graf Zeppelin airship. She removed a dark cotton slip from the basket; it looked like it was streaked with moss. "This weather! *Merda!* How we're expected to live with damp seeping from the walls and clothes that never dry I'll never know. And now the mail steamers are stranded. I've been waiting to send letters home for days to let them have our change of address."

The young woman at the window smiled politely but did not reply. Instead she kept her head down and squeezed another cupful of water into the tin bucket. She continued humming her tune. There was a slight blush to her cheeks and a small beauty mark on her chin. A few freckles were sprinkled beneath her blue eyes and her hair came to crescent points, kissing her cheeks. She had graceful gestures which matched the elegance of her knife-pleated, low-hipped skirt.

The girl with the painted eyebrows remained silent for a few moments, then announced, "May I introduce myself? My name is Izabel Perera," she said, drawing in a deep breath and speaking quickly. "We moved into the top floor flat last week. We're from Barreiro, just south of Lisbon. It took us thirty-two days to get here. We made seven ports of call en route including Algiers, Aden, Bombay and Colombo – what a filthy place Bombay is, decrepit and full of flea-bitten people. We came on the Peninsular-Oriental Line – spent most of the time on the sundeck, writing letters and sipping beef tea. Nice cabins and very clean, but the food!" She made a face. "Sausages, red cabbage, grilled liver! Not nearly enough fish. The fish in Barreiro is wonderful. Barreiro is wonderful. Have you ever been? It's about six miles from Lisbon and is right on the sea. There's a lovely church square and a red-roofed town hall and beautiful little white houses that look onto the quiet port. I have a big family there, many cousins. I miss them terribly, especially my brothers and sisters and my cousin Anna." There was a short pause as she took another breath. "My husband is in the fabric export business. His office wanted him to start buying Shantung and Chinkiang silks and, because Canton is regarded as the centre of the silk-trading world, we ended up in Macao. What's your name, by the way?"

The girl at the window took a few moments to digest the astonishing amount of information. Eventually she said, "Nadia. My name is Nadia Shashkova."

"Are you the new maid?"

Nadia, conscious of her bare feet, smiled. "No . . . my uncle's the landlord here. We run the tobacconist across the road and rent out these rooms. The previous owner forgot to mention the indoor swimming pool when we bought the place. It happens every time we get a bad storm. Have you met my Uncle Yugevny?"

"No, my husband, Carlos, negotiated the rent." She looked hard at Nadia. "You are not *Portugues*?"

"*Russo*," Nadia conceded.

"But you speak Portuguese. . . ."

Nadia squeezed another cupful into the bucket. "I learnt it at school. Took me a while to master all the swear words."

Izabel laughed at this, causing her olive cheekbones to redden to a carmine velvet. "*Meu Deus*. I'm so sorry. I didn't mean to sound rude, calling you a servant and complaining about the damp walls. In Portugal we are so used to the dryness. Sometimes we don't see rain for months. It's been raining here since we arrived." She watched over Nadia like a protective *pombo* hen as water gurgled from the cracks in the window hinges. "Please, let me help you with that." Izabel grabbed a dry towel, and hitching up her loose cotton dress, squatted on her haunches.

"No, there's really no need."

"I insist," said Izabel. A rivulet of water swelled around

11

her polished beige shoes. She started mopping, glancing at Nadia through her eyelashes. "I like your dress. It's the cat's meow!"

"Thank you."

"Were you born here, in Macao?"

Nadia shook her head. "Russia." She felt impelled to offer a similar level of detail as Izabel had. "In a village near Tver, about two hundred miles south of St. Petersburg. When I was seven we moved to a city called Chelyabinsk, just east of the Ural Mountains, to live with cousins. We lived there for four and a half years until, eventually, my mother and I came here to be with Uncle Yugevny." Her voice trailed away as she watched a tiny snail crawl up the wall.

Izabel got to her feet and picked up the almost-full bucket. She shuffled over to the washstand, weaving through an area crisscrossed with flopping strings of washing, and emptied the contents into the basin. When she'd replaced the zinc pail on the floor she cocked her head to her right shoulder and gave a single slow blink of the eyes. "And your husband? What does he do?" she said.

Nadia couldn't prevent an involuntary flick of the head. "I'm afraid I'm not married," she said cheerily.

"What? A pretty girl like you?"

Nadia smiled, shrugged her shoulders.

"A single Yelena, eh? Just like my cousin Anna. Well that's just *doocky*." Izabel looked fleetingly out of the window, into the brightening sky. "I remember the days when I was single. Full of parties and dancing until daylight. With two little children running my life now it's all a distant memory. Still, Carlos and I set aside a few evenings a month to go out and enjoy a good dance or two. Are you out most nights?"

"No, usually I stay at home."

Izabel made a face. "Sounds terribly dull."

"Dull?" Nadia said.

"Yes, a good-looking thing like you should be out teasing the boys, showing off your new, short hairstyle, your legs, your *garconne* look. That's what being a flapper is all about, isn't it? Being vibrant and enjoying yourself. Before I was married with children I was out all the time. Enjoying *men*." She gave Nadia a nudge with her elbow.

"How do you relieve the boredom?" Izabel asked.

"I read."

"What, periodicals? I love periodicals." Izabel glanced at the magazine on the floor. "I've been reading this wonderful article about the design for the new Zeppelin. They've decided to make a picture show about it. Do you know they're going to print their own on-board newspaper?"

"No, I meant books, mostly modern American novelists . . . Scott Fitzgerald, Sinclair Lewis, Sherwood Anderson. I've just read 'The Sun Also Rises' by a new, young author called Ernest Hemingway. Have you read it?"

"*Merda*, if only I had the time! My children are little monsters. Where they find the energy I simply don't know."

"How old are they?"

"I've got two boys, they're five and six." She paused and gave Nadia a conspiratorial look. "Maybe we should go out. You, me, and Carlos."

"Go out?"

"Yes, to try the local giggle water."

"Giggle water?"

"It's American slang for alcohol. I picked it up from one of the stage show magazines. "

Nadia smiled, looked a little surprised. "There's a strict etiquette of chaperonage in Macao. . . ."

"Phooey!" she said, waving her hand. "Etiquette is for old ladies and pale, skinny men who read Oscar Wilde."

Nadia continued to look surprised; she didn't want to say that she often read Oscar Wilde.

"Well we're a fine pair! Me with two brats and a hoggish husband from Barreiro. You, an unmarried recluse from Russia . . . and here we are mopping up water that belongs in the South China Sea."

Nadia laughed.

"What made you come here? Why come to Macao, of all places?"

"My Mamuchka wanted to be with her brother, my Uncle Yugevny. I think she wanted a fresh start, felt she had to leave Russia, leave the past behind. . . ."

"What year was this?"

"November, 1911."

"Did you come by ship?" said Izabel.

Nadia shook the hair out of her face. "The final part of the journey from Vladivostok was by passenger ship."

"Well that sounds *just doocky!* – that's another American expression by the way – so you arrived in Vladivostok then came here by boat. I bet you had to learn Portuguese pretty quickly. What were the first words you learned, apart from the swear words?"

Nadia smiled at the memory. "Mamuchka and I used to have breakfast in a little Macanese café around the corner. The owner was this tiny man with a huge nose who talked in a high-pitched voice. He's returned to Porto now, sadly. Every morning he'd ask us the same question: would you like your eggs *fritos* or *escaldados*. So the first words I learned were *'Fritos, por favor.'* "

Izabel laughed. "One day you must try my Barreiro omelet. I prepare it with shrimps and sweetened apples." They held onto each other's elbows for support as they rose from the floor. There was a tight clap of churchbells in the distance. The pealing chimes stopped just as Nadia wiped up the last remnant of rain with her foot.

"Seven-thirty already," said Izabel, looking out the window. "The rain has stopped. I'd better wake the monsters." She began climbing the steps. Small flies gave up their places on the stairs as she approached. "It was nice to meet you," Izabel said, placing one hand on the door.

Nadia disengaged herself from the wet towels and looked up into the landing. "If the weather clears there'll be a town parade tomorrow morning, with firecrackers and acrobats. Maybe even a lion-dance. I can take you if you want?"

Izabel paused at the top of the steps and looked at the doorknob. She closed her eyes and gave a laugh that shook her tomboyish hair. "A lion-dance," she said. Her throat made a soft warm sound. "I used to read about lion-dances when I was a child."

"It's a date then?"

"I'll have to ask Mrs. Lo from across the hall to see if she'll look after the children . . ." She nodded. "Yes, all right."

"Afterwards we'll have an early lunch at the café around the corner."

"And watch the acrobats and tumblers perform along the streets." The honeyed thrill of her words spilled down the stairs and settled in ticklish swirls by Nadia's feet.

3

The light was failing by the time Nadia returned from the fruit market. She was very pleased with her evening's bounty. A fresh shipment of Burmese mangoes – Uncle Yugevny's favourite – had come in and she was glad to have snapped up five of them before they'd all gone. She ran, lifting her skirt through the downpour, over the pools of water left by the post-monsoon showers.

The door to her house was dappled and paint-chipped. Nadia squeezed the lapels of her raincoat together and clasped her scarf against the wind. She was standing in mud. Her black shoes, more functional than elegant, dented the springy wet ground, unleashing rude sucking noises with each step. The rain-filtered streetlights made it hard for her to see the keyhole. The stench of the open drains made her want to cover her nose with a handkerchief, but instead she stooped and felt for the keyhole with her fingers. On the third attempt she got the doorknob to twist and open.

The cavernous ground floor was cool and quiet. A crystal chandelier hung stiffly over the tiled floor, and Nadia could see the ubiquitous spiderwebs that mingled amongst the many tiers of glass. She peeled off her coat and removed her shoes, feeling the coolness of the floor on her feet. She wound her way through the still corridor, past the warren of small rooms that led to the shop, rippled shadows of lantern light trailing her every step. Some of the chambers were painted pale yellow, others a bold blue. At the end of the hallway she looked through the door that opened onto the cigar store, into the wood-panelled dusk of the Tabacaria. Her Uncle

Yugevny was closing for the night, putting up the sign in the window, and she heard the clicking of door locks and the scraping of a heavy drawer. Uncle Yugevny had mad-professor hair that prodded out at all angles from his head; it was a look she had grown to love. She gazed briefly at the glass cabinets, the tidy stacks of cedarwood boxes, the cartons of Abdullahs, the teapoy in the corner; she saw the white porcelain jars labeled with Mild Virginia, Zubelda, Spirit of St. Louis, the bell-shaped packets of pipe tobacco, the 20-unit cartons of Fatima, the carved briarwood and corncob pipes that hung from pegs on a revolving stand. She listened with a faint frown of concentration for the metallic fall of the key followed by the forceful closing of the drawer.

"I've got a surprise for you," she said, waiting for him to emerge from the darkness.

"A surprise?" he said, from somewhere within the gloom.

"I have," she said theatrically, "five mangoes from Rangoon, fresh off the boat."

Uncle Yugevny stepped into the light and put a hand on her cheek. He adjusted his glasses and looked into the brown paper bag. "*Fkoosniy*," he said, nodding his head. "*Zamyechateel'niy!* Have you had *oozhin*, supper? You will eat with me?"

"No, I'm exhausted. I was up at five. The typhoon woke me and I was worried about the flooding."

He took the bag from her and scuttled back into the shop. "How is the basement across the road?" he cried. "All dry now?"

"All dry. I met one of the new tenants this morning who helped me mop the floor. Her name's Izabel. She's very nice."

"By the eyes of the *domovoi*, I am glad. Tell me, did the mail sloop come in today? My subscription to Pravda is due. I hear a rumour that Stalin is planning to form collectives throughout Russia. What will happen to the kulaks? The man is dangerous, I tell you."

17

"No, the mail boat is due tomorrow."

"Tomorrow it is then."

"Well, good night, Uncle, *spakoynenawche*," she called, and from within the lamplit dark of the Tabacaria came a reply that resembled the quickly fading cough of a chimney pot.

She climbed the steps to the second floor in the dark. On every sixth stair was placed a poison-box to snare cockroaches. It was a compact, old house; the breaks in its substructure were so ancient they'd been naturally resealed over the decades with compressed grime. There were cracks along the walls and layers of wallpaper that had grown ochreous with time. The floors had been laid with hand-hewn teak planks shipped in from Java. Broader and thicker than any present-day Southern-Chinese oak, it was sturdy enough to withstand numerous resandings. The problem, as Nadia knew all too well, was that it creaked horribly. The spring of the dilating wood beneath her feet often made her feel like a tightrope dancer. She tried to walk now with a light tread, eager not to disturb her mother. But then she heard the singing.

Her mother's bedroom door was open. For a minute, perhaps more, Nadia stood listening to the old world music, surrendering to her Mamuchka's soft voice. She did not want conversation; she was too tired for talk. She just wanted to hear the sounds that made her think of rolling country, fields of wheat and rye and corn, golden-haired village children taking the cows to pasture, dishes of pickles, potato soup, steaming-hot piroshkis. Nadia waited for her mother's voice to trail away, for the Russian folk song to taper off. When things went quiet she lingered in the breathless silence for an additional minute before approaching the door. Treading softly, she entered and saw a spacious armchair in which a large, grey-haired lady was fast asleep, her mouth partially agape, a cluster of knitting discarded on her lap. Nadia removed the long metal needles from her mother's fingers, laid them next to a small bundle of photographs on a coffee table, and covered her legs with a blanket. She looked at the face she knew better than she knew her own. Her Mamuchka's hair, usually fluffy and unruly, was gathered in a bun using a comb and hairpins, and the bridges of her spectacles had slid to the tip of her nose. Nadia's love for her mother was strong. The pride she felt in her little family sifted down on her like silver dust; it brightened her apple-cheeked complexion and squeezed a smile from her eyes.

She looked again at the photographs on the coffee table and for the first time in ages she saw her father. He was standing by a fountain, slouching a little, a straw hat tilted at a rakish angle on his head. Before him, on a stone step, were sitting Mamuchka, grandma and grampapa Petrov, and a little white dog. Their faces were radiant and full of laughter. She stood motionless for perhaps half a minute, then, not wanting to rouse her mother, slipped the bundle into the pocket of her skirt.

Unhurriedly, she moved away. But then she heard her mother speak. "Senhor Pinto, the judge, came to call on you this afternoon," Olga Shashkova said in her pebbled voice, cutting through the silence like gravel. "He's promised to donate HK$80 to the White Russian Widows charity."

"I thought you were sleeping," Nadia said. Under her skirt the photographs pressed like a weight against her thigh.

"*Kto rano vstayot, tomu bog prodayot – God gives to those who wake up early. Anyway, the senhor promised more pledges in the future. He said maybe we should hold a charity ball or a cake bake to raise more money." Olga's eyes remained shut. "He left you a set of embroidered handkerchiefs. Beautiful little butterflies, all satin stitched.*"

Nadia saw his calling card on the bureau with a corner turned down to indicate that he had visited in person. "He must be sixty, Mamuchka."

"Well, you're no spring flower yourself . . . what are you . . . thirty-five?"

"You know very well I'm only twenty-eight."

"*Only* twenty-eight. And just look at that hairstyle! You look like a stable boy from Mtsensk." Mamuchka's eyes were now open, and Nadia saw a hint of mischief in them.

"Must we go through this every time . . ."

"Go through what?" asked Mamuchka.

"Never mind."

"Your father would have wanted you married at twenty. He would have been so proud. . . . I was married at twenty and that was considered old then."

"I know."

"Senhora de Souza across the road says Pinto's annual income as a magistrate is at least fifty thousand patacas." Olga Shashkova looked dreamily at the ceiling. "*Choodeasne!* Imagine what I could do with fifty thousand patacas."

"Buy Senhor Pinto a pair of elevated heeled shoes to start. He only comes up to my shoulder."

"Not his fault that you're tall."

"He's a midget."

"A fit midget, nonetheless."

"How do you know he's fit?"

"He does all that pulling and grunting in his bedroom."

"Pulling? Grunting? What are you talking about?" Nadia sounded moderately shocked.

"Senhora de Souza says he has one of those contraptions in his bedroom. You know, it's secured to the wall and you have to puff and pull and twist, and then it springs back again."

"How would Senhora de Souza know?"

There was a pause. Olga pressed her lips together. "*Bawzhemoy!* I never thought of that."

"Mamuchka . . . I'm not interested in that old mountain goat."

Olga's face loosened. She started laughing, crinkling the wrinkles on the sides of her mouth. "I know, Nadrichka. . . . I'm only teasing. Anyway the old fool should know that giving handkerchiefs causes tears." Nadia glanced at the coffee table, at the empty space where the photographs sat only seconds earlier. "I've upset you," said Olga.

"No you haven't."

"I didn't mean to."

A moment of silence passed.

"I left some food for you in the kitchen," Olga said.

"I'm too tired to eat. I think I'll go to bed."

"But it's not even nine o'clock? You must eat something."

"I was up before five this morning." She leant forward and kissed her mother's cheek.

"Goodnight Nadrichka, *spakoynenawche*."

"*Spakoynenawche*."

In her own room Nadia glanced at the ikon of the Virgin hanging on the wall of the north-east corner, the so-called 'beautiful corner'. It looked heavy and awkward in the dark-gravy light. She bowed to the waist before the image and said a quiet prayer to Saint Nikolai Chudotvorets and to the Holy Mother of God. After crossing herself she pressed her forehead to the cool floor then got to her feet. She thought of her Mamuchka again, how she would sit each day behind the shop counter, playing with her hair, always in a long-sleeved, black organdie dress. "I've sat here for so long," she'd say to customers, "that I think I'm growing roots." Nadia smiled to herself, amused by her Mamuchka's dry humour. Her personality pulled people into the shop like nails drawn to a magnet.

She undressed, pulled on a nightgown and hung up her skirt behind the door. The photographs slid from the pocket and fell onto the floor. She knelt to retrieve them, peering at each as she arranged them into a neat stack. There were pictures of her old house, the gardens, Papashka in his white flannels, Mamuchka in bloomers holding a tennis racquet. She leafed through them one by one, but then stopped when she came to a folded piece of worn paper. It was a letter written in Cyrillic. She'd read the words a hundred times before, but seeing the doctor's signature at the bottom of the letter now filled her with sadness and deep frustration. She squeezed the letter to her breast and then, along with the photographs, pushed the bundle into the bureau drawer and readied herself for bed.

She pulled the chenille bedspread onto the floor, unfurled the mosquito net and climbed under the sheets. She began thinking about her mother again. If only, Nadia thought, she could find herself a man that she liked. It would please Mamuchka so much. She remembered all the high-hatted and high coloured suitors who used to arrive at a rate of one every fortnight – that was when she was in her early twenties. Things had tailed off considerably since then. It had been assumed by her Uncle Yugevny that Nadia would marry, but the Carvalhos, Ferreiras, Redondo-Wongs and da Fonsecas, to name but a few, had bored her, stifled her even. She had rejected them all, discarded the idea of marrying them as one discards a fountain pen when it draws dry of ink. Was she capable of mending lace curtains? They'd asked. Did she know how to cook *arroz de polvo*? Or *rabanadas*? Could she prepare sardines stuffed with crab? Did she know anything about raising a family? Did she worship Our Lady Santa Ana or attend catechism class? Had she ever been to Lisbon? Nadia's replies to these questions had always been a firm no. Yet despite the fact that she couldn't do any of this Portuguese housewifery, they still pursued her.

It took a few months of puzzled conversation with Uncle Yugevny before Nadia realized that she simply did not want to marry. She liked men; she liked talking to them, looking at them, even occasionally kissing them, but everything beyond that was out of the question. She put it down to some psychological block; something to do with what she'd witnessed in Tver when she was a little girl, something she had seen on the night of the great fire – she carried with her a mental image of a brutal ambush, a ferocious assault – and it left a deep, complex scar. And now it was abundantly clear to everyone who resided around the Largo da Sien that the pretty Russian girl with the short-haired flapper look and the sea-blue eyes would forever be single.

If only, Nadia thought, pulling at the mosquito netting above her head, she could meet someone who reminded her of Papashka. Someone with his strength, his kindness, someone who could make her feel alive with joy. Maybe then she would reconsider marriage. And for that she was prepared to wait. Who cares if I'm almost thirty, she thought, if a man can't give me what I want in life then I'll simply stay home and quietly run the Tabacaria. To hell with these *gloopee* Macanese bachelors and their garlic-stuffed shrimps! To hell with black olives and authentic Portuguese cooking! Give me borsht and vegetable *goluptsy* any day! Nadia exuded a deep, long sigh, suddenly deflated. I'm twenty-eight, she thought once more, and my life has reached a dead end.

For a while Nadia lay on her back, staring at the cracked plaster lines on the ceiling, then, feeling her body finally relax, she bit her lip gently and closed her eyes. She dug into a pocket of her nightgown and furled her small fist over something the shape of a crown; a piece of cloudy glass, weathered and smooth, the colour of aquamarine syrup. It was a keepsake, a lucky charm given to her by her father. The edges were rubbed soft. She felt the polished, fluid texture in her palm. Held it to her mouth.

A heavy rain had started again outside. The emptiness of the night presented itself to her. She considered getting out of bed and scrubbing the bathroom walls, cleaning the sinks, but thought better of it. She pulled off her nightdress and imagined the sheets of water that lashed at the windows were soaking her, dousing her, cleansing her of something.

Unclothed, on the edge of sleep, curled into a ball, she started to dream. A smell of scorching filled her thoughts. Pine cones exploded. Stone walls glowed. The sun disappeared beneath a sawtoothed layer of black cloud. No sooner had the images appeared behind her eyes than Nadia found them quickly fogging up, like breath on a mirror. Somewhere in the back of her dreams she began remembering – a yellow manor house, an estate deep in the forest, misty lean skies, bowls of lumpy *gogol-mogol* pudding, and, high in the trees, jewel-eyed blackbirds pushing their blue wings against the wintry air.

4

When Wednesday morning arrived the sky was a crisp pink and the veins of pale cloud on the horizon resembled streaks of light in an over-exposed photograph. It was eight o'clock and Nadia was standing in front of her uncle's shop looking at the pistachio-shaded fąade, the display bow window and the sign above with the emporium's name – Fillipov Taba-caria. The colonial-style, three-storey building was looking even more ramshackle than usual, she thought. The black wooden shutters on the second floor looked broken and the balcony on the third floor appeared to be sagging more than ever.

She breathed in the tired post-monsoon air, heard the sound of passing rain on leaf, on the broad palm leaves in the Largo da Sien. Close by, she could see activity in the Senate Square. The curator and his minions were busy opening the doors and gates to the art gallery, courtyard garden and library. Just a minute earlier, she'd been watching the coolies digging into the clogged-up storm gutters with their emery-grey hands, and counting the lines of children returning to school. She could still smell the stench of the open drains. She covered her nose with a handkerchief and waited for her new friend, Izabel, to appear.

From the main road, through the colonnades, Nadia could see Senhora de Souza in the window of her dress boutique purposefully fastening corsets to mannequins. Inside, she knew, there would be drawers full of rayon bloomers, picoted lingerie, chiffon hose. Turning, Nadia saw that, in the hair salon opposite, a Chinese girl was having her braids touched up with tassels of silk, and by the tea-houses she spotted a couple of men chattering to their pet songbirds, tilting their bamboo cages in return for a tune.

Across the road, Izabel emerged from the darkened interior of her low-rise apartment building. She was wearing a sleek, loose-fitting dress, the same beige shoes with the closed toe and pale cotton stockings turned down to the knees; in her hand she carried a furled white-laced parasol. Nadia looked down at her own dark shoes, at the bare flesh between her socks and skirt – she knew Izabel was going to roast in such thick stockings and wondered why she wasn't wearing her rayon ones. She wanted to say something but felt that she didn't know her well enough to give advice. She watched Izabel sniff noisily at the air and rub her eyes, wondered whether her Mediterranean body clock took time to adjust to the subtleties of morning.

"*Bom dia,*" Izabel said, taking in a large gulp of air then proceeding to choke on it. "Sorry I'm late. I had to drop the children off with the lady across the hall."

"*Alo,*" said Nadia. "The parade's already started."

Izabel nodded. They began to stroll from the smart boutiques of the Avenida de Almeida Ribeiro, through the arcaded sidewalks, towards the Rua Central. All around them they saw brightly painted shop signs made out in Portuguese and Chinese characters. Nadia began to point them out one by one. To the left was the Ming Fung Mercearia and Yu Chong Hing's Dentista (picturing a cartoon hippopotamus with a great maw of pink gums and white teeth), to the right the Barberia Li & Lo with its turning blue-and-red pole. Because of the heat, the doors to each was open agape and Nadia could see framed portraits of Cheng Kai-shek on the walls, often next to ones of King Manuel II, the last of the Portuguese monarchs.

Nadia introduced Izabel to Senhora de Souza, who was still struggling with a mannequin, and then, a little further down the road, they encountered an egg distributor called

Carlos Ferreira, whose business comprised of three types of eggs – the ordinary kind with chalky pale shells, a second type which seemed to have been wrapped in strips of grass and straw and immersed in dried clay, and finally black-onyx-coloured ones with a translucent tar-like coating.

Izabel grimaced at the black eggs, held her tongue.

"Tastes fine if you douse them in vinegar and rice wine," Nadia said, turning away to smile.

They pushed into an alleyway filling up with people. The narrow *travesa* smelled of linseed oil and wet, old vegetables. Shoeless urchins kicked a feathered shuttlecock up in the air, striking it with the soles of their feet. Professional letter writers took dictation from their clients. Nadia and Izabel carried on walking through the bright and tawdry festive market. The air bent again with new and curious perfumes. From here there came a smell of joss sticks and burned paper offerings, from there the quite startling aromas of fried eels and rancid bean curd.

"Which way?" asked Izabel. Perspiration beads were forming on her brow and upper lip.

"Follow me," said Nadia, taking her hand. And from somewhere high above, on a second or third floor balcony, came the clap, the resonant tile-on-wood slap of mahjong playing.

"It is like two worlds that have collided headlong," Izabel said, as she spied an old Cantonese lady on the street corner reading a week-old copy of the *Jornal Acoriano Oriental*. Next to her an elderly Portuguese man was sucking on a crescent of Chinese pomelo, checking out the headlines over the old woman's shoulder. "You know," said Izabel. "I still find it amazing how 15th century Portuguese traders managed to get here from Europe."

They walked past a group of ear-cleaners who were setting up their stalls, lining up bottles of ethanol and home-made wire plungers.

"Even more amazing," Nadia said, "when you think how

successful they became in China. Within fifty years of first arriving, the Portuguese were doing such brisk business all along the Chinese coast that they made a deal with the local Mandarins making Macao their base. It was only once they signed the treaty that the Portuguese ships began arriving in force from Goa, overloaded with all kinds of things."

"Such as what? Indian cotton?"

"Silver inlay from Arabia, African Ivory, cinnamon from Malacca, rhinoceros horn from Java, and all sorts of European merchandise. After that, for a few years anyway, Macao became one of the wealthiest places in the world. Now it is just a dilapidated old city full of girls, gambling and opium."

"How on earth do you know all that?" said Izabel.

"I told you, I like to read."

A man on a bicycle rattled past, eyelids skipping on the cobblestones; a block of ice was propped on his handlebars on its way to one of the hotel bars. He bellowed at the crowd to make way.

A little further on, the girls paused at a street market. Amahs in white tunics and housewives in cloth pyjama-suits jostled to see what chicken feet or pig entrails the butcher might be selling on the cheap. Raw meat hung from hooks, live quails trilled from bamboo cages, dried-seafood merchants displayed triangles of sharks' fin and cuttlefish. Some of the housewives shouted out their orders in Cantonese, others cried out in pidgin-Portuguese.

A Chinese man with a round straw hat was placing row upon row of dried salted fish onto rattan mats. Their skins resembled crinkled tree bark, or the hide from some ancient elephant. *"Bacalhau,'* said Izabel. "Dried cod, just like you find in Lisbon." There were baskets of tiny whitebait too, while lines of ogre-faced ling fish hung from footpath rails. She shook her head disbelievingly. "What you must have thought when you first arrived here from Russia . . . I can't imagine. Was your father in the diplomatic service? Is that why you came?"

"No. My mother and I travelled alone."

"Alone? What was your mother thinking?"

Nadia's eyebrows knotted at the carelessness of the remark. "Unfortunately," she said, "we had no choice. My Uncle Yugevny came to collect us when we reached Irkutsk, near Lake Baikal." She stopped abruptly.

"Sorry, I didn't mean to pry. Have I upset you?"

Nadia shook her head. There was a silence. "No," she eventually said. "You haven't upset me." But the fine lines around her eyes had deepened.

A group of sun-tanned children came barging into them, caught up in the excitement of the market. They were laughing and giggling. Nadia remembered it being like this in Russia – when aged five, playing in her garden, her arms and legs as brown as a gypsy, her chest full of laughter.

Neelzya, she heard herself say, trying to sweep the memories aside, but the images kept coming, and once again she saw the scattered fields of barley, the thatched cottages and the winding country lanes. There were silver firs and mountain ash that veiled the hills, sandy paths where cattle boys drove herds to water. She recalled the chattering birds that played in the trees and the molehills on the lawn that drove her father to despair and the pine smells of the forest that carried through to the house on gusty days, bringing with it the wet-earth aromas of the soil and the summer fragrance of freshly picked cotton.

The house sat beside a pond with a thin pebble surround, set back among a grove of spruce and pine, fifty yards from a mountain stream, pale against the darkness of the hills behind. Nadia remembered that there used to be a fountain, skirted by lawnchairs, spluttering in the front garden, while in the back garden a vestibule and paved courtyard looked onto pear and apple orchards planted against the slope. There was a dovecot with windows shaped as crescent moons and stars. She used to call the daisies curling in the flowerbeds 'her drowsy old gentlemen' and the blackbirds in the trees her 'shiny-beaked ladies'.

Izabel's smile, fixed at first, shrank from her face. She lifted her hands apologetically, as if in a gesture of peace. "I'm sorry if I said something wrong."

Nadia glanced around at the faces of the crowd. The children had vanished. She felt a physical hollowness in the pit of her stomach. "Wrong?" she said, blinking quickly. "No, sorry, I was just daydreaming." The childhood memories faded, leaving her with a feeling of grief and remorse. Grief at what she had lost and remorse at what she had failed to do all those years ago. Looking at the sky she remembered the charm her father had given her mere days before the fire, and the words he had whispered in her ear; she had learnt the words off by heart: *The problem with us Russians is that we spend all our time reminiscing and forget about the present. We must love what we have now before it has vanished forever.*

Nadia shook her head slightly to clear her mind. She heard a sudden stir of activity and pointed towards a mass of colour and movement. "Over there, Izabel. Look! The parade!"

The clash of cymbals and the thud of cudgel on drum carried clear in the damp air. Commotion was everywhere. People walked along the top of roofs to gain a better view. Children swarmed along the front of the road – there were gongs and discs and acrobats stripped to the waist holding swords that glinted in the feeble sunlight. Three lions made out of bamboo and papier mache cavorted to the cymbal and gong melody. The lion heads were as large as wine vats: they had red, fleece-lined mandibles and round, protuberant eyes. The drums followed the lions; the cymbals followed the drum-players and the stilt-walkers followed everyone else. The huge eyelashes of the lions blinked and fluttered to the rhythm of the throbbing noise as its torso pounced and weaved in rapacious rage. A wailing toddler grew separated from her parents and squatted on the ground, covering her head with her hands for protection. It was a holiday crowd that had come in from the villages of Coloane and Taipa to celebrate the festival. The din of the lion dance grew louder.

Nadia had to cup her hand over Izabel's ear to make herself heard. "Let's move closer to the temple," she cried. A latticework of bamboo scaffolding enveloped some of the bigger buildings. The tall structure of the Taoist temple only served to catch the noise and throw it back at them – the laughter of the multitude, the sharp bangs of the sparklers and pinwheels exploding, the manic tinkling of pedicab bells. "See that over there . . ." said Nadia, "that's what the Chinese call Big Step Street."

"Strange name for a street."

"There's no tree cover here. When it gets really hot in the summer the barefooted rickshaw boys have to race through as fast as they can otherwise the soles of their feet get burnt."

Izabel stooped and grazed the ground with her fingers. "Feels like a furnace already."

They went into the *praca*, a vast square area flagged with shiny pale cobblestones. Around its edge were hundreds of people watching the show that took place at its centre; men wearing dragon-heads cavorted and whirled, clutching reptile tails made of teak; women handed out decorated parcels of long-life rice. Gymnasts from the various martial arts schools were performing feats of strength and agility. Their muscled arms were adorned with sandalwood paste as they formed human pyramids and snapped wooden boards with their fists. Long strings of firecrackers exploded, filling the square with choking smoke, and a band made up of trawler fishermen played unmelodious Cantonese music using bizarre wooden instruments.

After half an hour the parade moved on, down towards the Praya Grande, passing the gates of the Hospital S. Lourenco. Nadia noted the air was beginning to smell as the morning sun intensified and she could see that Izabel's face had pinkened from the heat. The sulphureous stink of firecrackers competed with the stench of the nearby soy sauce factory, where vats of condensing soya beans were putrefying in the open air. She leaned forward and placed the back of her hand against Izabel's shoulder. She noticed that Izabel was staring at a rattan basket hanging outside the hospital gates.

"What is that?" asked Izabel, lines etching into her face.

Nadia looked at the basket. A palm leaf was fastened over it to shield its contents from the elements.

"An abandoned baby."

"What do you mean, a live baby?"

"Yes."

"But it will die in this heat."

"Sometimes the hospitals will take them in . . . other times not."

"How can you sound so nonchalant about it?"

"In China there are baby towers where infants are thrown to their deaths. It happens all the time. At least here, with the hospital, there's a chance the baby may survive. You get used to it, I suppose. It's hard to change what's ingrained in their culture."

"Nonsense!"

All of a sudden Izabel was pale. Her forehead was crumpled and frowning. She raced up to the gates and pulled the basket down, dislodging the rope that secured it to the metal bars. But the pannier was empty.

"I don't understand?" said Izabel, blinking into the sunlight.

"Perhaps the hospital people took the baby inside."

"Perhaps . . ." said Izabel with a nod. She shut her eyes and let out a breath, gently running her fingers along the lining of the basket.

"Would you like a break?" Nadia said. "Let's go somewhere quiet for a cup of tea."

They descended the large stepping stones into the Rua de St. Lourenco, their ears ringing with noise. The town fell away below them, a hodgepodge of red-and-yellow tiled roofs angling down to a shimmering chocolate-coloured sea. Sailing junks passed gracefully, tacking along the inner harbour waterfront, their burnt-sienna masts leaning away from the wind. Dockside activity was minimal. Away from the festival, the city had changed tempo. There was an undertow of langour now, merged with a certain thirst-provoking world-weariness; a type of tropical inertia. This was the Macao Nadia was used to, the Macao she liked. The *travesas* grew sleepy, the street life laconic and slow. Frayed clotheslines hung slack. Coolies sat on rickety-looking walls, puffing blue smoke through bamboo pipes. An aged lady washed her cabbages on the steps of her front door as her husband slumbered in a wicker chair.

Nadia found the café she was looking for - a little *cha lau* with a sprawling white verandah and views of the Pearl River estuary. The two women found a table in the shade, where the breeze cooled their slender arms and an adventurous sparrow hopped about feeding on crumbs. They ordered iced mint tea with limes and sat amongst the working men having their breakfasts of chorizos and congee and assorted dim sums. The cold tea arrived with icy droplets of water sliding down the outsides of the glass tumblers. Toast and fried eggs made their way along the table. And when they shared stories about their lives they spoke as if they'd known each other for years.

A man with red hair sat nearby with his shoulders hunched and his elbows on the table. He was reading a copy of the *South China Morning Post*, a Hong Kong newspaper, and perspiring profusely. Nadia's eyes returned to him from time to time, deeply engrossed as she was in her conversation with Izabel. Once, she thought she caught him looking over at them, but the man looked away quickly, his eyes shining. When she was done eating her toast, she offered him a sideways glance only to find that he had gone, leaving a small roll of one pataca banknotes as payment for his coffee.

Nadia shrugged and her gaze returned to Izabel.

"I simply cannot forget what they are doing to those babies," Izabel said. "It's horrible. Nadia, we must do something to help them."

5

Nadia had an unsuspicious nature and it would never have occurred to her that she was being watched at the *cha lau*. It was only when the same red-haired man came into the Tabacaria the following day with a roll of one pataca bills, wanting to buy a carton of Lucky Strike, did she think that there was something familiar about him, and something peculiar too. To start with, his voice – all chopped vowels and abrupt syllables – was unimaginably exotic. He spoke Portuguese in a way that she had rarely, if ever, heard before. She could hear a distant land in his voice; there was a ruggedness, a gravelly, chalky earthiness to his tone. It made her think of rain-rinsed sand.

"Can you recommend a mild tea-towel?" he said, having paid for the Lucky Strikes.

What an odd question, she thought. Nadia shrugged her shoulders and repeated the word, *"Chatoalha?"* – tea towel?

"Sim, chatoalha."

"The fellow's an idiot." Uncle Yugevny said in Russian from across the room, his mad-professor hair sprouting from his head at all angles. "By the eyes of the *damovoi*! Last week he was in here looking to buy a dozen kettles!"

"Don't get excited, Uncle Yugevny. Remember your heart."

"Excited? This nincompoop wants you to recommend a mild tea-towel and you tell me not to get excited?" As he said this, his glasses steamed up and he had to wipe the lenses with his thumb.

"Do you mean *charuto*?" Nadia suggested to the man.

"Sim, sim, charuto," exclaimed the stranger, at once pointing at a set of cigars.

Nadia could not take her eyes off him. She saw a man in his early thirties with turbulent red hair, short-clipped with a side parting, and lean, pale cheeks that were only very slightly freckled.

"My name is Sutherland," he said in Portuguese, pushing back his head to reveal a flushed face with dark, sun-kissed eyes. "Iain Sutherland. Sorry, my accent's bloody awful."

"Don't worry. You're just a little off-key."

"Do you speak English?"

"I do," said Nadia. "But I'm a bit out of practice."

"Thank God for that," he said, reverting to his mother tongue. "'Fraid I never managed to get my head round Portuguese. It's like learning to speak Gaelic backwards."

He stood between the rosewood glass cabinets; there was an exotic scent of orange peel and rose water lifting off his flesh. Nadia gazed at him with a puzzled look. "So, how may I help you?" she asked.

"Aye, well, I was hoping you could help me choose a cigar, something not too strong in flavour."

She approached a row of patterned cigar boxes from Cuba and selected a petit corona for his perusal. "I can recommend Hoyo de Monterrrey," she said. "Subtle and mild, it can be enjoyed at any time of the day."

Sutherland held the cigar under his nose between thumb and index finger. The cream collar of his shirt was a little loose against his neck. Nadia could see the dappled patina of heat rash on his ivory throat. "Smells of cedar trees and moist coffee beans," he said. He was staring at her with such familiarity that she had to lower her gaze.

"If you find it too overpowering I can show you a Cifuentes which is a much lighter smoke." She ran a finger lightly across the counter.

"No, this'll do fine," he said. Nadia smiled against her will. She didn't find him especially handsome, yet there was something engaging about him, particularly when the light caught the whitewood edge of his cheeks.

He leaned his elbows on the counter, amongst the boxes of cigars; on either side of his arms stood two lamps, holding thick, red lampshades. The only other light came from dim bulbs from the four corners of the room and a stain of sunshine that radiated through the display bow window.

"So," he said. "Do you live here?"

Nadia sat down on a stool opposite him, "Why do you want to know?"

"Cos there's a Tarzan film on at the Dom Pedro and I don't feel much like going alone."

"My mother's free. I'm sure she'll go with you."

He smiled. "But I'm asking you."

"I don't know you."

The ceiling fan rotated languidly, made soft clicking sounds, cooled the backs of their necks. The silence filled the room.

"So is that a no?"

"It's a no."

Sutherland sighed. "How embarrassing." He slipped the cigar into his jacket pocket and looked at his hands. "I suppose I ought to be going then."

A tall, middle-aged lady with a good figure entered the shop. She asked for a box of matches and a packet of Richmonds. Nadia served her and placed the change on the counter. She returned to stand by the rosewood cabinets.

"What's your name?" asked Sutherland.

"Nadia," she said.

"Nadia what?"

"Nadia Sviazhsky Shashkova."

"Na-di-ahh," he repeated.

She laughed. "You say it as if you're gargling with pins."

"I'll have you know that pin-gargling is a very respectable past-time in Scotland. My cousin Murdo was the pin-gargling champion of Troon."

Nadia laughed again. "Are you some sort of crackpot?"

"Aye," he said, smiling back. "Oh, I almost forgot, maybe you can help me. I'm supposed to be meeting a Senhor

Lazar. . . ." He dug his hand into his trouser pocket and pulled out a torn piece of paper. "He lives at number 16 Rua dos Mercadoda . . . Mercadala. . . . God how do you pronounce it?"

"Rua dos Mercadores."

"Aye, thank you. Do you know which house number 16 is?"

"Not only do I know the house," said Nadia. "I've been inside it."

"Oh?"

"Senhor Lazar is my uncle's brother-in-law."

"Really?"

"Uncle Yugevny was married to Senhor Lazar's sister. It's the reason Uncle Yugevny settled in Macao. Auntie Amelia's dead now, sadly."

"I'm sorry."

"Anyway," Nadia said. "Rua dos Mercadores is the next road down on the left."

"Will you be in tomorrow?" Sutherland asked. "Around say ten o'clock?"

"I might be," she replied. Her breath was taut and high in her throat.

"Want to catch the early showing of Tarzan and the Golden Lion?"

Her heart quickened. She smiled. "I already told you, no."

"Perhaps we can go out dancing sometime," he said, replacing the hat on his head. "Can you do the Charleston?" He bent and straightened his knees, kicked out a heel.

"I love the Charleston," she said.

"So shall we go out? There's a good Filipino band at the Rex."

"No."

"Your mother's very welcome to join us as a chaperone." He looked round and tilted his hat at Nadia's mother who had recently appeared in the shop. "Oh, I forgot. Flappers don't call it chaperone. What's the word you like to use?"

Nadia paused. "Fire-extinguishers."

"Aye, well, your mother's welcome to join us as a fire-extinguisher."

"I don't think that would be a good idea, but if you want to get into her good books you can make a donation to the White Russian Widows charity." She scraped a tin box across the counter. "We send what we collect every year to an organization in Shanghai."

Iain dug into his pocket and dropped some coins into the slot. "Well, some other time maybe." He crossed the room and walked out of the shop through the glass-tinted double doors, allowing a delicate white light to flood through the shop. After he had gone, Nadia was sure the room lingered with an exotic perfume of orange peel and vetiver oil. His smile had made her grip the sides of the counter firmly. She suddenly felt an overriding urge to start cleaning things; she decided to go and scrub the bathroom floor.

Iain Sutherland returned the following morning armed with a small bouquet of flowers for Mamuchka. He went and stood in front of the counter and looked at Nadia who was standing behind the cash register. "Come closer," he said, leaning forward on his elbows.

"Come closer?" she said.

"Aye. What's your name? Nadia?"

"Yes." She folded her arms over her chest.

"You want a dram of whisky, Nadia?" He removed a hipflask from his jacket.

"No!" she said. "Not especially."

"The thing is," he said, "we were going to have this official dinner at the embassy on June 3rd to celebrate King George's birthday . . ." He cleared his throat. "And I didn't know who to invite."

Nadia smiled nervously.

"And I was thinking maybe you would have liked to come. But the dinner's now been cancelled."

Nadia didn't say anything.

"What would you have said if, say, the dinner was still on?"

"I would have said no."

She turned to replace some cigar boxes on the shelf.

"Don't turn away. Come closer. We're too far apart to talk."

She leaned forward on the countertop.

"What about tea? You girls like tea."

"Mr. Sutherland, I don't want to go out with you."

His little finger reached out and tickled her forearm. "Tea with honey? You like honey, don't you?" He started laughing. It was a wicked, hushed laugh that made her smile involuntarily.

"You know, there's something very wrong with you," she said.

"Aye."

"You appear to be trying to toy with me. Are you?"

"Am I?"

And for the best part of an hour he tried to persuade Nadia to join him for lunch. When she refused, he winced and promised to be back. The next afternoon he arrived with a tin of Scottish biscuits from Nairn, and twenty-four hours later appeared with a phonograph record, a 10-inch seventy-eight, by a man called Jimmy MacKay. Uncle Yugevny removed it from its paper sleeve and played it on his 1921 Brunswick. It turned out to be accordion music performed by a one-legged man from Oban.

"What do you think?" said Sutherland, doing a little jig.

"It's a little grating . . ." Nadia said. She didn't mind the music so long as the man from Oban didn't sing. At one stage she was sure that the accordionist had trodden on a cat.

"You should hear him on the bagpipes . . . tremendous!"

"Don't you have any records by Ethel Waters or Bessie Smith?" she asked, feeling besieged.

When Iain left the shop he blew her a kiss and touched her chin with his fingertips. Her lips parted and began to itch. She felt as if they'd become enamelled with turpentine.

6

A fortnight had passed since the heavy downpours of Quasimodo Sunday, and when he wasn't in the Tabacaria, Iain Sutherland was entrenched in the airless office on Avenida da Republica, which he shared with his Chinese assistant, Peter Lee.

The hot, steamy air of summer filled the streets. The sound of cicadas mushroomed over the ruined church of St. Paul's, and from the line of Banyan trees on the promenade the sparrows began to call. It was the first morning in weeks that it hadn't rained and the sun, white-rimmed and severe in the sky, was burning off the moss, the lichen and the pools of scummy water from the lanes.

Seated at his clerical desk, under a fan, Iain peered fixedly at a set of nautical charts of Hong Kong and Macao's waterways. The charts were pinned to the walls by the window and were encrusted with red and pink tacks. The red pins indicated known drop-off points, the pink ones make-shift jetties where sampans and walla-wallas picked up their illicit cargo. Not for the first time, Sutherland noticed that the maps were beginning to grow yellow with mildew.

Since the weekend, Iain had started a new routine. He'd arrive at his office in the British Consulate at first light, produce a small notebook from his desk, light a cigarette and stare for over an hour at the words TOBACCO, CODEINE, MORPHINE, OPIUM, and PAPAVERINE at the top left-hand corner of the chalk board. No one else he knew had his ability of concentration, of keeping so still, of working systematically through a problem, as one might explore a new, yet dangerous, puzzle. Every surplus thought, distraction, smell, sound, mood was pushed aside to tackle the obstacle at hand. The room became a closed world, his secret hideaway. Under the heading SMUGGLERS' ROUTES, he would scrawl the names of people, their organizations and their locality, with question marks beside each one.

Today he wrote the letters L-A-Z-A-R in thick, white chalk. Beside it he added *floating body*, *skeleton foot*.

"Why you come into office so early last few days?" said Lee, typing furiously, not raising his eyes. "I work for you over one year and you never come in to office so early." He attacked the keys with nine of his ten digits, the little finger on his left hand useless and broken since childhood, sticking out at an ugly right-angle.

Iain paused, long enough to light another cigarette, before walking to the far end of the room. Once there, he turned back and paced slowly towards the chalkboard, never taking his eyes off the scribbled letters. *Lazar*, he said to himself with each step, *Lazar*, *Lazar*, *Lazar*. Now, nearing his target, he trusted that his intuition would reveal something insightful, something overlooked. But nothing materialized; at least not yet. Sutherland noticed most things; it was just that some things didn't register until later.

"You have unsoemiac sickness, *lo baan*? Cannot sleep?" asked Lee.

"Army training. I always rise early. Also, I'm getting these migraines . . ."

"You were in army?"

"Royal Scots Dragoons."

"Hey! Me dragon too. I born in 1905. Same you too?"

"Be quiet, you ninny." Sutherland approached the chalkboard one more time. He glared at the name, rolled the l and the z around on his tongue. He consulted his notebook, selected a pen from his inkstand, and made a few jottings in the margin. Then he heard a loud knock on the door.

"What do you want?" he demanded.

"Mail deesh-patch from Hong Kong, from Breetish Colonial Department," said a snub-nosed, sway-bellied man leaning against the doorcase, a straw hat held by his side.

A purplish shadow fell across the brass plate on the door; the words 'Passport Control Office', the SIS operative's overseas cover, grew distorted in the billowing light. Sutherland kicked a rush-bottomed chair towards the man with the boater. "Take a seat, Costa, and keep your mouth shut. Lee, please leave us."

Costa raised an eyebrow slightly. "Bad mood again, *Vermelho*?" he said, handing Sutherland a brown package and letters embellished with British postage stamps. Both men sat as Lee left the room and closed the door behind him.

Sutherland recognized the handwriting on the letters, and the wax-stamped seal on the brown package, embossed with a royal crown underpinned by a lion and a unicorn, belonged to Government House. He noticed the wax seal had been broken on the package and threw it beside the Remington typewriter. "Have you been reading my mail again, Costa?"

"Naturalmente."

"Why can't you keep your fat fingers out of my things?"

Costa lifted his shoulders, let them fall. "It's a seeckness, I think. I can't help myself."

Iain pinched the skin between his eyes and shook his head. "Well go on then, tell me what it says."

Costa reached over and removed a few sheets of paper from within the brown parcel. "I have here the fortnightly Confidential Report," he announced.

"Yes, I know, you fool. Read me what it says."

"You want me to read it to you?"

"Aye."

"In Eenglish?"

"No, you bloody twit, in Swahili. Of course in English!"

Costa gave a groan then cleared his throat noisily. "It says that there's been fall in opium prices," he said tentatively, blinking hard at the words. "The price of the colony's opium, shold through the Hong Kong government monopoly, ish falling because of illegal shupplies. The Breetish Colonial Department estimates opium to account for only 11% of the government's total income for the year."

"A drop of 3% from last year," said Sutherland. He shook his head. "Clementi's not going to be pleased. The monopoly's meant to be managing the traffic. With His Majesty's Government so reliant on official opium revenues, it's no wonder he's cracking down on smuggling."

"Internal reports show shmuggling shindy-cates are thriving. Illicit trade valued at Hk. Tls 135,000 is thought to have been brought into Hong Kong seence Chinese New Year. And seex weeks ago, 2000 catties of a tobacco/opium mixture, packaged in bundles, was intercepted by the Hong Kong Police in a swoop in Wanchai. They shuggest that the contraband material ish coming through from Macao." Costa stopped talking, wiped a lustrous bead of sweat from his cheek.

"And?"

"And what?"

"Why have you stopped?"

"My Engleesh. It's not so good. It's tiring for me to read like this, *Vermelho*."

"Stop whining, you great lump, and get on with it!"

Costa made a sour face and lowered his eyes to the sheets of paper. "It says here seex names are extracted from those that are arrested. One, a Mr. Takashi, ish a Japanese entrepreneur with hotel and gaming interests; he hazh already been brought in for questioning and ish on remand. Intelligence information indicates that Takashi ish head of the Golden Tiger triad syndicate – a very dangerous man. Files show he hazh three business partnersh. One of them is called Mr. J. P. Lazar."

"What do you know about Lazar?"

The Macanese man thought for a moment, stretched his fat legs toward the window. He was slow-moving but not lazy. "About shixty, hotel owner, operates two, maybe three unlicenced gambling halls. His sister married a Russian tobacconist, some man called Fillipov. She died about five yearsh ago." Costa shrugged and got up from his chair. He went over to the windowsill where a row of men's toiletries – some bay rum, a jar of hair cream and a dark green bottle of Musgo Real Agua de Colonia – stood basking in the sun. He picked up the bottle of cologne and looked closely at it. "I've been into the shop. There's this beeg Russian woman who serves behind the counter, great beeg booshoms! Like melonsh. But I cannot remember her name." He gave the bottle a shake. "What is my *colonia* doing in your office?"

"She's called Olga Shashkova."

Costa sat back down. He repeated the name and then raised a finger to the sky. "You think Lazar and the tobacconist are involved in the opium. In this triad business? Ish that what you are thinking, *Vermelho*?"

"I'm under pressure to put a stop to this opium smuggling as it's eating into the Government's profits. I'm looking at every possible angle. That's why I've been trying to get information out of the daughter."

"Lazar hazh a daughter?" said Costa, leaning forward in his chair.

"No, Olga Shashkova's daughter."

Costa, still leaning forward, watched Sutherland closely. "She ish good-looking?"

Iain paused, shuffled some papers on his desk. "Sort of . . ."

Costa smiled at the ceiling. Sutherland ignored the look on his colleague's face. "I want you to pay Lazar a visit today," he said. "Two thousand catties of tobacco is huge. Let's find out whether there's any connection between the tobacco and Lazar and this Shashkov fellow. Maybe the Tabacaria is a smokescreen of some sort. I'm going to keep on talking to the daughter."

"So that ish why you borrow my *colonia*. You like her, eh?" Costa grinned, at the same time removing a fruit-scented handkerchief from his pocket to wipe the sweat from his face. He also extracted a bag of pistachios from a filing cabinet and started peeling away their shells. "You want to dance the midnight rumba with her, *Vermelho*?"

"No," said Iain. Something in his throat tightened. "I'm just doing my job."

"You go to shleep at night with a pounding heart, eh?" Costa's face flushed with delight. He was nodding and full of laughter. "*Amor, amor!*" he sang, and when he laughed his mouth grew wide and childlike.

"It's the smuggling ring I'm interested in, not the girl," Sutherland said with emphatic sobriety. "And then there's this body that was found floating in the harbour . . ."

Costa, worn down by years of port and heavy aromatic food, shrugged his shoulders and grunted. "Maybe it was a shooishide." He began eating his pistachios.

Sutherland got to his feet and moved to stand before the slatted window. "You don't bind your hands with rope, stuff rosary beads into your mouth if you're going to top yourself. And why was the right foot stripped of flesh?"

"You think it ish a triad killing? Maybe to do with Takashi?"

"Maybe. Lee and I are accompanying a police detective to the mortuary tonight to look at the body, which will be fun. You know how I love the smell of a three-week-old corpse."

Costa threw a pistachio into his mouth and gave it a crunch.

Morning sun slanted through the wooden blinds, whirling grains of golden dust in its rays. In the street below the hubbub of coolie calls and shouts soared above the fountain in the middle of the promenade square. Sutherland could see the sweep of the Praya Grande in the near distance, could hear the waves beat against the age-old rocks of the seawall. He began thinking about Nadia. Tall, composed, a little proud, there was certainly something unusual about her, as if her body concealed a secret. Was it a naivety, a virginal confidence? Why did he think she was a virgin? The woman was in her late twenties. It was something he couldn't put his finger on. Perhaps it was the way she held herself; maybe it was the wistful, artless slope of her mouth. He certainly liked her laugh, thought it was a pretty one. And when he pictured her face – the beauty mark on her chin, the sprinkling of freckles beneath the eyes, the loose strands of hair that kissed her cheeks – a feeling ran through his blood like a hot wind through brittle leaves.

"Amor, amor! Tell me something about this Shashkov girl," said Costa.

"There's nothing to tell."

"Entangled in desire . . ." Costa sang. *"Oh, my sweet lady friend, won't you lend me your lips . . ."*

Iain Sutherland bowed his head. He felt a pistachio shell strike the back of his neck, another ricocheted from his shoulder. A glimpse of a smile spread across his face. "You really are one of the most annoying men I know."

"Sweet lady friend, sweet lips of paradise . . ."

Three whole pistachio nuts pinged off the window pane. Sutherland looked round at Costa with a flashing look of pique. Costa squinted back at him like a gunslinger in a cheap cowboy movie, baring his teeth in a smile. He shut one eye as a hunter would when taking aim at his prey and hurled another nut at the Scot. Sutherland lunged at him, grabbing him by the shoulders, attempting to pull the shirt over Costa's head. The two men grappled. Costa teetered from his chair. Spontaneously, he threw his arms into Sutherland's chest. The chair landed with a thud on the parquet as they crashed to the floor and rolled, scattering paper, nuts, straw hats, pens, paperclips, blotters and ashtrays. "You are meshmerized by her melonsh," cried Costa, giggling. They were breathing into each other's faces, both laughing now. Costa bit him on the elbow.

"Get off me, you fat weasel," yelled Sutherland. Their heads rolled and banged against one another. It was a moment of pure intoxication. Two men in their very early thirties, old companions, wrestling, acting like children again.

"Wait!" hissed Sutherland, with hoarse intensity. "Someone's coming." He heard the door begin to scrape open; it was a thick door and its wood juddered against the floorboards. Sutherland and Costa froze. Mrs. Chan, the consulate administrator, filled the threshold. She held a crystal vase in her hands, containing a pretty arrangement of yellow flowers. A look of horror and astonishment darkened her face as she surveyed the scene before her. Keeping her eyes fixed on the two men, she bent down slowly and laid the vase on the floor, then eased herself upright once more. Without speaking, she squeezed the tops of her fleshy arms, unsure exactly where she should put herself. Costa's hands were still clasped round Sutherland's throat. Sutherland's fingers were in the other man's hair. They must have looked huge and wild and ludicrous.

"Ahhh, Mrs. Chan," said Sutherland standing up. "What have you got for me today?" Costa clambered to his feet too, shirt disheveled, potbelly swaying. Cloth, wood, metal and newspaper were strewn across the floor – a mess of confidential documents lay liberated from their cardboard shrouds.

"I thinking . . ." she said, whispering, "that maybe your room need a little colour."

"Very good of you, Mrs. Chan, I'll put it on the table by the window later. Senhor Costa was just showing me some new karate moves."

She stared at him, her lips quivering with displeasure.

"Anything else?" he asked, embarrassed, turning his attention momentarily to Costa who, he noticed, had a great split down the back of his trousers.

"Yes," she said. "Police Commissioner is waiting for you in next room."

7

At about six o'clock that same evening Iain and Lee arrived at the Hospital St. Lourenco. The mortuary was below-stairs in a bright, low-ceilinged anteroom. The skull-white walls were adorned with charts of the human nervous-system and pictures of the Virgin Mary. On the lime-washed shelves were specimen jars containing livers, hearts and intestines swimming in formaldehyde, together with numerous sets of grinning faceless teeth mounted on wood. In one corner hung a pig carcass suspended from a meat hook. On its rump, stamped in blue ink, were the Chinese words *'slaughterhouse approved. 60% lean meat'*. The hairy snout brushed the smooth floor. The room was very cold.

Following his meeting with the police commissioner, Iain and Lee had been given special dispensation to be present at the autopsy. They were accompanied by a police detective named Poon.

"You will need this," said Lee, handing Iain a tiny red-and-gold tin of Tiger Balm. "For the stinky. Put under each nose hole." Iain applied the camphor ointment.

Seconds later, the refrigeration unit hissed as the autopsy room door slid open, emitting a strong smell of sulphur dioxide and ammonia.

"Mr. Sutherland? Mr. Lee? Det. Poon?" asked a short Chinese man in a laboratory coat.

"Yes," they replied.

"My name is Koh. Please come this way. Oh, and forgive the pig, my niece is having her *moon-yuet* celebration tomorrow. Only place to keep it fresh." He took a few neat little steps forward. "I was informed that you are not a policeman, Mr. Sutherland. Very rare for us to have a civilian present at our PM's, you know."

"So I gather. I'm here representing HM Government Hong Kong."

"Yes, very hush-hush and classified. Don't worry, as witnesses your names will not appear on the paperwork."

The autopsy room was equally bright, lit by a series of overhead bulbs, its floor liberally covered with sawdust. At its centre was a metal operating table fitted with twin grooves on either side to allow for the drainage of blood and other bodily liquids. On the nearby worktop Iain saw a sink basin, a hot and cold tap, a pedal for a shower hose, electric sockets, and a range of stainless steel tools – scalpels, bone saws, sheers, toothed forceps, needles, skull chisels and rib cutters.

Iain folded his arms over his chest.

"Is this your first forensic autopsy, Mr. Sutherland?" asked Koh.

"Aye."

"*Lo baan* was in the army before," said Lee. "He not scared of dead people."

"Actually, ever since the war I've been a little uncomfortable around corpses."

Another man entered the room. The refrigeration unit hissed again, excreting additional odours of sulphur and ammonia. "This is Ah-Kuen," said Koh, "he is what we call in our business the *diener*. He will move the body, photograph the subject and take samples of hair and skin scrapings."

Ah-Kuen went over to a tall white cabinet and opened up one of the hatches to the cold chamber. Inside, Iain saw trays of bodies stacked three-levels high. Koh looked at his notes. "Ah, yes, number B188. One of our long-staying residents."

Iain took a step back. Ah-Kuen transferred B188 to a wheeled stretcher and brought it to the autopsy table. After cleaning the body, Ah-Kuen left the room.

Koh started making visual observations. "Male, aged early thirties. Race: Chinese stroke Macanese. No visible birthmarks. Mole on right upper leg. Right foot stripped of all flesh up to the ankle, first to fifth metatarsal bones intact. Flesh of lower leg corrupted in parts. All distal and proximal phalanxes appear undamaged. Lateral cuneiform has signs of indent. Evidence of external interference – possible bite and gnaw marks. Looking further up, we see a wound to the throat and an entrance wound to the chest. Scar-tissue consistent throughout. Tattoo on left forearm. Both wrists have noticeable abrasions, probably caused by ropes or handcuffs."

"What kind of tattoo?" Iain asked.

"An image of a red pole carrying a blue lantern, and the number 426," said Lee, leaning forwards to see.

"What does that mean?"

"It means he a member of a secret society. Wo Cheung Wo triad. The red pole and number confirms he a 'fighter'. The blue lantern confirms he loyal to his leader."

Ah-Kuen returned with a camera and started taking photographs. The flash popped several times.

"Now I will make an internal examination," said Koh.

Ah-Kuen came forward and placed a body-block under the spine of B188 so that the arms and neck fell backwards. "This pushes the chest upwards, elongating the skin," said Koh with a smile. "It helps to facilitate the cutting."

Iain instinctively turned his back to the proceedings.

"You ok, *lo baan*?" Lee asked, standing close.

"No." Iain swallowed. "I saw a lot of death in the war. I don't like being reminded of it, regardless of what form it comes in."

"Hey, but you big army man. Scottish Dragons. Why you scared?"

"I'm not scared, Lee."

"Then how come you look as white as octopus?"

"It's the memories."

"My Ma-Ma says that best way to not scared of memories is to talk about them."

Koh said, "Now I am making a deep Y-shaped slit from left shoulder to breastbone to right shoulder."

Iain heard the quiet tearing of skin and flinched. After a few seconds he said, "Lee, let's wait outside. We don't have to see this. Det. Poon can supply the details."

Iain laid a hand on the door handle. The door hissed open and he stepped into bright, low-ceilinged anteroom. He stood amongst the jars of livers and hearts feeling tired and off-centre.

Inside a minute, Lee had joined him and was now staring dumbly at the pig, as if hypnotized. The two men treated each other to a long period of silence.

Eventually, Lee spoke. "Pigs always remind me of my fadder. He used to work in the abattoir," he said, prodding the hog's snout with the tip of his shoe. "Every evening he come home, stinking of bwud. His clothes were always dirty and stained from his work. When he come to my bed to kiss me goodnight, I used to push him away.

"Then one morning, a temple day, he put on his best shirt and cleanest trousers to go *bai sun* and give respects to his ancestors. He carried two oranges in his hands. I thing I was late or something. Anyway, he get hit by car. In those days there were very few cars in Macao. He was not used to crossing the road. The police give my Ma-Ma back his glasses, his shoes and his two oranges. You not the only one, *lo baan*, who has been angry with the Gods."

Iain drew in a breath. "But I saw a lot of it, Lee. Far too many of my friends . . ."

"Maybe it worse when they die by accident, like my fadder, because you not expecting it."

"Maybe," Iain said. There was a long pause.

Through the door, Iain thought he could hear the sounds of sawing.

"You ever kill someone during the war, *lo baan*?"

"I'll kill you if you don't stop with these questions." Iain wiped his face with a handkerchief. "Look, let's change the subject. What do you know about the Golden Tiger triads, Takashi's outfit?"

"Them big in gambling and drug distribution. Mainly *pen yan*, opium."

"Are they in direct competition with the Wo Cheung Wo?"

"I thing maybe."

"Do you think we have a gang war on our hands?"

"I thing so."

"Do they usually dump bodies out in the open?"

"No, usually someone just disappear. Tied to rock and thrown to bottom of sea or hide undergownd."

"And why stuff his mouth full of rosaries?"

"Maybe it a Catholic symbol?"

"Maybe it means get the fuck out of Macao."

"Hey *lo baan*, we have to be careful, you know, or they maybe kill us too." He raised his eyebrows at Iain. "But you no worry, before I learn *hung kuen*!" He made a fist. "And also I know crane kung-fu." Lee stood on one leg and stretched his arms out to form a crucifix.

"I feel reassured already," said Iain. Behind the door came a nauseous, gurgling sucking: the sounds of a hydro-aspirator at work.

"What the hell do you think Koh's up to now?"

"I thing he taking fluids out of lungs."

"Look, when this is over we're going to meet up with Costa. The fat man talked with Lazar this afternoon. Let's see whether he has any additional insights."

The seconds passed.

Finally, Koh reappeared with Poon at his elbow.

"What?" asked Iain.

"The man died of drowning," said Poon.

"I could have told you as much," said Iain.

"But he didn't drown in salt water, Mr. Sutherland,' said

52

Koh. "The police report said he was discovered floating in the sea, yet we found his lungs were filled with fresh water not salt. Strange that, don't you think?"

Later that night, having met with Costa, Iain returned home. He walked along the *Rua Central* with Lee in tow.

"So you thing the man was drowned in the sewers?"

"Yes. It would explain how the rats got to him. Costa's going to ask for permission from the PWD so that we can take a look at the storm drains. There may be something down there."

"Did you ever see man drown during the war? I hear in trenches, everywhere was wet mud. Did soldiers get shot and drown in mud?"

Iain remembered having to leap from corpse to corpse, stepping onto the backs of the dead, otherwise his boots would sink in the quag. "Lee, what is this bloody fixation you have with the war?"

"I no have fissation. I love action, I love American gangster films, excitement. That is why I take this job."

"So, you're a fighting man. Is that how you broke your finger?"

"What this?" He held up his crooked left digit. "Kung-fu! I was in big street fight against rival gang. The man I fight was master of drunken monkey *kuen*!"

"Oh, really."

"Yes, really." A moment passed. "No, not really. When I little boy I put string to finger and tie to chicken neck. Chicken was my pet. I like to take for walk. But then came a naughty cat and the chicken run like crazy. *Wahh!* So strong, almost pull my finger off!"

Iain laughed.

They stopped in front of a *dai pai dong*, an open-air street restaurant, and ordered two bowls of wonton noodles. The smell of steamed *char siu* and roasted *lahp cheung* wafted from the stoves. They collected their wooden chopsticks from a bamboo receptacle and ate standing up.

"You know, *lo baan*, I joke about kung-fu and everything, but we must be careful of the Wo Cheung Wo triads."

"How so?"

"They are very dangerous, very well informed, some people say they have even in-few-trated the police. They like to intimidate their enemies. Scare them into submission. Only afterwards they try to kiw you."

"I think I can handle it."

Lee pleaded, "Just promise me you keep your eyes open, ok?"

Iain gave a resigned shake of the head. He fed thick filaments of noodle into his mouth. "Alright . . ."

Satisfied, Lee tilted the bowl to his face, slurped the broth from the noodles. "I must not eat too much. My Ma-Ma cooking *haam-yu-gai-faan* tonight. My brudder is joining us. Hey, *lo baan*, you have brudders or sisters?"

Iain paid for the noodles and together they crossed the road, approaching Lau Ming Street from the south. The tinny trill of Chinese opera music disturbed the hot night. Pungent incense bundles burned from shophouse shrines; some dedicated to local deities, others to Guan-Yin, Goddess of Compassion.

"Two brothers."

"Tell me story about them. Did they fight in war too?"

Iain sighed and nodded absentmindedly. "I used to share a bedroom with them. James and Callum. We used to pretend that the scuffed carpet was our battlefield. James' infantrymen and lancers against Callum's fusiliers and my dragoons. We had over fifty of them."

"Fifty of what?"

"Soldiers, which we kept in large Colman Mustard tins. James, the oldest, used a hunting knife to carve the figures out of green holly – there were pipers, battery gunners, infantrymen, Royal Scots, King's Borderers, Bombay Lancers, and a general from the Duke of Connaught's Own that we'd painted blue. Sometimes James wet the wood or immersed it in water and it was my job to dunk the figure in the tung oil which we got from the old man that ran the tackle shop on Strathnaver Street.

"We played all morning if there wasn't school. We were not from a wealthy family. There was no land to speak of; just a vegetable patch, which mother took care of, and three chickens that Callum looked after. James was great with his hands. A talented footballer too, an inside-left. He had trials for Aberdeen at seventeen. He died taking a bayonet to the chest in Verdun in 1916."

They walked along in silence.

"I'm sorry, *lo baan*. I should not ask questions if answers are sad for you."

They got to the entrance of Iain's building. "Do you want to come up for a nightcap? A dram of whisky perhaps?"

"No, I go home and talk with Ma-Ma. She cooking *haam-yu-gai-faan*."

"See you in the morning."

"Hey *lo baan*," he said, looking up at the first floor window. "You leave light open in your house this morning?"

Iain peered upwards and saw that a white pool of light was blazing within. He shrugged. "Might've done. Anyway, see you tomorrow, Lee."

He climbed the stairs. Somewhere inside the building a baby was crying. He was advancing towards his door and had started to extend his arm when he got a sense of being watched. He looked to his left, up the banister, along the line of steps to the next level. The fringes of shadow seemed to slide, to swirl very slightly. But beyond the darkness he saw nothing.

He inserted the key into his door and had only a split-second to recognize the shotgun shell in the rat-trap. The door activated the trip wire. He saw the springs trigger, the metal crossbar fall. Iain tried to duck his head. The shotgun shell went off.

8

It was Sunday morning and the Tabacaria was closed for business. Uncle Yugevny was relaxing in the back courtyard. It was a small area, largely taken up by the outdoor privy and the gnarling roots of a tall bauhinia tree which split the blanket of pavestones with diagonal fissures. The calm that pervaded between the walls of the courtyard was broken only by birdsong and cat meows, and Uncle Yugevny enjoyed the stillness, the tranquility, and the rich smells of the ocean that drifted across from the esplanade. He squatted on a low bamboo stool, feeding the stray cats that loitered around the washing lines. When he'd finished with the cats he picked up a letter from the table and held it in his hand.

As he read the opening line, he heard a voice shout, "I'm going to do it!" from within the wet kitchen. He sent his blue eyes shimmering towards the door.

"I'm going to do it!" repeated Izabel as she stormed into the courtyard.

"Do what?" said Nadia appearing at her elbow.

Izabel drew in a deep breath. "I'm going to save them." Her bow-shaped lips tightened. "I'm going to save the abandoned babies."

"The ones left at the hospital gates?"

Izabel nodded. "I can't let it go on any longer. A child won't live a day in this heat. And what if it rains? I'm going to Government House to talk to somebody."

"Who?"

"The Health Minister, the Chief Justice, the Governor. I

don't know who, but I have to do something. It's ludicrous, I know, but I can't let it go on. Will you come with me?"

"You want me to do what?" she said laughing at the foolishness of it all.

"Come with me to Government House."

A crease appeared between Nadia's eyes. She hesitated. "But what do you expect me to do?"

"I don't expect you to do anything," Izabel said, "just stand next to me and give me moral support."

Nadia met her friend's radiant, challenging stare. She shrugged. "All right," she muttered.

Izabel looked round to see Uncle Yugevny seated beside a lithe, athletic Chinese gentleman whose generously fleshy lips were smiling at her. "Oh, hello, Yugevny," she exclaimed with surprise. "I didn't know you were out here."

"*Bom dia*, Izabel. This is my friend, Ping."

Nadia groaned, "Oh no, not him again."

Uncle Yugevny ignored his niece and went back to his reading. Earlier, a letter had arrived off the mail sloop and was delivered by Miguel Soong, the weekend postman who was on his way to church anyhow. Uncle Yugevny recognized the orderly handwriting and double-ring Cyrillic postmark immediately; the letter was from cousin Zossima from Chelyabinsk.

It spoke of the country picnics they enjoyed during the summer holidays whilst growing up in Russia. How, after the last of the August rains, his old housekeeper Marianma would take the children, including his sister Olga, into the woods and lay a thick rug across the grass, never more than a dozen yards from the troika, in the middle of which sat Fyodor, the household stableman. Out of a great wicker basket, Marianma would remove a seductive, mouthwatering array of dishes. Cousin Zossima reminisced about the apples from the Crimea, Kiev sweetmeats, pickled apricots, pears dipped in honey and flash-fried in butter, jars of creamed berries, smoky flavoured cucumbers drizzled with salt, and bottles and bottles of sugared lemon juice. Afterwards, they would take a rowing boat across the vast pond to a summerhouse for tea, collecting coloured fossils and pebbles from the nearby stream, followed by a soak in the bathhouse, submerged in tubs of steaming, aromatic water infused with wormwood, rosemary and horseradish.

The letter also mentioned how hard life currently was under Soviet rule. *'Sad how we now hardly get any fruit in the summer months. The best we can hope for are potatoes, turnips and more potatoes,'* Zossima wrote. *'Well, it is time for me to sign off now. You asked in your last letter about Boris. Our beloved son shows no improvement. His illness continues to eat into his mind. Soon there will nothing left of him.'* Uncle Yugevny read the words with a heavy heart. He felt a hand in his hair, gently easing his locks to one side.

"May Ping begin?" asked the Chinese man, laying out his tools on the nearby table.

"*Da, da,*" Uncle Yugevny said in Russian, sipping a cup of hot, apricot-scented, Oolong tea. He removed his glasses.

Ping began inspecting his collection of white-tipped, toothpick-thin, wire plungers.

From a few yards away, from within the confines of the wet kitchen, the jarring clang of pots and pans suddenly shattered the semblance of peace.

Both Uncle Yugenvy and the Chinese man looked round.

Nadia, standing by the window, was frowning, giving looks of disapproval. The stench of grain alcohol had grown stronger and Izabel, standing beside Nadia, was peering through the cracks in her fingers, trying not to look. "Why must you put yourself through this, Uncle," said Nadia.

"Scouring out one's ears is vital to good living," he replied in Portuguese, "and at my age you cannot be too careful with hyzhiene."

"There's nothing more *un*hygienic, if you ask me. Heaven knows who else has been using those tools."

"By the eyes of the *domovoi*," he sighed. "Must you make such a *vaznya*. Ping here requires a steady hand."

Ping cleaned ears for a living. All that he carried with him was a cylindrical elmwood receptacle full of metal probes, a miniscule feather duster called a *shuxeen*, a white towel with a huge hole at its centre, a copper tuning fork and a bottle of grain alcohol. He had been cleaning Uncle Yugevny's ears for seventeen years.

Nadia and Izabel both decided to take a seat in the courtyard. Izabel was in a short skirt, with turned-down hose; there were dabs of powder on her knees. Nadia was wearing a fringed skirt with Peter Pan collars at the waist, and she had on her favourite, low-heeled shoes, what she called her 'finale-hoppers'.

They talked for a while longer and watched as Ping started delving into Uncle Yugevny's inner ear.

He began by drawing back Uncle Yugevny's unruly hair and caressing the skin around his earlobe with a squat, blunt knife. "Dis will stimulate da acupuncture points," said Ping soothingly. The girls stared, fascinated, as he twirled the *shuxeen* into the ear tube with a surgeon's care and precision, removing it seconds later to insert a cotton-tipped copper wire.

Izabel winced, unable to watch any longer, and looking up into the sky, asked Uncle Yugevny how it was that he ended up in Macao.

"My *dyedooshka*, my grandfather, was in the tobacco business," he said. "He manufactured cigarettes, what we called *papirossi*, in small ferkshops in St. Petersburg. When I was old enough to dzhoin the family business there wasn't much for me to do, so my father suggested that I travel and look for new types of tobacco. So I dzhourneyed east, past the Urals, sampling all sorts of tobacco – *Samsun, Izmer, Bursa*. I then tried my luck in the Orient. He said there was good smoking tobacco in Siam, in the Philippine archipelago, even in China. Well, I travelled *vyeazdye* and sent hundreds of samples back to Russia, but I rarely returned home. And then one day I was in Hong Kong, convalescing from a long boat dzhourney from Siam, when I met a young woman called Amelia Lazar. She liffed in Macao." Uncle Yugevny paused and looking as though he was the victim of a great injustice, sighed. "By the eyes of the *domovoi*, the rest is history."

"And it was you who persuaded Nadia's mother to come to Macao?"

Uncle Yugenvy was silent. His head was very still. Ping was scouring his inner ear with a *qeezi*, a type of copper pipe-cleaner. "She wasn't persuaded," he said finally, his tone suddenly austere. The letter from cousin Zossima trembled ever so slightly in his hands. "Olga made that decision all by herself."

There was another long silence. Nadia grew worried. She saw two horizontal lines cut into his forehead. Uncle Yugevny didn't say another word, but started nodding his head, which made Ping withdraw the *qeezi*. He nodded and nodded, his face getting redder and redder, the veins on his neck bulging. Nadia took a deep breath, got up from her chair and walked over to the tall bauhinia tree. She started picking up the dead leaves that had accumulated within the splits in the paves-tones, wondering anxiously if he was going to have one of his fits. When she had collected a good handful, she shot her uncle a look. His nodding routine was over and she began to think that they'd weathered the storm, but then Uncle Yu-gevny's voice barged in. It was a yell verging on the falsetto. "By the eyes of the *domovoi*, they were bloody murderers! *Oobeetsa!*" he cried, jerking his arms up and breaking Ping's hold on him. He hurled the letter to the floor.

"Uncle Yugevny, please calm down."

With a violent motion, he replaced the glasses to his face. "You think they left Russia because they wanted to? They were forced out! The bloody *muzhiks* were torching estates, burning farmlands. They came and burned down their house."

Nadia let the leaves fall back to the ground.

"Burned down the house?" said Izabel. "Why?"

It was something Nadia asked herself all the time.

Uncle Yugevny wasn't even listening now. He was looking at his trembling hands. "It was 1907," he said. "The crop had failed again. Russia had just lost a war to *Yaapawnya* and there was anarchy in the countryside and ferker uprisings in the cities." A cool wind rushed across the patio and hurled itself at Nadia's bare ankles. She got goose-pimples on her arms. She shrank back from her clothes, let herself smile. It was a forced smile, and she hoped that Izabel didn't see how uncomfortable she'd suddenly become.

"Were people hurt?" Izabel continued.

"Hurt?" said Uncle Yugevny. "*Kanyeshna*, people were *hurt*." The way he'd answered, Nadia knew right away he was livid. She wanted to step in front of Uncle Yugevny and tell Izabel to keep quiet, to smother her voice. Instead, she took Izabel's hand and shook her head.

"It was a rabble," said Uncle Yugevny, breathing hard, his face puce, "fifty strong, armed with pitchforks and hunting daggers, and they stormed the country estates, attacking everyone and everything. Like animals! Like those filthy rats we saw a couple of weeks ago! Filthy bloody rats," he repeated, the rage in his voice beginning to falter to a whisper. Within seconds, his anger dissipated like drops of water over a fire. "By the eyes of the *domovoi* . . . even after all these years, I feel the pain."

Nadia felt how hot her own face and neck had become. Once again she saw the mob led by delegates from the Peasant Union, their torches burning the summer sky, grandma and grampapa Petrov being hauled into the garden and beaten, one of the servants howling at her to run. The front end of the house was collapsing. People were scattering in all directions. She remembered Mamuchka screaming her name, over and over, the blaze of bright phosphorous heat, the yellow walls turning black, the dandelion seeds dancing in the thermals, the blur of smoke as she ran from the house through the grounds into the woods. The men with long sticks were charging after them. She didn't even know who they were.

Eventually, she and Mamuchka took cover under some bushes facing out to the river, blood pounding in their ears. Eyes screwed tight, seeing nothing, mouths stretched wide, wanting so much to scream, they hid for hours on the clay-crusted verge, their faces dark with mud and ash except where the tears ran down. They'd found a place on a ridge, hidden by trees, beside a long border of berry bushes. Mamuchka treated the painful burn on Nadia's arm with dock leaves and berry juice. She'd been wounded when the banister fell down and the flames ran up her arm. There were also streaks of what looked like strawberry jam on her legs – scratches from the thorns and spines that littered the forest floor. When it grew dark they listened to the wind and the rustling leaves and for the twig-snap of a footstep. Nadia could see the pinkish light coming through the trees too, knowing it was her house that was illuminating the horizon, and then, seconds later, the little thuds of noise, gunshots that sounded like pine pods exploding in the heat. She remembered little bubbles of sounds – voices crashing against the evening sky, becoming one, and then spreading like fire; yelps of grief breaking as if washed ashore, and she remembered waiting for these sounds to go away, the sounds of the villagers to die out, the sounds of birdsong to return. Waiting for whatever was going to happen next.

If only, she thought, if only they'd gone back earlier to look for Papashka.

Her mind went white.

She looked at Uncle Yugevny, saw his eyes squinting angrily. He caught her looking at him and his eyes jumped away. She wanted desperately to change the subject. Nadia watched her uncle's expression as she spoke, saw that the line of his jaw tightening. She felt her cheeks burn. "I think it would better if we don't talk about this now. Remember your heart, Uncle Yugevny," she said.

The old man grew silent, picked up a pebble from the ground and tossed it hard against the wall. The cats scattered.

"And now look at the country," he said. "After bloody revolution what do we have? Stalin! A Georgian madman! He's now planning to resettle all the Russian Jews in Birobidzhan, a small town on the Russian-Chinese border. Why? So that he can murder them all quietly? He changed his name from Dzhugashvili to Stalin, meaning 'man of steel' – that says it all does it not!"

A minute passed. Nadia gave him a nervous glance. He looked red-faced and uneasy, but a little calmer now. The two horizontal lines on his forehead were receding. "I hear that they're doing a new dance in New Orleans," Nadia said, turning to Izabel "Do you know the Black Bottom?"

Izabel must have seen the look on her face because she responded quickly, apologizing with her eyes. "Of course," said Izabel.

"Can you teach me?"

Izabel got to her feet and pulled on Nadia's arm. They took half a dozen steps and reached the far corner of the courtyard. "The thing you have to do," she said, "is sway your knees. Begin by standing up straight with your legs about a foot apart."

"I'm sorry," Nadia whispered, talking through clenched teeth as she rotated her hips. "He's gets very . . . my grandparents were killed, you see."

Izabel nodded, frowned, understood. "You don't have to explain," she whispered back. "You've both suffered terribly." She held onto Nadia's sleeve. "On the first count sway your knees to the right," she said loudly. "At the same time remember to raise the heel of your left foot. Remember the knees have to be kept together. On the second count sway both knees to the left and raise your right heel, yes, that's good. The art is to combine two slow, swaying movements and quickly follow them up by three very fast swaying movements."

Nadia, who had been watching her feet, looked up, saw Izabel smiling. "Like this?"

"Just like that, very good." Izabel began to laugh. "How would you like to try it out tonight?"

"What's happening tonight?"

"Carlos is taking us dancing," said Izabel with a mischievous smile. "Because of the children we rarely ever go out, but this evening's an exceptoion. We're going somewhere called Club Camoens. And I think I have found you the perfect dance partner."

Nadia stood there, looking at her friend, trying to imagine what her 'date' would be like. A small sharp burst of restlessness, of excitement, crossed her face. The Club Camoens was in the more daring, racier, part of town, in the Pleasure District. Close to a street named Rua da Felicidade, or Happiness Street; it was somewhere Nadia had never been before at night. She swallowed, looked down at the heavy shadows on the patio floor. It had been months since she was last out dancing. She worked her fingers into her skirt pockets.

"Who is he?" she said, a little wary. "My date, I mean?" She was staring at the ground now like a shy little girl.

"Well it's not my cousin Anna." Izabel laughed and gave a quick shrug of her shoulders, shook her head. "Oh, you'll see . . ." she said.

Nadia hissed, "Tell me." But Izabel's shadow had turned from her, vanished so that only Nadia's dark shadow remained on the patio floor. And when she looked up Izabel was already gone, disappeared through the door that led into the wet kitchen and beyond.

"Going out tonight?" asked Uncle Yugevny from his bamboo stool. The ear-cleaning session had ended and Ping was rinsing his tools in alcohol.

"Yes, to Club Camoens."

Ping stopped what he was doing. Both he and Uncle Yugevny stared at Nadia.

"Club Camoens? On Happiness Street?"

"Veewy naughty pwace," said Ping, shaking his head.

"You'd better let your mother know."

"Oh, come on, Uncle Yugevny, I'm a grown woman. How bad can it be?"

9

That evening, Nadia crossed the road from the Tabacaria and climbed the stairs of the building opposite, up to the rooms at the top, passing the ochreous wallpaper and the bait boxes filled with cockroach poison. She knocked on Izabel's apartment door. Her husband, Carlos, showed her in, smiled, and ushered her down the narrow hall. A kind-faced man with the loose, droopy eyelids of a bloodhound, Nadia liked him for his courteousness and for accepting her wholeheartedly as Izabel's new friend. They approached the children's bedroom. Izabel had a big storybook open and held it in her hands, facing her two boys. Nadia grinned when she looked up, said hello to the children as their heads shot around to take her in.

"Mrs. Lo should be ready for you now *meninos*," said Izabel. "You're to go straight to bed when she tells you to and you'll do precisely as she says. Do you understand?" She took both boys in her arms and hugged them.

Nadia went along the corridor and waited in the small drawing room as Izabel said her goodnights to the children. She turned to look in the direction from which a faint scratching noise was emanating. On a chiffonier she saw a mantis that was hopping about in a square, bamboo cage. Round and round the dark wooden bars the insect went and, not for the first time that evening, she was reminded of her father, Ilya Shashkov. The way it danced on its hind legs, swaying like a leaf in the wind, was curiously similar to the way he used to dance with Nadia when she was about five years old, holding his little girl by the arms, elbows kinked awkwardly to compensate for Nadia's lack of height. After several seconds' hesitation, she remembered what she was like when she first came to Macao – how desperately she wanted to be grown-up, to make her own decisions, how strange it was that her father was no longer in her life; she hadn't taken well to being a child once Papashka had gone.

The wall clock struck eight. Izabel came running into the room. "Before we go," she said breathlessly, putting her hand on Nadia's arm and handing her a sheet of paper, "take a look at this."

"What is it?"

"A petition to the Governor about the babies left out on the streets. I wrote it this afternoon."

Nadia gave Izabel a quelling look. Her eyes glided over the page. "Are you sure you want to go through with this? I mean, it's not really the done thing to confront the Governor. There are rules and conventions . . ."

"Phooey! I don't give a rooster's doodle-doo about conventions. Anyway, it's too late. I've already sent copies to the Governor and his ministers. I'm going to Government House first thing Tuesday."

"What are you going to do if he turns you down? Demonstrate, picket?"

"If I have to, yes."

"By yourself?"

"No, with you of course."

"*Bawzhemoy!*"

"You'll do it, won't you? You said you'd help me."

Nadia's powdered cheeks reddened. "Izabel, I mean, come on now, it seems a bit extreme."

"You said you would help me!"

Nadia saw Izabel frown. She laughed at the futility of the idea and shrugged. "Fine, fine," she said, if only to indulge her friend. "I'll do it."

"Promise?"

Nadia sighed. "Yes, I promise."

Holding her friend's eye, Nadia stepped out onto the landing while Carlos sloped down the stairs to hail two coolies from the rickshaw rank. They waited by the banister.

"Who are we meeting tonight?" Nadia asked.

"You'll have to wait and see," Izabel said with devilish glee. Nadia noticed that Izabel had used a number of different tints on her face, and had rubbed a powdered pink blush onto her cheeks. She was wearing a lovely rust-coloured dress trimmed with red sequins, so short it gathered an inch above the knees, and a long rope of pearls, tied in a knot across her chest. Nadia noticed, too, that the bumps of her friend's knees had been dabbed with rouge.

"*Bawzhemoy*, look at me," said Nadia, smoothing the front of her outfit. She wore a green silk brocade cheongsam adorned with plum blossom and bamboo patterns. It was calf-length and sleeveless and featured a mandarin collar with cloth buttons running down the side. "Compared to you I look like a twig of grass."

"Phooey, what nonsense. You look just *doocky*!"

"No, I don't:"

"Wait here a minute," Izabel said, rushing back into the apartment. She returned with a pair of shoulder-length evening gloves and a black velvet headband with ostrich plumes. "Try on these."

Thrilled, Nadia held the headband in place with a soap-stone pin and pulled on the gloves. "*Choodnee*," she said in Russian, as she covered the scar-tissue on her right arm. "Wonderful."

"Ready?" said Izabel.

"Yes, oh, just one last thing," Nadia said, diving into her little glass-beaded purse and extracted a tiny essence bottle. She drizzled scent on a handkerchief and handed it to Izabel. "You'll need this for the rickshaw ride," she said. "Hold it to your nose when we go through the *gai sih*, the fish market."

Ten minutes later they were stepping off the rickshaw

onto the crescent-shaped Rua de Felicidade. Although not much more than a thousand yards from the Largo da Sien, the mood of Happiness Street was vastly dissimilar. All along the narrow road oil lanterns hung from hooks, and in the doorways of the three-storey buildings with the carved red lacquer facades, the prostitutes were flaunting their brazenness unashamedly. They beckoned to Carlos good-heartedly. Seeing the peach-cheeked women, Nadia was undisguisedly embarrassed, if a little humbled. She had expected them to be morose and surly; instead their expressions were full of mischief and laughter, not what she had anticipated at all.

Izabel smiled, a wry little twist of her lips. "Fascinating, don't you think?"

"I think it's this way," said Carlos.

Nadia stepped through the cobbled street, over globules of spit and cracked melon seed husks and puddles of paraffin oil rainbows. At the end of the crescent-shaped lane, in a large three-story building with a green-tiled roof and curved eaves, there stood a huge door made from burnished brass and steel. Carlos banged it with the side of his shoe. A peephole in the door opened. Nadia was aware of a face watching her; the red-flecked eyes in the window had pupils that were gorged with opium. Nadia tried to peer into the room. All she caught was a crush of people, slippery pools of lamplight and whirling spirals of smoke. Carlos thumbed a five pataca note through the peep hole. Half of the man's face broke into a smile. The window of the peephole was drawn shut. The bolts of the iron door slid open, allowing the swinging gate to bite its edges into the floor.

Once inside they were led into an expansive foyer and were each given a steaming hot towel to clean their hands, followed by a complimentary glass of cold mint tea.

"Excited?" asked Izabel.

"Very," said Nadia, as they strolled from the foyer into the main hall.

"I wish my cousin Anna in Barreiro could see this. She loves places like this."

The rectangular, high-ceilinged room was full of vast mirrors, elaborately carved ironwood chairs, and twenty-foot-long gambling tables covered in light brown, grass matting. The people were well-dressed and noisy, laughing and shouting with equal gusto. Nadia could smell the rose-water scent that masked the cigarette smoke and the piquant aromas of Cantonese cooking. High above her, to her left and right, on two separate levels, were a series of balconies where guests played fan-tan while they dined, lowering their bets and pulling up their winnings via wicker baskets on strings.

"*Onde e o bar?*" Izabel asked.

"The bar and main restaurant ees thees way," said Carlos. At first Nadia thought there was only one long table, but then, as her eyes focused on the far corners of the hall, she saw two, then three, additional games taking place. By each table there was a railed-off area and a high chair for the cashier. Beside him a small blackboard was erected where the stakes were marked. As the odds were written up, the *t'an kun*, or banker, dressed in a shiny-blue pyjama suit, placed two large hand-fuls of white bone buttons under a silver bell-shaped cup. He then allowed the players to place their bets in one of the four squares, numbered 1,2,3, and 4. Once all the bets were laid, the cup was turned over and the beans removed four at a time until there were four beans or fewer left on the table.

"Do you want to play?" said Nadia to Izabel.

"I don't know how."

"Watch the banker as he scoops up a handful of buttons and places the cup over the pile. There are probably between thirty and forty buttons there. Your job is to guess how many are left over after he's drawn the buttons away four at a time."

"The restaurant is through here," said Carlos with impatience, about ten paces ahead of them, looking back over his shoulder.

"I think there'll be two buttons left over," said Izabel, ignoring her husband.

"So stick your money on square number 2," Nadia said.

Izabel removed some money from her purse. "I used to play the weekly lottery back in Barreiro," she whispered. "Carlos never knew."

"What in *ceu* are you doing now?" he asked peevishly.

"*Uma minuto, Carlos!*" said Izabel. She placed her bet. A few seconds later a bell was tinkled and the bell-shaped cup upturned. The *t'an kun* raked the beans, four at a time, to one side of the table using a tapering blackwood rod that resembled a small backscratcher. A two was marked on the blackboard as the winning number. Izabel yelped with delight.

Carlos, encouraged by his wife's windfall, began telling them what he knew of the place. "Not only do they have fan-tan here, they also offer baccarat, poker, thirty-seex card *ch'a t'an*, dice, dominoes and eeven quail fighting. I'm told the birds are furnished with metal spurs."

As Izabel leant forward to collect her winnings, Nadia noticed a waiter hurry by carrying a tray laden with plates of steamed garoupa with ginger, mui-shui pork with taro, and crispy fried shrimp rolls on saddles of baby bak choy. Distracted by the aromas of Cantonese cooking, aromas that reminded her that they still hadn't eaten, Nadia led Izabel away from the table. "Can we eat soon, Carlos?" she asked.

"*Sim, sim,*" said Carlos, nodding vigorously. He led them along the middle of the room to a place where a vast satin curtain with a dragon motif came down from the ceiling. He pulled it to one side. Holding out his hand, he took Nadia's arm. Stepping through, Nadia entered a large suite where the walls were matt black and draped with antique Hanlin scrolls. She saw red prayer flags and embroidered tapestries depicting wispy golden carp and graceful waterfalls. Six sprawling opium daybeds made of intricately sculpted dark wood were spaced evenly across the suite. A silent figure, a slack-muscled man, lay calmly on his side on one of the beds. His shoulders were being massaged by a pretty Chinese girl. Nadia saw him rolling a ball of black opium between his finger and thumb, noticed the long ivory pipe by his hip with the jade mouthpiece, the small, glass lamp, and what appeared to be a set of metal needles arranged on a piece of cloth. The man squinted vaguely at her as she walked past.

"Through here," said Carlos. In the adjoining room they sat at a small, round rosewood table encircled by samphire-green pillars. The accompanying hardwood chairs were backed with marble. Songbirds twittered in cages hung from the ceiling. There were ivory chopsticks, cloisonné-handled spoons and two bowls of pickled ginger already set out in front of them. A waiter, dressed in loose, black *fu*, felt slippers and a mandarin jacket made from red embroidered silk placed four small glasses and a broad-necked bottle of *saam sair* snake wine on a sideboard; he then proceeded to pour monkey-picked oolong tea into delicate bone china bowls.

"Today shoo-wimp very fwesh. Plegty good," said the waiter. "Only fee guest tonight?" he said, placing the teapot on top of a methylated spirits lamp at the centre of the table.

"No, *quatro*," said Carlos.

"Who's the fourth?" asked Nadia.

"Me." The gravelly, rain-rinsed voice came from behind one of the samphire-green pillars.

Nadia looked around. There was suddenly a strong whiff of orange and vetiver oil in the air. "*You!*" she said.

"Aye."

"*Bawzhemoy!*" Nadia turned all the way back around to look at Izabel as if she'd just seen a madman. "What are you trying to do, kill me?"

"He was very persuasive," said Izabel. "He came knocking on our door yesterday saying you were in love with him, and something about you being too shy to admit it. Other than that I wasn't sure . . . his Portuguese is appallingly bad."

72

"And you believed him? Why didn't you ask me?"

"I thought it would be a fun surprise," Izabel said playfully. Iain pulled out a chair and sat down next to Nadia. She noticed that one side of his neck was heavily bandaged. He offered Carlos a cigarette and ordered a round of drinks, asking the waiter to fix him a very dry Gibson, straight up, with a twist of lemon peel. From the dance floor behind them came the sound of clarinet and piano music, a rising melody under the warbling voice of a male vocalist. Nadia felt something touch her wrist and discovered Iain's little finger worming its way up her forearm, tickling her. She slapped his hand away kittenishly. Her initial shock at seeing him had given way to feelings of anticipation and curiosity. A glow had spread inside her. Despite herself, she offered him a thin smile and his pale face lit up like a big baby.

10

Iain danced with Nadia. He was moving her around the dance floor, his eyes glancing at all the profiles around him, wondering if he was being watched. Satisfied that he was surrounded by friendly faces, he unclenched his jaw. "Great band, don't you think?" he said.

"What?"

"I said, isn't it a good band?" She wasn't listening to him, preferring to look all about the room than into his eyes. She was intrigued, delighted even, that Iain had taken such a keen interest in her, yet she wanted to appear cool.

Iain continued to dance and smiled, as though to himself. He noticed that her neck muscles were taut, could see how she was fighting with herself. He didn't say anything for a while. He was thinking.

He tried to shuffle Nadia away from the band, to where it wasn't so noisy. The dance floor was filling up. Soon he was surrounded by grey-haired men, black-haired women, men with pitted skin, girls with wide, painted eyes. A man's face next to his was shouting loud Cantonese words to his partner. Everyone clasped each other tightly.

"What happened to your neck?" Nadia asked.

"Razor burn. What I'd call a close shave."

There was a long silence.

"How's business at the shop?" he asked eventually.

"Fine, thank you."

"And your Mum's charity?"

"We raised 300 patacas last month."

"Has Senhor Lazar been in lately?

"Lazar?"

"Yes, has Lazar been into the shop?"

"No, why should he have?"

"Doesn't he do a lot of trade with your uncle?"

"He doesn't even smoke."

"I head he purchased two thousand catties of raw tobacco from the Tabacaria."

"I don't know where you heard that from."

"What about a man called Takashi . . . ever heard of him?"

"No."

Iain's eyes scanned the room again. The booby-trapped door in his apartment had sharpened his instincts to a knife. He saw a boyish-looking man staring at them from across the floor. Next to him stood a Chinese woman with a snub nose and shawl draped over her shoulders. The woman's eyes were piercingly dark, as black as boot buttons. The man took two quick strides forward and put his hand into his jacket pocket. Iain felt a vein on his forehead twitch. Every nerve in his body came alive. Stiffening, the man caught Iain watching him and pulled out a cigarette case, turning to sit at an empty table.

Iain relaxed. His hand met the slim muscles along the small of Nadia's back. He spread his fingers slowly, pulling her hips against his, very gently. He could feel her though the silk. He sensed her soft flesh pressed against him, the tremor of her breathing, her ribs rising and falling, his own heart hammering, quickening. He thought he felt her shudder against him.

He opened his mouth to ask another question about Lazar, but then closed it. Instead he began to question what he was doing with this girl. He had no destination, no idea where he was taking her. He wondered what he would do once he got all the answers. Would he disappear, wash away the footprints in the sand, leave no trace? That was the nature of his job – it made him feel as if he could be many people, that he could never be himself; as though he was always acting, diluted, disseminated, as if every part of his life was influenced by the circumstances of his job. He was a man whose innards belonged to Whitehall, without roots, with no core.

Yet when Iain was with Nadia, this twenty-eight-year-old girl with large blue eyes and an unpronounceable middle name, he felt genuinely happy. He found his facial muscles were sore from a curious involuntary grin that he'd worn the last ten minutes. What was the matter with his mouth? Why did she have this effect on him? He felt tenderness for Nadia, and the more he held her and danced with her, the more his feelings were at odds with his professional duties. His lips felt dry from all the smiling and from the Gibson he'd drunk earlier. She turned to look at him. He wanted to take her face in his hands.

"Are you all right?" she asked.

"Yes. Why?"

"You're not dancing."

"I didn't know I'd stopped. Sorry."

There was a big spotlight on the singer so that everyone could watch his face as he sang. Iain didn't know the name of the song but he noticed Nadia mouthing the words.

> *It had to be you*
> *It had to be you*
> *I wandered around and finally found*
> *The somebody who*
> *Could make me be true*
> *Could make me feel blue*

"Who's the song by?" he asked.

"What?"

"I said who's the – "

"The Isham Jones Orchestra."

The name reminded Iain of his school days.

"I used to share a set of rooms with a boy called Peter Isham-Wood," said Iain. "He had the annoying habit of carrying a white marble with him wherever he went. He used to keep it in his jacket pocket. During matins he would drop it on the stone floor and say, 'Oh hell! My glass eye!' "

"You're full of silly stories, aren't you, Mr. Sutherland."

"Call me Iain"

"Where was this school of yours, in Scotland?"

"Sussex, England."

"Did you enjoy it?"

"No. I was an outsider. Isham-Wood was one of the few boys I liked. He didn't tease me about my accent or background. The others called me a Scottish 'prole'."

"I don't know the word."

"Karl Marx," said Iain. "Comes from the word 'proletarian'. The prefects threw mud at me shouting, 'Shove off back to Scotland, McProle!' "

Iain knew he wasn't like the other boys. Furthermore, he knew he wasn't just any Scotsman, he was a Sutherland. The Sutherland clan were pure Gaelic, theier clan crest displayed a Scottish wildcat. They had a bold green-and-blue patterned tartan, and a clan chief known as 'the Great Chait'. Iain knew he came from a long line of proud, fighting people, but his father was the Helmsdale river bailiff which, in the eyes of his schoolmates, made Iain working-class and unsophisticated. It also made him tough and resourceful.

"So why were you sent to a school in Sussex?" Nadia asked.

"I was awarded a bursarship thanks to one of the proprietor's of the Helmsdale river who had connections with a Mr. Healy of the Foreign Office. One afternoon I met Healy, who was still dressed in his fishing waders, over a cup of tea at the Achantoul Estate, a few miles up the strath. He asked me about my academic interests, about a possible career in the F.O., my loyalty to Scotland, to Britain, and the Crown. A month later I was entering Christ's Hospital in Sussex in the fourth year, aged fifteen."

He deliberately omitted telling her he'd left Helmsdale in

disgrace; that he'd arrived off the Inverness train in a drab tweed jacket, slicked-down red hair, carrying a cheap set of suitcases and an inferiority complex the size of Loch Naver; that he'd been prickly, querulous and easily offended. And that over the course of an academic year he'd been ordered to the headmaster's office three times and punished for fighting, once for breaking an elder boy's cheekbone.

"And when you finished school, what did you do?" Nadia said.

"After Christ's, I took up my one-year apprenticeship with Mr. Healy at the F.O. But then, in the autumn of 1917, at the age of nineteen, the war took me to Amiens and the Somme with the Royal Scots Dragoons, where, after a year of wading through the narrow trenches along the front lines, I was demobbed following the armistice and transferred back to the Foreign Department."

Instinctively, he left out that he was ushered into Group Sections in a building in Kensington, followed by a 10 month stint with M.O.5 (c) – the records, personnel and port control department. Not long after he was sent to Kuangchow, China, as a cadet officer to learn Cantonese, before finally being elevated to the status of Passport Control Officer for South China – the SIS operative's normal cover when abroad.

Iain had arrived in Hong Kong from Kuangchow hidden underneath a brown umbrella. Within an hour of his arrival, he'd been introduced to the Colonial Secretary and the Chief Justice. He recalled being told to sign the Visitors' Book at Government House, then being lectured on the perils of cholera, Chinese girlfriends and Hong Kong Foot – an itchy fungus that grows between the toes – by a self-important official called Fielding from the Interservice Liaison Department. 'If you're idiotic enough to marry a local girl,' Fielding warned, dabbing his thick red lips with a handkerchief. 'You'll be called upon to resign. Is that clear? If you want a bit of fun there are licensed brothels on Lyndhurst Terrace.

I'm told they're rather civilized places, nothing vulgar or coarse, with a decent mix of French, Italian and Hungarian tarts. You can go and fuck the White Russians too if you want, just don't go making a show of it. We try not to mix with them socially. Is that clear?' Iain remembered feeling contempt for the man and his dirty white rag of a handkerchief. It was one of his few clear memories of his first day in Hong Kong – that and seeing the rain on the windowpanes, thinking that it resembled liquefied silver.

The more Iain thought about this, the tighter he held Nadia. She was staring straight before her. He found he was holding her protectively and felt her squirm a little as they danced. In his arms she seemed so frail, so graceful. So bloody beautiful. He moved her hand in his as they danced. First slowly. Then quickly. He saw the question mark in her eyes.

The band started playing *I'm Just Wild About Harry*. Iain and Nadia began to dance the Charleston. He cleared his throat. "That's enough about me. Tell me a little bit more about Lazar. Am I right in thinking that he has no association with your uncle whatsoever?"

She turned her head a tiny bit to look at him. "They fell out a few years ago, soon after Auntie Amelia passed on."

"Supposing Lazar wanted to buy a load of tobacco, he'd still go to your uncle though, wouldn't he?" The pictures of his old life made Iain suddenly afraid. He was talking much louder now, almost shouting above the music.

"Why are you so interested?"

"No reason."

The singer started singing a song called *The Varsity Drag*. Iain was looking at Nadia's face. She was what people back home would have called mickle-mouthed. Her mouth was big and full. He noticed that she never closed it entirely, the lips were always just that little bit parted. It was a pretty mouth, he decided. The petal-bruised lips made him think of the chocolate cream bars he used to love as a child. I wonder, he thought to himself, whether her mouth would taste like that – all mintiness and flaky cream chocolate.

A waiter walked past with a tray of caramel tarts and fudge squares.

"Are you fond of chocolate?" Iain asked. Nadia's chin was by his left shoulder, he could see that her neck remained taut. "In Helmsdale there used to be a sweet shop on Strathnaver Street, built out of Brora stone. I remember when I was about five years old I'd walk down the Old Caithness Road, with the sun cracking through the deep grey sky, and peer into the shop's window, ogling at the chocolate violet creams and *soor plooms* and shiny glass jars full of peppermints. When I close my eyes I still see the old faces, the narrow streets, the tight rows of low lime-washed houses."

"Mr. Sutherland . . ."

"Iain."

"Iain, why do you ask such peculiar questions?"

"How do you mean?"

"Last week you asked me if I liked honey, now you want to know about Lazar and whether I'm fond of chocolate."

"It was a harmless enough question."

Nadia was putting up a front. Behind the mask of detachment was a smile. "I just find it odd."

"Odd?"

"Yes, odd!" She made a face.

"Why are you screaming?"

"I am *not* screaming."

"Yes, you are."

Nadia looked at him with intense, smiling eyes. "You don't give up easily, do you? Don't think that I'm not angry with you, Mr. Sutherland."

"It's Iain, please. And why are you angry?"

"I told you I didn't want to go out with you . . . I thought I had made it quite clear. The next thing I know you have the *chivaanstva* to show up at my friend's home – "

"*Chivaantsva* . . . what's a *chivaanstva*?"

"You show up at my friend's home to tell her that . . . that I . . ." She contorted her face. "That I love you. *Love* you? Are you completely insane?"

"I think it's Russian."

There was a long pause.

"You think what's Russian?"

"This *chivaantsva* word you keep using."

"*Must* you be so exasperating?"

"Who's being exasperating? I was merely asking about – "

"I'm going back to the table."

"But you never answered my question?"

She sighed. "What question?"

"Whether you liked chocolate?"

"If you must know, I don't."

They were still dancing, clasped close. He kept his left hand on her back. His fingers started tickling her ribs.

"Please stop doing that. I hate being tickled. And what is that awful cologne you're wearing? You smell like a fragrance factory."

"That's your father's fault, that is."

"My father? What the *praklaateeye* does my father have to do with this?"

"If a father can't spoil his daughter with a spot of tickling and chocolate then I don't know who can?"

She shook her head and said something to herself in Russian.

"You're an only child, aren't you?" he said. "Usual problem . . . father spoils little girl incessantly but grows guilty that he's neglecting his wife, he backs off, overcompensates, becoming aloof, resulting in resentment on both sides. Is that how it is with your father?"

Her look of surprise turned to distaste. "How dare you!"

"How dare I, what?"

There were tears welling in her eyes all of a sudden. She tilted back her head in defiance. "How dare you bring my father into this?" She slapped him hard across the face and stormed off the dance floor. He watched, quite stunned, as she headed out of the restaurant, with her friend, Izabel, not far behind. Her black velvet headband with ostrich plumes had fallen to the ground.

11

Nadia knew that her anger had been childishly undirected; still she set off at a furious pace with no idea where she was going. She ran from the club and crossed into an alley where massive circular moon-shaped doors beckoned her to enter. Poison-green candles, dripping wax like wreathing pythons, hung from the open portals. She made her way up the raised steps and went in.

Her tears plopped down on the pounded-earth floor. Black ash from paper offerings floated and stirred by her bare ankles, some fragments still alight. She found herself in a temple, before a simple altar.

The interior was extremely small, enough for a dozen people at most, with only a single window to allow in light making the air smell heavy with worship. There were no pews, only low slabs of wood by the altar for people to rest their knees on. Joss sticks smouldered in profusion. Incense coils hung from the roof. Oil burners gave off sickly sweet smells of java flowers and frangipani. On either side of the doors stood ancestral tablets lined up against the wall – plain, oblong pieces of blackwood with the name and age of the deceased etched in red. Nadia knelt, legs tucked under her, in front of the image of the shrine. Blades of light crept in through the tiny window, illuminating the altar; brass, silver and stone gleaming timidly. She was full feelings of absence and loss, as though she was holding her breath and didn't know how to let go.

Time seemed to stand still. Incense sticks, plunged into great urns of sand, burned before the figure of Tin Hau, the

Queen of Heaven and Goddess of the Seas. Nadia watched the smoke drift over the effigy's solemn face, over the rich burgundy lacquer and gold leaf headdress, rising heavenwards to blacken the bamboo laths of the temple ceiling. A gong, hung up at the side of the shrine, reflected the quivering candlelight as a fever of hope and renewal rose up within her. She heard Izabel enter the temple through the moonshaped doors. She was aware of Iain's presence too. Izabel approached Nadia quietly and knelt by her side. Nadia felt her friend's hand take hers, holding it tightly. She wanted to be strong but the pressure that was tearing her up inside, pressure that had built up for years, began to boil over. Her mind grew full of images of her Papashka. Her cheeks and face were burning. She began to weep for the father she hardly knew, weeping to keep his memory alive.

There was a long silence in the temple. Eventually, Izabel said, "I want you to tell me what's happened. What has upset you?"

Nadia picked at her fingernails, looking at the ground. "It's hard to explain." She lifted her gaze and saw Izabel's concern. "I get overwhelmed sometimes," she said.

"Why?"

She closed her eyes briefly then looked again at Izabel. "There are times when I get angry and confused with what's happened in my life. Sometimes I break down trying to make sense of it all." Nadia fixed her stare on a pool of lamplight on the altar table. "Do you remember what Uncle Yugevny told you about the fire that burned down our home?" She felt a fierce throb of emotion in her throat. "Well, the peasants not only razed the house, they also dragged my grandparents and my father into the garden, beat them with sticks." She hesitated for a moment. "I remember sitting in the kitchen, eating my *uzhin*, the evening meal – potato cakes with mushroom sauce – I remember cutting up some sweet boiled cabbage that was set on a side dish. Then cook rushing to the window when we heard the dogs barking

84

and the screams. I rose quickly from my chair, not knowing what I had just heard."

Izabel stroked Nadia's hair then rested her elbows on her knees, cradling her friend's head in her hands. "That night," Nadia said. "When they set fire to our home I thought I'd lost everything. The mob separated me from my parents." Nadia once more saw the mob on her doorstep, their faces streaming in a frenzy of destruction. She saw the yellow smoke, the flaring eyes, the rampaging sweating bodies descending on her with cudgels and horsewhips. "I thought Papashka was in his study," she said. "I heard Mamuchka calling me but I had to try to save him. I didn't know that they'd taken him into the dovecot and poured paraffin onto his clothes. I remember screaming his name, over and over, trying to get into his study but the banister had fallen down and there was smoke everywhere. The floor had started to shift and groan. The noise was petrifying, with sheet glass rupturing as it warped and tinned food exploding in the kitchen. I couldn't see anything, and then I felt the flames run up inside the arms of my shirt. The pain took my voice away. That was when my mother grabbed me and fell on me with her overcoat. We ran through the garden listening to the housemaids wailing for their children – the mob was attacking everybody – and then we fled into the woods.

"There were people screaming and shrieking everywhere. I remember seeing a man assaulting one of the servant girls, pinning her down by the potting sheds. Her name was Svetlina. She was one of my friends. It was . . . terrible. As we ran we saw that the grounds were crowded with people fighting, cheering, two men were climbing the spruce trees to affix ropes. They were the trees I used to climb. By the main driveway Marit, one of our kitchen staff, was hanging by his neck, feet dangling. His face was purple and his swollen tongue was sticking out of his mouth. Someone had slashed his stomach open. His distended entrails were fluttering in the breeze. I remember my mother covering my eyes. I was only seven years old," she said softly. "Later, we hid under the cover of some thick bushes by the river, waiting for the sounds to go away."

"The day after the fire, we returned to our home. It was just a blackened shell. Mamuchka and the estate manager, Mr. Bogdanov, cut the bodies of my grandmother and grandfather down from out of the spruce trees. Mr. Bogdanov only survived because he hid in the nearby church."

"Why did the peasants suddenly rise up? What made them behave so viciously?"

"There were many reasons. In 1904 Russia went to war against Japan for control of Korea and Manchuria. We lost. Worse, we were humiliated, lost the entire Baltic fleet. The economy was ruined. The collapse led to revolts by industrial workers, demonstrations, railroad strikes, mutinies, and Bloody Sunday."

"What was Bloody Sunday?"

"A massacre that happened in 1905 in St. Petersburg. Over 200,000 peasants and workers gathered in a peaceful march to deliver a petition to the Tsar. They demanded an eight-hour workday and an increase in wages. But the army panicked and opened fire. Some say over a thousand men, women and children were killed. A few months later, the peasants began to rise up all across rural Russia."

"What happened to the culprits, the people who attacked your home?"

Nadia sighed and shook her head. "There was an official enquiry. The prime minister, a man called Stolypin, made a statement which Mamuchka read to me. In it he blamed 'the tragic loss of life and property to a band of scoundrels and rogues that had infiltrated the many peasant communities to drum up sedition and insurgence in order to overthrow the Tsar and his government.' About a thousand citizens were hanged by Stolypin. His gallows were known as Stolypin's necktie."

"And your father? What happened to your father?"

"We looked everywhere for Papashka's body. Had it been left in a ditch, under a pile of stones, or thrown over the *avrak* onto the rocks below? We didn't know. Perhaps he'd been burned up along with the house, his ashes rubbed into the earth – there was no way of telling. We checked every hospital, every neighbour's home, every barn and stables, but found no trace of him.

"Eventually someone was sent from the city. A *gorodvoi* from the Imperial Russian Police came with his white-and-black hat and showed us photographs of peoples' bodies. Charred corpses, lying in rows, wrists and arms and legs in tangles. He said thirty-seven people had been killed in our area. Mamuchka identified four cadavers from the photographs: a count and his wife from one of the neighbouring estates, a doctor that lived beyond the stream, and our servant-girl Svetlina, whose naked body was found a mile from the house."

"And your father?" Izabel asked again, gently.

"Papashka wasn't amongst them but Mamuchka didn't give up looking for him. After burying my grandparents, we stayed for a time in Mr. Bogdanov's cottage. But with the aftermath of such violence none of the *muzhiks* were willing to cooperate. She searched and searched . . . but nothing. She didn't give up though. She knocked on villagers' doors, turned the forests upside down, was constantly writing letters to the Imperial Police asking for information, but nobody seemed to know anything. With each passing day she grew more desperate. Most of the time I just clung to her, frightened that the peasants would return. Eventually a senior *gorodvoi* came to see her and told her that Papashka was most likely dead.

"A few months afterwards, Mamuchka and I travelled east with what was left of our lives to stay with cousins in Chelyabinsk. I didn't want to go. I remember beginning to cry and shaking with the crying, me hugging my arms and Mamuchka hugging me. I didn't want to leave Papashka behind, didn't want to leave the memory of my grand-parents behind. I made life hell for her. It was exhausting for both of us.

"When we got to Chelyabinsk we stayed for three long winters. Eventually, four years passed, and with still no word about Papashka's remains, Mamuchka decided she had to leave Russia. Everything about that day kept replaying in her head. My mother would see Papashka standing by the manor house, his tanned face against the sun-crinkled stone, waiting for the mob of villagers to come and take everything away from him."

Nadia's eyes took on the cheerless light of the Siberian sun. She folded her hands and placed them on her knees.

"Is that when you came here?" asked Izabel, her voice deliberately quiet and calm.

Nadia nodded. "Yes. In 1912 we journeyed further east to meet Uncle Yugevny in Irkutsk. We went by train, skirting the southeastern shores of Lake Baikal to Chita, then on to Harbin, and Vladivostok. From there we boarded a ship to Macao." Her face paled a little. "After a few years in Macao we heard there'd been a revolution in Russia. We stayed in close contact with our cousins in Chelyabinsk. Then one day we received a letter with a different postmark."

Nadia looked down. Bits of her hair fell into her eyes. "It was a moment I'll always remember. It was a Thursday morning, February 21st, 1919, a cool day with blue, cloudless skies. I was eighteen years old. Mamuchka read me the words, saying they were from a doctor at the Alexander II Homeopathic Hospital in St. Petersburg. They'd found him. They'd found my father, Izabel. And he was alive."

12

Either side of the main altar, the wax candles burned bright. Nadia was rubbing her eyes, which were stinging a little from the joss stick smoke. She and Izabel were still on their knees.

"Papashka had been found some years earlier. The hospital had treated him, but for a long time they couldn't establish who he was." Nadia could feel her eyes beginning to pinken again. She felt as though she was lost on the edge of some wild jungle. There were small tears in her eyes. "The day of the fire, he'd been set alight in the dovecot and dragged behind a horse into the forest. They'd left him to die in a stream. He was covered in burns. But it was the cool water that saved his life. He was found by a man, a beekeeper," Nadia gave a short laugh. "Can you believe it? A beekeeper had kept him alive by dressing his ravaged skin in honey and herbs.

"He'd suffered terrible injuries, his legs had been burned up to mid-thigh. Worse still, for a while his brain had been deprived of oxygen. He was half-blind, he couldn't speak and his memory was badly impeded. He'd stayed in the care of this beekeeper for years, three, four years maybe, I don't know how long. Then some doctors from the city on a charitable mission discovered him, and he was moved to this specialist homeopathic hospital in St. Petersburg." Nadia stopped talking. She thought about what her Mamuchka had said, that time heals everything. But Nadia knew better – time didn't heal, it simply picked at the scab, scraped at the sore, until fresh blood appeared. And if she was honest with herself, she didn't want to be healed; she embraced the sorrow, accepted it, because it was the sorrow more than anything that kept Papashka's memory alive. Without it his face would blur into nothingness, a circle of featureless dough.

She shook her head. "Everything just went misty for a long time after that. The whole process of not knowing his fate, and then grieving for him, having gone through hell picturing and imagining how he might have died, wasn't easy. And then finding out years later that he didn't die at all, that he'd been so badly hurt . . . the feelings of grief and sorrow came rushing back again . . . you'll never know how hard . . ." Her voice failed her. She took a deep breath. "Mamuchka wrote letter after letter to him and to his doctors. We wrote to the Portuguese Embassy in Shanghai, to the offices of White Russian solicitors, to Soviet state ministers in Moscow. But there was no way of getting him out of Russia, not with the current regime in charge. My father is alive, Izabel, but we will never be a family again.

"Over nine years have passed since we received that first letter . . . nine years is a long time for a family to live like this . . . sometimes I can't work out what's going on inside my head. Do I have a father or not? I don't know what he looks like, or what his voice sounds like anymore . . . it's like a dream. Maybe some people would have run away from the problem. I can't run away from the situation because of Mamuchka. And it isn't an option, for me, to run away. It's not my nature. So I write to him once a month, telling him of my life, my hopes. Some of the letters get through, and only very occasionally do I receive a reply. He must be getting people to write for him, because the handwriting is rarely ever the same, opening each letter with *My dear little chimp*. It was what he used to call me as a child. "

Izabel looked at Nadia in a new way now, with caution in her eyes. "Where do you write? Where is he now?" she asked.

"Blagoveshchensk."

"Where on earth is that?"

"On the Russian/Chinese border in Manchuria."

"How did he get there? And how did he find you?"

"It's a long story. We've had to rely on scraps of information, half a dozen letters from various people; the news has been sporadic at best. But we've managed to reconstruct the lost years nevertheless. While he was in hospital in St. Petersburg, he was being treated by a German-Russo doctor, and there were clear signs of improvement. He and the doctor, a man called Riedle, became friends and Papashka had already started to recall huge chunks of his past – things like his name, his family, his old home, but it was our whereabouts that flummoxed him. That was until he remembered our cousins in Chelyabinsk. It was through them that the hospital managed to find us.

"Our Chelyabinsk cousins offered to take care of him, but they have a mentally ill son who needs constant attention. It wouldn't have been fair on them or on Papashka. In 1920 Papashka was moved to an asylum, but in 1921 it was forced to close from lack of funds. After that Papashka went to live with Doctor Riedle and his family on a small farm in the Urals. But then in 1922 we received a letter from Doctor Riedle saying that, with the formation of the collectives in Russia, the Riedle family had to leave their land, otherwise they would be sent to labour camps. They headed east with the rest of the German-Russo diaspora, and Papashka went with them. They now live by the Amur River somewhere near the border with China. Riedle works in the small hospital outside Blagoveshchensk."

"And there is no way of seeing him?"

"No." She sighed. "At first, I had nowhere to put my anger. I'd walk the nearby hills up to Guia lighthouse for an hour every morning just to get rid of all the frustration and fear. Now I keep it bottled up. Sometimes, of course, it boils over."

The temple once again grew silent. A fly flew around the joss sticks and landed on the altar table, on one of the kumquats. It crawled on the pitted skin, stopped to wash its face with its front legs.

"Do you feel better having talked about it?" said Izabel.

"Yes . . ."

"Nadia, these are terrible and shocking events. I feel for you so much," said Izabel, cradling her friend once again.

"Thank you."

"Phooey, for what?"

"For listening," Nadia said. "I haven't spoken about this for a long time."

"Will you be alright now?"

"Yes."

Izabel nodded hard, smiled. They embraced.

A few more minutes went by. Nadia felt her mouth pulling into a shape of a smile. "Don't you think you ought to find Carlos? We don't want him wandering the Rua da Felicidade without an escort, do we?"

"That's a good point." Izabel gave a wave and was gone. Nadia heard her footsteps recede down the *hutong*.

A moment later Nadia got to her feet and started walking towards the circular moon-shaped doors. She saw Iain kneeling by an oil burner, his jacket folded on the ground. She'd been aware that he'd been in the temple too but she'd been so wrapped up in her own memories that she didn't really care that he had heard her monologue. He stood up and they looked at each other for a few seconds. "Hello," he said. She looked away. The air was filled with the sound of cat meows and distant music, somebody on a nearby balcony was listening to a gramophone record. "I'm sorry," he eventually said. "Will you forgive me?"

She turned her back to him, and when he tried to touch her hand she wouldn't let him.

"I'm so terribly sorry about your father, Nadia. I really am. I never meant to upset you by talking about him."

There was gentleness and compassion in his voice. She turned and looked at him. He had another cigarette in his mouth, his forehead was furrowed and his red hair was damp with perspiration.

"Did you come in with Izabel?" she asked, knowing full well that he had.

He nodded.

She noticed how his sweat-soaked shirt clung to his back. "You've been waiting quite some time for me then."

"I'd have waited all night if necessary." His eyes fell from hers in embarrassment.

She smiled. "How's your face?"

He gave his cheek a rub. "You pack quite a wallop for a wee lass."

They began to walk back to the club. "You know, I know so little about you, Mr. Sutherland," she said. "Tell me a little about yourself. Your home in Scotland, this Helmsdale, where is it?"

"Way up in the north, on the east coast, fifty miles from John O'Groats."

"But you don't sound very Scottish?"

"My Scottish accent was hammered out of me at school. Christ's rinsed the 'Scottishness' away." And in its place, he wanted to add, had come something alien, something anxious and impatient; a hot stone to fill the hollow void.

"Ah yes, the school in Sussex. Do you have any family here?"

"No, not here in Macao, but back in Scotland I have a mother and two brothers, well one now. His name is Callum. My big brother James was killed in the war."

"What about your father?"

He hesitated. "I have a father as well, but we don't . . . we don't speak."

"No other dependants?"

"There's a barman at the Rex who's quite dependent on me, but no, nobody else."

"So, we're both living with loss," said Nadia. Conscious of a sense of fellow-feeling, they fell silent. They strolled past the buildings with the carved red lacquer facades and the painted Cantonese girls in the brightly-coloured cheong-sams, past the oil lanterns suspended from hooks and the urchins playing with bamboo hoops. Midnight bells chimed somewhere in the distance. The white scar of a youthful moon shone vivid in the sky like a wise, slow-moving eye. It was the start of a new day.

13

The following morning Iain, Costa and Peter Lee boarded a ferry to Taipa Island, the rural retreat a mile to the south of the Macao peninsula. They went swimming, diving into deep water off the rocks nearest to the boat jetty. Iain was an able, spirited swimmer and was not afraid of choppy seas. Costa, too, was accomplished in the water. Lee, however, never having learned to swim, remained on dry land, his light flannelled trousers rolled up to the knees.

As soon as they had established a beach towel camp, under a lean-to amongst the shade of some trees, Lee extracted the binoculars, charts and maps from the canvas grip, while Iain went to change in the nearby Nissen huts. He burst into laughter when Costa appeared, sporting a striped one-piece swimming costume with shoulder straps that hugged his grotesque belly like a dark, greasy merman's skin. "Christ almighty!" Iain roared. "A hippo in a leotard!" Costa was having some trouble with the garment catching at the cleft of his buttocks. "Your arms and legs look like giant cocktail sausages!"

Iain, by contrast, preferred to swim in a pair of old long johns. And despite the salt-sting to his neck wound, he loved the feel of the cool water as it coated his body, the freedom of the tides caressing his muscles, his limbs rejoicing in the challenge as he fought against the swells. Below the tide level Iain chanced upon clusters of sea urchins, and on the rocks that made up the small cliffs he found slippery weeds and several delicate flowers which succeeded in growing in the little crannies: a type of purple gerardia, a species of sea lavender, and tiny yellow flowers with indigo leaves often too small to see with the naked eye. Iain snatched a long train of gerardia from the rock face and kept it in his hand.

When Costa climbed out of the water, scrambling across the shingle of loose pebbles, bedraggled and panting, Iain offered the big man his shoulder for support. With Costa clambering to his feet, Iain surreptitiously slipped the trailing loop of gerardia he'd kept in his hand into the V-shaped ravine of Costa's ass cheeks. The gerardia drooped down the backs of Costa's oily-smooth thighs like a purple tail. It gave Iain a curious pleasure to see his friend, his face framed by sea-weed hair, advancing up the beach like a huge, capsized troll, the thin purple plant jutting out from what looked like two over-ripe glistening guavas. Iain listened to the giggles. He tried not to laugh. Only when he heard the guffaws from the local fisher-women, perched on the edges of their sampans, did Costa reach behind him with a curse.

The surf washed Iain ashore. Out of the water, he laid his hands on the sand and proceeded to perform fifty press-ups.

"What are we doing here, *Vermelho*?" asked Costa, slumped on the dune like a marooned sperm whale.

"What does it look like we're doing?"

"Right now it looks like you are fucking the ground."

"It's called blending in. If we're being watched, I want it to look as though we're enjoying an outing."

"Oh, you mean like a company field trip. How shweet! I should have brought some teacups and a leetle cake!" He scrubbed sand off of his belly as if they were sugar grains. "Tell me," he said. "What wass the final verdict from the coroner?"

Iain hissed with the intensity of effort, relishing the hot burn racing through his muscles. "Koh thinks our victim, B 188, was probably suspended by the wrists, his mouth stuffed with rosaries. Somehow he drowned in fresh water."

"A cruel way to die. How many is that?" said Costa.

"Thirty-four . . . only sixteen more. Shut up and let me finish!"

"*Vermelho*, why do you have to be so intensh about everything, eh?"

"Why? Because somebody booby-trapped my house and tried to take my head off. And they're bound to try again."

Costa glanced at Iain's neck. "A mere scratch." He looked up into the cloudless sky, at the early pinkish sunlight, then quickly down to his toes. "Argghh! Crab!"

"Stop whining you old lump, it won't bite."

Costa started hopping from foot to foot.

"Can't you just act like any normal person would at the beach?"

"Sorry, *Vermelho*."

"Now when I'm done I'm going to race you down to where Lee is . . ." as he said this, he realized that this was how he loved to live his life – to the full. Whether it was performing press-ups, or preparing poached eggs for breakfast, or taking a walk in the mountains, or delivering a speech to the ombudsman, he did it as best he could, never one to cut corners. It wasn't in his nature to do otherwise.

"Again with the competitiveness. When we play golf or tennish, you try to thrash me. When we go out drinking, you drink like a sailor in a rumshop, always wanting to get me ass-hole drunk. And what is that Scottish saying you taught me? The one I now yell at my neighbours at three in the morning?"

Iain completed his forty-third press-up. "*Slainte mhath!*" he grunted.

"That's right – '*Slainte mhath!*', '*Let's have a kiss!* Now, it is like a reflex for me, I yell it every time I arrive home! My neighbours think I am a hooligan!"

Iain started laughing. His laughter grew infectious. Soon Costa was laughing too. "You are a shtrange potato, *Vermelho*. Sometimes you make me shout for joy and I adore you like I adore a child, other times I can wring your neck."

Iain carried on laughing. "Forty-nine. . . . I'll give you a five second head start. Loser pays for lunch. Ready?" Costa thundered away.

Iain completed his fiftieth press-up and scurried after him.

As soon as he and Costa got to the lean-to and beach towels, Lee was talking excitedly. He'd unfurled one of the Public Works Department maps and pinned it down with stones. "Look at this, *lo baan*!" He was trying to draw attention to several points on the map all at once. "These are the four areas where the storm sewer flows out into the sea. One, in north side, flows into *Canal dos Portos*," he jabbed his finger at the top of the folded sheet. "Another, we have it coming into the *Porto Interior*, the third," he moved his hand to the right, "we have *Porto Exterior*. And last one is this," he stabbed at the expanse of water between Taipa and Macao. "Barra Point, at the southern tip."

Iain stood in the sun, drying his hair. "Four exit points. Yet if you study the sea currents, only one of them fits the criteria. Only one could have taken the body to where it was eventually discovered."

"Barra Point," trumpeted Costa, panting, still pulling his swimming costume from between his ass cheeks. A shower of sea water droplets fell from his arms and splattered the map.

"That's right. The undertow from the Taipa Strait kept the body from floating out to sea."

Costa picked up the binoculars and peered through them, searching for something across the stretch of water, towards the column of Indian fig trees. "So what necksht?"

"We search every storm drain that runs its pipes through to Barra Point."

The rolls of fat seemed to quiver about Costa's jowls. "I'm not going into any fucking shoe-wer."

"Yes, you are fat boy. An old turd like you ought to see the sewers."

"Can I come too?"

"No, Lee, you go home and spent time with your mother. This is big boy's work."

"I fucking show you I big boy too!" Wind-tossed and shirt flapping, Lee jumped to his feet, spraying sand across the maps and towels. "You look! *Haaa-chaaa!*" He snatched at the air with his hands, coiling his left knee. "Praying-mantis kung-fu! *Horrr-chorrrr!*" He kicked at the sky and fell over.

Costa shook his head and sighed. *"Deus!* The lunatix you hire, *Vermelho!*"

That night Iain stood alone in the darkness, trying not to make any noise. The Rua da Barra was a narrow, quiet avenue on the waterline that marked the southern fringes of the city proper. Beneath an inclining umbrella of Indian fig tree, Iain drew on a cigarette. He had advanced cautiously, eased himself silently into the shadows to observe the coolies loading wooden crates off the pier. By Ponte No. 23 the sampans and wallah-wallahs knocked against each other as they slid with the glassy current. Delicate leaves littered the ground. Looking not at the floor but at the brittle tide, he watched a pair of kerosene lamps emerge from the black water in the distance like pinpoints, growing closer all the time. The swollen yellow lights danced and blurred soundlessly, making their easy approach to the shore. A little way away, a heavily muscled man in a singlet threw a coir rope into the water. Iain saw the ridges of sinew on the man's shoulders pull taut as he anchored the sampan to the pier. And then, quite abruptly, the lamps were extinguished.

A foreman who stood by the godown across the street shouted a question in harsh Cantonese syllables. Voices murmured then died away, footsteps sounded on timber and vanished. For a while Iain turned the cigarette around in his hand, hiding the crimson glow within his palm. He'd learned to smoke this way in Amiens, concealing the cigarette within his hand, to prevent snipers from homing in on him at night. He waited for the godown doors to open and shut, for the trolley cart to drive its deep grooves into the beaten-earth ground. He made out four, perhaps five head-shapes, but then the night clouds came over the moon, and made everything turn pitch. There was a momentary stillness. Iain remembered it being like this during the war, when every branch that the wind lifted, every rustle of a leaf, sent a whistle of alarm through his chest. Even the cicada's chattering sounded like the feathery scrape of a knife. Someone lit a tiny flare and he saw now that the trolley cart had been pushed to the end of the small pier; it gaped empty and forlorn. They were working quickly.

When the wind shifted direction, the salt air spray blew directly at Iain; he let the spume cool his face, then glanced furtively around to see if he was being watched. The light improved as the moon reappeared in the sky, freeing itself from behind the clouds. The alleyways were deserted. Satisfied, he turned his attention back to the water's edge. He looked at his watch – a quarter to two. All about him the croak of tree-frogs began to fill the air with loud reports. Iain glanced sharply round. He saw that the men were using ropes to lower the crates into the little craft, which seemed to ride lower under their weight. There was a cough of diesel, a compression of air in cylinders, a *chak-chak-chak* of metal-on-metal. The engine spat into life with a cackle and with a pronounced shiver the sampan began to move, parting the thick, dark water of the bay like the head of a Yangtze alligator. It cut into the low swell, squirmed and creaked, dwindling, before losing itself in a knot of blackness.

Despite the breeze, the night was hot, the humidity close to ninety percent. Sutherland removed his jacket and held it with two fingers over his shoulder. He was perspiring freely, the sweat covering his chest and neck forming prickly heat spots. He left the security of the Indian fig tree and circled around, retreating fifty yards to a spot where a stationary vehicle was parked. Just as he got to the Packard Sport Phaeton it started to drizzle. He climbed in, left the door open and squinted through the windscreen.

"What do you think?" he said.

Costa was leaning an arm against the window, cradling his head in his hand. His melon-bellied gut was growling and so was he. "What do I think? *Filho da puta!* I think we are crazy to even consheeder going down the shoewers at night. There might be river alligators down there!" The colour had gone from his face. "Do you have a gun?"

"No."

"Here, take this. It's A Webley Mk VI."

"I don't need a revolver."

"*Vermelho*, have you any idea how big those shoewer rats are? You remember what they did to that man's foot? They'll go right through your shoes and nibble away your toes. Nibble, nibble, nibble!"

"All right, give it here. What about you?"

Costa flourished a Colt 0.45. He waved it towards the warehouses. "What makes you think this is the shpot."

"Those men from the godown are up to something. I think we're getting very warm," was all Iain said in reply. He took the metal hand crank resting by his feet and walked round to the front of the automobile. A few seconds later, the double-beam headlamps blazed awake and the eight cylinder engine shook to life.

In the darkness, nineteen feet underground, Iain and Costa made their way through the subterranean ducts, flashlights in hand. Every step took them deeper into the main tunnel, passing under brick arches that rested on brick buttresses. A rivulet of black water rippled past them, full of fast-flowing solid matter. The walls dripped with moisture, rats scuttled along the handrails. The stench of shit grew stronger with each passing moment.

"Join the Breetish Colonial shervice," Costa's breath

quivered. "Enjoy the glamour of the Empire. Journey to fascinating, exotic play-shes . . ."

"Quiet!"

Iain raised his torch. They were climbing a gradual slope.

They reached a drain duct where it appeared as though some of the exterior wall had broken loose and the innner pipe had been damaged. Iain shone his torch at it. "What do you make of this?"

Costa stooped in order to get a closer look. "I'd shay either extreme water pressure hazh caused this or something big and solid was clogged here. It's bent the mouth out of shape."

"Do you think you can fit inside?"

"Me? In there? These are brand new trousers!"

"Come on you fat lump, if they get ruined I'll buy you a kilt to wear." He pulled on Costa's arm. "Follow me."

The pipe was 40 inches in diameter, just large enough for Costa to squeeze through on his haunches. They entered the narrow tomb in a crouching walk.

"What if I get stuck?" said Costa.

"Than I'll fetch a corkscrew."

"You are a fucking *bastardo*, you know that don't you, *Vermelho*?"

"I know."

Their voices echoed within the piping. A stream of cool, clear water ran past their ankles. Costa grunted hard each time he drove his knees forwards. Happily, the conduit seemed to widen the higher they climbed the gradual gradient. Costa started coughing. "No air down here. How much further?"

"Ten feet, maybe twenty, and then it should lead into an internal catchment basin."

Iain pushed forward. The walls of the slender tunnel were getting slippery. He had to dig his fingers into the glazed clay grooves of the pipe to get any purchase at all.

A few minutes later they flopped into a reservoir of

stagnant rain water, holding their arms above their heads to keep their flashlights dry.

Like a pair of soggy spaniels, they pulled themselves out of the water and shook themselves dry, walking along the narrow perimeter, feeling their way through the darkness. Rats plopped in and out of the water. Cockroaches and white millipedes dribbled up and down the slime-encased ramparts. Iain aimed his torch towards the ceiling.

"What are we looking for?" asked Costa. Both men were perspiring heavily.

"A large metal hook."

Iain crouched, looked along the line of his torchlight. "There," said Costa, pointing with a fat, wet finger. Iain trained his eye.

On the far side of the tiny reservoir, hammered into the brick wall, were a series of elongated iron spikes.

"Keep a look-out for king rats," Iain ordered. He skirted around the outer edge of the water. Brushing close to the wall, he placed the ends of his fingers against the smooth upsweep of a spike, and said over his shoulder, "They're like meat skewers." Costa's flashlight bit sharply in his eyes. "And what do you suppose is this?" His hand tugged at a loop of knotted cord-like fibre.

"Part of the rope that held our drown veectim."

"Exactly." Iain's mouth tingled. Twinges of fear, no more. "So this is where they killed him."

He felt Costa squeeze his arm. "I theenk I know what happened." The fat man looked from an open storm duct to Iain then back to the open duct again. "Over here," he stomped forward, illuminating the wall directly above with light, "on the night of the beeg typhoon, the water came rushing though from the street. It wash like a river, powerful, strong, tearing our dead man off of his hook. He must have fallen face down and drowned in the fresh water. Later, the shtorm drains must have clogged. The water level started rising. Remember all the rats? They were in a panic. Some-

103

how they must have eshcaped through the maintenance tunnels."

"But why would the storm drains clog? Our friend, B188, didn't clog the drains otherwise he wouldn't have been flushed out into the sea. No, there's something else."

"Look!" said Costa. His torch shone on a flat metal panel, about half way up the wall.

"It's a kind of floor hatch or trap door. I'll bet that's not in the Public Works records."

Hoisted on Costa's shoulders, Iain tugged at the iron facing. "Jammed shut. Probably locked from within."

"Can you shee any hinges at the edges?"

"Yes."

"Shoot out the hinge barrels," said Costa, holding Iain's ankles. "And for *punheteiro's* sake hurry up! Your shoes shmell of sheet!"

Iain paused, handed Costa his torch, rebalanced himself on the big man, before unclipping the revolver from his belt. He grasped the joists of the door with one hand to stop himself from being thrown backwards and lined up the gun muzzle to the hinges. He fired three times. The gun's recoil threw him sideways. He almost overcompensated but corrected himself just in time. Seconds later, the twin hatch panels squealed obdurately and the trapdoor dropped out, falling into the reservoir below with a splash.

"What's up there, *Vermelho*?"

Craning forwards, Iain broke the news in a whisper. "Looks like a laundry chute. Here," he uncoiled a rope-ladder that was fixed to the wall, "come see for yourself." His voice echoed in the hollow chamber. Costa climbed the rope-ladder and together they pulled themselves up the chute. Iain's heart was pounding, the gunshot was still buzzing in his ears. "Where the hell do you think this leads to?"

They pushed their way through to the top of the chute. Costa's torch illuminated the chamber. Their torches hosed the walls. They were in a plain, oblong, windowless nook with a wooden door at its centre. Everything stank of footsweat and old tea. In one corner were five or six large water-proofed bags.

The flesh across Iain's eyes tightened. Inside the bags, he found a jungle of wood straw which served to protect hundreds of thickset rectangular packages hidden within. These were neatly stacked, encased in brown paper, with bamboo twine tied round them.

"Dar o rabo!" Costa cried, spraying light in all directions. He mopped his face with his shirt, bent down and brought one of the packages to his nose. He threw back his head. *"Vermelho,* this is all opium!"

14

They gathered at the situation room in the basement of the British Consulate. It was nine in the morning and the sun had risen thickly from the sea. Ten feet separated Iain Sutherland from Utaro Takashi, the head of the Golden Tiger secret society. Takashi sat hunched at a table, hand-cuffed, a sly smile imprinted on his loamy face. He had humped shoulders, a beak nose and tapering eyebrows that curved down sharply like half-moons. Iain thought that he looked like a hooded vulture.

Iain and Takashi were staring hard at each other, like rival huntsmen.

"Why did you stuff his mouth with rosaries?" Iain asked Takashi.

"A message. Rosaries are a Cazzolic symbol. The Golden Tigers are at war with the Cazzolic gangs."

"A little melodramatic, don't you think?"

"I will remember you, Suzzerland" whispered Takashi. "I do not forgive, I do not forget. In many years time, when you least expect, I will find you and kill you."

"Send me a postcard from prison, won't you?"

"Maybe you laugh now, but we will see who is laughing when I put a knife in your chest."

Behind them Costa toyed with a cup of coffee and looked immensely hungry. When the Police Commissioner appeared at the door, striding in, wringing his hands with delight, Iain jerked his gaze away and got to his feet.

"Top-class job, Mr. Sutherland," the Commissioner said.

The banks of telephones began to ring.

Iain handed over a short hand-written report. He explained the situation to the Commissioner: "Whenever there was a police raid, they sealed the bags of opium and threw them down the chute, through the trap-door. Then they plugged up the hole and rolled the carpet across. Someone down below later secured the bags onto the hooks and left them overnight until the coast was clear."

"What happened on the night of the typhoon?" the Commissioner wanted to know.

"The water pouring in from the storm drains was so heavy it must have first ripped our dead friend off of his perch, and then carried the bags off . . ."

"Which clogged the drains."

"Hence the rats."

The two men exchanged looks. "I will instruct my men to officially charge Takashi for opium possession and smuggling. Oh, yes, and we have also arrested a armourer linked to Takashi, a man who specializes in booby-trapping shotguns. There won't be any further attempts on your life." Iain received a firm handshake.

Nadia and Izabel arrived at Government House early. There were two armed Angolan soldiers at the front gates who stared through them as though they did not exist. They climbed the stone steps into the gently echoing foyer and made their way through the azulejos-tiled atrium. Potted hinoki-trees and gigantic oil portraits of past-Governors lined the walls. The receptionist nodded in greeting.

"We are here to see the Health Minister, Senhor Queiroz," Izabel told the receptionist.

They were kept waiting for over an hour. Then they were shuffled from one imbecilic clerk to another. After a further bout of mindless waiting, Izabel could stand no more. She abducted an undersecretary and claimed she was from the Red Cross Society. Within minutes, she and Nadia were led up a flight of red-carpeted stairs to an office at the end of a corridor defended by a guard in full regalia.

Without knocking, Izabel barged through the door and found a fastidiously dressed man napping fitfully at his desk. "Are you the Minister of Health?" she demanded. "Are you Senhor Queiroz?"

"*Que? Quem?*" croaked the man, who in panic, lunged for his telephone.

"We are here," said Izabel forcefully, "to make a formal complaint about the babies. I have in my hands a petition. A petition I sent to your bureau in triplicate a few days ago."

Queiroz rubbed his nose. He was holding the telephone receiver to his lips. His baffled, watering eyes looked beyond the women towards the door. "Who . . . who are you?" he asked.

"I am Senhora Perera." She sat down opposite Queiroz and removed her gloves. Nadia drew up a chair too. Seated, her cloche hat as tight as a bottle cap on her head, Izabel frowned hard at the minister.

Looking skittish and bug-eyed, his hair like concertina wire, Queiroz attempted a smile. "If you're here to complain about noisy babies from adjoining apartments," he was stabbing at the dark, "then you have come to the wrong man. You should be speaking to your landlord or the Housing Minister."

"I'm here because of the abandoned babies that hang from the gates of your hospitals," Izabel said, hot-faced.

"Oh," he said.

"How long do you think a baby can live without food, exposed to the elements? And what about the rats? We all know about the rats!"

His tone became assertive, affording a muscular timbre. "I assure you, our hospitals do what they can but we simply do not have the facilities to – "

"Nonsense!"

"You have to understand that hundreds of infants are left

on our doorsteps each year. If we had the manpower we would take them all in, but we simply cannot . . ."

"So you leave them to die. Just like that. Without any moral qualms, you let them die of heat or cold or hunger. I hear their damp yelps, Senhor Queiroz. They are tiny little things. These infants are two, three days old, their bare feet are purple, most will still have their birthing cords still attached – "

"In China baby girls are burned, smothered, thrown to scavenger dogs."

"This is not China! We are a Portuguese colony! This would never happen in Lisbon."

He gave her a long, mocking look. "Then I suggest you go back to Lisbon."

"How dare you! You little worm!"

"Senhora Perera, listen to me, you're wasting your time."

"What you mean is that I'm wasting *your* time, that's what you're really saying, isn't it? Where's the Governor? I want to speak with him."

Queiroz busied himself arranging his shirt-cuffs. "He is out of town."

"I demand to see him! Otherwise I'll be taking this up with the Portuguese Colonial Office, the Colonial Secretary himself! If necessary, I'll take this to the judges committee. Your name will be plastered all over the *Jornal Acoriano Oriental*!"

Senhor Queiroz's voice changed – reflecting uncertainty, dismay and an unquestionable desire to bolt for the door. "Senhora, please, you must understand. There's only one orphanage in Macao."

"So build another! We're not talking about stray cats here! These are children! Children! Their lives rest in the palm of your hands and you choose to pull them under, drown them!"

"I haven't drowned anyone," said Quieroz.

"It's a metaphor," said Nadia.

"You just wait until I speak to the Colonial Secretary. My husband has connections you know!"

"Calm yourself, Senhora."

"Calm myself? Calm myself? There are three-day-old infants dying on my doorstep and you tell me to calm myself?" Izabel was spitting tacks. She slapped her hand against the desktop. "You tell the Governor, he hasn't heard the last of this!" She rose and marched out of the office with Nadia in tow.

They stomped down the flight of red-carpeted stairs, both women swinging their arms with anger.

"*Bawzhemoy!*" Nadia said, unable to repress a smile.

"Was I any good?"

"Any good? I can't believe you were haranguing him like that. You were like a possessed madwoman in there!"

"That hateful man!" Izabel kept repeating. "Hateful!"

Their heels echoed angrily across the azulejos tiles.

"Where are we heading to now?" asked Nadia.

"To see the sign-board maker on Rua do Gamboa. Do you know anything about forming a picket line?"

A little later on, up in their office, with Lee installed in the corner, busily typing out aide-memoires, Costa reclined in a rush-bottomed chair, picking his teeth with a thumb nail. His feet were perched on a filing cabinet and he was staring at Iain.

Iain was thrumming his fingers against his leather-topped desk. The tension from the previous night still pulsed through his veins.

"You should learn to relaksh more, *Vermelho*. Tensh nerves lead to tensh shoulders that lead to tensh assholes. Next thing you know your shit ish like stone, hard as broken beer bottles, and you're straining on the *toalete* all day, pulling at the laces of your shoes."

"What the hell are you talking about?"

"Constipation. A lazy colon. The beeg push. In Portuguese we call it *obstipacao*."

"Obstipacao."

"Yes. A terrible business. If you're not careful the pylorus shnaps shut and then your shtowmach fills up with gashh. You Scots people probably suffer from it all the time. It's your diet. Olive oil ish what you need. It shtops things from drying up. Olive oil."

"Oh God," muttered Iain. "I'd forgotten you were a failed medical student."

"But of course I have the perfect cure-all."

"I'm sure you do." Iain watched with disinterest as Costa lifted his ham hocks off the filing cabinet and began rummaging through one of the lower drawers.

"For lubrication," he said with a wide grin, setting two glasses and a half-drunk bottle of port on the clerical desk.

"You ridiculous fool. It's only just gone ten o'clock, for God's sake."

"So?" Costa looked offended.

"Aren't you meant to be interrogating that melon man this afternoon?"

"Meal-on man?"

"You know, the fellow who tried to smuggle two pounds of opium in hollowed-out melons."

Costa's face contorted into a mask of suffering. "What am I supposed to do until then?" He looked at the leftover scraps of pistachio crumbs on the desk. Licked up a few specks with a damp finger. "Maybe I go and fetch some breakfast, eh? Maybe I go get a custard bun."

"Please."

Costa cleared his throat and played with the two shot glasses for a few seconds. Then, with a resigned sigh, he scratched the back of his neck and shuffled out of the room.

"Lee," said Iain, standing. "Stop what you're doing and come with me."

Screwing up their eyes against the sun, Iain and Lee ambled down from Avenida da Republica towards the Praya Grande, towards the dappled shadows of the banyan trees.

"Where we going, *lo baan*?"

"To a jewellery shop."

"Jewery shop? Why?"

"I need your bargaining skills."

When they came to the Governor's mansion and the shotgun toting Angolan sentries, they bumped into Izabel Perera. "Ola!" she cried, flourishing a scroll of paper in Iain's face. "Please sign this petition," she said feverishly. "It is for the children." Iain wasn't too sure what she was talking about but signed his name regardless.

"Has you been seeing Nadia?" he asked in his hillybilly Portuguese.

"I left her with the sign-maker."

Iain nodded, confused. "I want me to be going now," he said.

Five minutes later Iain's back was soaked with sweat. At the junction of Rua Lisboa he hailed a rickshaw and gave the puller the necessary directions. He and Lee climbed over the shafts and into the apple-green vehicle to sit on the rattan padding. The red pram-like hood gave them some relief from the sun. The puller lifted the shafts and proceeded to struggle slowly up the Estrada do Penha towards the imposing church on the hill. The spoked wheels turned, began a slow trundle round the tree-lined Rua da St. Lourenco.

The route took them past a little park with lotus gardens. He felt his body relax, his shoulders go slack. He took in the tiny pond, the rockery, the artificial grotto, the azaleas and bougainvilleas. He saw a group of *fah-wong* women squatting on the lawn clipping the grass with scissors and the barefooted local gardener with a pair of watering drums slung from a bamboo pole balanced on his shoulder.

"Curious, isn't it," he said to Lee, "that Chinese gardens are always built around water."

"You have gardens in Scotland?"

"Not many. It's pretty barren around Helmsdale and Golspie, not much around Brora either. There are some

Versailles-inspired gardens at Dunrobin Castle that spring to life in the summer, but they belong to the Duke of Sutherland."

"Is Duke your fadder?"

"No."

"I saw that you receive letters from home today?"

Iain nodded. "From my mother. She wanted to know if I wanted another package of Nairn biscuits and Orkney oatcakes."

"Do you feel nostalgia for your mudder?"

"Aye." He felt nostalgia. He missed seeing her at the stone sink in the kitchen, rinsing potatoes and turnips. He missed her large square hands rubbing his ankles after a football match. He missed the tweedy roughness of her embrace, the smell of fried herrings in her hair, the sound of her infectious laughter, the trill of her voice as she sang along to the music playing on the phonograph. More than anything, however, he missed talking to her.

"Tell me *lo baan*, what is she like?"

"The most sweet-tempered soul I've ever known."

"And your fadder?"

Iain tried to picture his father's curled-lip expression and his broken-toothed smile; as a boy, he'd lost a few teeth playing shinty, resulting in a grin which made his mouth resemble a crossword grid. Iain sighed. He felt incapable of talking about his father. His mood darkened.

He visualized all the old faces, the narrow streets, he peaty water, the predatory crouch of the cormorants, the Sunday service at the Cross Free Kirk, the silent congregation of men and women in grey tweed. He heard again the calls of the Helmsdale trawler men as they pushed their dinghies out to sea, the familiar voices of the ladyfolk pinning up their washing, the children playing tug o' war in the gorse with some unfortunate woman's bedlinen. These recollections came to Iain more often of late, and then something occurred to him: it had been sixteen years almost to the day. . . .

He saw the train heading south for Inverness; he saw his tearful mother waving her goodbyes with a white handkerchief, the stationmaster cocking his blue cap.

The smell of the heather blooming was everywhere that hot August; the purple and red-tipped flowers swaying and wrinkling the heathlands, the oystercatchers dancing in the distance, flecking the horizon. His thoughts took him back for what must have been the thousandth time to that day on the strath. He replayed the scene again: he saw the rush of the river, the water the colour of cobalt, the stars low in the uncrumpled sky. He pictured himself climbing the cattle fence, making his way through the shrubbery. And then he was standing by the river again, under the protective canopy of a large birch tree, near the Kildonan Falls. He knew nearly every stone, every fencepost along the beat. The clearing was full of deer tracks, rotting pine cones. There was the smell of churned mud and the wet leaves had grown slippery under the soles of his waders. He saw himself securing one end of the 10-foot net to the earth using wooden stakes, crossing the river at its narrowest point with the other end still in hand, sinking it with rocks; he followed this by throwing stones into the downstream pools to scare the fish upstream into his trap. He repeated this six, seven, eight times. His haul grew until he had four grilse and three salmon lined up under the birch tree, like seven bars of silver, almost more than he could carry. Then he heard a twig snap.

His father had made almost no noise on his approach. He remembered turning toward the figure coming out of the undergrowth, out from the woodland path, lifting his head, seeing his father's bewildered face, feeling absolutely helpless. The light of the moon lifted off the water. His father, the river bailiff, was the huntsman, he the hunted. He remembered the poaching net trembling in his fifteen-year-old hands, the glinting salmon, dead on the crumbling bank. Both men standing frozen to the spot. The look of disbelief on his Daa's face. The incalculable and incomprehensible shame.

Iain Sutherland closed his eyes. Sixteen years ago, he reproached himself, sixteen bloody years.

The road forked at the top of the Rua da St. Lourenco. The rickshaw turned into Rua Central then slowed to a wobbling halt fifty yards from the line of jewellery shops and gold outlets.

Iain alighted and paid the rickshaw boy.

"I need you to get me a big discount," he said to Lee.

Lee nodded.

Iain felt a strange sensation building within his chest – a curious, unfamiliar mixture of exultation, excitement and fear. He saw again what he'd chosen in the lighted window – it was snuggled on a little velvet cushion next to an elaborate string of pearls – and parting the red, beaded curtain with his hands, entered the shop, sweat streaming down his back. He guided Lee towards the display cases full of ivory and jade and diamonds set in platinum. He told the proprietor, an elderly Chinese man, what he wanted and asked to see it. The proprietor smiled a broad gold-toothed smile. He indicated a chair and called through the door for his wife to bring tea. "You number one custama for today," he said, grinning. "I giff you number one spesso pwice."

15

A day or so later Iain went for a walk with Nadia up Guia Hill, with its views of Taipa and Coloane, famed for their firework factories, matchstick makers and black sand beaches. Nadia pointed out the broad tracts of coarse farmland, the pitch and roll of the low, green hills, the little huts made of bamboo-and-wattles.

At the top of the footpath Nadia began passing out leaflets calling for the end of infanticide and urging the Government to act. On the reverse of each flier, printed with orange crayon, was an advertisement publicizing the charity bake sale to be held in the gardens of the St. Lourenco church. Although initially apathetic, Nadia was now swept up by the cause – Izabel's dedication to it was proving to be infectious.

Having handed out half of the fliers, they visited the white-washed lighthouse. From the observation platform they looked down and saw the ground dropping away, the sweep of pine trees, and the outer harbour full of silhouettes of slow-moving fishing junks heading in and out of the open sea. They also saw three tiny figures marching back and forth along the gates of Government House, white signboards flashing in the sunlight. "Oh God, don't tell me that's who I think it is," said Iain.

Nadia nodded. "Izabel, Mamuchka and Mrs. Lo."

"How did she rope your Mum into this?"

"She offered to buy her lunch."

"Why aren't you down there?"

"Me? I'm passing out the fliers."

"You're quite commited to this now, aren't you?"

"Yes."

Later they took in a Hollywood matinee at the Roxy on Rua Victor. It was so hot in the theatre that almost every person was waving a paper fan or newspaper. When Nadia handed out more fliers, people wiped there foreheads with them, complaining bitterly about the stifling heat. At which point the screen came alive with newsreels showing the civil war in China – fighting in Hailufeng, Chiang Kai-shek's troops killing Communists in Shanghai, houses burning in Ninggang County, Kuomintang Nationalists singing as they advanced through the paddy fields of some southern province – and the carping ebbed to a muted whisper.

They didn't stay for the whole show, preferring to retire to a little *restaurante* on the corner of Rua Direita. They ordered spicy African Chicken and a plate of grilled fish and both thought at the time that only the intimate could eat together and be this happy. It made him want to appreciate her, reveal things to her. Over a bottle of *vinho verde*, they disclosed little secrets to one another, tiny hidden thoughts, making jokes about their bizarre food cravings. He admitted a passion for hot sauces and a weakness for chocolate violet creams, Caramel Bullets and 'soor plooms'; she confessed to hating black olives and liking pickled beetroot with custard. But it was what she revealed over coffee that really surprised him – she spoke about her early childhood in Russia and the deep feelings she had for her family.

She told him about her summers spent playing in the enormous haystacks that dotted the meadows, diving in and out of them like a trout in a stream, and how in winter her father would build her a toboggan run made from ice that stretched from the first floor balcony down to the pond. Her blue eyes started laughing in the sun. As she spoke, Iain saw not the woman in the restaurant, hands gripping the table, but a little girl running with her father through the cornfields, her arms clamped around his shoulders, teeth glinting with laughter. She was vulnerable, soft, devoid of cunning. It made Iain feel rotten about himself because his initial approach to Nadia had been professional and deceitful, a fact of which she was unaware. He wondered whether he ought to tell her about Lazar.

Oblivious to Iain's disquiet, Nadia sat sipping carbonated water, peering at the cardboard menu; she was genuinely excited. There was so much she wanted to know about Iain. So many questions she wanted to ask. She felt in the top half of her head, just above the eyes, a lightness; a thrill that was extending across her skin and surging outwards from it, illuminating the room. It made her want to smile.

Nadia looked at him. "Tell me", she said. "What exactly is it that you do?"

He paused, thought for a moment. "Oh, this and that . . . I work for His Majesty's Government. I guess you could call me a sort of licensed rabble-rouser."

"Oooh . . ." she said, eyes brightening, playfully veiling her face behind her napkin. "You mean you're a spy, a mole, a *shadow*."

"Nothing of the sort." He took a long gulp of beer, draining the glass. She laughed at his visible unease, feeling oddly satisfied.

A moment passed before he said, "Nadia, I've been thinking about your father. Can you tell me more about him?"

Her eyes looked away. A waiter brought a fresh basket of hot bread rolls and a plate of paprika-coloured sausages. "What do you want to know?"

"Anything really. What can you remember?"

She thought for a moment and laughed, covering her mouth with a hand. "He used to call me his little chimp because I used to climb the trees in the garden like a monkey."

Iain smiled and seemed pleased with himself. "His little chimp, yes, you've mentioned that before. What else?"

Nadia leaned back in her chair. She had broken a bread

roll in half and was hollowing it out, digging a hole in the centre with her thumb. She took in a breath and heard herself sigh. "He was a good-looking man, four years older than Mamuchka. He was dark, his face slender with the same blue eyes as mine. Back in Russia people always teased Mamuchka that she was lucky to get him. And Mamuchka said that he made people laugh, never at their expense, or by showing off, but by poking fun at his own faults. Someone once said that when he looked at you it was as if the sun was shining on your face. But I think the reason people liked him so much was because he possessed a frailty which people couldn't quite identify. It was as if he needed you. He met Mamuchka at a playhouse in Moscow, in between scenes of Moliere's *Bourgeois Gentilhomme*, when he fell through the floorboards of the dress circle into her lap. Papashka said it felt as if he'd fallen onto a thick foamed layer of eiderdown. The look of horror on her face made him laugh. They fell in love instantly. Woodworm was to blame."

Nadia could still hear his voice sometimes. Deep, tender, with a flutter of mischief.

"Do you miss him?"

Nadia looked at the bottles that lined the bar and thought hard about this. She was pressing a sausage into the hollow centre of her bread roll. "I don't know," she eventually said. "I really don't know anymore. Sometimes there's a pain in my heart." Her voice tailed away, enfeebled by the nearby bark of an alley dog.

"Don't you want to hug him, don't you want to be a family again?"

"My father disappeared when I was seven years old. Much of what I remember of him are merely images from photographs. Not knowing him through that transition of childhood into adolescence then into adulthood, not having him around to witness my achievements, my disasters, seeing me fall in love, fall out of love, all the questions you wish you could ask your father, it's a – I don't know the

English word for it. In Russian we say *oorezeevats*. Like a cutting off."

"A curtailment."

She nodded and took a bite out of her sausage sandwich. "It is a curtailment that never leaves you. One of the most influential characters in the story of my life was written out of the plot too early. It has left me floundering a little bit, made me unsure what I want to do with my life. And I hate it."

"Surely it's not too late to – "

"It's been twenty years, Iain. I just want some sort of resolution now. For me to live my life, I've had to let a piece of him die. Sometimes I think what it might be like if he was to walk through the door – I don't know how I'd react. A part of me yearns to have the past back, even if it's only for a few minutes. But there's another part of me, a darker part that wants to bury it, just so that there's no more pain."

"What about your mother? How does she feel about it?'

"Mamuchka?' She sighed again. "Mamuchka's spirit is like a tree slowly shedding its leaves . . . her heart will take a long time to die. I think Mamuchka would do anything to see him again. Anything."

"You say he's living somewhere on the Amur River?"

"With a family called Riedle. His letters are postmarked Blagoveshchenck. But his letters say he is in a village called Elychoko. The handwriting is rarely ever the same, so he must be getting someone to write them for him."

"Blagoveshchenck." Iain said, trying to picture a map of Manchuria in his mind. "That's on the Amur's left bank, I think. It's a huge stretch of water that freezes over completely in winter; about two, maybe three miles wide, and very hazardous to cross in the summer months. The nearest city on the China side would be Heihe."

Nadia didn't seem to be listening to him. "Strange isn't it" she said, deep in her own thoughts. "First we were separated by fire, now by water."

"Do you still think about that day the fire took your house?"

She placed her half-eaten sausage bun onto the plate. "Sometimes, I do. Yes."

"Is that how you got the wound on your arm?"

Dazed at the suddenness of his question, Nadia involuntarily ran her fingers along her forearm, felt the hard bumps on top of the granulated skin – a reminder of my past, she thought.

She jumped a little when she felt the touch of his hand on hers. And she saw for the first time that it wasn't because of his looks or his strength that she liked him; it was his tenderness.

"I'm sorry, Nadia. I'm a bloody fool. I shouldn't have brought it up." He reached over and caressed a strand of her hair away from her eyes.

The touch of his hand stayed with her for the rest of the day.

16

The next afternoon Iain took Nadia swimming in Taipa. "Aren't you on flier-duty today?" he asked.

"No," she grinned. "Today's a rest day. Izabel's got blisters on her feet from marching too long!"

They changed out of their clothes in the Nissen huts that fringed the far end of the beach, hanging their things on hooks. Nadia took a couple of turns around the drab grey concrete floor, which was polished shiny with use, unsure whether her costume might be a tad risqué. She wore an open-necked outfit with ruffles, with her arms bared and her legs exposed to mid-thigh. A yellow scarf was knotted to her head, gypsy-style. She was more than a little embarrassed about showing off her legs in public.

Iain jumped off the high rocks into the deep water with a splash, while Nadia bathed in the torpid shallows, in the glorious silkiness of the currents, away from the froth and boil of the creaming cauldron of waves. There were little fish patrolling her knees, showing off their bright golds and speckled greens, while matchstick-thin eels searched the stones and grasses for food. With a moan of pleasure, she swam on her back, on her front, even under the surface for a time, holding her nose, but the water was too opaque to see much. When she and Iain tired, Iain picked up a string of seaweed and threw it at her. She leapt out of the water in hot pursuit of him but stopped abruptly. Iain dashed out of the surf and looked around, was waiting for her on the sandy shore.

"What's the matter?" he said.

"I'm not coming out of the water until you get me something to put on."

"Why?"

She cupped her hands over her breasts.

He went over to the Nissen huts and returned with her sandals, dangling them on the ends of his fingers. She started laughing. "I meant a towel, *byeazoomyets!*"

He stood, watching her, the surf receding from his ankles, feathering his toes.

"No towels," he said, shrugging. "Sorry."

She stood defiantly in the water for several minutes. Then unravelling her wet scarf and wrapping it round her thighs, she raced out of the water to sprint after Iain with a handful of seaweed. When she caught up with him, they embraced at which point Iain twirled her about on the sand as if they were dancing. He lolled her head back in a tango move and she laughed. They looked into each other's eyes.

Afterwards, they spent time on the cliffs overlooking the fishing junks soaking up the sun, making little stick figures out of grass and small conifer saplings as thick as a man's finger. Nadia slipped her blouse over her swimming costume, feeling her wet arms snag and pull on the sleeves. Later, they went gathering pebbles and shells, picking them out of tide-soaked hollows and tidal recesses, and carrying them in the apron of Iain's loose white shirt. Searching for the stones, which were so smooth-grained, so variably coloured, pleased Nadia as much as the swimming. Some of the pebbles were mountain ash grey and had long, slanted pink lines running across them; others were rich chocolate brown with raspberry blushes bursting to the surface. Most of them, however, were a dark, deep blue and marked with blotches of silver or stripes of white.

When they wearied of collecting pebbles, they strolled to the little ferry pier and sat upon the wooden anchored floats, dangling their toes in the sea, splashing water at each other in little sprays of blue. Looking down from the floats, into the water below, they saw tiny pouches of seagrass softly waving with the tide and tiny translucent fish swimming between their ankles. When they got to their feet, they noticed a Chinese woman with a snub nose and piercing mascaraed eyes standing by the landing stage, evidently waiting for the next ferry boat. She had a shawl draped over her shoulders and a fat bouquet of wet, white lilies nestled in the crook of her elbow. Iain said hello and nodded in her direction. The woman nodded back.

Turning to Nadia, Iain smiled a tiny enigmatic smile. Self-conscious, he folded his arms across his chest. "Nadia," he said with care, inclining his head briefly. "Your father . . . Papashka . . ."

She looked up from the water, her little girl's eyes, edged in gold, expressing a few moments of confusion. "What about him?"

"There's something I want to know."

"What?"

"Something about his character – what was he like?"

She looked suddenly unhappy. "No," she said. It was a quiet 'no', not a sob, but a refusal that slid away with the sea. "It's been so long, Iain. I don't wish to discuss it."

"Why not?"

"I just don't."

He wondered why she was reluctant to talk about her father. Was she keeping something from him? Hard little thoughts bobbed about inside his head, tiny fragments of doubt. When he'd asked her before whether she missed him, she'd answered that she really didn't know anymore. Yet Iain had to make sure. If he was going to go through with his plan, he had to be certain. He swallowed hard and let out a breath.

"Nadia," he said, delicately. "Was he a good father? Was he a loving husband? You told me that if he were to suddenly walk through the door, you wouldn't know how to react."

Nadia looked back down into the water and rubbed her cheeks with the back of her hand. She started squeezing out the wet hem of her scarf.

"Nadia, talk to me."

"He's gone, Iain, he's a part of the past."

"He's not gone. You told me he still sends word to you. You write to him. Tell me. Please. Was he a good father, Nadia?"

She exhaled deeply, looked almost helpless.

She took in a breath to collect herself. "Yes," she said. That was when she turned to him and looked right into his eyes. "Yes, he was. He was kind, he was funny." She stopped, then, softly, she said, "He was the centre of my world, Iain."

Soothed by the tidal throb as it lapped against his feet, Iain said, "I want to help him."

"*Help* him?

"Yes. Nadia, what would you say if I told you I could reach him." His eyes were assessing her. "My job, the people in my field . . . they can do things, open doors."

Nadia looked at the horizon. She shook her head. Her voice was a distant, shaken whisper. "You can't – no one can."

"That's not true."

Nadia opened her mouth to speak but no words would come out. For so long she had told herself that the past was no more, just a mass of darkness, that there was nothing to be done. It was what she had tried to believe. But she was wrong. It was always there. In her heart she was still the devoted seven-year-old girl, lingering at the foot of Mr. Bogdanov's doorstep, waiting, looking at the kink in the dirt road, at the outline of trees, wishing, praying – praying that a troika would round the treeline, its great wooden wheels turning, kicking up dust, just as Mamuchka came running out of the house, screaming with laughter and joy. And then the tears would squeeze from Nadia's eyes, taking the hurt away. Because Papashka had jumped out from the troika, arms outstretched, reaching forward to throw her high into the air, squashing her to him, with the words, *I'm home, little chimp, I'm home*, ringing in her ears.

Nadia looked at Iain now. This was her chance, she thought, her chance to have her life whole again, without the darkness, the pain, the broken-edged past. For a moment her spirits leapt and galloped. But then she saw the futility of it all, remembered all the bitter moments she'd spent with Mamuchka, sobbing with dumb frustration, when all their dreams of celebration came to nothing.

Her heart sank. She pictured the awful blackness of previous failures, the despair and rage that came with all the let-downs. She knew from experience that when people talked about helping Papashka – the embassy officials, lawyers, the diplomats – they had always fallen short. This was old, well-trodden ground; a path that always led to disappointment. And she resented Iain suddenly for talking about it. She fixed him with a stare.

"I can find him, Nadia."

"Don't say that!" she said, starting to rise from the wooden decking. "Don't say that if it's not true."

He grabbed her arm. Like a fish, she wriggled past him, and got up from her knees.

Her voice was trembling. She shivered hard, as if it was winter outdoors and not the moist heat of summer. "Don't you dare try to sweet-talk me by making rash promises, do you understand? Don't you ever do that!"

"I'm not trying to sweet-talk you, Nadia. I mean what I say. I can help you, I know I can. I can get your father out of Russia."

Izabel made a thin, startled sound and started laughing. Nadia's cheeks reddened.

"What does he do?" asked Izabel.

"I'm not really sure. He's attached to the British Consul. He speaks several languages – Cantonese, a bit of French." She paused. "Maybe he's a spy."

"A spy? Phooey." Izabel repeated several times. "The only thing he wants to spy on is your laundry."

At that moment Nadia realized how much she was enjoying herself. There was a period not long ago, she thought, when everything seemed dull; when doing ordinary things meant little, when doing little things felt ordinary – the daily walk down to the vegetable market, the donning of a pale blue blouse, the state of her bob and how it fared in the wind. These used to be mundane concerns. Now everything took on a new importance. She realized she might bump into Iain at any time; the white muslin dress with the moth holes by the sleeve, the ancient scar-tissue along her right arm, the old black shoes that sagged from overuse, the unsightly droop of her buttocks – now took on fresh significance. And why was it that when she walked down the street she smiled for no reason? Smiled big, like a nincompoop, prompting strangers to smile back at her in return. How strange, how wonderfully strange, she decided, that he could make her feel like this, as though she'd spent the night at sea, with the floor swaying beneath her feet. It was a peculiarly heavenly feeling, yet at the same time it made her feel quite sick.

To her, Iain Sutherland was a mystery; he didn't fit her typical mould of a Scotsman. He didn't wear a kilt and have wooden teeth, didn't stagger about drunk on Friday nights, he didn't have moths living in his wallet, nor did he suffer incorrigible bouts of dourness and introspection – in reality, he seemed to Nadia to be quite the opposite in nature. He was generous, exuberant and candid. In fact, in her view, he appeared to have not a worry in the world. Yet, there were times, whenever he looked deep into her eyes, when he seemed to be a very contemplative, profound person. He seemed, as her Mamuchka would say, *saversyhenstva* – the complete package, almost perfection. The backs of Nadia's hands usually grew sticky with perspiration when she thought about this. Perfection was a word she used to describe a Russian fruit cake or a Mozart aria – not a man.

For all that, there were moments, late at night, when Nadia pulled her emotions apart, yanking at threads of conversation, trying to search for meanings in his words. Often she squinted into the darkness, wanting to sleep yet never feeling so awake, finding few answers, experiencing a host of contradictory things: fear, excitement, joy, expectancy. Maybe, she thought, she ought to just try and put him out of her mind, convince herself that it was simply a passing infatuation, but because she had so much time on her hands, memories of him trickled into her thoughts night and day, without warning. It usually added a glazed-over sheen to her eyes.

"You're thinking about him again aren't you," said Izabel, who was securing a Red-Indian bandana to her son's head. A good two minutes of silence had passed.

Nadia tried to hide her embarrassment but nodded nonetheless. "I can't seem to help it. I wish I could just shoo the daydreams away, but I can't," she said. "You know, before I met Iain I was a little scared of men, but when I'm with him it's different. And the more I think about him the more I want to settle down. I envy you, Izabel, as a wife and mother. For the first time, I feel tempted . . ." Her mouth smiled as she spoke.

"Would you like to have children?"

"One day, yes. Doesn't every woman eventually want children?" She could feel the throb of contentment in her chest. "God, listen to me. I sound ridiculous."

"Phooey! I felt exactly like you when I first met my Jorge."

"Jorge? You're married to Carlos. Who on earth's Jorge?"

"Jorge was the butcher's son. He used to deliver meat and

sausages to our door. I remember I was nineteen and infatuated with him throughout that long, hot summer. Twice a week he used to drive the cart right up to the door and I'd wait by the window where he couldn't see me and watch as he ambled up the garden path, basket in hand, with a bundle specially wrapped for my mother, all tied up with paper and string. Simply thinking about him would make me all tingly and flustered.'' She broke off her narrative just as her youngest child, Jiao, came in to demand biscuits. When Jiao had gone she leaned in close to whisper, ''I enjoyed a little kiss with Jorge in one of the back alleys once, but then one of the neighbour's girls said he couldn't get it up . . . so I lost interest.''

''Izabel!''

''It'd be like going to a restaurant and ordering a good hearty plate of *chourico* only to get a lukewarm bowl of cabbage soup, don't you think?'

They were still giggling when Carlos walked in. He had heavy eyelids which made him look dozy, like a kitchen hand who has just seen all the potatoes he must peel. The girls left Carlos with the children and danced downstairs and across the road to Nadia's apartment, where the kitchen was warm with the smells of cooking. The countertop was replete with containers of sugar and diced garlic and ground meat – all immersed in larger bowls of water to keep the ants away. Mamuchka was in her apron arranging crispy-fried piroshkis in a blue ceramic dish. She was getting some help from her friend, Mrs. Lo, the lady who sometimes child-minded Izabel's boys.

''Have you heard the new Hoagy Carmichael song?'' Izabel asked Nadia.

Nadia shook her head. ''I wish I could get Iain interested in music. I'd do anything to get him to swap his Jimmy MacKay records for some Bessie Smith or a bit of Kansas City jazz.''

Nadia's mother smiled at Izabel and gave her a wink.

"*Chtonovava?* What nonsense are you two talking about now?"

"We're talking about boyfriends," said Izabel.

"Oyo," Mrs. Lo said to Nadia. "You finally have a boyfriend? Wahhh!" She took Nadia's head in her hands and made spluttering noises, '*tchoo, tchoo, tchoo, choy choy, choy*'

"Why is she spitting on you?" asked Izabel, her eyes wide.

"To celebrate good luck and ward off evil spirits," said Nadia

"Who is name of man?" asked Mrs. Lo.

Nadia looked at Izabel, as if to decide what to say.

"Not the magistrate, Senhor Pinto, I hope?" said Mamuchka in a teasing tone.

"No, he too short," said Mrs. Lo.

"And old," said Izabel.

"He not so old."

"What do you mean, not old," Mamuchka contended. "When he smiles his skin crackles like a *gorodvoi's* patent leather boots!"

"A face that launched a thousand groans," said Nadia.

"What year he born?" asked Mrs. Lo. "Is he a dragon year? If he born in dragon year, tell him he must wear red underpants until new moon comes."

"I don't think I know him well enough, Mrs. Lo, to offer that kind of advice," said Nadia.

"My son a dragon," said Mrs. Lo. "Red underwear bring him plenty luck."

Nadia knew that Mrs. Lo liked to mention her son quite a lot. "How is Lennox," she said. "He's doing very well, I hear."

Mrs. Lo beamed from ear to ear. "Oh, he doing fine. He bring in soap and other top, top things from Portugal. You see that soap in the shops called *Musgo Real*? That's my Lennox. Business is prospering."

Satisfied she'd made Mrs. Lo's day, Nadia turned to her mother. "Mamuchka," she said. "You're a woman of the world. How would you go about winning a man's heart?"

"Food," she replied. "You win a man's heart through food. Biscuits usually work, dzhust feed him some biscuits."

"He's not a sheep dog, Mamuchka."

"Is he Russian?" asked Mrs. Lo.

"Scottish," said Nadia.

Mrs. Lo shook her head. "Ayaa, Scottish very dry people."

"*Lyubov'zia, polyubishi kozin* - love is blind," said Mamuchka.

"Russian marrying Scottish no good. A chicken can not talk to a duck."

"Scottish?" Mamuchka said, as though suddenly realizing something. "You don't mean the red-headed fellow who was asking all those questions about Lazar, do you? *Bawzhemoy!* Why didn't it occur to me before?"

"What?"

"The man's a fraud."

"What do you mean?" said Nadia.

"He's a fake. I heard it from Lazar, himself. He's a kind of policeman, interviewing all sorts of people about opium smuggling. All this talk about love is dzhust nonsense. He's stringing you along so that he can get close to Lazar. He's playing you for a fool, Nadrichka!"

Nadia was more used to thinking than acting, but her anger would not be restrained. She walked all the way to the British Consulate, her cheeks burning. With every step, she heard her mother's voice, reminding her that she'd been played 'for a fool' and taken advantage of. Everything that Iain had done appalled her: the stealthy questions regarding her family, the conceited attempts to charm her with lies, the false kisses, the fictitious and deceitful promise that he could help get her father out of Russia. She'd thought she was in love . . . thought she was loved.

By the time she reached the Avenida da Republica, she felt as if her tongue had been honed into a kitchen knife. She marched straight upstairs and raised herself to her full height. "Where is he?" she said, barging into Costa at the top of the steps. Angry pulses of perspiration appeared on her lip.

Surprised, Iain got up as she entered his office. He studied her face for a few moments. Her look of disgust seemed to suck the light from the sky. "Are you sick?" he said.

"You're the one who's sick," she said, her hands clenched into fists. Her mouth was like a chamber-pot. *"Zhri govno i zdohni!"*

"What's wrong?" he exclaimed.

"What's wrong?" she repeated, her tone was piercing and strange. "What's wrong is you, that's what's wrong. You're an imposter. A bloody two-faced lying . . . arggggh!! Did you ever think I wouldn't find out?"

"Find out what?"

She stared at him. In her anger, she swayed slightly. Her face contorted. "You're a bloody shit," she said.

"Ha!" laughed Costa, entering from the hallway. He struck a match to light a cigar. Nadia watched the flame. A greater heat simmered in her chest.

Nadia glowered at Costa, before turning back to Iain. "How could you lie to me? Say those things about helping Papashka when all you wanted was to get close to Lazar. I feel humiliated, ridiculed."

"Lazar? Is that what this is all about? Lazar was just a lead. The man we were really after was Takashi. He's in jail now." Iain stepped forward. "Look, I never lied to you. I just didn't . . ." he hesitated, "I just didn't tell you the whole truth – "

"I see. And that's ok is it?"

"What I said about your father is true. I still mean to help him. To help you."

"You're a liar! A liar!"

"Pants on fire!" Costa sang, puffing on his cheroot.

"Will you shut up!" Iain shouted. Costa winced and backed out of the door.

133

"Well, at least now you'll have an amusing story to tell your friends," she said, sharply.

"For God's sake, Nadia, the whole Lazar episode was before I got to know you."

A pained light entered her eyes. "Before you got to know me?" She snorted. "You don't know me, Iain. And you'll never get to know me."

He was speechless. She walked slowly out of the room.

Iain followed Nadia down the staircase and watched her board a bus. He called out to her but she wouldn't turn around. He watched the bus buck forward as it accelerated away, spitting up dust.

In a deep funk, he turned back towards the Consulate gates. With one eye on the fast-disappearing bus, he noticed Peter Lee coming down the steeply sloping road that connected the Praya to Barra Hill. He was carrying a clay pot in his arms.

"Hey, *lo baan*!" he shouted. "My Ma-Ma make you some *haam-yu-gai-faan*."

Iain was about to thank him, but all of a sudden stopped short. Something appeared out of the corner of his eye. It was someone he'd seen at the ferry pier a few days before, the snub-nosed Chinese woman with the white lilies. The scent of the flowers rose to Iain's nostrils as a host of pointless questions surfaced in his head: Was the woman lost? Was she following him? What was she doing with these flowers? Was she trying to sell them?

He experienced a moment of cold confusion.

The woman half-ran, half-marched up to him. Mascara muddied the skin beneath her eyes. Iain stood still, expecting her to say something. Instead, the woman snatched back her shawl and pulled out a pistol. The white lilies fell from her hands, spilling. Now she held the gun at arms-length, aimed at Iain's chest. As she squeezed the trigger, her mouth exuded a hissing sound.

The next few moments came in waves. There was a loud scream. Lee jumped in, holding up his crooked fingers as a means of defence, pushing Iain to one side. A gunshot split open the air. There was a stifled howl, a rain of blood. Lee went sprawling, his head breaking open, his gaze huge, looking far away, ivory white.

Then Costa's hands were on the woman's throat, his thumbs against her windpipe. They were both on the floor. Costa was squeezing with all his might. She gagged, making wheezing noises. First her cheeks, then her whole face turned from red to deep puce to blue. Her legs kicked frantically, heaving, hauling, jerking. Baring her teeth, her lungs gurgled.

She went limp.

Iain knelt down at Lee's side. He cradled him in his hands, watched the lights in his eyes grow thin and fragile and timid. Iain felt his friend's urine warm his knees.

The bullet had bitten a chunk off the side of his head like he was a half-eaten apple. Lee gulped for breath. His stare swelled; the real fear in his eyes unutterable, intractable. He flung an arm out and dragged Iain close. At almost the same moment, death came, very suddenly. Iain laid his hands on what was left of his assistant's face. "My God,' he said. "My God."

People stood around, unsure what to do. Some of them crossed themselves three times over. A shudder washed over Iain A dark chamber inside him opened, set his arms and legs quivering. Memories of the war – slippery duckboards, gunfire, explosions, the countryside bombed black by shells – came back to him. He let out a wail.

18

Iain stood at the window. On hot mornings like this the stench of sewage and sour cinnamon lifted off the open gutters and hovered over the city like a wet veil. His office felt small and the ache in his head was sharp, making him want to lose his stomach.

"Yesterday's killing of Peter Lee," the Police Commissioner said, "merely highlights how dangerous it is for you to remain in Macao. I'm afraid we made a terrible miscalculation. The woman was one of Takashi's people. A trained assassin. She may be one of many."

The sun was low in the sky and the windows of the houses behind were obscured with lines of washing. Iain could hear the Hakka women in their black lampshade hats chattering in the street below; their serrated voices pounded his head purposefully; it was market day and in his foggy mind he could visualize the makeshift stalls strewn across the broken brick sidewalk, see their assorted wares – fried cinnamon dumplings, temple incense and fruit. He could hear the talk of politics and minor warlords, about the retreating Communist party, the failed Nanchang uprising, and how businessmen in Shanghai and Peking were throwing money at the Kuomintang Nationalists. He could also see the bloodstains on the road left behind by Peter Lee.

Iain placed his palm on the back of his neck and dryheaved. The smell from the cinnamon dumplings seemed to stick to the roof of his mouth. A peculiar chill flooded his brow followed by a pinching so extreme he creased over.

"We think it prudent," the Commissioner continued, "if

you went away for a time. Let us know your decision." The policeman left the room.

Iain turned his gaze away from the road. After a while he closed his eyes and said, "He was only twenty-three."

"You're in danger if you remain in Macao." It was Costa's voice spilling out of the shadows. He had a cup of steaming *café preto* in his hand and a brown package with a torn red wax-stamped seal. "The grey suits are talking about moving you."

"I don't want to be moved."

The big Macanese nodded. "That's what I told them."

"I expect they want me back in Hong Kong."

Beached like a walrus in his chair, Costa said. "Whitehall's shtarting to worry about the Japanese and this Shantung incident," he said, scratching his belly through his shirt. "There was a bloody, yet brief, armed conflict between Japanese forshes and the Kuomintang southern army. The Kuomintang emissary was killed."

"I suppose Whitehall expects there to be more skirmishes."

Costa shrugged. "It looks like they want somebody in Tsingtao."

By *somebody*, Iain imagined that Costa meant Paul Katkoff his colleague in Shanghai, which was four hundred miles from Tsingtao across the Yellow Sea. "You mean Katkoff, I suppose."

"No."

Iain looked aghast. "Not me, surely?"

"Yes, you."

"To Tsingtao?" Iain shook his head. "Who rubberstamped this?"

"Du Maurier in Sh-tation C, Peking. He asked for you shpesh-ifkly. Read the report yourself if you don't believe me."

"Who's the liaison officer in Tsingtao?"

"A fellow called Fielding from the Administrative Service. Do you know him?"

"Aye, I know him. He was the liaison officer the first time I landed in Hong Kong. The man's a prick, a *trusdar*. What about in Dairen. Do we have a man in Dairen?"

"Cooke," said Costa. "The man in Dairen is called Cooke. Why?"

He rubbed the skin between his eyes. "How long do you think I'll be gone?"

Costa shrugged and ran a hand through his mesh of sweaty hair. "Seex months, maybe longer. Who knows? For as long as it tayksh for things to cool off here." He leaned forward, exposing parts of his pink belly where a shirt button had popped.

"Why don't they send Katkoff?"

Costa looked at Iain incredulously. "It's 1928, *Vermelho*. Perhaps you've forgotten there's a war going on in China. The anti-foreign rampage has already claimed the British concessions in Hangkow and Nanking. And Shanghai is still unshtable – only a year ago the Municipal Council declared a State of Emergency. Remember there was that fighting near the Settlement between the Nationalists and the Communists? Katkoff can't be risked."

"But I can?"

"You'll be shafer in Tsingtao than here. Of course, you could always take offee-cial leave."

Iain thought about this and realized that because of the civil war in China, he hadn't taken a holiday in three years. "Yes, I could take official leave." Iain got up and approached the window. He looked across to Government House where he could see Izabel Perera marching with a face like thunder. There was a Chinese lady picketing as well, but he couldn't see Nadia. Then he spotted her standing by the seawall, staring out into the ocean, her hands balled into fists.

"Tell me," said Iain. "How far is Tsingtao from Heihe?"

"Heihe?"

"Heihe, Manchuria. On the right bank of the Amur River."

"How should I know?"

"You must have some idea?"

"Why are you always ashking me these difficult questions, *Vermelho*?" He closed his eyes, as if trying to picture a map in his head. "At a guess, I would shay about a thousand miles." Costa raised his eyebrows. "Why do you want to go to Heihe? Is that where you intend to go on holiday??"

Iain said nothing. A plan had already formed in his head.

19

The very next evening, Nadia and Mamuchka were in their kitchen. They were planning on making 100 rambutan tarts for the charity bake sale to be held in the gardens of the St. Lourenco church. Earlier, they'd heard about Peter Lee's death outside the British Consulate – something that the press put down to illicit opium trafficking – which made Nadia push all thoughts of Iain even further away.

"Horrible, isn't it, Nadrichka?"

"Yes, horrible."

"Turning this peaceful place into the Wild West . . . I'm so glad you have nothing to do with Iain any more."

Nadia did not reply, instead she broke open a hairy-skinned rambutan with a thumbnail and, spreading the sections like petals, squeezed the white marrow out – luscious, translucent, pulpy, shimmering with juices.

The kitchen was an old room, floored in pale wood with a dust-covered bulb in the middle of the ceiling that gave off a faded light the colour of grubby tea. Nadia and Mamuchka were standing at a long oak table; it was draped with layers of green gingham tablecloths. The whole house seemed to swell with the aroma of cooking.

A basin of milk was full of soaking custard powder, a curlicue of honey was running off a thick wooden spoon, and a batch of cornflour and desiccated coconut was on the stove. There was also a platter of chopped rambutan and black persimmon – their chewy seeds removed – a salver arranged with apple crescent moons, a tin of Banania tapioca and a fat pitcher of freshly whipped cream. Plates and saucers were piled up high. Nadia added teaspoonfuls of honey and knobs of butter into the milk and custard mixture, stirring it as it simmered, feeling something black and hot smoulder in her heart.

"*Beris'druzhno ne budet gruzno* – many hands make light work," said Mamuchka.

"When the baking is done, Mamuchka, will you join us down in Government House?"

"Nadrichka, let me be honest with you. Much as I support Izabel's intentions and admire her conviction, I don't think we should get involved."

"Why do you say that?"

"People are already starting to talk. They're branding her a troublemaker."

"But it's an honourable cause. I feel ashamed that no one has done anything about it before."

"That may be so, but you know how people are." Her voice was intense yet gentle. "They're like sheep. Everyone's afraid to buck the system. And don't forget that we're outsiders. Despite living here for almost twenty years, we'll never be regarded as Macanese. The last thing I want is for the authorities to brand us as troublemakers too. There's nowhere for us to go if they kick us out, you know."

"Don't be so melodramatic, Mamuchka."

"I'm not being melodramatic, I'm being sensible. Put these in the oven for me, will you?"

Just as Nadia was preparing to slide the tray of pastry shells into the wood-burning oven, she heard a knock on the door.

Uncle Yugevny's eyes were heavy-lidded and dozy. He looked like a grumpy, bespectacled bear roused from his cave. There were grease marks on his spectacle lenses and, blinking like a pothole dweller, he wiped his hand on the tablecloth and leaned on one leg to remove something from his trouser pocket. It was a small present, square in shape and wrapped in shiny red paper.

"For you," he said to Nadia.

"What's this?"

"That red-headed, nincompoop friend of yours left it at the counter. Wait. There's a letter that goes with it."

"Wh-what did he say?"

"He said something about a vegetable."

"A vegetable?"

"By the eyes of the *domovoi*, you know what his Portuguese is like? I think he was trying to tell me he was going on a journey."

"Is he still downstairs?"

"No, he is gone. He mentioned having to catch the afternoon steamer to Hong Kong." Uncle Yugevny returned his eyes to the bowl of olives. "He also asked for some photographs."

"Photographs?"

"Yes, he wanted something to remind him of you, and asked if he could take the one of you as a little girl standing with your father by the fountain in Vadra."

"Did you let him have it?"

"I did. At first I was reluctant to give such a precious thing to him, but he promised to give it back and take care of them. Why? Did I do wrong?" When Nadia did not reply, he scratched his head. "I will be in the shop if you want me," he said, walking out the door, wiping his glasses with his thumb.

Nadia tore open the envelope and read Iain's words. *Dear Nadia, I have had to go away,* said the note. *The other morning, when we were sitting in the square under the big banyan tree, I was going to tell you something.* She felt her face burn and flare, and she set her mouth tight, determined not to cry. *Something I had rehearsed for hours. But as soon as I started to speak . . . well, needless to say, I lost my courage. If I have hurt you in any way, please forgive me. It was never my intention to deceive you. My heart has belonged to you from the moment we first met. Keep this gift close to your heart. Remember me always. Yours, Iain.* She removed the top of the little red box. Inside she found a cirrus of cotton wool, and inside the cotton wool, sitting on a bed of tissue, was a tiny, jade monkey pendant, carved into the shape of a banana leaf. It was attached to a gold chain. Her hands began to tremble; she felt the stifled air rush out of her lungs with a gasp. Her anger towards him dissipated. "Oh God," she said, fighting for breath and turning away from her mother.

"*Bawzhemoy!* What is it, Nadrichka?"

"He's gone."

"Who has gone?"

There followed a forlorn silence. Then Nadia whispered the word *Papashka*. She said it with a hooded breathlessness, as though it was a secret blown across a jagged beach. She made to leave the room but her mother blocked the doorway with her body.

"What do you mean, Nadrichka. What are you talking about?"

Nadia raised both hands, palms upturned. Her mind felt like two birds flying in opposite directions, one out the front door of the house, the other out the back. "Oh God! Mamuchka!" Nadia looked white in the face. "I think Iain's gone to do something very stupid."

"You're not making sense, Nadrichka. Why are you looking at me like that?" Nadia went to hurriedly remove a bottle of port from the shelf. She laid out two Russian glasses, set them down right next to the jade monkey pendant. There were all sorts of knots and tangles inside her stomach. Anxious, with unfounded hopes, she yanked the cork off the bottle and said, "I don't want to say this. What if I'm wrong?"

"What is it? What's the matter?"

"Maybe it's something that I've imagined . . . but . . . I think Iain's gone north."

Mamuchka shook her head. "I don't understand."

"I think he's gone to get him."

Mamuchka stared at her, as if Nadia had somehow betrayed her. Her voice quavered now. "Get who, Nadrichka?"

She covered her trembling mouth with a hand and closed her eyes.

"Nadrichka, why are you crying? What are you trying to tell me?"

"Papashka, I think Iain's gone to get Papashka."

PART TWO

Autumn 1928

1

Within a week of Iain's arrival in Dairen, Manchuria, the weather had turned bitterly cold. In the three months that it took for him to journey north and arrange what needed to be arranged, rain had turned to snow and freezing air had begun to blow in from the high table-lands of the interior.

During that time, Iain had been very busy. To begin with he had to gain an extended leave of absence, attain the necessary entry visas for travel through the Three Eastern Provinces, then make contact with his SIS counterpart in Manchuria and find temporary accommodation. He also acquired several maps of Northern China, a Commercial Traveller's Guide to the Far East, and bribed several people to keep his movements quiet to avoid suspicion. Everything began moving quickly after that.

Bundled up warmly, wrapped in a woolen scarf and coat, his red hair crinkled in windswept waves, Iain waited for Cooke to arrive. He was breakfasting in the square opposite The Yamato hotel. A bowl of steaming noodles sat on the table before him. He ate little of it.

In the distance he could see the ocean. A torrent of sampans, lighters, cockboats, double-enders, wallah-wallahs and shallops crammed the docks cheek-by-jowl. Ships' bells clanged in the filthy harbour.

He didn't like Dairen; at one time part of a Russian-leased territory, it was now controlled by the Japanese, with a Japanese governor general, and aside from the former Russian Governor's Palace and the properties in Nicholas Square there was little to admire. Iain thought it charmless and ugly

– every other building was either a gas works or a sulphuric-acid factory. It reminded him too much of Glasgow.

Cooke, a veteran of Amiens, was tall and slim with a fresh healthy face and thick earlobes. He emerged out of a rickshaw at the circular plaza and came forward now, greeting Iain with a wave. Cooke only had one hand. His left paw was a stump, severed at the wrist like a snapped-off icicle.

He sat down, looking preoccupied. A pot of tea was set before them. Cooke drew in a breath and ran his good hand through his oiled hair. "Well, I think I've got everything you asked for," he said.

Iain rummaged in his pocket and extracted a cigarette, stuck it in his mouth. "Including a guide?" he asked.

"Yes, I found a Russian-speaking guide who can get you across the Amur River."

"What about guns?"

"I've found you a pair of M-1891 Cossack rifles. They are standard Russian infantry rifles used during the War. You'll want to blend in, so no point carrying British weapons."

"Yes, that's good. Well done." His thoughts hurried ahead. "And furs? You've got furs. Good. How cold do you think it'll be?"

"If there's no wind, minus five on a good day. Minus thirty-odd when the weather closes in for the winter. I strongly advise that you to get in there before then. However, there are Red Guard river patrols out in full force at the moment, so your best bet would be to wait for the Amur to freeze over and cross it on foot. How many people are you looking to bring back with you?"

"I don't know for certain," he said. He was thinking about the Riedles. "I know for sure that I'll have one passenger, a very frail one at that. There's a chance of two or three others."

"The danger is that if you cross too early the ice won't have set and you might fall through it, too late and your sick passenger's liable to freeze to death. It's a small window of opportunity."

Above them, a clock struck the quarter hour.

Cooke pulled a watch from his pocket and both men rose from the table. "Let's take a walk," said Iain.

They made their way across the square and headed into some backstreets. With the advent of winter, the snow fell like drifts of sifted flour. Beggars and pavement-dwellers, wrapped in tattered animal skins, huddled under lean-tos, scratching out life from the slush.

"Rickshaw! You wan Rickshaw?" bellowed the touts from every corner. Despite the wafting snow and harsh wind, dozens of sleet-covered Mongolian ponies and coolie-carts were out on the streets, dragging gunny sacks of grain, rice, melon seeds, blackened bananas, straw braid and lumber from north to south, east to west.

Iain and Cooke continued to walk straight ahead. The route took them past buildings with walls punctuated with Chinese graffiti: *Down with Imperialism! Abolish unfair treaties! Boycott all Japanese Goods!*

Their feet crunched against the thin snow. The twinkling ice stretched along the street like a long sheet of shellacked tin. Overhead, dark clouds gathered.

Cooke reached into his overcoat and extracted a pair of train tickets. "I've got us a late evening departure, leaving tomorrow. Means we can sleep a bit if we want. We'll change trains at Mukden and I'll accompany you as far up as Changchun. That's where the guide will meet you. We've arranged a truck to take you to Heihe from there."

Iain thanked him again. After a pause he asked, "What's your section saying about Soviet Russia? What's the current political climate? Do I need to worry?"

Cooke was expecting the question. He pulled his watch from his pocket once again and twirled its chain round his finger. "Stalin's government seems to be in a state of organized chaos. They've been trying to put forward the idea of a collective farm system, but they've come under heavy resistance. Last year there wasn't enough grain being produced in Russia, so now there's a bread shortage. It might lead to another famine. Stalin's blaming the kulaks."

"Who?"

"The kulaks are the wealthier peasant class. Last year's grain harvest was three million tonnes less than the year before. The kulaks were accused of hoarding. They've refused all along to sell grain at state-fixed prices. Chances are Stalin may invoke a state of emergency and confiscate kulak land and cattle and turn it all over to the collectives. There's going to be widespread resistance. I'm told there's rural discontent, a lot of suspicion and widespread resentment."

"So I should watch my step."

"The countryside's swarming with urban-party cadres and Red Guards. It's a rotten time to enter Russia uninvited. Things are getting ugly there."

They crossed the street. By the bus terminus, they witnessed a procession of shorn-headed Chinese men wearing wooden blocks round their necks being paraded through the streets of the city. Their legs were in shackles. The message on their block-collars read: *'Condemned to death for opposing The Japanese Imperial Army.'*

A little further on, they looked on as three White Russians were systematically beaten up in front of a Caspian tea house. The Japanese soldiers were demanding to see their papers but all they had were outdated Tsarist identity-documents. With no jurisdiction or consulate to protect them, their statelessness rendered them easy targets.

"Things are getting ugly here too," Iain said.

"It's a cakewalk compared to what's happening in Russia." Cooke scratched the back of his head. He let his hand fall to his side. "These people you want to go in and get," he said, looking puzzled, "who are they? Why are you doing this?"

Iain didn't reply for a while. The questions hung in the air. He felt a pang. Should he confide in Cooke? Would he understand? Should he admit to wasting SIS resources?

To being a fool? A romantic? Searching his heart, he only found more unanswered questions. His conscience flooded his throat like sour milk. He had to say something. He decided to tell Cooke the truth.

"I'm trying to reunite a father and daughter. I'm hoping to help a woman, a woman who means a lot to me." Then, to his surprise, he added, "I'm also trying to ease my own guilt having destroyed my own family."

They found an empty compartment, sagged into their fitted seats which folded down into beds, and opened several bottles of beer. Their passage north to Mukden took 8 hours by train; it was followed by another long rail journey to Changchun, the northern terminus of the South Manchuria railroad. During that time, to calm Iain's nerves, he and Cooke played a variety of pen and paper games such as squares, battleships and hangman, and occasionally, when very bored, they played fan tan using a cupful of melon seeds acquired from the dining car.

Relaxed by the beer, Iain allowed his mind to conjure up images of Nadia. He knew that she wasn't speaking to him at the moment, yet he tried to picture her standing by the sea wall with the sun on her shoulders. He tried to imagine the joy in her heart when he returned with her father. But he could not. Instead, the burning sense of anticipation in his stomach grew and grew. And the closer they got to Changchun, the more uneasy Iain began to feel, so that soon it started to show on his face. As he peered into the darkness he thought of all that Nadia had lost – the life that she never had. Her home, her childhood, her father had been snatched away by fate. She'd been robbed of something. It made him remember the day he had stood on the railway platform as a boy, leaving Helmsdale in disgrace, Iain believed it echoed his own life in some respects. But in his case, fate wasn't to blame, the blame was all his, harsh and bleak and brutal.

"Another couple of hours to go," said Cooke, eyeing Iain

narrowly before gazing out the window. A shred of red light came through the narrow mountains. The sky was raw now. Dawn was approaching fast. "Are you sure you're ready for this?"

"I think so." In the subdued light Iain held his head in his hands. He let out a long breath. "What do you think my chances are?"

Cooke fluttered his eyes and sucked in a breath. "Let's look at the facts: you're entering a hostile environment; you're searching for a family called Riedle in a village called Elychoko near Blagoveshchensk, but you're unsure where they live; if you were to find them, there's no way of telling how they'll react to your advances – chances are they'll think you're dangerous and inform the authorities; but let's assume they're friendly and take you to Shaskov – you've never met Ilya Shaskov before, so there's a risk he won't believe a word you say. Now, you claim Shashkov is ill, do we know how ill? Can he walk? We don't know. Will he survive the trip? Again, we don't know. On top of that there are armed Red Guards swarming about, you don't speak a word of Russian and yesterday's wind chill temperature in Heihe was estimated at –22 C. All in all, I'd say your chances were pretty slim."

Such doubts weren't new to Iain – he'd been persistently troubled by them for weeks. He didn't like thinking about this, so he gave a mirthless laugh. "Thanks for the vote of confidence."

Cooke gave Iain a searching look. "You said earlier that you were hoping to help a woman. Forgive me Iain, but who is this girl?"

Iain started to answer, but drew back and said nothing.

"I presume she's White Russian and that she's Shashkov's daughter."

A silence. The volume of the train's chugging rose and fell. Then. "Her name is Nadia."

Bemused, Cooke said, "You obviously care for her otherwise you wouldn't be doing this." He waited a beat. "But are you sure she's worth it?"

"Yes." His voice rang full and true.

"What about the Riedles? I presume you'll take them with you? What will you do with them once you get back across to China?"

"There is a Lutheran Mission in Harbin who help Russians from over the border."

"And if you make it back, do you intend to marry Nadia?"

Iain's lips grew tight as though there was grit in his teeth. His heart ratcheted in his chest. He shrugged slowly.

"Do you think that's wise?" Cooke asked.

"You tell me."

"Marrying a White Russian," he said bluntly, "may cost you your job."

For a while they didn't speak or blink or even appear to breathe.

An hour and a half later, as they approached the city's edge, the porter knocked on the compartment door and came in with a tray bearing cups of hot tea and a plate of Chinese buns. As soon as he left, Cooke shook his head and brought a cup to his mouth. He watched Iain over the steaming brim.

"They'll execute you as a spy if you're caught. Either that or you'll spend the rest of your life working in a Siberian salt mine. The Soviets don't treat espionage lightly."

This was a phrase he'd heard repeated before. Iain felt himself grow cold. There was something in the way Cooke said 'they'll execute you' that made him quiver. It prised open a weakness in him he didn't know existed and for a brief moment he resented Cooke for his honesty.

Cooke opened his briefcase with his good hand and removed a square of folded paper. "Look," he said, "I realize this is an unofficial operation, and we usually only hand these out to our field operatives, but it might just save your life." Iain unfurled the note. It was made from lightweight paper, measuring 13 by 16 inches, designed to be folded into eighths. It contained both English and Cyrillic text.

"What is it?" he asked.

"It's what we call a Blood Chit."

Iain studied the pointee-talkie language chart and the English-Russian pronunciation guide at the bottom: 'I am a British citizen. Please help me return to the Chinese border. The British Government will reward you. You will be paid handsomely in gold for my safe return.'

There were also phonetic translations for the Russian words 'don't shoot', 'far, near', 'food, bread, drinking water', 'doctor, medicine', 'sleep, hide' and 'I will pay you'.

He pursed his lips, felt himself tense up. His eyes settled on Cooke's invisible left hand, at the shiny-pink rub of skin. It would have been a grenade, thought Iain, either that or a sniper's bullet. Had it happened at night? Was he smoking at the time? Had the cross hairs focused on the crimson glow within his palm? The shock would have been brutal and swift.

They'll execute you.

Iain scraped his palms together and pushed them through his hair. He sat stiffly quiet for a long time. His own hands, he noticed, were quivering faintly.

Iain squinted out the window. The road ahead looked as black as the midnight sky, but his heart knew where it was taking him. Iain's eyes glinted in the window; there was no retreating now. He was ready.

2

Sunrise. The Amur Valley became a land of mirrored frost, of boundless swards of ice stretching to the horizon and beyond. The frozen water, covered by a thick surface skin of ice, seemed to ripple with the violence of the changing light – the sky was predatory, even the sun looked raw with cold.

Iain put his hand up to his eyes to stop the glare. Tiny scuff marks of animals marked the tableau, ruining the pristine snow. To his right he saw a strip of river, cut from stainless steel; to his left a stretch of trees, of which only the tallest of the pines showed any hint of green. A gale sent snow powder swirling off the tips of these trees onto the ground. The wind was like a whip. Iain grimaced as miniscule chips of ice spat into his eyes. He walked on, head down.

A week had passed since his train journey from Dairen. In that time he'd grown a stubbly beard, a dusty red fleece with pinpoints of gold, and although it helped to keep out some of the wind chill, his cheekbones, despite being framed by an aureole of rabbit fur, were chilblained and had turned the colour of tinned salmon.

The compressed ice squeaked as he walked. Iain paused to scrape the ice fragments from his eyes. He couldn't quite believe he had crossed over into Soviet Russia. To his left, he saw a sika deer stretched out, frozen stiff, by the edge of the road, its head and greyish forelegs only just visible above the snowline. Iain looked behind him. Beyond the river were some scattered distant houses of a village and what might have been a skinning farm. Iain took a few seconds of cautious thought to evaluate what he was about to do. He'd made a calculated guess that he and the guide could carry Ilya Shashkov for half a mile without having to rest. It meant that they were going to have to stop between six to eight times.

The day before he had driven up from Sunwu to Heihe, passing gold mining towns along the old route that ran from Hsi-gangshi towards the Amur River. The truck belonged to the Manchurian warlord Chang Hsueh-liang. The men in the truck – a driver, three armed toadies, and a Russian-speaking guide – were all on Chang's payroll. Now, four of the men, including the driver, waited for him on the Chinese side of the Amur, while Iain and the guide made their way through the outskirts of Blagoveshchensk. Iain had no choice but to trust the warlord and his men.

Dressed in dog hides and fleeces, with blanket rolls draped over their shoulders, Iain and the guide each carried a rifle, water skins, and long wooden poles with a strip of canvas slung between them to be used as a drag sledge.

Some time in the middle of the morning they came to a smooth hollow, verged on either side by banks of trees, and then, moments later, climbing a hill, they reached a hamlet. Iain saw men with features ridged by the Siberian wind, emerging from their homes to gather wood for their fires. Their faces resembled wrinkled sacks. Iain kept his eyes low and hooded.

"Ni khuya sebye. We haff arrifed," said the guide, pale ghosts of steam escaping from his mouth. "We haff come to the weelage of Elychoko. We must be most careful now. Do not speak to the weelagers. I will do all the communicating." As he said this a man on horseback rode by; he carried in his arms an Amur leopard.

"Who is that?" asked Iain, wondering whether the horseman was a Red Guard.

"Ye vaw? He is a hunter. He uses the leopard to bring down wild deer."

Crowded together, one and two storey houses made out of

thatch and earth and silt – silt streets, silt courtyards, silt-and-mud walls – Elychoko was a little village which turned dark at night because there was no electricity and grew quiet enough to hear a marmot burrowing in the snow outside. It was a place with crooked, rough-stone lanes that had never seen a motorcar, a place shrunken from the world. It was also home to a small monastic church, which had three low apses, with white stone walls and narrow, deeply splayed windows.

"Follow me," said the guide. "We haff to ask for information. We try in the church." Making their way under the eaves, Iain was directed under an archway, through to the main door of the church via a Judas gate; out of respect, he and the guide left their guns at the vestibule. They entered, out of the cold wind, into the dark, bleak interior. It stank of animal hides and unwashed men. There was the sound of a woman coughing, a baby crying. He saw candlelight on the far side of the altar; a small group of people standing with their backs to him, a few of which had bowed down to the ground.

The guide, two paces ahead, stamped his felt boots to shake off the snow. Iain did the same, rubbing his hands to ward off the cold. The people turned their heads towards the noise, blinking their eyes at the strangers. Iain searched the row of bewildered expressions. Some exchanged secret looks. He continued forward, everyone's eyes upon him. Was he interrupting a service, he wondered? And where was the clergy? But then he saw a propaganda poster on the wall depicting a peasant with a rifle. The peasant was sitting on a giant egg protecting his harvest; he was surrounded by a greedy-looking kulak, a priest and a boot-legger with a knife. The church was no longer sacred; it was now a recreation centre.

A man with huge whiskers walked out of the shadows wearing an unsavoury smile and a pelt made from bearskin. He wore an arm-band emblazoned with a bright red star. He looked conspiratorial and slithery. "*Zaluba*. Party cadre," the guide whispered in Iain's ear.

Iain noticed he had a round face and a long, bony nose like a buzzard's bill. He had the wide, wet eyes of a spaniel and a brown fringe was plastered to his forehead like bacon to a greasy pan.

"*Nyeznakormets*, comrades," the cadre said to the congregation.

People gathered round: babushkas with covered hair stared with trembling eyes; peasant youths, their mouths dark and brooding; elderly men wearing ushanka hats and horse skins, baring their teeth.

Iain stood quite still. The noise of breathing was all around him, mixing with the smell of oppression and tyranny. The party cadre continued speaking; his tone remained harsh, mildly argumentative. Another man with a rifle appeared from out of the blackest part of the church and stood beside the first man. They had moustaches like a thick hairbrushes, as untamable as hedgehog bristles. They appeared well-fed. In contrast, the ordinary people in the crowd looked as if they were starving.

Iain saw the cadres' eyes flash at the crowd of people, their lips curling – was that scorn he recognized in their faces? Iain watched with narrow attention. He kept his eyes on the first man, who was now gesturing with his hands. He spoke slowly and deliberately. There were grunts of derision from the assembly.

The cadre began to harangue the congregation, thumping their fists into their hands. Iain recognized the Russian words for 'Communist Party' and the word *khlyeb*, meaning grain.

After several moments one of the party officials appeared to ask the crowd a question. He gazed expectantly into the sea of faces. Someone raised his arm and said something, but the Red Guard standing beside the cadre pointed his gun into the gathering and the man lowered his arm. The party official put the same question to the people. This time there was a hush of silence. People bowed their heads, dropped their gaze. The babushkas cowered. Nobody raised a hand.

The Tsar's overthrow was eleven years behind them, thought Iain, yet the countryside still shook with fear like a vulnerable flower.

The official continued to glare at the crowd and allowed some moments to pass before speaking. As Iain listened, he thought he heard something about the kulaks and handing over of *khyleb*, but he couldn't be sure. A minute later the cadre dismissed the congregation.

Gradually, the people disbanded, moving about in the velvety darkness, lighting candles that had already burned halfway down and rearranging chairs. Iain noticed a few babushkas handing each other jars of preserved fruit, exchanging loaves of black bread, radishes, strings of dried herring. In one corner, he noticed two men flipping through the soft covers of a book, as if discussing the lines of a poem. In another corner a small group of children were playing with a hoop of wood. With the cadres gone, the church, Iain soon realized, had been transformed into a type of activity centre.

Iain watched the babushkas stuff their food into their coats, saw their relieved smiles. Others made their way outdoors, their faces crumbling with glum dismay.

"The goffernment haff urged the peasants to deliver increased amounts of grain and get paid less for it," whispered the guide.

"I thought as much," Iain replied.

Out in the cold, the guide went up to an old man to ask about the Riedles. The man shook his head and walked off. Seconds after, Iain saw a donkey cart trundle up and watched several peasant boys being led away under escort. A woman ran up to one of the boys and covered his shoulders with a quilt. A Red Guard pushed her to the ground and bundled the youths into the back of the cart.

Two of the young men were taken aside and the guards

searched their coats for weapons, throwing a small hunting blade into the snow. One of the boys was whistling through his teeth, trying to remain calm, but Iain could see the fear in his eyes. A moment later the whistler stood up in the back of the cart and shouted, *"Khuy sinim!"* only to feel the butt-end of a rifle crash against his shins.

These were neighbours and friends, thought Iain, being hauled off to God-knows-where, yet people did nothing. They were all too scared to move.

The guide whispered to Iain, *"S'khuyali?* Punishment for hoarding sacks of corn and other food."

Careful not to stare, Iain glanced away. Seconds later he saw the guide approach a man across the village square. As they talked Iain saw the man look over at him. Iain felt uneasy and lowered his eyes. The stranger looked dirty and ill-fed, with boils on his face. The guide spoke in a hurry, his voice hushed. Iain looked on, concerned. The stranger kneaded his forehead and pointed clandestinely towards a hill. The guide squeezed a bank note into his hand.

He said his name was Nikolai. They followed him as he led them away from the church. For a few moments they stood outside a tavern before entering. Once inside, Iain took in the solemn expressions, the menagerie of eyes that could have belonged to homeless dogs. He noted the cups that had blackened with age, the sparseness of the shelves, empty but for a tin of boiled beef and a sad-looking loaf of bread. "We haff to order some wodka to get them to talk," whispered the guide. Iain studied the grey-faced muzhiks. Pressed into their coats, many appeared tired of breathing.

A bottle of vodka was placed on the bar. Smiles rolled across a few of the faces. Every man in the tavern was given a tumblerful and soon the smiles turned to laughter. The ill-fed Nikolai nodded at a tall man standing across the way. He wore a fur hat with long earflaps. They glanced at each other and then out the window, moving their eyes rapidly. The Red Guards had melted away for now.

Moments later, Iain found himself fighting against the wind again, one eye closed against the cold, trudging through the snow towards a solitary farmhouse on a hill. The tall man was taking them up the slope. Iain trudged through the snow and as he looked up he saw a majestic sight appear from out of the bleak landscape. It was a male elk standing proudly against the snow-whitened birches. He had a set of glorious antlers that were over four feet long and Iain could make out its thick red coat and the buff colourations on its rump. It stood posturing for several seconds before disappearing back into the woods.

"*Smeerne!* I think we are close now," said the guide.

Filled with anticipation, Iain began thinking about Ilya Shashkov. The old photograph in his pocket showed Ilya with Slavic cheekbones and angular shoulders – would he still look the same, would he have his daughter's eyes, her nose, her character? Iain glanced ahead, to the top of the rise. He saw a tiny cottage with woodsmoke swirling out of its chimney. Was her father at this very moment watching them, he wondered, through his window, seeing them struggle up the hill? Iain had a mental picture of shaking Ilya's hand, explaining who he was, seeing the old man's face burst into smile. The fact that, soon, Ilya and Nadia were to be reunited made Iain's heart thump against his chest. He held tight to this thought, trying hard to rein in the urge to run to the top of the hill.

The farmhouse stood on a crest of rock that jutted from the edge of the woods. They began their ascent in silence, up a yak track that was laden with animal horns to shepherd trekkers through the winter snowfalls. Rimes of frost formed on their beards and eyebrows.

They entered the farmhouse, letting themselves in without so much as a knock. Iain noticed there were no locks on the door; a person kept no secrets from Soviet Russia. The walls were pea-green and damp, fringed with aspen wood beams;

it resembled something out of a Chekhov short story. In the semi-darkness, Iain saw a log-lined hall with Karelian birch chairs, stained wooden floors, a ticking mantel clock, and numerous unvarnished icons on the wall of St. Paraskeva, the Nativity of the Virgin, and the Crucifixion.

Despite the glare from the snow outside, the light within was murky. Iain smelled a log fire burning from somewhere within and followed his nose down the long corridor. He turned into the kitchen, found a square wooden table and a fireplace next to a tall mirror. A tin milk bucket hung by its handle on a metal bar by the fire; potatoes were softening in the boiling water. Sitting at the table, staring at the open fire, wearing a woolen cardigan thinning at the elbows, was an elderly man with a tense line for a mouth. "Who are you? Why are you in my house?" he demanded in Russian.

He was a man of about sixty with scraped-over white hair, sunken cheeks and a soft-spoken, academic manner. A pencil and a blue sugar ration card rested on the table before him. Standing behind him was a pumpkin-faced woman, with a scarf wrapped over her head.

Iain came slowly, respectfully, forward, his hat in his hands.

The guide drew his arms up to his chest and bowed. He apologized for intruding. "You are Riedle?" asked the guide.

"*Da*," said the white-haired man, his mouth tense once more.

"You live here, alone?"

Riedle gestured to the woman. "I have my wife, Nina, with me and . . ." he stopped himself.

"And who?" said the guide.

"Nobody else. My son is married now and living in Vladivostok. We are alone."

"We are looking for a man called Shashkov. Is he with you?" said the guide.

Knees stiff, Riedle got to his feet. The sugar ration card dangled from between his finger and thumb, and slid to the floor. He started shaking his head, shaking it for a long time. Iain heard the guide say the word *"Breetanskeey."*

"Breetanskeey," Riedle repeated, a perplexed smile of muted expectation forming. "You haff come to help us?" he said speaking in English, directing the question to Iain.

"I have," replied Iain.

"What is it?" came a voice from another room, croaked, sounding weak. Iain turned to find a narrow man with spindly shanks for legs appear at the door. He had dull blue eyes, partly clouded with cataracts, and skin as pale as milk; half of his face appeared to have fallen in on itself and his left arm swung without life. Yet despite the obvious signs of stroke, there was something noble about the way he held himself – his back was upright, his head was lifted high and bravely straight. "Who are these people?" he insisted. Shuffling forward on sticks.

"Go and rest, *tovarish*," said Riedle, still suspicious. "Nothing here concerns you."

"Is this man Shashkov?" asked the guide.

"Niet, niet," replied Riedle. But the pause he'd allowed before answering told Iain otherwise. "He is my brother. He is visiting us from Lensk."

Iain came forward and took the frail man by the right elbow, searching his face, the many tones and transparencies of his skin.

"I am a friend of your daughter,' he said to Shashkov in English. "Your daughter Nadia Shashkova. Look, I have a photograph. Please you have to listen to me." He sat Ilya down and kneeled in front of him. "We don't have much time."

Iain started drawing things out of his satchel – postcards of Macao, a photograph of Nadia, train tickets. Ilya Shashkov looked at Iain. He was silent. Riedle, too, had gone quiet. The mantel clock ticked in the hallway.

Icy surprise had greeted Iain's words. They were sitting at a table in the sitting room. The tall man with the fur earflaps had departed and the potatoes in the pot had cooled and remained uneaten.

Iain examined their scared eyes in turn. Mrs. Riedle laid a hand on Shashkov's forehead to feel his temperature. "I am here to help you, all of you," he repeated.

He'd rehearsed his lines before starting to speak. It was never going to be easy persuading them to follow him, to trust him, but Iain did what he could. "Your house in Russia," Iain said, "just outside of Tver. Nadia told me all about it. She told me about the fire, about Mr. Bogdanov, the estate manager, about the lucky glass charm you gave her." He showed them a recent photograph of Nadia. Ilya's hands hesitated as they reached forward. Iain saw the blood throbbing at his temples – he could smell his warmth, hear his breathing. The old man's eyes grew tender; he appeared to understand. "She mentioned the toboggan run you made from ice that led down to the pond."

"This cannot be," said Nadia's father in Russian, but the tremor in his voice belied his words. His lips parted. Words fell out of his mouth, skidding like perplexed sighs. His eyes blinked. His confusion was clear.

Iain produced more images from his satchel, handing Ilya the one of Nadia as a little girl standing with her father by a fountain.

Ilya gazed at it for long moments. "This was taken in our garden in Vadra!" he said. There was glee in his chest now. He laughed out loud before collapsing in a fit of coughing.

"You must come with me," said Iain.

Riedle shook his head vigorously. His voice was like dry wheat. "Ilya will never surwife the trip."

"But he must come. What is there for him here?"

Lowering his voice, Riedle said. "He has not seen his family for twenty years. Nina and I are his family now. Can you not see how *balnoy* he is, how sick? He can not go."

"Isn't that his decision to make?"

"I am his *vrach*, his doctor. I am also his friend."

Iain looked back over his shoulder at the guide who was standing at the window. *"Smeerne.* We haff to hurry," said the guide. "The weather is getting bad and I fear the Red Guards will find out about us. If you don't hurry *nam khana."*

"I'm doing my best," shot Iain.

"What is to become of us?" asked Riedle.

"We can take you across too," said Iain. "I can get you to Harbin."

"Byazrasoodnye! We haff considered escaping many times before, but it cannot be done," said Riedle. "If they catch us they will zhoot us."

Ian would not be deflected.

"What's left for you here? There's talk of collectivization. They're starving all of you slowly. Bread, flour, sugar, salt – all these aren't available in the free market."

"Things will improve."

"No, they won't."

"It is true," said Nina Riedle in Russian. "Things are getting worse here. The ration cards are hopeless. People have turned to the black market instead even though prices are hugely inflated. Women in the towns hide little sacks of flour or sugar under their skirts for bartering."

"Please be quiet, Nina!" cried Riedle.

She ignored her husband. "And now bread is baked with cornmeal or ground beans. It is often inedible. Some of the bread is mingled with straw."

Iain looked at Nadia's father and thrust the photographs back into his hands. "Your daughter is waiting for you," he said. His face was pink with pleading.

Shashkov's tears made tracks down his cheeks.

"But what will happen to us?" said Riedle. *"Byazrasood-nye!* Nina and I will be stateless. We haff no money . . ."

"Last year the Lutheran Mission in Harbin took care of almost a hundred Mennonites who had crossed over from Russia."

"We are not Mennonites."

"You'll be offered the same opportunities, the same help. There are numerous charities sponsored by American Mennonites that will help you. I have already made enquiries. President Hoover's administration will approve your emigration to America. You'll be offered a fresh start in the Mennonite Brethren settlement in Fresno, California. Think of all that American milk and beef and ice-cream."

"A fresh start. *D'ermo!* At our age? By the Spirit of Lenin . . ."

"They will take good care of you. Trust me, please." Iain's voice floated over the room.

"*Smeerne!* I see horses," said the guide. "I see horses!"

"We need a decision from you," said Iain. "The longer we stay the more dangerous it gets." The mantel clock in the hall struck a single lonely toll.

"The horsemen are riding up the hill!" the guide called out. "I can see Red Guards! I can see their armbands! I think they know strangers are in the weelage."

"We must hide you!" said Reidle. He shepherded Iain and the guide into the kitchen. There was a low wall made up of loose logs for the fire. "Here!" he said, "Crouch behind the logs." Riedle threw saddle blankets over them and then some broken tinder on top. "*D'ermo!* Do not move or make a sound!"

The heat from the open fire reddened their cheeks. They waited, squashed against each other like peppers in a heated pan. A distant hush of quiet voices sounded through the house. Riedle stood in the corridor, looking back behind him into the kitchen over and over again.

The guide suddenly gazed at Iain. "What about the rifles?" he hissed. "I haff to get them."

"Where did you leave them?"

"*Zaluba!* In the sitting room, with our zhoulder bags behind the door." He covered his head with his hands. Then came fresh sounds – the rumble of hooves and shouts –

166

followed by a rush of wind and the thud of footsteps down the corridor.

Feeling the throb of his heart against his chest, Iain's breath pulled tight.

Through a crack in the logs, Iain could see the front part of the kitchen; he blinked and stretched his neck. He watched something dark move in front of them. A man's hobnail boots, black and wet with snow, crossed the room, stopping at the larder. A hand reached inside and took out some bread and onions. Not far away, standing by the door, was another man, ice dripping from his long overcoat.

"*Durak neshtiasny!* Where are they?" cried one of the Guards.

"Two men were here, saying they were from the North, from Tugur. They were demanding food and shelter. Comrade, I think they were counterrevolutionaries." said Riedle. "I gave them some beets because I feared they might harm us. They were carrying rifles. Comrade, do you think these are the Whites or Solidarists looking to overthrow our blessed Soviet government?"

"*Blin!* Did you see which way they went, *starik*?"

"They followed the fenceline away from the village, heading against the sun."

Iain could hear Mrs. Riedle yelling from the sitting room. She was shouting at the men, her voice stern. The men in the kitchen turned to her and handed back the onions they'd shoved into their pockets.

"We are searching every house from Elychoko to Blagoveshchensk." said the Red Guard, scowling towards the door. "If you see the *svoloch* again, go down the hill to the church and ring the bell. *Vrubatsa?*"

Riedle's face was expressionless. The hobnailed boots banged against the floor. Iain heard the front door bang and the horses quickening their pace as they rode away. Iain turned and stared at the guide. The mantel clock ticked in their ears once more.

3

The mournful cries of the lotus porridge vendor radiated from the cobbled streets below, '*Leen sum bak tong juk,*' he sang, his voice forlorn, like a sailor who'd lost his rum bottle in the fog.

Nadia was in the kitchen adding up all the signatures that Izabel had received. "With all this support the government will have to go ahead and build a new orphanage. Two hundred and sixty eight names so far. Not bad," she announced. "We'll present it to Government House on Monday."

"Izabel is going to get into trouble over this. You mark my words."

"I don't see why."

"Nobody likes having their bottom spanked and that's exactly what Izabel is doing to this fellow Quieroz. You too. I heard some gossip from Senhora de Souza that they may look to charge Izabel with being a public nuisance. You ought to be careful."

"Nonsense, Mamuchka. We're doing what's right. It's our duty to see this through."

But Mamuchka had stopped listening. Her gaze had dropped to the bundle of old photographs which she held in her hands. "These are all I have left of your father," she said. The images had faded to the colour of an earthy yellow. "Cousin Myshkin gave them to me. All our photographs perished in the fire."

"Why have you taken them out?"

"Because of Iain. Because you said he's gone to bring Papashka home."

Nadia tucked her list of signatures into a folder and approached the stove. "Let's not get our hopes up."

"Please come and look at the photographs."

"Take a sip of soup first," said Nadia. She removed a ladle from a clay pot and placed a bowl of beef broth in front of her mother. "Look what I've made. Solianka, the same kind I used to prepare for you when I was about fifteen. Do you remember?"

"I remember." There was a moment's hesitation and then Mamuchka asked, "You used to add those fat Chinese mushrooms, those *doong goo*. They were your trademark." Mamuchka sighed. "Those first few years were unbearable," she said. Her eyes had fixed at a point on the far wall. "I was lonely and frightened. You were so young. We were like shipwrecked sisters." She sighed. *"Zhizn' prozhit' – ne pole peretyi* – life was never meant to be easy."

They were seated at the long oak table in the kitchen, the plates and saucers cleared away. The jade monkey pendant and its luminous red box lay between them on the polished wood. It was a talisman, a precious thing, something to banish the fear that Iain might not return.

Mamuchka saw her looking at the pendant. "Have you forgiven Iain?"

"Yes," she said. "I think I have." Nadia reached across and locked her fingers in Mamuchka's and squeezed.

On the wall behind Mamuchka she saw the little horizontal lines of ink, and recalled all the times she had stood there in her early teens, shoes off, Uncle Yugevny, measuring her growing height, placing a ruler flat on her head and marking it off with a scribble, followed by the date. The marks were still there, faded now.

She remembered their first days in Macao. Her mother transferring her irritation from one thing then to another – she disliked the food, the smells, the foreignness of everything, the tangle of streets. "Where are all the trees, the open fields," she'd say. For Mamuchka, Macao was a place to mourn her memories. For Nadia it was a place to bury them.

Mamuchka stared at the steam coming off the bowl of Solianka for several moments. "For years, wherever I was, the first thing I'd think in the morning was, 'I wonder if it is raining in Tver.' After a while, of course, I learned to cover up my feelings, pretending to be busy with this and that."

"Soup's getting cold," said Nadia. Mamuchka took a spoon and dipped it into the beef broth.

"Too much pepper? If you don't like it, I get run down and buy some lotus porridge from the hawkers."

"No, it's very good, Nadrichka."

They both looked at a photograph of Papashka, taken when Nadia was three years old. She must have looked at this photograph a hundred times over the years and, like a favourite poem, it was the one she returned to time and time again. In it he is looking away from the camera, a shadow thrown over one side of his face. "He was very handsome," she said, absorbed.

"Lionel Barrymore," mused Mamuchka. "Not quite as heavily-built."

Nadia pushed her chair back and went round to give her mother a hug. "I still remember," she said, "the day you told me you thought Papashka was gone."

"Yes. I remember too."

Looking back, Nadia saw herself aged seven again. It was an autumn night, a few months after the fire, and Mamuchka was telling her how her father might have died. The *gorodvoi* had just left Mr. Bogdanov's cottage. Again there was no news of Papashka's body. They were making plans to go and live with their cousins in Chelyabinsk.

Mamuchka and she were sitting by the hearth in the estate manager's cottage. The embers gave the plain, living room a pale, almost delirious glow. She said that Papashka was like the tiny moth in the story 'Little Caterpillar and the Fire'. She said the little moth had translucent wings.

"What's translucent?" Nadia asked. She was dressing a

doll in a canary yellow dress; it had been a gift from the *gorodvoi*.

"It's when light can pass through it," said Mamuchka.

"You mean like the way light passes through a ghost?"

"Can I continue the story?" Nadia nodded. She was playing with one of the doll's shoes. "Once upon a time a little caterpillar and a tiny moth with translucent wings lived together in a matchbox. They were boiling soup in an eggshell when the tiny moth fell in and burned herself to death. When the little caterpillar saw this she began weeping loudly. The moment the samovar heard the crying he said, 'What's the matter, little caterpillar?'

'Tiny moth has burned to death.'

The samovar began to whistle violently.

Then a passing thundercloud said, 'What's happened, samovar?'

The samovar said, 'Tiny moth has burned to death, little caterpillar is weeping.'

The thundercloud began to rumble and rain started to fall.

Then the river said, 'Is something the matter, thundercloud?'

The thundercloud said, 'Tiny moth has burned to death, little caterpillar is weeping, the samovar is whistling.'

'Oh,' said the river. And he broke his banks and flooded the land with water, carrying the burned tiny moth out to sea.

'Why did you do that?' asked the thundercloud.

'So that the sea can soothe his burns and purify his soul.'

The thundercloud hovered over the drifting moth and watched – saw its wings floating, spread out on the waves around him, hanging limp. And slowly the restless water caressed the limbs of the tiny moth, spilled rain onto his translucent wings, brought light to the darkness. The soft mouth of the sea was lifting him off the ocean surface and soon the moth came alive once more and flew up towards the moon, circling the earth one last time."

Sitting there in the soft lamplight of the kitchen, trying not to imagine how her father was dragged by the ankles into the dovecot and set alight, Nadia retrieved a small object from her dress pocket. She remembered the day he had pressed the little piece of smooth glass into her hand, still warm from his own touch. They'd been fishing by the river and when she opened her hand she saw something the shape of a crown; a piece of cloudy blue glass, the colour of aquamarine syrup. It seemed to her to be a truly intimate gift.

All of a sudden she felt like a little girl bathing at the beach who'd been so absorbed in herself that that she'd forgotten about the currents. It was as if she'd lost sight of the land. Her father's words, whispered in her ears years before, now rang loudly inside her head: *The problem with us Russians is that we spend all our time reminiscing and forget about the present. We must love what we have now before it has vanished forever.* The thought froze her, sobered her. She looked fiercely into her mother's eyes and wondered why the only face she could see was Iain's.

4

They agreed to wait until dawn. It didn't seem right to sleep, so Iain stayed by the window and watched for any signs of trouble.

As soon as the light outside turned grainy, they were out in the open, pushing their way forward through the snow. The guide nodded towards the yellow rind of sun and he and Iain settled Ilya Shashkov into the canvas harness of the drag sledge. The guide fastened his hat under his chin, grabbed the poles and began to pull.

They walked for an hour before stopping. The Riedles had packed hurriedly by oillight, without making a sound, stuffing their most prized things into an assortment of bags. Scrambling across the tall snow, they pumped and heaved their legs, steam wisps curling from their mouths.

By eight o'clock they'd made it to the banks of the Amur. Through the clearing they saw the river. Everyone's breathing grew more and more laboured as they broke into a run. Then the poles snapped. And Shashkov's arms and legs fell to the ground with a thump.

"We'll have to carry him," said Iain.

Crossing the frozen river, however, would be more treacherous, explained the guide. "There is no cover so we will be completely exposed. Anyone could be watching out for us, including Red Guards. Their long-range rifles are accurate over a range of 200 yards."

With one arm wrapped round Ilya Shashkov's frail body, Iain grabbed hold of a handful of coat, and half-carried, half-dragged him through the snow. They were yards now from the water's frozen edge and Iain's face was breaking out into wild grimaces of delight – the thrilling taste of escape was intoxicating.

"Wait!" The guide hissed.

"What is it?" said Iain.

"Do you hear them?"

"No."

"Can you not smell it?"

"Smell what?" But as Iain said this, he knew exactly what the guide was talking about. The stink of horse dung was sharp.

In the distance, dogs were barking; Iain was sure he could now hear other sounds too – the trailing shouts of men, the neighing and whickering of horses, the thrumming of boot-clad feet trampling the ground. "Are they on to us?" he asked.

The guide lifted his rifle.

Muscles quivering, their lips blue, all of them dropped to the ground and hunkered down by the stump of a felled tree. Curled up in their fleeces, they struggled to control the tempo of their breathing.

Nadia's father began to wheeze and cough up blood. His entire body throbbed and trembled. "He is very sick," said Riedle. "We must get him to drink liquid. His pulse is very weak."

"Do you see any Red Guards?" Iain said.

"Not yet. But I hear them. Keep low and they will pass."

"Are you not listening to me?" Riedle cried. "This man is dying."

The veins on Shashkov's temple were throbbing violently through his skin. Iain comforted him and rubbed his back. "Breathe," he said in English. "Breathe deeply. And here," he withdrew a skin of water from his satchel. "Drink this," he said to Ilya. He tilted the skin to his lips. Ilya Shashkov nodded, appeared to understand. He extended a pink tongue, thick and fat like a slice of gammon. Some of the water had frozen, but a few droplets managed to find their way down Ilya's throat.

"*Nadia,*" he said out of the corner of his crooked mouth as he drank, spilling dribbles down his chin. "*Mnye noozhna pamatryet Nadia.*" He gestured with his hand that he wanted to look at her photograph again.

"Later. You will see her later," said Iain. "I promise you. Don't fall asleep, Ilya. Don't sleep."

Mrs. Riedle put her hand to Shashkov's forehead. "He is burning."

"He will not survive this," Riedle said. "We must get him indoors." Extricating himself from his wife's arms, Riedle got to his feet quickly, like a marionette being pulled up by strings. "Get down!" said the guide. "They will see you!"

But Riedle was already half-way up the embankment.

Iain reached out and tried to grab him. He'd scarcely moved when a large cat bounded past them, followed seconds later by an enormous black horse. The horse hurdled them all, including the stump of the felled tree, and galloped away, pounding past them at speed. The rider was sitting in a forward position in the saddle, holding the reins in one hand, whilst clutching a curved saber in the other.

"What the hell was that?" said Iain.

"Deerhunters!" said the guide.

"Deerhunters?"

"Did you see that cat? It is a leopard. It belongs to the woodsmen. They use it to hunt sika deer."

"So they're not Red Guards?"

"No."

"In that case, let's move! We've got to get Shashkov across now!"

Iain could hear and taste and feel only the wind.

Overhead clouds had turned parts of the sky dark blue, bruising the heavens like a subcutaneous contusion. A thunderclap shook the air and there followed a few seconds of suspenseful silence. They were half way across.

The blizzard had dropped onto them quickly.

Lurching crablike into the spindrift Iain pushed forward. He wrapped his arms around Ilya Shashkov and exhaled deeply. Engulfed in a maelstrom of storm debris, the white-out enveloped them like a giant hand, tossing them, rolling them.

They were mid-river, traversing fractured young ice. Iain knew that they might fall through at every step. Crack-lines appeared everywhere across the frozen river's surface.

Nadia's father was desperately tired, slumping to the ground every few steps. Iain didn't dare proceed at pace, lest they dropped through into the freezing water. He flexed the fingers of his left fist. Heart pounding, he realized his hands were beginning to die, succumbing to frostbite. They kept advancing, one step, two steps, testing the fissuring, latticed crust for its weight, heading into the unknown. Despite being −15 C, their clothes were wet with perspiration, a wet-ness which quickly turned into a thin film of frost on their skin whenever they stopped moving. A few minutes later, the guide cried out. "Follow my voice. Do not get separated!"

A little after that, Ilya began coughing up a red mucus again. Bones trembling, Iain lifted him onto his shoulders, so that Ilya's cheek rested against Iain's ear. Almost there, he kept telling Ilya, almost there.

They crept forward.

Iain asked Shashkov how he was doing. There was no reply.

The guide cried out once again; his shouts vanished instantly in the storm.

Iain's voice was calm. "Say something, Ilya." But Shash-kov remained silent and the thickness of the silence crushed his ears. He wanted to put him down and shake him. "Ilya Shashkov!" he shouted. The words emerged from the pit of his stomach. "Don't you dare die on me!"

Iain pushed on. Squalling sheets of snow formed in front of his eyes. He was walking into a wall of white so blinding that it hurt his eyes. From somewhere ahead came the sound of an engine. And then he saw the truck and the four men approaching, faces chalked with snow, appearing like ghosts out of a mist.

He felt them take Ilya Shashkov off of him, spreading their blankets over him.

He felt their arms clasp tight round his waist. His mind clouded. He could rest now, he said to himself. He could rest. Seconds later he passed out.

5

"That will be fifteen patacas and thirty avos, Senhor Pinto," Nadia said, placing a varnished box of Culebras cigars into a paper carrier bag.

"We should spread our magical wings and glide away together," he whispered, slipping her a few notes and coins.

With Iain gone so long, a number of men, including the magistrate Senhor Pinto, had started to take an interest in Nadia again.

"Perhaps," continued the short, little man with the skin-crackling smile. "We can start by taking a stroll by the Praya and enjoy the sunset."

"I'm very busy with the shop. With Uncle Yugevny semi-retired, I'm running it now." She glanced at her ledger. As it happened, she'd learned much in the past three months: how to manage inventory and stocktaking, how to gauge seasonal demand, and what it meant to secure credit from a bank. She'd even taught herself to replace the lever at the side of the cash register, which allowed the till to ring again.

Senhor Pinto placed his hand on top of hers. His skin felt cold and lizard-like. "I have some embroidered handkerchiefs for you. Beautiful little cranes and swans, all satin stitched. Not as beautiful as you though." Nadia felt her insides shrink. "May I give them to you?" he asked, twirling his moustache.

"You are too kind, Senhor Pinto, but I prefer not."

"Why? You think I am too old?"

"Handkerchiefs bring on tears," she said.

"Nonsense, you think me old. But I am young. Look, look

at this *musculo!*" He flexed his arm, urging her to squeeze his bicep. "Every day I do *muito exercicio.*" She pictured the old man huffing and puffing in his bathroom, pulling on his spring-loaded contraption, dressed only in his underpants. The image made her smile broadly.

"You see?" he said. "Pinto can melt even the most frigid heart."

Senhor Pinto kissed her hand and bid her farewell just as Mamuchka and Yugevny emerged from the paint-chipped corridor. As always, Mamuchka was dressed in a long-sleeved, black organdie dress. "*Adeus*, Olga," he called, making a hasty retreat. "I'm off to court."

"*Adeus*, Pedro." Mamuchka sat in her usual chair by the teapoy in the corner. "More offerings of handkerchiefs?" she asked.

Nadia nodded, jotting some numbers into her ledger before returning to her Christmas project.

"Why are you wasting your time with window displays?" said Yugevny.

"I'm trying to make the shop less stuffy, more modern. A display with a Christmas tableau will bring in more customers."

"Well, I think it is stupid. This is a tobacconist not a toy store."

"It's called progress."

"Progress? Progress died when they murdered the Tsar." He went off in a huff.

Nadia shook her head. She'd spent most of the morning working on the window display, giving it a bright, nativity theme. There was a marble painted in gold to symbolize the guiding star. A lush carpet of hay forged from Montecristo cigar labels. Papier mache wise men wrapped in silver leaf. She'd even formed the words *Feliz Natal* and *Happy Christmas* out of cigar bands, draping the banner over the window frame.

When the shop bell tinkled a few moments later, her

mother offered a pebble-voiced welcome. Without looking, Nadia continued with her task, pinning paper poinsettias to a strip of silk bunting.

"Mamuchka," she said, "can you serve the customer."

"But ish you I wish to speak weeth," the voice announced in English. "I have something to geeve you, Senhora."

She turned and saw Fernando Costa standing by the door, his huge bulk almost dwarfing the glass cabinets that housed the porcelain jars and briarwood pipes.

Costa bowed his head. From somewhere deep within his enormous overcoat he fished out a letter.

"The deeplomatic bag arrived this morning with mail from the north."

"The north?" Her eyes widened with expectation.

"In it wash thees letter addressed to you." He held the envelope high in the air.

She took a step forward, reaching out. "Give it to me."

Costa continued to hold it above his head, out of Nadia's grasp. "Not until you tell me something first."

"Let me have it!"

"Where ish Iain? Tell me where he ish heading?"

"I don't know. I haven't seen or heard from him in four months. You're his friend, surely he must have confided in you."

"No. I shuspect he did not tell me because he knew that I would try to dishuade him."

"Well, I don't know where he is."

"Are you shoor? He didn't mention anything about Manchuria?"

"It will probably say in the letter."

"It doesn't."

"You mean you've already read it?"

A desultory grin. "Of course." He handed it to her. "The letter came via the British Consulate in Dairen. Sent almost five weeks ago. Did Iain ever tell you where he wash going, what he wash planning?"

Nadia hesitated. "Months ago," she said, frowning, "he mentioned my father."

"Your father?"

"He mentioned going into Russia to rescue my father. But I never believed . . ."

"*Putanheiro!* He'll be shkinned alive! No wonder there's been no word."

"Are you saying Iain's gone missing?"

Costa looked her straight in the eye. "It appears that way. None of our stations have heard anything since Dairen." Nadia stared at Costa. "The theeng is, you shee, we want to inform him that he can return to Macao. You remember the man who was trying to kill him, Utaro Takashi, the head of the Golden Tiger secret society? Well, he hash been deported, handed over to Osaka police. Iain can finally come home."

The day after Christmas; a powder-blue sky. Izabel's boys were playing football in the square and the church bells rang long into the morning. Nadia, alone in her bedroom in Macao, at her bureau, cut off by brown curtains from the world, surrounded herself with old photographs of her family.

She drew open the brown curtains. The sun was lifting off the horizon. There was a telegram from the Great Northern Telegraph Co. on the chenille bedspread. Nadia stared at the piece of frail, blue-tinged paper. With her index finger she traced the words one by one. The days and weeks without Iain had become a wasteland. A chasm had been left behind. After an eternity of waiting and more torturous waiting, living day after day without word, the communiqué had arrived wholly without warning. She had to read and reread the message over again and again if only to convince herself that it was no lie. Not wanting to cry but ultimately unable to stop herself, she cleared her throat and heard her own quivering voice announce once more:

ARRIVING MACAO ON MERCHANT NAVY SHIP TAIBU EVENING DECEMBER 26 STOP VERY MUCH LOOKING FORWARD TO HOT BOWL OF PORRIDGE STOP IAIN

Finally, after 152 days she would be able to hold him once more, feel the muscles of his arms envelope her, wrap her in his love. It had felt like a lifetime; she was determined never to be apart from him again.

She shrugged back her shoulders, momentarily feeling a nervous pressure infect her. She ought to have been ecstatic, yet something hot and troubling was making a home inside her chest. That's when it struck her. Why was there no mention of her father, she wondered. Why had Iain left this vital question open and unanswered?

Nadia gathered up the jade monkey pendant and her piece of cloudy glass, shaped like a crown – her two most prized possessions – and pressed them to her lips. She gazed up at the image of the Virgin, hanging on the north-east corner of the wall, and said a prayer to Saint Nikolai Chudotvorets and to the Holy Mother of God, thanking them both for their miracle-making. After crossing herself and bowing to the waist, she scooped up the telegram and raced down the stairs to see her mother.

Nadia found Mamuchka sitting in the hallway by the kitchen, a console table at her elbow. It was well beyond noon yet she hadn't changed out of her billowing, tasseled nightdress, its plumes rising and falling with her breathing; she looked stranded, like a marooned jellyfish, the piled, flouncy cloth of her dressing gown resembling the blue float of a Portuguese man-of-war. She was in a plain wicker chair that looked out of the tiny window and onto the street below. Her body, her posture, was held rigid, her face taut. In her hands she held the bowl of soup Izabel had given her an hour earlier. The soup was untouched, cold now.

Nadia placed her hand on her mother's back. Olga Shashkova raised her head and looked into her daughter's eyes. They both smiled hugely. Nadia brought the jade monkey pendant to her mouth with satisfaction and kissed it, just as Mamuchka emitted a great, staggered sigh. She did this several times, drawing in a great breath and sighing, as if breathing was a struggle for her.

"How do you feel?" Nadia asked.

"Oh, the way any wife would feel if she was about to meet her husband again after twenty years. Terrified mostly."

"Mamuchka," she said, hinting at caution. "There was no mention of Papashka in the telegram."

"Your father is with Iain, Nadrichka."

"Mamuchka, please, I urge you . . . don't build your hopes up."

There was a moment's pause. The sounds of the streets emptied into the house, voices floating in from the cobblestoned lanes. Nadia, restless and intimidated by her mother's stillness, by her laboured breathing, needed to break the silence. "What are you thinking about?" she eventually asked.

"What, right at this very moment?"

"Yes."

"I was just thinking whether we ought to make up the spare bedroom. We'll need to change the bed linen. Otherwise where will your father sleep?"

"Won't he be staying in your room?"

"I haven't laid eyes on him for almost a quarter century! I can't share my bed with a *nyeznakawmets*, a stranger!"

Not for the first time Nadia felt disjointed. For years she had reeled away from the heartache and grief of losing a parent. Now, all of a sudden, his resurrection was staring her full in the face. What would she say to him? Should she hug him, kiss him? Maybe Mamuchka was right, she realized. Perhaps he was a stranger, an outsider – there was no way of guessing what type of man he had become.

"You know," said Mamuchka, "your father always hated

travelling on boats. He would always get terribly seasick, poor soul. Do you think he will be alright on this merchant navy ship?"

Nadia shook her head and smiled. She relieved Mamuchka of the cold soup. She didn't know this about her father – that he suffered from seasickness. There must have been dozens of facts about him that she didn't know. Would she be discovering dozens and dozens more similar facts in the coming weeks, she wondered? She placed the soup bowl on the console table and with her hands she massaged her mother's shoulders, working the tension out of them, saying, "Let's go see what the ladies are preparing for Iain's home-coming, shall we?"

Along the hall, within the kitchen, Mrs. Lo, Izabel and her two children were putting up Chinese characters in red ink, posting eighty-eight symbols of *Shou* (longevity), *Fu* (good fortune) and *Ai* (love, affection) across the wall and trailing them all the way down the stairwell to the ground floor. Nadia saw that the best silver was laid out and the food – two thick loaves of fresh white bread, steamed buns, a suckling pig flavoured with sea salt, a tureen of *caldo verde*, a dish of roasted almonds, garlic mussels, sausages with green beans, marinated herrings, a fat wedge of imported Portuguese cheese called *Queijo da Ilha*, a mountain of quavering strawberry jelly, some fruit and three bottles each of red wine, beer and seltzer – was spread out on the kitchen table. There were also dainty bowls full of eggs dyed red with *yen chih*, for luck, placed in each corner of the room.

When Mamuchka saw the range of dishes she gasped and said, "*Bawzhemoy!* Are we expecting a regiment of soldiers?"

Mrs. Lo clapped her hands with brio and said, "Ayah! We forget to cook fish. Fish is for good luck. I should cook fish for your hussbun and give him the cheek to eat!" then she said to Mamuchka, "Olga, what year your hussbun born in? If he born in year of pig, we must all wear purple colours for good luck."

Taken aback by the question Mamuchka had to think hard about this, before concluding, "1865 . . . he was born in 1865 . . ."

"Him an ox! Wahhh! He a very speshow man! He very stable husband with strong heart like a bull! My son Lennox is a dragon. He also a very adaptable and careful character."

Mamuchka smiled and said, "*Vek zhivi, vek uchis* - you live and learn."

"Maybe I still have time to buy fish," said Mrs. Lo. "One with big cheeks."

During this exchange, Nadia had to remind everybody three times that there was no certainty that Papashka would be on the boat. "Iain might be alone," she said.

"What?" said Mrs. Lo, now resigned to opening a can of sardines. "You think Iain will come back empty handed? Like a beggar? *Choy! Dakka laisee!* Oyo, I no think so!"

Nadia challenged everyone with her eyes. "All I'm saying is we might be disappointed."

Izabel who had been silent for some minutes decided to speak out, arching her already arched set of eyebrows higher. "Look, whatever happens, we know that Iain is safe. Isn't that what really matters?" She rubbed Nadia's arm. "Am I right?"

But who would she actually prefer to have back, Nadia wondered, Iain or her father? She thought about this for several seconds. Iain was her future. Her father was her past. If she had to choose between them she would opt for her future. She felt grateful to Iain, she felt committed to him. Yet something perverse made her hate him for going into Russia, for putting himself at such risk.

"Am I right?" Izabel repeated.

Nadia nodded.

"Do you think we need more wine?" said Mrs. Lo, "We better buy a few bottles of *vinho verde* . . . and some fyer-crackers, maybe some flowers too."

"Camellias would look just doocky!" said Izabel.

Mamuchka, who was torn between rapture and apprehension, tried and failed to get into the spirit of things. She said, "Yes, flowers would be nice. No yellow ones, though, and make sure you buy odd numbers. Russians believe that even numbers are for funerals."

Moments later Uncle Yugevny entered the kitchen. He gave out a yelp of delight when he saw all the food. "Oughtn't we be celebrating by now? Where is the wodka?"

"The boat doesn't dock for another four hours!" said Mamuchka.

"So? I am thirsty!" he said. "By the eyes of the *domovoi*, since when did a Fillipov need a reason to haff a drink?"

"*The joy of Russia is drinking*," said Nadia, quoting Prince Vladimir, the 10th century Russian monarch.

"*And without drinking we cannot be*," finished Uncle Yugevny.

"We could have a little port, I suppose," said Nadia.

"Phooey!" said Izabel. "Why have a little when we can have a lot."

Taking his cue, Uncle Yugevny uncorked a bottle of Sandeman and started filling glasses to the brim, Cossack-style. As he did so, he broke into song. He sang a melody about old Mother Russia. After a while, they all shared in the singing, including Mrs. Lo, who tried her hand at Cantonese opera.

Sitting around the kitchen table, laughing, they all decided a second bottle of port would be a bad idea. Instead they passed around the dish of roasted almonds, and debated whether they should all go to receive Iain at the pier or if it should be left to Uncle Yugevny to meet the ferry alone.

Three hours and a bottle of red wine later it was determined that Uncle Yugevny would go and the women would stay behind and wait. Nadia, her mouth as dry as a communion wafer, applied some make-up to her eyes and changed into a pale yellow cotton dress with an Empire waist and a short hem. She looked into the mirror and took it straight off, putting on a Cheruit-inspired dress instead. Tiny butterfly wings were beating wildly in her chest. She felt vulnerable and squeezed with anxiety.

In the cavernous entrance of their home, under the crystal chandelier, surrounded by red Chinese symbols and taffeta party balloons, Nadia and Mamuchka stood by the front door. They watched the entrance and the shadows that passed along the window, not quite knowing what they expected to see, listening out for the footsteps that would echo in a brand new, uncertain world. They gripped their sides with their arms.

Inhaling a breath, they heard a hand rattle the doorknob from the outside and a key being inserted. The doorknob twisted.

Their ribs felt crushed.

They did not cry. They would not cry.

6

Nadia saw Iain, bearded and smiling, and then this grey old man behind.

Afraid to say too much, facing each other, they stood there a long moment, unsure whether to embrace. But then Nadia held her hands out wide, almost as a petition. Her father's face, so corrugated and rucked with lines, so white-haired, crumpled even more now as their bodies met. They gathered each other; his worn hand on her cheek, her hands pressing against the middle of his back. Stroking and stroking. Stroking the sadness out. He was all bones. Behind her, she sensed Mamuchka's arm on her shoulder, rubbing, consoling, kneading, as if her hand did not know where to put itself. There was so much emotion in the room, it felt like a physical obstacle. Each of them wanted to speak, but the words simply would not form in their mouths. Instead, they cried. They held onto each other and wept sharp, monumental tears that spilled down their cheeks. "I never stopped believing," he said, quietly. Nadia had never felt such happiness; she had never felt such sadness. The years of loss would take years more to heal.

In the days to come, Mamuchka filled the rooms with hustle and bustle, keeping the windows wide open so that everyone could witness her happiness. She hosted tea-parties and soirees, charity lunches and lucky draws. It was as though, after all those years, she was alive again. She placed a notice in the local newspaper, saying that her husband had returned, she told the butcher, the baker, the *char siu* supplier, the seamstress she hadn't spoken to for ten years, as well as the rat-catcher and ear-cleaner. In the throes of her exhilaration, she even donated a statuette of the Virgin Mary to the church. While outside, in the square now with New Year bunting and strung flags, she stood on the steps of the square smiling, laughing louder than everybody else.

Papashka, meanwhile, stayed out of harm's way and rested in his room, laying on his blankets.

It wasn't easy for Mamuchka however. Though Ilya's arrival, for all its emotional drama, had given her a renewed sense of self, it also brought its difficulties. Having got used to her routine over the years, her husband's return meant that she now had to care for an invalid. She had to shop for him, cook his meals, bathe and shave him, dress him, put clean linen on his bed; she even had to help tie his shoe laces. And despite Nadia's tireless efforts to help, occasionally the responsibility overwhelmed Mamuchka.

Only late at night, over a pot of hot cocoa shared with Nadia and Izabel, would she suddenly confess to being confused by this man in her house who shuffled about rearranging her things and forever saying, 'Please help me with my shoes, Olga,' or 'Can you please bring me a pillow, Olga,' and 'Fetch this, fetch that.'

"He's been through a lot," said Izabel.

"All he does is rest, rest, rest," said Mamuchka. "And when he's awake all he does is think and think some more about Russia. You'd think he'd left his family behind."

"In a way he has. Do you think he's awake right now?" asked Nadia. "I want to speak to him."

"He was staring at the ceiling a few minutes ago when I left him," her mother replied, picking up her cluster of knitting only to put it back down again.

Nadia climbed the creaky stairs to the second floor and stood in the darkness for several moments. "Olga, is that you?" her father cried from behind the guest room door.

"It's me, Papashka." She pushed her head into the room

and saw her father in bed, the thin covers drawn across his chest. Tired lamplight illuminated his face and hands.

"Nadia, come in, please, come in and sit."

She settled down alongside him. "Mamuchka says your doing a lot of thinking." He looked at her then looked away. "Is this true?" He nodded. "Only people that are unhappy think all the time. And sleep all the time. You shouldn't be unhappy. Are you unhappy?"

He turned to her again and lifted his hand to softly touch her cheek. "Nadia, my Nadia. No, I am not unhappy." His eyes were warm, smiling now. "What I am is worried . . ." He paused. "I am worried."

"Worried about whom?"

"I am worried for the people I left behind in Harbin, Nadia. The Riedles were my family for so many years. I owe them my life. They are like a brother and sister to me. I need to know where they are. I need to know if they are safe."

He hadn't said much to her about the Riedles, but she knew instinctively how important they were to him. "Iain said the Lutheran Mission in Harbin was taking care of them," she said.

"But it is my responsibility to ensure they find safe passage to America, to California." He climbed out of bed and started buttoning his shirtsleeves. "And to ensure that once they get there, they are given what was promised."

"What are you doing?" asked Nadia. "You need to rest."

"Rest, zhest! I have been resting too long. I am going to talk with your Iain. I need assurances that my friends are safe."

"What, now? But it's almost eleven o'clock?"

"So? These things cannot wait. I need to talk with Iain."

"You can use the telephone in the shop."

"Telephone? I have never used a telephone in my life. Pass me my sticks and help me with my trousers, will you? And then go outside and hail a rickshaw."

"Where are you going?"

"*We* are going to see Iain."

"But Papashka, you can't go out into the night. You're far too frail."

"Nonsense. I haven't survived twenty-odd years as an invalid by being frail. Now, fetch me my shoes. It's time you saw where you got your strength of character from."

Two hours later, having read through Iain's correspondence and numerous Western Union telegraphs from the Mennonite Brethren in Fresno, California, Ilya concluded that the Riedles were indeed in safe hands. According to the paperwork, Peter and Nina Riedle were currently on a ship sailing to San Francisco Bay. The thought made Ilya smile. Perhaps Nina was tasting American ice-cream for the first time, he mused. He rested his palms on Iain's kitchen table and got to his feet. "You may take us home now," he said.

When they reached the Tabacaria, Ilya said a hasty goodnight. He refused any help as he struggled up the staircase. No sooner had he reached the landing when a finger-wagging Mamuchka confronted him at the top of the steps. "What time do you call this?" she yelled. "Just who do you think you are, out gallivanting til the early hours like an old tomcat! To bed with you!"

Downstairs, in the cavernous ground floor, Iain smiled at Nadia. She threw him a strange look. They made their way along the corridor and into the cigar shop. Nadia switched on the lights. They stood amongst the white jars of Zubelda and Mild Virginia, looking at one another.

"We haven't talked much since I got back," said Iain.

"No."

"You haven't kissed me either."

"Iain," she said firmly. "We need to talk."

"Talk about what?"

"Things . . . you . . . the way you just go off and do things without asking me first. It annoys me. What you've done annoys me."

"What do you mean?"

"The trip north . . . it was unfair what you did, toying with our emotions like that."

"I don't understand. I never toyed with you."

"You're playing God with our lives, Iain. Who gave you permission to go and rescue my father? Who said you could send the Riedles half way across the world."

"Permission? What are you talking about? I don't need permission."

"He's my father."

"I got him here in one piece, didn't I?"

"But what if you hadn't?"

"I don't think you have any idea what we had to go through."

"Actually, I do Iain. My father told me about the blizzard, about the Red Guards, how you never once let go of him. But did you think about the risks? Did you even once stop and think that the journey might have killed him . . . or you?"

"Of course I did. Why are you acting as if I'm the villain of the piece?"

"Look, Iain, if we're going to be friends, I can't have you making these sorts of decisions without consulting with me."

"Friends? Is that what we are? Friends?"

She looked at him as her words sunk in. "Yes, friends. Have you forgotten what happened before you went north? I called you a liar and an imposter. Don't tell me you've forgotten all about Lazar."

"No, I haven't forgotten about Lazar."

Reaching into her coat pocket she went over to the Tabacaria's entrance and, following a clicking of locks, pushed the front door ajar.

"You want me to go?" he said, raising his eyebrows.

She held the door wide open.

Iain stepped out into the cool night.

He walked briskly across the Largo da Sien. A stray dog

lifted his leg across the road. He listened for the cries of *'hey mista, you wan ride?'*, but there weren't any rickshaws in sight. Iain stood in the darkness for several moments and stared at the ground.

Three minutes later he banged on the cigar shop door.

"You also called me a shit," he said.

"A bloody shit if I remember correctly."

"I've thought long and hard about you, Nadia Shashkova," he said. "Long and hard."

"And?" She folded her arms across her chest.

"There used to be a hot stone in here." He pointed to his heart. "It was something alien, something anxious and impatient filling a void. But it's gone now. You made it go away." She unfolded her arms. "They want to send me to Hong Kong. Maybe not right away, perhaps in a couple of years time. There's even talk of returning to Scotland."

"Then you should go."

"I want you to come with me."

"That's not going to do your career any good is it? Bringing back a White Russian."

"It's a gamble I'm prepared to take."

"Well if it's gambling you're after then perhaps you should try your luck at the fan tan tables." She looked at her watch. "Club Camoens will still be open."

"I'd choose you over my career any day. I'd choose you over anything."

"Are you saying you want to marry me?"

He tried to kiss her mouth, but she pulled away.

He stopped and looked at her. "I don't know, am I?"

"My mother always said you were a flatterer and a deceiver."

"You're mother's no fool."

After which a smile spread across her face. "Do you know," she said. "When you were away I used to ask myself that if only one of you could return to me, would I rather have you or Papashka?"

"And? Which one of us did you choose?"

Nadia laughed, tickling his ribs with her fingers. Then she looked him in the eyes. "I'm grateful for what you've done, Iain, I really am. Don't get me wrong. But don't you ever take a risk like that again. And don't you ever play God with my life. Never again, do you promise me?" Her words were spoken through softened eyes.

"I promise."

"Goodnight then."

"Goodnight." He turned and walked once more into the night and like a rush of warm water, a sparkle of contentment fell over her. She pressed her nose to the glass and watched him disappear into the blackness.

For the next few weeks Nadia's life was serene and contented. But like a marsh snake in a flooded paddy-field, trouble eventually found its way to the surface.

It was during one of Mamuchka's cocoa-nights that Izabel burst into the kitchen and started tossing pots and pans onto the floor.

"Izabel!" cried Nadia. "What are you doing? Stop it!"

After staring at her friend for several moments, Izabel let out a scream and the colour left her face.

"What's happened?" asked Nadia. "Has something happened to the boys? Is it Carlos?"

"The police have sent me a summons." Izabel choked a little as she said this.

"What are you talking about?"

Izabel sat, gripping her thin elbows with her hands. "They are charging me for being a public nuisance, for disturbing the peace. They say that my marching bordered on harassment."

"Harassment? That's ridiculous. All you did was walk up and down the Praya. You weren't chanting insults or banging drums. You didn't accost anyone or abuse anyone."

"I called Queiroz a worm."

"So have hundreds of others, I'm sure."

"Do you think I'll go to jail?"

"Of course not, Izabel, you've done nothing wrong."

She shook her head. "What am I to do?"

Mamuchka interrupted. "Can anyone help us? What about Iain? Can he do anything? Do we know anybody who works for the law?"

"They might send me back to Portugal," said Izabel. "What's going to happen to Carlos? What if he loses his job over this, or his club membership? The shame is not worth thinking about."

"Maybe someone in the Government can help us," Mamuchka said.

"I know nobody in the Government."

"Or someone in the judiciary . . ." Mamuchka tailed off.

In the semi-darkness of the kitchen, a thick silence settled over them.

Suddenly, the whites of Nadia's eyes grew large. "Senhor Pinto," she said. "*Bawzhemoy!* Why didn't I think of it before? He's a magistrate. I'll go and talk to Senhor Pinto."

The following morning Nadia paid Senhor Pinto a visit at his Rua da Colina offices. The brass plaque on the building read '*Supremo Tribunal de Justica*'

Nadia knocked lightly and pushed the doors open, and as she entered, the judge came forward and welcomed her with a boyish grin.

"Sit," he said, pulling his chair close. She handed him a parcel, wrapped in silver paper.

"What's this?" he said.

"Oh, nothing really," she said. "Just a little something." Nadia cast a quick glance at the room as Senhor Pinto unraveled the paper. His law chambers were furnished sumptuously – Regency furniture, heavy velvet curtains, leather tomes in opulent carved bookshelves – and cooled by twirling ceiling fans.

"You've brought me some embroidered handkerchiefs," he said, delighted.

"Yes, beautiful little chrysanthemums, all satin-stitched," she said.

"But I thought you told me that *lencos* bring tears."

"These will only bring you tears of joy."

He thanked her and tugged at the end of his nose. "Well," he said. "What exactly can I do for you?"

Pinto was in his judicial robes, made of pearl buttons and black shiny cloth. Wearing his court medallion low against his chest, he studied Nadia closely as she related Izabel's story. His eyes travelled up and down her face as she spoke. She felt like a bug in a jar. "So you come to me for a favour, hmm?" he said, leaning back in his chair.

"Yes."

There was a long moment when neither spoke. He drummed the desktop with his fingers. His eyes were aglint. "And if I grant you this favour, what will you do for me?"

Nadia looked at the floor. Her face reddened. After several moments she raised her head to find Senhor Pinto shaping his mouth into a grin.

"I am toying with you," he conceded. He held out his left hand to her which she took and kissed. "Come back at noon tomorrow. I will see what I can do."

Nadia met Izabel in a cafe near Big Step Street; it was the same *chau lau* they'd gone to months before when they'd first met. Both women ordered iced mint tea with limes and sat staring at each other.

"What did Pinto say?"

"Not much," said Nadia.

Izabel, dressed in a pale slimline linen dress and silk scarf, removed the scarf from her throat and brought it up to her eyes. "What am I going to do?"

"Can you show me the summons?"

She reached into her handbag. "Here."

Nadia read the arraignment. It stated that Izabel was required to appear in *corte* 21 days after the issuance of the summons and if she failed to show up the court would order a judgment in favour of the prosecution.

"Carlos is livid, of course."

"I'm not surprised."

"He says we should have been more respectful to Queiroz."

"We were doing something we believed in. It's something we still believe in."

"You're right."

"However, I think we may have to find you a solicitor."

"*Merda!* A solicitor will cost money. Carlos won't like the sound of that."

"Can Carlos not talk to Queiroz himself? Don't they belong to the same sports club?"

"He already has. Queiroz called him a fool and told him to *coma a merda e morra.*"

"*Bawzhemoy!*"

"And there's more."

"What?"

"Queiroz mentioned something about you."

"What?"

"He said he was going after you too, Nadia. He said he's going send you packing back to Russia."

At noon the next day, Nadia entered Senhor Pinto's law chambers once more.

"Please sit down," he said, gesturing unsmilingly.

Nadia looked at him with eyes wide with hope. "A-any thoughts?" she eventually asked. "Any thoughts on my friend's problem?"

Pinto shook his head. "I can not help you," he said.

Nadia's heart sank.

Pinto stared at the floor. But then his face cracked into a grin. "Haaaahaaaa!" he yowled. "I fooled you, eh? Of course, I will help you." He smiled, face crinkling. "It just so happens that I share your friend's opinion. What's happening to these babies is a disgrace. The problem must be addressed either by the Legislative Council or the Health Ministry."

"But what about Queiroz? He has a point to prove . . . his honour has been challenged."

"Nonsense! Queiroz is being sent back to Lisbon in two months. His three-year posting is drawing to an end. His opinion holds no weight around here."

"But what about the summons?"

He got up from his chair and took Nadia's arm, guiding her to the door. "You leave this to me, Nadia. And tell your friend, Senhora Perera, to tear up that summons. I have spoken to the Governor about this matter. From this moment on it has become void."

"Really?"

"*Sim*, really."

"Tell her *Juiz* Pinto, circuit judge of Macao's court of appeal, has taken the matter into his own hands."

"I don't know how to thank you – "

"Also I wish to help with this orphanage."

"You wish to help?"

He lifted a finger aloft to underline his words. "We will have a new orphanage set up here in no time. Mark my words."

"I can hardly believe what I'm hearing."

"Ah, believe, believe, my dear. Old Pinto still has some pull around here, no?" He flexed the bicep muscles in his arms.

Ecstatic, Nadia wrapped her arms round the old man and kissed him hard on the cheek. Senhor Pinto blushed and looked to his right and left. "Please, Nadia, I have a reputation." He pulled out a comb from his hip pocket and ran it through his hair several times.

"Thank you, Senhor Pinto! Thank you!" She raced out of

the office and down the stairs, taking two steps at a time.

Outside, Iain was waiting patiently, swinging a folded umbrella about. He pretended it was a golf club. When Nadia saw him, she rushed into his arms. "How did it go?" he asked. Nadia's lip parted in a broad smile. Feeling proud, she said it went well. They turned from the gates of the chancery and walked towards the Praya, eyes looking off into the distance, sunshine spilling on their shoulder, their future bright, full of new hope. She paused midway down the street and looked back. Standing at the second-floor window, she saw Senhor Pinto. She gave him a wave as she took Iain's hand. Pinto smiled and flourished a satin-stitched *lenco*. She removed her own handkerchief from a skirt pocket and held it high to the sky, watched it flutter freely in the breeze.

She had never felt so alive.

PART THREE

1937

1

Nadia's first impressions of Scotland were not good. On a morning in early February, Glasgow was biting cold and wet, smelling of mud and smoke and puddly streets. The terrain was grey, its landscape cheerless, with endless silhouettes of power stations, warehouses and crummy industrial chimneys. To Nadia it resembled a worn-out shoe.

Nadia stepped down the narrow covered gangplank separating ship from shore. It was drizzling and the landing stage was teeming with humanity; a bustling sea of tweed coats and skirts and steamer trunks. The strong wind blew her shoulder-length hair across her eyes, stinging her cheeks, making the skin tingle. Reaching into her overcoat, she brought out a silk scarf. Under the shadow of ropes hauling baggage from the ship's hold and groaning pallets being winched high into the sky, she secured the headscarf under her chin and strode into the roaring maelstrom of stevedore cries and clanging bells.

"Guid day McCleish! Ye bampot!" came a shout from above, "Dornt stain arooond lookin' glaikit, gie those bags aff jist loch 'at!"

Nadia turned her face forward. She had to push through the throng of salty dock-hands and porters and people watchers in order to catch up with Iain, who was several paces ahead. She wanted to stick to him like a burr, but he kept moving away. Bumping hips, and arms and shoulders, she weaved through the traffic, hurrying after him. Crowds trailed behind her and from nearby she heard the skirl of bagpipes – a welcoming band perhaps – as passengers and long-shoremen ran round her. But where was the Scotland from the guide books, she asked. She had half expected to see moated castles, thistled hillsides and horse-drawn trams advertising Nairn's Handbaked Scottish Oatcakes – not this; anything but this.

After a long time of standing around at the Dock Offices and not recognizing anybody, Iain eventually put up his arm and waved. Abandoning Nadia and the luggage, he sprang forward, winter coat tails flapping, to embrace a man with shimmering dark eyes and Iain's lean build. The two men stood admiring one another for several moments, sizing each other up. "Nadia this is my brother, Callum. Callum, meet my wife, Nadia."

Callum, clad in plus fours and a tweed coat, dipped his head. He peeled off his flat cap. Nadia shook his hand – a big hand, calloused and broad – then offered her condolences. "I'm sorry for your mother's passing," she said.

"Och, she was a guid lady. Cannae really believe that she's gone, tae tell you th' truth, e'en though it's bin nearly three months. Aam glad you'll be with us fur th' memorial service."

"That'll be on Sunday?" Iain asked.

"Aye. Sunday."

Callum threaded through the crowd to fetch the car, a Hillman Minx. After securing the luggage to the roof, Iain climbed into the front with his brother, who was driving. Nadia sat in the rear.

Callum pulled the starter and the car moved off.

"Fancy motor," said Iain.

"Aye, better than th' sheep trailer ah usually get tae drive. Look," he said taking both hands off the wheel. "Look hoo well it holds th' road. Wish it were mine, but it belongs tae th' estate," said Callum. "Borrowed it fur th' day. Our petrol allowance has bin cut tae practically naethin' however."

"You been keeping busy all the same?"

"Och aye. We hud a busy night with th' steward and th'

204

ghillies, clearin' up some ay th' fallen trees around Baden-loch. That's why aam still in mah work clothes."

From her isolation in the back seat, Nadia watched avidly as the city panned out before her eyes: through the pillows of haze, she saw line after line of hunger marchers and pick-eters and boarded up mills, shop windows covered with newspaper, children scavenging in shoes without laces. An electric tram pushed drearily through the rain. Further ahead, Victorian tenement buildings, brown with soot and rusted metal, in various stages of ruin, reared up like neglected tombs.

She saw drayhorses propped against viaduct walls; labourers in baggy blue boiler suits rolling their own cigar-ettes; two drunkards fighting over the remains of a whisky bottle; gangs of jobless men, standing in clusters, milling about on railway tracks or under bridges. She heard their guttural vowels, their jumpy snaggle-toothed voices against the roar of the subway trains. By then she understood the meaning of the expression 'the Great Slump' – for these were victims of the depression, of economic decay, and it seemed to her that the rot was spreading.

Callum kept glancing at her in his mirror. "So, Nadia, ah gahther this is your first time in Scotland. Whit do you think of it so far?"

"Wet," she replied.

"Och, the drizzle's guid fur your skin. Does wonders fur the complexion." Callum Sutherland kept talking. "Scottish lassies ur knoon fur their bright an' rosy cheeks, you know. It's the drizzle, ah tell you, the Scotch mist." He laughed. "Isnae tha' right, Iain." He turned and punched Iain in the arm. Nadia thought she sensed a tinge of resentment in Callum's voice. Was it because Iain never made peace over his father, she wondered? Never tried for some kind of reconciliation?

"How long hae you both been married noo? Six years? More?" Callum craned his neck to get another look at Nadia through the mirror. "What about wee uns? Any signs of having bairns yet?"

Staggered by the baldness of his tone, Nadia shifted uncomfortably in her seat. Noticing that Iain's face had turned away, she shook her head as she spoke. "Not yet."

"Mebbe your trews are too tight, Iain," he said punching his brother in the arm once more. Again, Nadia sensed an undertone of disgruntlement.

"What're you waitin' fur?"

She took a breath. "We're not waiting for anything," she replied.

Innocent as the question was, it stung her. She realized it shouldn't have, but it did. *We're not waiting for anything* – the words sounded so small ridiculous to her all of a sudden. She was thirty-six years old! She was desperate to give her parents a grandchild. How much more time did she have, she asked herself. Could women get pregnant after the age of forty? She didn't know anyone that had. And didn't older mother's risk miscarriage? Breech babies? Mongols?

She wondered what was going through Iain's mind. She knew that, like her, he desperately wanted children. But why couldn't she conceive? Their marriage was strong, not perfect, but strong; nevertheless she couldn't help but feel as though she was letting him down. And now especially, having worked with Izabel at the orphanage, her longing to hold her own baby was greater than ever.

For the next few hours, as the car headed north, through towns such as Dunkeld, Pitlochry, and Dalwhinnie, Nadia thought time and time about her condition. She used to love being self-sufficient, used to dread the idea of becoming a mother, fearing the responsibility, the sacrifice, the loss of freedom. Now she yearned for it, practically ached for children, yet, for some unknown reason, she could not conceive – and it wasn't for the lack of trying. It was, she knew, quickly turning into an obsession.

At first her mother dropped subtle looks and hints, reassuring her that it was only a matter of time. But after a while, Mamuchka had begun to ask questions, sifting through her laundry, enquiring about her monthly secretion – was it punctual, was it uniform in colour, was the discharge cloudy or creamy or lumpy, what was the pain like? Sharp? Or a dull ache? Why did it hurt when she went for a pee? Did she always feel nausea during her period? And why were her hands always clammy? Papashka would tell her to stop interfering, but soon, she was saying that Nadia was too skinny, that she wasn't eating properly, that she ought to avoid meat products and consume more alfalfa, pumpkin seeds, avocados and wheat.

"What about coffee?" Mamuchka would ask.

"What about it?"

"Avoid it." And when that didn't work, Mamuchka took Nadia to the see the local herbalist on Rua da Palha. The herbalist told her to avoid hot baths as that could change ovulation. He advised that she drink lots of pear juice to alleviate the pain in her bladder whenever she peed. In the meantime, he prescribed an infusion of yellow dock, chamomile and Chinese angelica to be sipped twice daily and for a balm of wild yam to be rubbed on the stomach each night before bed. In addition, he suggested that she remain on her back with her legs raised in the air for twenty minutes after the male had ejaculated. After a month they returned and this time he prescribed an herbal formula consisting of licorice and false unicorn. Yet, still, nothing happened. Her menstrual flows continued.

It was extremely frustrating.

"Perhaps it is the husband who is at fault," suggested Mamuchka, scrambling for any explanation.

The herbalist nodded. And in no time Mamuchka was adding flax seed oil into Iain's food without him realizing and feeding him copious amounts of cooked clams and pine nuts and sesame seeds for their zinc. Soon after, Iain began complaining of a metallic taste in his mouth and nausea, so she was forced to cut down on her dosage.

"Got your beak in a book, hae you? You like readin' then?'

Nadia looked up and saw Callum's eyes in the mirror. "I'm sorry?" On her lap was a copy of *A Passage to India*, opened to chapter one. She had yet to read a line of Forster's novel.

"Hoo about a cuppa and a bit ay lunch?"

"My brother wants to know if you're hungry," said Iain, glancing round and smiling.

A side road emerged through the trees. Turning off at a town called Aviemore they stopped at a restaurant overlooking the Cairngorm Mountains where they rang a lunch gong and ate Cullen Skink with cheese crackers.

The men talked about golf and rugby and the ten-point stag that was shot on the Achantoul Estate. Nadia wrote a postcard home, confirming their safe arrival. For a while she studied the inky whorls which made up her distinctive hand. She held the postcard against the window, trailing the flight of a distant cormorant hovering high in the clouds. The bird must have abandoned its nest, she decided.

Already, she missed her mother.

It was her first afternoon in Helmsdale. The small cottage was cool and dry; its walls trimmed with roebuck horns, decorated with quilted tartan. Nadia liked her room – the doors creaked, the upholstery itched, the pipes beside the washstand growled (the water ran brown with peat), the old black wireless crackled – it made her feel welcome.

Nadia sat with Callum's wife, Jane, by the window-bay looking out towards the sea. Shafts of sunlight spilled through the glass, speckling the room with gold dust. Nadia followed a nimbus of cloud streak across the horizon. The north-sea sky looked anaemic to her, like marine ivory, and there was a sheen of frosty dew that settled upon the blackthorn like sun-bleached sand.

After a while her gaze turned to Jane. She was a slight, busy-looking woman of about thirty with sharp eyes and a kind-hearted tongue. Her hair was straggly, like a bundle of straw. She enjoyed talking with Nadia about her recent sea voyage, asking questions about the ship and the stops it made out of China. She was eager and quizzical, and though she seemed to be tied to the land, as though bound by its earth and roots, Nadia could tell that she longed to get away from the restraints of village life. After years of being confined to the local gossip, she was hungry to hear about other, new, things.

"I'm so glad you're spending a wee while with us," said Jane, her accent and intonations nowhere as meaty as Callum's. There was a need-to-impress urgency to her voice. "We never ever have visitors from abroad and I've heard so much about you from Iain's letters. A Russian woman living in the Far East! It sounds so exotic! I had to look on the map to see where Macao was. I didn't realize it was only forty miles from Hong Kong. And I hear you run a cigar shop. You'd do well here, almost everybody smokes." Nadia noticed Jane's long fingers which were clutched tightly round a white cotton handkerchief. The fingers tripped about whenever she grew animated and she seemed to talk without stopping. "And who would have believed that you'd come all this way to be with us in wee-tiny Helmsdale. I mean, I have cousins who come to see us at Christmas – they live in Oban – and we have the Highland Games every year in Inverness but we seldom have people travelling from across the world!"

Nadia looked at Jane fondly and smiled. "You're part of our family. Coming here was a pleasure."

Jane then talked a little about her own children, who were six, eight and eleven, all currently attending the local school, but Nadia managed to steer the conversation toward Iain – his job, his hobbies . . . anything in order to avoid hearing that dreaded question, 'And what about you, Nadia, don't you want to have a baby of your own? Don't you want to hear the pitter-patter of tiny feet?'

As they talked, Nadia found that they had similar interests. She soon realized they would get along just fine.

"Callum mentioned that Iain will be going to Edinburgh in a fortnight," said Jane.

"Yes, he's meeting with some old colleagues. Then we're off to London for ten days to meet with more of his superiors."

"Will you be going too? You're very welcome to stay until he returns."

"That's very kind of you." Nadia felt her heart sink. She remembered her appointment with Dr. Goode, the fertility expert. "But, I think I should accompany him." After that she fell silent, listening to the seagulls in the bay.

"You'll love Edinburgh. It's a beautiful city to explore. You'll have a grand time."

"Yes," said Nadia.

Once again she grew silent, as though the anticipation of meeting with Dr. Goode had smothered her. She was terrified of being told that she could not conceive. Why was it, she wondered, that there were some women, like Jane, who were like baby-factories, squeezing out six, seven, even eight children over the course of a lifetime, while others were desolate. Was she desolate? Did she bear only withered fruit? The idea made her heart ache. What was wrong with her? She tried to repress the black feelings.

"Well then," said Jane looking at her watch, "I expect the men won't be back from the pub 'til after three. There's a wee bit of tension between them that needs sorting out. We don't want to lose the whole day waiting for their return, do we? Would you like to go for a walk around the village before the weather breaks? We could pay our respects to Iain and Callum's mother." She gave a little sigh. "Poor old thing, up to the very end she was upset that Iain never made peace with his father."

"Yes, I know. Tell me, how did he die? Iain's father, I mean. Iain doesn't like to talk about it."

"Liver cancer. He left us in 1935."

"Oh."

"Poor Callum took it quite badly. After James died in the war and with Iain away abroad, he and his Daa grew very close. I don't think Callum has ever forgiven Iain for breaking his father's heart." She sighed. "Anyway, what's past is past, God rest his soul. I was wondering whether you 'd like to go for a wee stroll?"

Nadia set down her thick tea cup. "I'd like that, yes."

"There's not much to see really, just the church and the early-spring salmon leaping about at the mouth of the river. Callum's the factor at one of the estates. He's got the rest of the afternoon off today, as you know, but I could get his permission to show you the grouse moors if you like. I'd also like to take you to the little house where Iain and Callum grew up."

"That sounds lovely."

"But we can't have you walking around dressed like that, can we?"

Jane's words took her by surprise. Nadia looked down at her slim-line, woolen skirt and pale yellow sweater. It was what she called her Myrna Loy look. "Why, what's wrong?"

"You'll have all the children in the village following you around, that's what's wrong. They'll think the Duchess of Argyll has arrived."

"Too bright?"

"Come," said Jane, taking Nadia by the hand. "Let's get you into some country tweeds and wellies."

The graveyard was on a small headland. It rested on level ground at the top of a slope, looking down onto the dark, pebbly beach.

The Highland sky was grey, darkening quickly as a mizzle of rain swabbed the spiny gorse and yellow broom. Looking behind her, Nadia saw a barren little hill and a fringe of lonely, whitewashed cottages along the shore. Oystercatchers swooped. Seabirds and herring gulls flew in downward arches.

It was late-afternoon and the herons were taking up positions on the edges of the cliff.

Nadia, clad in a pair of green Wellington boots, knelt down by a white headstone. The tablet was new and unblemished and as she read the inscription, she recognized the name. SUSAN VALENTINA SUTHERLAND 1874–1936, it said, BELOVED WIFE AND MOTHER. Next to it, a mere yard away, was the grave of Iain's father, dead two years. The pink and canary-coloured flowers she'd purchased from the village shop skipped and hopped in the gale. Nadia planted them under a stone.

Behind her, Jane stared out into the ocean. When the wind was like this, blowing in from the north, it smelled of rockweed and periwinkles and sweet hand-scythed hay. Callum's wife was watching the fishermen as they hauled their short wooden currachs into the sea.

The surf roared, throwing tiny specks of water into the wind, misting the fishermen's faces. Each man braced as the bow met the swell. Further out, beyond the roll of waves, a group of boats floated serenely; spatulate thumbs worked hard, as the fishers, burdened with coiled ropes and keepnets, baited their lines with mussels, 150 hooks per line.

After a while, Nadia and Jane came down from the headland, descending the narrow hill path that led to the sea. In the distance they could hear the calls of the lobster men over in the tiny harbour – a frisson of excitement as they fed the seals who were coming out of the water, taking the fish straight from their hands.

Nadia hung onto Jane's arm as they forded the shallow surf, feeling the water tug and suck at their boots. Their hair whipped across their eyes. The two women held between them two little wooden boats, replicas of Chinese junks, filled with lighted incense sticks. Sea-grass baskets and cast nets bobbed in the shingles as the surf rushed up like a greedy outspread hand, washing away their footprints. Cheeks wet with salt-spray, they pushed the boats into the foamy water. "Incense to purify departed souls," Nadia whispered.

The waves clapped. The ocean sang. The tiny boats danced on the beads of froth until they fell into the curls of the sea.

2

The Cross Free Kirk was on Strathnaver Street. Its stained glass windows shone like a butterfly amongst the blackthorn bushes. Iain, seated at the front of the marigold-scented church, felt his wife's fingers search out his hand. He looked at Nadia who smiled at him.

Everything to Iain seemed shadowed with memories – the narrow lanes where he and his brothers learned to play football, the old plane trees which they used to climb, now so much taller and their limbs thicker, the weather puckered walls of the small school on Rutherford Terrace. Was the chemistry master's yellowing lab coat still hanging on a hook in the assembly room, he wondered? And what about the gentle-faced vicar stood before him? Was he really the same wild-eyed man that used to warn the Sutherland boys about fire and brimstone and being sent into the pit?

Turning to sneak a glance at the congregation, Iain dipped his eyes, his breath so shallow it came in nips and drams. There were little puddles of melted snow all across the chapel floor. He saw heads bowed low and arms crossed, braced against the frigid draughts that swept through the unheated church. Everyone wore black for his mother's memorial service. There were a few uncles and aunts, a cousin too, but nobody else he really recognized. Only his Uncle Johnny stared back at him, with what to him looked like a glare of hostility, but his eyes were so blinkered and cataracted that Iain guessed he could see little distinctly.

They sang a hymn. Mrs. McManus, a retired teacher from Rutherford Terrace, played the organ as accompaniment.

Moments later, the vicar recited the ritual benedictions. Kneeling in prayer, hands gathered by his forehead, Iain tried to take in the vicar's voice.

He listened for a while, only half-registering the echoing words, wishing for all he was worth that he could kiss her again and say one last goodbye.

An hour later Iain was in a pub, invited there by Callum for a *gab-and-chat* drink with the local men whilst Nadia went for a stroll along the shore with Jane. The pub's walls were painted in the navy and green colours of the Sutherland Highlanders Regiment and as the raw afternoon light skipped off the polished wood of the bar, stinging his eyes, Iain took in the additional surroundings: worn oak tables, sawdust floors, frayed red curtains, spittoons, gantries with inverted bottles, and a motley collection of damp smelling dogs curled by the open fire.

No-necked men in leather caps and tweed stood staring at Iain, whisky tumblers in hand. Watching them watching him, Iain wondered whether he ought to try to make polite conversation. He nodded and smiled. Hardly anybody smiled back.

"Must be odd fur ye, comin' back here efter aw these years," someone eventually said. It was his creamy-eyed Uncle Johnny, his father's brother.

"It's good to be back."

"Ye expect us tae believe that dae ye? Efter abandonin' yer mother, betrayin' yer own people, it's guid tae be back, ye say. Weel we're nae sure we want ye back, laddy."

"I returned to pay my respects to my mother . . ."

"Ye didne pay her much respect when she was alive, did ye? Ye coulds hae come over tae comfort her efter your father died in '35, but ye didne."

"I live half way across the world. I can't undertake such a journey at the drop of a hat. Look, I'm here to say my final goodbyes to her, not to interfere with your lives."

"Och, ye willnae be interferin' wi' anythin' if I hae my way with ye."

"Meaning?"

"Meanin' ah'd fling ye out of town if ah coulds."

"Don't worry, I'll be gone in a few days."

"Ye know what folke are sayin' about ye, don't ye?" Uncle Johnny continued. *"There goes that Sutherland fellaw, Callum's brither. Th' one with th' sassenach accent, all hoity-toity noo and wrapped up in himself. Too proud tae call himself a true Scot."*

"It's not like that at all and you know it. I'm proud of my heritage."

"Like buck ye are. Ye're nae like us. Ye don't belong here anymore!"

Iain pedalled backwards with an involuntary step. He glanced at Callum for support but got none. His brother's eyes were as bulged as Uncle Johnny's.

A strained silence fell over the bar.

After several moments Callum spoke. His voice quivered. "Och look, Iain, we're nae lookin' fur a fight or anythin' like that. We, weel Uncle Johnny and me specifically, we want to know why you did it. Why you did whit you did tae Daa. Tae us."

Iain looked first at Callum and then at Uncle Johnny.

"You're right, maybe I'm not like you anymore. Maybe I don't belong. But I'll tell you this. Not a day goes by when I don't think about Helmsdale and what I did to my family."

"Why'd you hurt Daa like that Iain? Why'd you dae it?"

Iain took a swig of whisky. "You want to know? All right, I'll tell you. I went poaching for salmon on six occasions. The first five hauls were successful, brought me almost thirty-two shillings in total at Cameron's Fishmongers in Golspie. Each time, I borrowed your bicycle, Callum, and carried the salmon in a sack across my back. When I returned home, I hid the money under my bed, in a Colman's mustard tin filled with wooden soldiers." He paused. "The sixth time I tried it, Daa caught me." He took another sip from his glass.

"I gambled and I lost. Why did I do it? I did it for James, that's who, I did it for James, our brother."

"James?"

"Aye, for James. Do you remember how badly he wanted to go for trials at Aberdeen when he was seventeen? Remember how he always boasted of becoming a great inside-left? He needed something like two guineas to get his act together – trainfare, accommodation, that sort of thing. Well, Daa wouldn't help him, said there was no future in association football. What would he do if he got badly injured, Daa asked, how would he feed himself, bring bread to the table? What would he do with himself after the age of thirty-five when his legs gave in? A footballer's career is short – did he have a back-up plan, could he think of a back-up plan? Unfortunately, James couldn't come up with a good enough answer, so Daa refused to lend him the money."

"You lent it tae him?"

"I gave it to him and I made him promise he'd never say where he got the money from. It was enough to get him to Aberdeen. The rest he'd have to earn working for the lobstermen in the village, which he did."

Callum laid his hand on Iain's shoulder. "But you ne'er mentioned-"

"Let me finish. After he died I felt protective of him. For a few months I even wondered whether I was responsible for his death because he was still in Aberdeen when he joined up with the Gordon Highlanders. It was silly, I know, but maybe if he hadn't gone for trials, if I hadn't given him that money, he wouldn't have made it south. Maybe he'd have joined another regiment, like the Dragoons with me and avoided that bayonet. And maybe he'd still be here today. Anyway, when I got news that he'd been killed, I swore that I'd keep this a secret. I didn't want to sully his name in any way, so I've kept it to myself for twenty years."

"You shoods hae told us, shoods hae told Daa."

Iain shook his head. "No. Daa would never have under-

217

stood. He loved this river as much as anything. For me to do what I did was unforgiveable in his eyes."

A minute went by, followed by another. Nobody said a word. Then Iain felt Callum's hand on his shoulder once more and he looked into his brother's eyes. "I'm sorry that I caused so much hurt . . . I never meant to."

Callum's face showed real sadness. He pressed his lips together as though to suppress a cry. "Ah jist wish you'd told us afore.'

"I know," said Iain.

The two men grabbed each other and hugged. An old man seated with his dog let out a cry of hurrah and clapped.

"This doesnae mean we hae tae like ye, though," said Uncle Jimmy with a laugh. "Och, whit th' hell, this round's on me! A dram ay whisky for everybody!"

On Monday Iain took Nadia fishing. Over rocky pots and gravel shingles they clambered. Emerging from the under-growth, a thirteen-foot greenheart in hand, Iain led Nadia down to the water's edge into the weed-beds. They both wore thigh-length angling waders and dark clothing. It was early morning and a long bank of cloud hooded the bright-ening sun. By the time they reached the river bank there was hardly any breeze.

"Which part of the river are we on?" she asked.

"This here is community water, anyone can fish here so long as you get a permit from the local angling club, but if you look over there," he pointed upstream in the direction of a fringe of tall, thin trees, "that's the Whinnie, the start of beat number one. Only the proprietors can fish beyond that point. The river's divided into six beats, shared equally between the estates."

They waded into the water. Iain stood on Nadia's left and showed her the workings of the fishing rod. "We'll be using two different flies," he said, "A Hairy Mary for the tail fly and a Jock Scott as the dropper."

Nadia looked down at her feet. Little iridescent bubbles emerged from the underswell whenever she moved. The deeper she waded the more her toes and ankles felt squeezed by the river pressure. "Right," she said sucking in a lungful of wintry air. "How do I cast?"

"Like this." Using a shortish line, he lifted the rod so that it was perpendicular to his shoulder and after a moment's pause threw the rod head forwards. With a swoosh the line sprayed out towards the centre of the fast water, straight as an arrow. He did it again for her to see. Nadia studied his wrists, watched the way his body moved. Holding her arms in front, she did a series of imitations with her own hands, mimicking him. "Just remember to pause on the uplift and don't crack the rod like a whip. If you do that the flies will snap off."

Nadia took the rod in her begloved hands and did as instructed. She heard the *shwish-shwoosh* of her back-cast sailing through the air. The line did a wobbly zigzag into the open stream. "Any good?"

"Not bad at all." He sounded impressed. "Next time aim at a forty-five degree angle and wait for the fly to come right around. Then take a good step forwards downstream after each cast. That way we get to cover the entire pool."

They fished the pool all the way down to a bend in the river. From time to time a salmon would leap high out of the water and do a belly-flop. Iain looked skyward and examined the clouds. "I think we're going to see some snow," he said.

After a pause Iain said, "Did you see that?"

"See what?"

"A fish came to your fly. I saw a boil in the water." There was a ripple of circles where a salmon might have surfaced.

"Really? I didn't see anything." But Nadia wasn't watching her fly at all. She was enjoying the scent in the air, the sounds of the birds, the rush of the water swaddling her calves. Earlier she'd watched an otter roll down the far bank and plop into the water. Behind her now, on the southern hill, she saw railway men at the steam depot unloading cattle from Thurso.

After a while she asked, "What do you think they'll say to you next week?"

"You mean the office? I expect they'll want to know if I'm committed to staying in Asia."

"Are you?"

Iain glanced at his wife. "You know I am." He assured her.

"What if they want you to return here permanently?"

"Why would they want that?"

"There's talk of war in Europe. They may need you in Paris or Amsterdam or . . ."

"Then I'll turn them down. Nadia, what's the matter? I'm not going to leave you if that's what you're worried about. Why would I want to return to Europe?"

"But this is your home"

"Not any more, not for twenty years. I could never settle here now. I've changed. I'm not like these people anymore. I don't act the same. I don't sound the same . . . Maybe because I've been away so long. Maybe it's also because being in Scotland reopens old wounds. A long time ago I hurt my parents and never had a chance to properly apologise." Nadia remembered him telling her how his father had caught him red-handed trapping salmon.

"Was it here that it happened? Is this where he surprised you?"

"No, it was near the Kildonan Falls. A long way further up the river." He looked at the point of her rod. "Cast again before you get snarled up in the weed." She flipped the line over her head and sent it sprawling across the water. "Hand-line it just a little to keep the fly moving," he said.

"Why did you say that just now?"

"Say what?" he asked.

"You said, 'I'm not going to leave you'."

"Well, I'm not am I?"

"Does that mean you've thought about it? Do you want to leave?"

"Of course not! Christ, what's got into you?"

She noticed his eyes grow large in their sockets. She looked away. "Nothing's gotten into me. It's just that I'm surrounded by all these women who are fantastic mothers – Mamuchka, Izabel, Mrs. Lo, Jane . . . maybe you want somebody who can give you children."

"Is that what this is all about?"

The question seemed to take on a life of its own, circling round them like a predator.

They moved along to the next pool in silence. They fished it down without saying a word to each other. A choir of oystercatchers accentuated the stillness that hovered uneasily between them. Nadia felt like screaming. She knew how much Iain hated talking about their childlessness and she wanted to scream because she imagined what he must have been feeling.

"I want a family, Iain. Isn't that what we all wish for – a family to love?" she said.

"You have a family." Iain slipped his hand under her tweed skirt and into her tights. Speaking in a whisper he said, "I love you Nadia Sviazhsky Shashkova. Whether we have a baby of our own or not won't change how I feel about you. And if you doubt that for even a minute then you're as mad as a March hare. You've got to stop torturing yourself over this." His fingers caressed the skin along the back of her thighs, trailed across her buttocks. She felt him rub the delicate fabric between her legs, touching the soft grooves of folded cotton.

"Stop," she said, sensing her own arousal. "Someone might see."

"There's no one around." He began to kiss her neck, her throat, her wet eyes.

She could feel the cold air where he had lifted her skirt. His touch was cool against her warm body. A purl of complaint crossed her lips. She was tempted to push him away. But then she felt him slide her knickers to one side, parting the thin material, and his fingertips were inside her, feathering a path between her legs. The sensation blinded her with stars. Her heart began drumming in her chest. Her legs turned to mulch and her body grew moist. The river ran thick and dark beneath her loins. She felt the corners of his welcoming mouth on her cheek. Felt his hardness through his trousers. She wanted to tear off his clothes.

She pulled him by his sleeve, wanting to guide him deeper, to suck him in. His hot breath warmed her cheek; she could smell the Vitalis in his hair.

Wrapped around each other, she was about to drop the fishing rod when they were shocked out of their embrace by a shrill sound.

GGTSSSSSSSSSSSSSSSGGTSSSSSSSSSSSSS............

It was the reel.

"Bloody hell!" said Iain. "You've hooked a fish."

Nadia hopped up and down. "What do I do?" she yelled. The rod was bending alarmingly in her hands.

"Keep the rod up!" He grabbed her by the waist and guided her towards the bank. When she was on firm ground he said, "Now, follow the fish and try to get as close to him as you can. Reel in as much line as he'll let you. Don't let it go slack. Keep the pressure on at all times, but if he wants to run, let him."

"*Bawzhemoy, Bawzhemoy!*" she said over and over again. The salmon threw itself high into the air, darted this way and that, making deep Vs in the water. The reel sang like a drunken soprano.

They ran thirty yards up the river. Then they did an about-turn and ran thirty yards back down. Her mind was spinning crazily, like a lug nut come loose from a fast-moving train.

She played the fish for another twenty-five minutes. Her arms tingled, her shoulders hurt. Her cheeks were rosy, flushed with excitement. There was ice-cold water inside of her boots. "He's tiring now," said Iain.

"He's not the only one!"

"Look, his head's appeared on the surface. That means he's almost ready. Christ, what a brute! Must be over twenty pounds!"

"Get the net!" she screamed.

"What net?"

"Didn't you bring a net?"

"I didn't think you'd catch a fish."

"Didn't expect me to catch a fish!?"

"No."

"How do you expect us to bring him in?"

"You leave that to me." His voice was quick and alert. "Just keep him away from the weed-beds. Keep your rod up. If the dropper gets trapped in there we'll lose him."

The salmon's tail slapped loudly against the water surface. It tried to make a break for it when it saw Iain closing in. Nadia pivoted. The reel screamed once more. "What do I do?" she shouted.

"Try reeling in some line. Hold your rod up high and keep it pointed upstream."

For a moment time seemed to stand still as the exhausted fish, with its mouth above the surface, was guided slowly towards the bank. Then with a flourish Iain grabbed its tail and heaved it onto the shingles.

"My God!" he said. "What a monster! It's a cock fish. A fresh one too. See that, that's sea lice."

She wrapped her arms round his neck and kissed him.

He started removing the twin barbs of the Hairy Mary from its jaws. His joy gushed and overflowed. "Who would've thought . . . who would've bloody thought . . . a twenty pounder! You beauty, Nadia! You bloody beauty!"

Nadia stared at the streak of glistening silver with a sense of awe. "It's so beautiful."

"I don't suppose you have a priest handy."

"A what?"

"A priest, a mallet to knock it on its head." Iain went over to the broken rockery to find a stone.

"You're not going to kill it," she said.

"Of course I am."

"Can't we throw it back?" she asked.

"You want to throw it back?"

"Yes."

"Why?"

"I just want to."

Iain looked at her narrowly, as if she was under the influence of alcohol. "You're sure?"

"Yes," she persisted.

He gave the stubble on his chin a scratch. "Alright. But first," he said stooping to wipe his thumb across the salmon's crimson mouth, "I've got to blood you." He smeared her forehead with a streak of red. "There you go. Your first ever salmon!" He wiped his hands on the frozen ground.

Seconds later he held the fish gently in the shallow water and it shot off out of sight; a gurgling chorus of silvery spray, dorsal fin disappearing like smoke in the wind.

The scent of salt and distant wood fire lifted off the sea. They crossed a bridge and turned right, up a flagged street with men in dark shops working tirelessly, bending metal and wood with their tools. They saw jowly old grannies at their windows patching socks and looking at the world like watchful night-owls; a line of women waiting for a bus in their best going-to-town clothes; fishermen boxing lobsters in crushed ice, destined for the big city restaurants. They passed tight rows of lime-washed houses, stuck together like clots of marzipan, and a sweet shop that offered all sorts of rainbow-coloured enticements perched in its window. They spied gum drops and jaw breakers and violet creams, prompting Iain to rush in and return seconds later with a Caramel Bullet for Nadia. She sucked on it like a delighted schoolgirl as light snow began to mizzle their faces.

Soon after that they arrived at the cottage. As they entered though the back door, the pantry clock struck four. It was already getting dark. The glow of dusk lit the interior of the house with crooked, teetering orange light. They scrubbed their hands in the stone sink, removed their waders and damp clothing and left them near the boiler to dry. Jane, who was in the kitchen preparing the evening meal, a potato and kidney pudding, fetched some blankets for them and they changed into a set of fresh clothes. Warming their fingers by the fireplace in the living room, they watched the flames leap and dance.

"The children will be back from school in about twenty minutes, so enjoy the quiet while you can," said Jane. "Callum gets off work at six."

Both Nadia and Iain were full of laughter, whispering into each other's ear indulgently, flirtatiously. For the first time in about a month Nadia felt as though a tranquil gaiety had overcome her. She was light on her feet and all thoughts of seeing Dr. Goode were wedged far away to the back of her mind. Instead, her talk was all about her fish – how strong it was, how beautiful its markings were, how well it played. She wondered what must have gone through its head when these twin monsters dragged it out of the water and what it would now be saying to its friends. And she still could not stop from smiling at Iain who grinned back at her, boyishly, indulgently.

Sensing the celebratory mood in the air, Jane went to put the kettle on and broke open a packet of Nairn oatcakes. She returned with three cups of Brodie's tea and a plate of 'oatie wafers' on a tray, together with a jug of ewe's milk. As soon as they settled into their armchairs with the scratchy upholstery, tea in hand, they heard the radio broadcast.

'Chinese sources have confirmed that Generalissimo Chiang Kai-shek, the head of the Chinese Nationalist Army, was indeed *kidnapped in December by agents working for former Manchurian warlord, Zhang Xue-liang, only to be released ten days later, unharmed. Chiang Kai-shek's ruling Nationalists, the Kuomintang, have been engaged in a bitter civil war with the insurgent Chinese Communist Party for over a decade. Some Sino-experts have claimed that Zhang detained Chang Kai-shek in an effort to persuade him to abandon his fight with the Communists and present a united front against Japan. Japanese troops have occupied vast areas of Northern China since 1931 . . .'*

Iain sat up straight.

"What does it mean?" asked Nadia. Jane was standing at her elbow. Her hands were pale with flour from kneading and shaping the pudding pastry.

He did not reply. He exhaled loudly through his nose, thinking, his eyes steady in the dull twilight.

"I suspect Japan's about to show its hand," he eventually said. "They're going to make a push into China."

"I don't understand."

"Japan's threatening to invade China and the smaller Chinese factions are panicking. Chiang's kidnapping will either unite the Nationalists and Communists or pull them further apart. Whatever happens, it's only a matter of time before the Japanese start to infiltrate further into the mainland. Their expansionist policy is well-known to Whitehall. I think both China and Japan are preparing to go to war."

3

Leaning against the back seat of the taxicab, Nadia watched as the driver took her down the West End, skirting the Caledonian Hotel and the Princes Street Gardens.

This is it, she thought, the crossroads of my life. The doctor will tell me everything I need to know: whether I'm fertile, if my cervical fluid is normal, if my cervix is positioned correctly, if my eggs are healthy, if I have any eggs at all. She read somewhere that one in eight couples had trouble conceiving. She tried to imagine all the Christmases and birthdays to come without the laughter of children surrounding her. And she also thought about Mamuchka – imagined her sitting in the back patio in Macao, feeding the stray cats under the bauhinia tree, contemplating her happiness while her grandchildren ran about her feet. Nadia couldn't bear the thought of depriving her of such pleasure.

Iain held her by the hand as they walked around St. Andrew Square. The trees in the square were spiky and leafless, brittle with frost. There was a small quadrangle of hard brown lawn and a path that cut right through it.

"I'm nervous," she said.

"You'll be fine. You're my tough little girl."

"I may seem tough. I may put on a good act that I know what I'm doing – but I don't. I'm as frightened as anyone."

"I know you are. But there's nothing to be frightened of. Are you sure you don't want me to come with you?" he said.

A knot formed in her stomach. "Yes, I'm sure." He took her in his arms and they embraced. He held onto her so tight she had to prise his fingers away when they parted.

Her appointment with Dr. Goode was for three o'clock at his surgery on George Street. She was twenty minutes ahead of time. Better to be early than late, she said to herself.

Now, as she stepped into the elevator to take her up to the fifth floor, she felt alone and vulnerable. She missed her mother. It was at times like this that she needed Mamuchka by her side. With a diminutive gesture, the elevator-boy pulled the cage shut and the lift ascended.

She took a seat in the waiting-room. From her coat pocket she removed a letter that she had received the day before from Izabel. It started by talking about the ball that she and Senhor Pinto were hosting in support of their little orphanage on the Rua S. Lourenco. She said that invitations had already been sent out to members of the Clube Militar and the Jai Alai Association, to the stewards of the Trotting Club and to the editors of local media; she had even asked all the the doctors and nurses and social workers in the surrounding area.

The letter also mentioned that her young cousin, Anna, had arrived safely from Barreiro. She spoke of the Chinese New Year party that she threw and of all the people that attended – saying that Uncle Yugevny and her parents were in fine form, staying up past midnight, that Senhor Pinto got a little drunk and attempted press-ups on the living-room floor, only to be outdone by Costa who let off a stream of firecrackers in the kitchen which blew a hole in the wall. That although it was a good party, everybody said it wasn't the same with Nadia and Iain gone and that they were to hurry back as soon as possible.

The letter released a jumble of images – Papashka so frail, yet still so full of life; Uncle Yugevny singing Russian drinking songs at every opportunity, Mrs. Lo proudly boasting about her son Lennox, Costa being Costa and causing mayhem, Senhor Pinto still handing out embroidered handkerchiefs, and Mamuchka smiling sweetly through the ensuing chaos.

A female voice broke her concentration. "Mrs Sutherland, Dr. Goode will see you now," said the nurse with an enigmatic smile.

The clinic was brightly lit and smelled of camphor and iodine. The nurse rapped her knuckles against a door and waited for a response. When she heard a voice respond from within, she turned the door handle with a click and ushered Nadia inside. The doctor was a slight-shouldered man of about fifty with a Kitchener moustache. He wore wiry spectacles and had white hairs sprouting from his ears. A cloud of pipe smoke hung over him like a veil. He had pale slender hands and wore a humourless expression on his face as she entered his office, but as soon as he sensed her apprehension, his eyes softened.

"Please sit, Mrs. Sutherland."

Nadia sat down, rested her hands on her knees, gripping them. She saw that his desk was neat, devoid of paperclips, fountain pens and documents; a glass inkwell with twin receptacles, adorned the work surface. Its silver lids lay open. Nadia could smell the drying ink. Dry, she thought to herself, just like me.

Dr. Goode began by asking her how long they'd been trying for children. He wanted to know her age and medical history, whether she had any allergies to wheat. After that he questioned her about her diet, if she consumed coffee, white flour, fatty foods or alcohol, whether she smoked, whether Iain smoked. He wanted to know about her menstrual cycles and if she had ever miscarried, whether she suffered from cysts in the ovaries, symptoms which included unpunctual or absent periods. Nadia answered as clearly as she could, all the time noticing the different photographs that were scattered all over the room, surrounding Dr. Goode; images of children, infants, toddlers – all the little people that he had helped to bring into this world.

"Do you experience acute pain during your menstrual flow?" he asked.

"Yes, sometimes."

"Pain like a knife cut or as though you've eaten something bad."

"Like a knife."

"And do you feel severe fatigue or nausea during such times?"

"Yes, both."

His fingers closed round the bowl of his pipe. "And during your menstrual flow, does it hurt when you urinate?"

"Sometimes."

"Do you feel pain during intercourse?"

"Not often."

"But sometimes?"

She nodded.

"What about hot baths," he asked, changing his focus abruptly. "Does your husband take them often?" She said that he didn't, that he preferred to shower. "He suffers from prickly heat in the summertime, so he showers quite frequently to cool down."

She felt her face redden. Was it the intensity of his gaze that made her look away? She wasn't sure. Her eyes wandered across the room, moved to the numerous medical diplomas and certificates that hung like medals across the wall. He began to explain the ovulation cycle to her. "Timing is crucial," he added. "Get it wrong and it's almost impossible to conceive. If I may use a snooker analogy, it's like trying to pot a ball with all the pockets sealed off."

Nadia nodded.

"Well, my dear," he said, tapping out the bowl of his pipe and resting it upside down. "I think we'd best have a closer look at you. No time like the present."

He led her to an adjoining room and motioned her towards a raised examination table. "There's a dressing gown on the chair," he said. "Kindly remove your clothes. I'll be back in a few minutes."

"But I have never undressed for any man apart from my husband."

His Kitchener moustache twitched. "Mrs. Sutherland, I am a physician. You mustn't feel shy with me. If you like, I will ask the nurse to be in attendance."

Nadia hugged herself as though she were cold. "Yes, that would make me feel better."

He yanked the privacy curtain closed.

Nadia returned the following day, a Wednesday, to have a series of more complicated and often painful tests, including a blood and urine evaluation. Following this, they took swabs of her cervical mucus and measured her blood pressure at regular intervals.

She returned to her hotel bed exhausted, burying her face in the sheets, hugging her pillow tight as she slept, only to come back the next day and go through it all again.

On Friday morning Dr. Goode struck a match and lit his pipe. "There's very little I can find wrong with you, Mrs. Sutherland," said the doctor, gazing at his ash-tray.

Nadia wanted to smile with relief, but didn't dare tempt fate.

"However," he continued, with a stroke of his moustache. "That doesn't mean I'm giving your reproductive organs a clean bill of health."

"Oh," she said.

"Yes, there's a great deal medical science can tell us about fertility. There's also a great deal that remains hidden from us. And one of these things concerns your fallopian tubes – whether they are working properly or not, whether they are twisted, or infected or obstructed. Conception usually takes place when a female egg is ejected from the ovary and travels down the fallopian tube. Somewhere along the way our egg meets the male sperm who fertilizes her. After that the cells divide and reproduce, eventually multiplying to create a little baby. The fact that you encounter acute pain during menstruation, and discomfort during intercourse, the fact that I discovered mild traces of inflammation and evidence of scar tissue along your cul-de-sac, indicates that you may be suffering from Endometriosis."

Fear crept into Nadia's eyes. She swallowed hard, shielding her trembling mouth. "And what is that exactly? This endoterminus."

"Endometriosis. It's an immunological disease which causes the cells that line the insides of your uterus to form elsewhere resulting in inflammation and internal bleeding."

"I . . . I see."

"I'd say that your problem, and please, this is only an educated guess, is that these cells have made a home in your fallopian tubes."

"Which means?"

He made a steeple with his hands, frowned at his fingers. "Well, the prognosis isn't good. It implies that your fallopian tubes may be blocked. In a few years they may discover some sort of way to treat it, perhaps find a cure but until then . . ."

Nadia felt her heart thud in her chest. Her eyes lingered on the twin inkwells on the doctor's desk. The ink was completely dry now. She waited a few seconds before asking desperately, "What are my chances of having children?"

"I'm afraid," he paused in mid-sentence, "it means that you may never be able to conceive."

The colour drained from her lips. She tried to respond, her voice stiff in her throat. But his words had blotted out everything.

Empty tables and wooden stools snaked along the length of the pub. It was eleven in the morning and the place smelled of stale beer, nutty pipe smoke and the previous night's cigarettes. The publican, a portly man with a mermaid tattooed on his left forearm, was still setting out clean beer towels and ashtrays, lining up the freshly washed tumblers along his shelf; he had still to change out of his string vest. There were only two other people in the establishment, both men, both nursing halves of McEwan's ale. The other early-birds, it seemed, had yet to arrive.

Iain sat across from Nadia, holding both her hands. They had taken a table against a window looking out onto the street. When he looked, he saw that his wife's eyes were misty with shock.

Parts of her were trembling. First it was her hands, then the muscles on her neck throbbed and twitched. She reminded him of a deer he'd once seen that had just been struck by a car. The animal walked away but he could see that there was something very wrong, that something inside of it had been badly mangled. Something awful, too, he knew, was happening inside of Nadia. The woman he loved was breaking apart.

"I want to go home," she said.

"I'll go and hail a taxicab to take us back to the hotel."

"No, I mean Macao."

"We'll be back there soon." Iain squeezed her hand in his. He wondered whether he ought to tell her the news.

His mind went back an hour to a dark office in Jamaica Street. There were four men in the room: Fielding from HQ in Regent's Park, London, whom Iain had previously encountered in Hong Kong; Bowman from Internal Security; Patterson-Mutre from Records; and Ridley from Briefing and Debriefing.

"How long've you been married now?"

"Seven years."

"You do realize that by marrying a Russian you went against policy etiquette." It was Fielding talking. His lips were thick and red like a toilet plunger.

"Why on earth are you bringing this up now?"

"My dear boy, you haven't had a full debriefing in almost twelve years. You're not stationed across the road, you know. We're simply running you through policy etiquette."

Iain told them he couldn't give a monkey's about policy etiquette.

"Couldn't give a monkey's? My dear boy . . ."

"Don't give me that *my dear boy* rubbish, Fielding." Iain stared at them with the cold calculating eyes of a man who'd heard similar bigotry for the best part of a decade. "This has nothing to do with you." He spoke with the authority of a thirty-eight-year-old man with an unimpeachable record. "I fell in love and I got married. End of story."

"You're lucky the grey suits on the 9th floor hold you in such high esteem, Sutherland," said Patterson-Mutre, "otherwise, in my opinion, you'd've been on your bike by now."

"Frankly, I couldn't care a damn about your opinion. I gained Home Office consent to marry my wife, who now holds a British passport, and I received the full support of both C himself and Section VII. As far as I'm concerned that's all that matters. If you have a problem with that, then you should take it up with C or with your respective department heads and I'd appreciate it if you didn't bring up my private affairs again, all right?" He let the sentence hang in the air for a brief moment. "So, without further ado, let's move on to the next topic, shall we?" Thereafter, Iain had held his ground, knowing he was in control of the meeting. It took him only a further twenty-seven minutes to secure the posting he was looking for.

His attention returned to Nadia now.

"Did the doctor prescribe any medication, can it be treated?" he asked. "Will the condition improve with time?"

Cardiganed and vulnerable, she drew her arms over her chest, hugging herself. "No, there's no treatment. And he wasn't hopeful anything would ever change." She thought about the little bottle of pills in her bag and offered him an indignant smile. "He gave me some aspirin for the pain."

"But you said he based his diagnosis on a guess . . . he didn't say for sure."

A pause.

Iain could almost read what was going through Nadia's

mind – it was as though her femininity, her whole existence was suddenly in question. She was filled with anxiety and despair and a fear of the future; a feeling of helplessness threatened to overwhelm her.

"Remember what I told you," he said as gently as he could. "It doesn't matter to me."

"But it matters to me, Iain. It matters to me that you are with someone who can give you children. Do you have any idea how this makes me feel as a woman? How this makes me feel as a wife? I want a family. And so do you, I know you do."

"We can adopt."

"I don't want to adopt!" She snapped like a pair of well-oiled scissors. "I realize it's selfish of me, especially being involved in the orphanage . . . but I simply want to have my own child. A baby that has our blood, a combination of you and me."

He folded his arms over his chest.

"I don't think you understand how important this is to me," said Nadia.

"I do, believe me, I do."

Nadia twitched at the sleeves of her cardigan. She shook her head. "I just want this week to be over."

Iain nodded. "What about a drink? A brandy will help you," he said, forcing himself to smile. He glanced over his shoulder and caught the publican's eye.

The publican brought two brandies and retreated to the till with Iain's money on a plate.

"Go on, drink it," said Iain. "It'll do you good."

Nadia took a sip but didn't stop trembling. Through the window she saw a ragman go by pulling his cart. "How was your morning? What did they say to you at the office?"

"Oh," he sighed. "The usual nonsense questions – how predictable were the Chinese Nationalists, was the region safe from Communism, could Japan be contained in the north. Nothing I haven't heard before."

"Did they bring up something new? Is it anything that concerns us directly?"

"Actually, well yes, there was one thing."

"What?"

He hesitated. "Perhaps this isn't the best time to tell you."

"No, tell me. I want to know."

"Well, the thing is, I've requested a posting to Hong Kong. They've agreed and want us to be there in time for the coronation in May."

There was another pause.

"The fact is, with Japan getting increasingly hawkish, it's better that all South China operatives should return to Hong Kong."

Silence.

"Hong Kong," she eventually said.

"Yes."

"Why?"

"Because it's safer. It will be safer to be stationed in a Crown colony."

"When? When do we go?"

"As soon as we get back."

"What about Izabel?"

"What about her?

"She's hosting a ball. I have to be there."

Iain remembered that the newly opened Hotel Bela Vista had been secured for the evening of 8th May. "We'll leave the day after."

"The day after," she said, numbly, eyes locked on something on the floor, appearing to be far, far away.

"Maybe, it will do us some good, do you some good, to have a change of scenery. Maybe it will help you . . ." He wanted to say *help you get over this disappointment*, but left the words unsaid. Instead, he touched her hand. He looked at her, but she was no longer listening to him. She picked up the brandy glass and put it straight back down.

There was another silence. Iain could see by the struggle in her eyes that she wasn't thinking about herself; she was thinking of her parents and Uncle Yugevny.

Nadia ran her hand through her hair and sighed. She kept sighing, not looking at him. Instead, she kept her eyes on the brandy. Slowly, she began to pat the crinkles from her cardigan.

Iain stood up. He stepped round to her side of the table and held her in his arms. Her mouth crumbled a fraction.

"It's all right," he said. "We're going to be all right."

Nadia looked at Iain and knew that he was being genuine. But she wondered as the days, years pass without a child whether he would always be so sincere.

4

Through their porthole they caught a glimpse of land, a small cluster of islands, dark and green and thickly wooded. "*O console dos Ladroes*," Nadia said, "It's the name the Portuguese first gave Hong Kong – the island of thieves." They went up on deck. It was nearly twilight. Water glittered at the mouth of the Chai Wan headland. A quarter hour later they were in the harbour, passing buoys, tiny fishing junks, lateens, sampans, wallah-wallahs. Hugging each other with delight because they were almost home, Nadia and Iain watched the emerald hills of the colony unravel in the setting sun.

Having dropped anchor in a score of ports – Alexandria, Aden, Bombay, Galle, Rangoon and Singapore – they were now a six-hour steamer ride from Macao. Their journey had been an exhausting one; sharing the boat with a ribald group of twenty Dutch timber merchants had been particularly trying, as was having to share a bathroom with three other cabins. Their fellow passengers were loud and bawdy by day, and, fueled by gin and schnapps, even louder and more bawdy at night. Still, she'd managed to finish *A Passage to India* and two other Forster novels. But after thirty three days at sea, enduring lumpy beds, regimented mealtimes, clotted-cream teas and endless toads-in-the-hole, reception rooms decorated with musty peacock feathers, and a shipboard social life that resembled a knees-up in a hencoop, they were, finally, almost home.

They took the overnight steamer and despite the noisy engine, slept for three hours in their tiny cabins, in reed rockers. When they woke at dawn they found that they were only half a mile from land. The welcoming committee was assembled on the dock, full of laughter and exuberance. Even from a few hundred yards away she could make out her parents as well as Uncle Yugevny with his mad grey hair, Mrs. Lo, Costa and Senhor Pinto. There were even representatives from the Pinto-Perera orphanage to welcome her home. Only Izabel and her family were absent.

As soon as ropes were looped over the mooring poles, the passengers disembarked in a hurry. Nadia embraced Mamuchka first, then her father. Papashka, though a little wobbly on his walking stick, was buoyed with excitement and brimming with questions – what was it like going through the Suez Canal, he asked, was Bombay teeming with snake charmers and astrologers, did they swim in the Red Sea, did they take curry tiffin in the Taj Mahal Hotel, what was the tea like in Galle, were they allowed to visit the Shwedagon Pagoda in Rangoon? Was there much news in Europe about a possible war with Germany? Was there talk of Russia going to war? In fact, it seemed to Nadia that everyone was trying to talk at the same time. It made her think of a bunch of cuckoo clocks all cuckooing out of time with each other.

Wearily, Iain thanked everybody for coming and announced that they both needed some rest. However, they should all meet for supper. Uncle Yugevny removed his hat to fan his face and paid three coolies to carry the trunks up the hill.

"*Kak dela?*" Nadia asked, holding onto her mother.

"I am well, *spasiba.*"

"How's the house?" Nadia said, climbing into a rickshaw.

"*Prevaskawdnee.* In the three months you were gone I went every day, did a bit of dusting and cleaning, just to make sure everything would be nice on your return," said Mamuchka, waving her off as the rickshaw trundled away.

"Thank you, Mamuchka. I'll see you all tonight!" Nadia

called over her shoulder. "Thanks for coming to meet us! *Dasvidanya!*"

The rickshaw made its way along the Praya. It had just skirted the mouth of the bay when Iain told the puller to stop. He alighted and went into an alley that housed a ramshackle assortment of buildings. Nadia waited for him in the shade, under the spreading limbs of a Banyan tree. She knew where Iain had gone. He was paying his respects to Peter Lee's mother.

Nadia and Iain lived on Penha Hill, just behind the British Consulate building. It was approached through a pair of metal gates and past a company of stunted maples and overgrown bamboo.

When they got to the house, Nadia walked from room to room, taking everything in as if for the first time; she felt almost intoxicated at being back in her own home again. After changing into a kimono, she flopped headlong onto her bed and emitted a sigh of satisfaction. The house was an oasis when contrasted with the bustle of the ship and the noise of the dock; a warm welcoming place compared to the chill of Dr. Goode's clinic. This, she thought, was heaven. Closing her eyes she blew out a deep breath, felt her muscles relax. But something hot and unpleasant writhed within her chest. Their move to Hong Kong hovered before her like some indistinct ghost. She didn't want to think about leaving this all behind.

As Iain took a shower the telephone rang and Nadia picked it up.

"Welcome back!" said Izabel. "Sorry I wasn't there at the pier to meet you, but I had to take two of the little girls from the orphanage to church. I'm back now and Cristiano and Victor want to see you. Can we come over?"

"Of course you can!"

"We'll be there before you know it."

For the next few minutes Nadia leant against her pillows,

listening to the sounds of Iain singing in the shower. When he finished, she went and splashed some cold water on her face. Then she emptied her pockets of loose change and placed the coins and small notes in an envelope marked *White Russian Widows Charity*, before slipping into a summer dress. At length, she busied herself with her travelling trunk, unpacking her things, hanging her safari blouses in the wardrobe and putting away her shoes.

She was still tidying up her evening pumps and satin lounging mules when she heard voices in the driveway. She turned to see Izabel's boys, aged fourteen and fifteen, pressing their faces against the window. "Auntie Nadia!' they called. Tapping the glass with their fingers.

Nadia raced outside and embraced them. She took each one in her arms. "And look how you've both grown! The two of you must be at least an inch taller. How is this possible? I've only been away twelve weeks!" After a pause she asked, "But why aren't you at school today?"

"It's Sunday," replied the eldest, Cristiano.

"Of course, it is. Silly me."

Izabel, whose hairstyles had changed with the times, stepped forward to show off her new coiffure. "What do you think?" she inquired, batting her eyelids like a matinee idol.

"Very Bette Davis."

"You like it?"

"Yes, I think the cut suits you."

"Oh, I'm so pleased. I think it looks just doocky," said Izabel, clearly chuffed. "And this is Anna, my cousin from Barreiro. Do you remember I wrote you about her?"

Nadia saw a tall, olive skinned woman with stunningly dark eyes; a raven-haired Greta Garbo, what her mother would call an 'explosive Latina'.

"Anna Lopes," she said and extended a hand.

"She's a nurse," Izabel continued.

"Delighted to meet you," said Nadia.

"And you," Anna rejoined, smiling broadly.

"Come inside, please," Nadia said, suddenly conscious of her messy hair and unmade face.

"Have you seen the invitations to the ball yet?" asked Izabel. Nadia said that she hadn't. Izabel handed her an elegant looking card printed in relief on thick, rich paper.

"They're beautiful," said Nadia. "Make yourselves comfortable and I'll go make some tea."

As they entered the house, Iain strolled out of the bedroom in a pair of linen trousers but no shirt.

"Izabel! How lovely to see you!" he cried in Portuguese, smoothing Vitalis into his hair. "*Como está?*"

"I'm well," she said. He gave her a peck on the cheek.

"Did you have a good trip?"

"Yes, thanks."

"Let me introduce you to my cousin, Anna." Nadia watched as Anna – tall, olive-skinned, stunning Anna – stepped forward. She saw them shake hands. Iain was looking at her admiringly. She also thought she saw something glint in his eyes. And if she knew one thing about her husband, it was that his eyes never lied.

Feeling an unexpected tinge of jealousy, Nadia excused herself and hurried off to the kitchen to put the kettle on.

She returned a minute later with an armful of gifts.

"For you," she said to Izabel. "I have some Irish-linen tea-towels. For you, Cristiano, a bull-whip from Bombay. It's made from genuine leather. Be careful not to take your brother's eye out. And for you, Victor, a spinning rod from Scotland. There's a box of lures for you too. You'll be able to fish off Barra Point. Do you know I caught a twenty pound salmon?"

"Really?" the boys said in unison.

"Yes. Uncle Iain was there. You can ask him. It took me ages to bring the salmon in."

"You should have seen her face when we landed it," said Iain.

"I thought my arm was going to fall off." She stole a look at her husband who had slipped on a shirt. Beside him, Anna was looking at his hands as he buttoned his sleeves. She was smiling at him.

He smiled back.

A sudden chill prickled the hairs on the back of Nadia's neck. Her mouth grew parched, as if she'd consumed a packet of intolerably dry biscuits. She had never felt this way before.

"*Bawzhemoy!*" she exclaimed. "The kettle must have boiled by now. I'll go and fetch the tea."

Dinner that night was held in a little open air *restaurante* which was known for its steamed garlic clams and cosy atmosphere. Everyone attended except for Papashka who was resting at home. On the sprawling red-and-white checked tablecloth there were jugs of sangria blanco, baskets of freshly baked walnut bread, a platter of Brazilian broad beans with roast pork, curried crab sprinkled with coriander, a fat ceramic tureen of lacassa (shrimp and noodle soup), piquant fried rice with salted cod, and, of course, the house specialty, finger-licking garlic clams steamed in white wine and lemon juice, served with toasted *broa*.

Nadia could see herself in the mirror that hung over the far wall. She thought she looked pale and splotchy; the red lipstick she'd applied earlier resembled a wound. She rubbed her cheek with the back of her wrist, brushing the smooth scar-tissue that ran along the flesh of her arm against her chin.

"You must be tired from your trip, Nadrichka," said Mamuchka who was seated beside her.

"A little."

"You haven't told me what the doctor in Scotland said."

For a moment Nadia felt scared of the words that might escape from her mouth. She had deliberately avoided broaching the subject. She had also failed to tell her mother about the move to Hong Kong.

"We'll talk about it later," she replied, placing her fork on her plate of untouched pork.

She glanced across to Iain who was seated with Mrs. Lo to his left and Anna on his right. He was telling jokes, recounting a story about a rope dancer they'd seen in Bombay. Over the years his Portuguese had improved dramatically. He'd gotten used to the ooshing and shooshing of the language. Nobody made fun of his accent anymore, Nadia observed, least of all Anna. Nadia's mouth turned dry again and the skin prickled across the back of her neck.

Her eyes fell on Anna. The girl was laughing at something Iain had said, covering her mouth coyly. Was it her beauty, her youth, her wantonness that threatened her so? She couldn't quite decide. Was it her ears, her lips, her breasts, her hair? Maybe it was her flat, olive-chocolate stomach? Or was it those dark eyes boring into her husband? Whatever it was, Nadia took exception to her. Here was a woman with her hand on Iain's arm, for God's sake!

"Iain," she said attempting to assert herself. "You should tell Uncle Yugevny about the fish. How I caught my salmon."

"Not now, darling," he replied, stifling her.

Hot-cheeked, Nadia felt a pain in her hand. She looked down to find her own nails had dug into the flesh leaving four red dimples on the mounts of her palm. She had her eyebrows raised. She was angry. She could almost touch the electricity in the air.

Nadia glared at Anna, offering her a thin smile of dislike. Anna in response moved her hands over her chest furtively, as hushed and sly as lust. Were those her nipples poking like strawberries through her thin cotton dress, she asked herself. What a blatant hussy! Why couldn't she have been pimply and buck-toothed and shaped like a duck?

Across the table, she saw Iain take a pen and scribble something on the paper menu. Anna laughed, threw her head back. For a moment Nadia had an unpleasant feeling that the note was about her. No, that's not possible, she thought, Iain wouldn't do that. He wouldn't be making fun of her, would he? Unsettled and feeling slightly wounded, she began to pinken, as pink as a guinea pig's nose, yet she kept staring at them.

Nadia was determined to find out what he had written, but just then Anna glanced her way and both women looked at each other for an instant. Nadia wanted to scratch the smugness from her eyes.

"What did Iain just write?"

"What?" said Mamuchka.

"On that piece of paper, what did he write?"

"What paper?" Her mother sounded baffled.

"The paper Anna's just hidden under the table. The bloody cow." Iain looked over towards her. It was the wrong thing to say and she knew it.

"Cow? What cow? What are you talking about Nadrichka?"

"Nothing. It doesn't matter."

A chill crept over Nadia and she felt goosebumps on her skin. She turned away, and focused her attention on the window that overlooked Rua das Lorchas. Her gaze fell onto the giant cinema poster across the street, a billboard promoting 'Anna Karenina', Greta Garbo's new film. Greta Garbo! Wouldn't you know it, she said to herself. Wouldn't you just bloody know it!

'The hell with it!' she decided. She grabbed her glass of sangria and downed the contents in three eye-watering gulps.

Noticing her sudden passion for alcohol, Costa drained his own glass and, wiping his mouth, ordered more wine. Soon a cry of 'Slainte Mhath!' rang around the table, followed by its Portuguese equivalent, 'Tchim-tchim!' and Russian 'Na zdorovje!'

The wine arrived in a chilled flask-shaped bottle. Costa topped her up and as she knocked it back, he hooted loudly; his laughter as deep and chasmic as a giant's cleavage. Just

245

this once, she decided, she was going to get thoroughly and extravagantly drunk.

After her fifth glass, Nadia tapped the empty bottle with a spoon to get everyone's attention. "I have something important to say," she said, climbing off her seat.

Her mother looked at her expectantly – could this be the baby announcement she had long wished for, she wondered? Mamuchka clasped her hands together and pressed them to her lips. But any hopes that the Shashkov home would soon ring with the pitter-patter of tiny feet were quickly drowned.

"I'm sorry if this comes across as a bit formal, but I wish to say a few words. This may come as a shock to many of you, but Iain has been offered a new posting." Nadia's mouth contorted, struggling to maintain her composure. "It is a great opportunity for us and although I will be very sad to leave you all, and to leave Macao my home, Iain and I hope to have your blessings. We will be moving to Hong Kong next month in preparation for the King's coronation." She settled back in her chair, regretting her actions almost immediately. Embarrassed and furious with herself, she wondered why she'd been so blunt, so cold – was it to get at Anna, had it been an attempt to claim her rights to Iain? Something trembled in her throat. The gathering had grown silent. Nadia's eyes made a nervous pass across the table then turned to stare at the floor. She didn't want to look at the expression on Mamuchka's face.

Nadia sat in the sunny corner of the little patio behind the Tabacaria holding her father's frail hand. His walking stick was leaning against the bauhinia tree, beside the swaying laundry drying on the line.

She tapped the toe of her left shoe against one of the thick gnarled roots that split through the pavestones.

"Papashka," she began. "I have some news. News which I don't think you're going to like. You know how I told you

246

about Iain's job, how one day he may be asked to move to another country. Well," she paused. "He's being posted to Hong Kong." She felt his fingers tighten around her hand.

He remained quiet for a while. Lifting his face to hers, he asked, "Your mother told me last night after your dinner. But what about your house on Penha Hill?"

"We'll sell up, I suppose." She shrugged.

"How soon will you be going?"

She gazed into his washed-out expression, at his pale, unsunned skin. "In less than a month's time."

The old man was blinking quickly.

"Papashka, it pains me to leave you."

"Nadia," he was looking hard at her face, drinking her in. "We've had nine wonderful years in Macao together – something I never thought would be possible, considering what happened to me in Russia. I may have another nine years or another nine months left, but this is not for me to determine. This is for our good Lord to decide. What I will tell you, however, is to be by your husband's side when he needs you. He is a good man, Nadia."

"I know he is."

Ilya gave his daughter an involuntary look of pride. "And you have grown into a fine woman."

"I will miss you, Papashka. Please forgive me for having to go away."

Shushing her, he stifled her apologies with a smile, softly smoothing away the lines on her forehead with his knuckles. "But, what are we getting all teary eyed about. Hong Kong is not on the other side of the world. It's only forty miles away. We can still spend our Christmases together," he assured her. "Maybe even meet up for our birthdays. I'll be seventy-two this year. We can have a big celebration. You'll come and visit me, won't you?"

"Of course I will, Papashka." She pressed her smooth glass charm, the one he'd given to her as a child into his good hand. "In the meantime, I want you to have this."

Ilya Shashkov touched it to his lips with tenderness. There were tears welling in his eyes. *"Chto eta?* Goodness gracious, I recognize this. You were only five when I gave this to you. I recall finding it in the stream. Look, it's still shaped like a crown. You've kept this all this time?"

Nadia nodded and closed her eyes. Remembering. Eyes still closed, she said, "I bought some Rangoon mangoes for Uncle Yugevny this morning. Let me go peel one for you. *Ya sichas virnus."* She made to get up from the chair.

"Wait," he said. He raised his bad arm and banged it against his side, laughing. "Still as useless as a fire hose in the desert. I was trying to give you a hug."

"Here let me help you." Nadia draped his clumsy arm over her shoulder and held her father with the sun streaking through the bauhinia leaves. A shadow fell over one side of his face. And for the briefest of moments she thought that he resembled Lionel Barrymore again, just as he had done all those years before.

5

The following Saturday, to take advantage of the beautiful spring climate, Izabel invited everyone to a picnic in Co-loane. Unfolding two deck-chairs, Nadia gestured to Pa-pashka to sit down while Iain unloaded the car, carrying in his arms a wicker basket and numerous rugs. The wicker basket was bulging with chorizo sandwiches, potted shrimp, cheese, boiled eggs, melons, apples, fava nuts and pumpkin seeds. There was also cold beer, and lemonade for the boys who were already making sandcastles and collecting shells.

They found a sheltered spot by the beach, on a stretch of grass shaded by a tree. Opposite them, across the strip of dirt road, a hawker stall was setting up, selling fried noodles and peanut dumplings. The vendor was busy erecting his canopy and heating his coals. Next to him, his wife polished her tin utensils using the leaves from a nearby sand paper vine. Soon the pungent, zesty fragrance of cooking wafted across the road, making hungry lips smack and tummy's grumble.

Izabel's husband, Carlos, reclined against the tree and started to strum the Portuguese guitar. As he played, Anna twirled her hair in the breeze and eased into song. Her voice was pure and affecting. It bloomed like a saffron sunrise. Afterwards Izabel cut up some melon with a knife and passed it around.

"What were you singing?" Iain asked.

"A song called *Bella Aurora*." She lowered her long lashes.

"It was beautiful," he said, looking a little red from the sun. "When I start singing all the birds and animals in Macao flee for the hills."

Nadia reached over with his hat. "Darling, put this on, otherwise you'll burn."

"I'm fine," he said, sounding annoyed at being henpecked.

Nadia moved away and found Cristiano and Victor kicking a football in the sand. As she watched them bounce the ball along the beach, she pinned her hair up. Then she let it down. A minute later, she pinned it back up again. Vexed by the tone in Iain's voice, she crossed her arms and glared out to sea.

After a while she was joined by Mamuchka.

"Did I tell you that we received a letter from America? The Riedles wrote to say they have moved from Fresno, California. He's still working as a physician. He managed to get his son and daughter-in-law out of Vladivostok. They're all living as a family now in Seattle, Washington."

"That's nice."

Mamuchka breathed in the air as if it was wholesome and nourishing, puffing out her chest as she inhaled.

"We also received a letter from our Chelyabinsk cousins. Boris, their son with the mental illness, has been taken from them and locked away in an institution. Apparently one of the local cadres didn't like the way he looked at him. It seems that life in Russia is worse than ever. The political repression and persecution is continuing unabated. I don't know what the bread situation is like there, but I put together a food package – some tins of corn beef and soup, that sort of thing – and sent it to them along with some money. *Choodeasne!* I just don't know what more I can do."

Nadia shrugged. "You've done all you can for them, Mamuchka."

They watched as Victor kicked the ball. It skewed off his foot and landed in the water. Cristiano scrambled after it.

Nadia said, "I want to do an Easter fundraiser at the Tabacaria, donating one day's proceeds from the shop to Izabel's orphanage. Do you think Uncle Yugevny will agree to that?"

"I should think so."

"Good. I will talk to him about it tomorrow." Nadia bent down and dug her fingers into on of the crab holes in the sand.

"Papashka looks well, don't you think?" her mother said.

"Yes, very."

"I think the warm weather does wonders for him. His arthritis is much better. He's not so stiff in the legs. Sometimes he doesn't even need his stick. It's the herbalist that's cured him, you know, the man on Rua da Palha?"

"I remember," said Nadia. "The same herbalist we visited last year," – and a fat lot of bloody good he did me, she thought with a tinge of resentment. The shock of Dr. Goode's prognosis had weighed on her for weeks. At first she had just wanted to hide somewhere and cry, to wrap herself in bed for hours. But her feelings soon turned to denial which lasted another week. She was currently entering the anger and despair phase of her seven stages of grief. Now, she was looking for someone to blame.

Mamuchka continued. "That medicinal tonic that he drinks every day has worked miracles."

"What's in it?"

"White peony root, sea bark, papaya, and *Bawg* knows what else. I've also been giving him hawthorn root which helps increase blood circulation, as well as some other catnip and huckleberry concoction for his eyes. Have you noticed that his cataracts have cleared a little?"

"I have, it's quite something. You've really grown to believe in herbal medicine, haven't you?"

"*Vsykomu ovoshchu svoyo vreemya* - every vegetable needs time to ripen" Mamuchka gave a little cough before saying, "He needs you, you know."

"Who?"

"I'm talking about Papashka. He's sure to start to deteriorate once you go away." She sighed. "And I really don't know what will become of the shop . . . or me for that matter.

I spend so much of my time looking after your father. I think I've lost my identity. All I hear in my brain now is 'fetch this, fetch that, bring this, bring that.' "

They watched the surf roll in, felt it flow smoothly around their ankles.

Neither said anything for several minutes. At last Mamuchka spoke. "Nadrichka," she said. You're life is so settled here. Iain's contented, you're contented. Must you go away?"

Nadia had been expecting this. She knew that her mother didn't want her to leave. "I have to go where Iain goes."

"I hear it's not easy being a Russian in Hong Kong."

"I've been a Macao citizen for years. And having married Iain I hold a British passport now."

"That's not the point. The English think we are beneath them."

"The English think everybody's beneath them."

"I read that there are kidnappings there, and cholera, and, and, disease-spreading mosquitoes."

Nadia shook her head. "Mamuchka, you know none of that is true."

"But why must you go?"

"Because I am married to Iain and it will make him happy."

"What about you? Will it make you happy?"

"I'm all right, Mamuchka." After a pause she added, "Besides, the aspirin takes the pain away."

After lunch and a short siesta, everybody, apart from Papashka and Uncle Yugevny, decided to go for a walk along the beach. The two old men, festooned in straw hats, continued to doze in their deck-chairs, smiling under hooded eyes.

Anna and Nadia wandered across the shingles. Stooping to wash her hands in the sea, Anna looked across and asked whether Nadia was going in for a swim.

"Maybe in a minute," Nadia replied. "I thought I'd try and work off that huge lunch." They carried on walking. Nadia could sense that they were both trying to be civil to one another, but it was awkward. After a brief silence Nadia said, "So you're a nurse?"

"Yes."

"Do you enjoy it?"

"What, my job?" she sounded defensive.

"Yes, do you enjoy being a nurse?"

"It's all right."

"I'm surprised you haven't been snapped up by a doctor."

Nadia refrained from asking ask her why she had come to Macao. Whether it was it to escape from something – a shattered relationship, a broken heart? Had she been spurned by a man in Portugal? Was she a homewrecker, forced out of her town? She wanted desperately to ask her all of these questions, but she held her tongue.

"I'm not interested in doctors," Anna said, looking away, scowling, lost in thought. "Or in getting married for that matter," she added. "I am happy the way I am, happy in my own skin." They were at the end of the beach now. Apart from the hawker stand and a skinny stray dog, the place was deserted.

"Well, maybe you'll meet someone nice at the ball." They exchanged economical smiles.

Turning, they retraced their steps. The sound of the gently breaking waves played in their ears. "I like your bathing costume," said Anna, sweet as a lump of liquorice.

"I'm glad you approve," Nadia replied. It was a 'Ladies Uplifter', moulded to the body with shoulder straps that could be lowered for sun-tanning. She'd purchased it at Whiteley's in London.

"Considering the style is for a much younger woman, you carry it off rather well."

Nadia stopped cold in her tracks. Her mouth opened in protest, but Anna had already turned away, mumbling something unintelligible as she galloped off towards Victor and Cristiano.

For a short while Nadia didn't know how to react. Did she mean to mock her? Was she being deliberately rude? Or was it merely a joke made in poor taste? Nadia shook her head in silence. Then a wave of hot temper enveloped her. "*Bawzhemoy!*" she hissed. "The bloody cheek!" She felt a cluster of hard fibrous knots form across her shoulders. Looking at Anna now, gallivanting in the sand with her young cousins, her face darkened. She wanted to thump her in the stomach with a pair of heavy steel-capped boots. "The bloody cheek!" She kicked the air with her right foot and marched out until she was knee-deep, then in one angry swoop, dived into the sea holding her nose.

She swam for twenty minutes without stopping. She swam until her arms ached and her heart shook in her chest, pushing her muscles to the limit, so as to drive away the angst.

The heavens clouded over. The noonday sun had given way in typical tropical fashion to a grey overcast afternoon. Thunderheads collected on the horizon making odd black patterns. Indifferent to the changing weather, Nadia swam on her back, listening to the ocean surge and rush below her, feeling the tide tugging at her arms and legs. She remained in the water, marinating in her own juices for almost an hour, trying to restore her own equilibrium.

Meanwhile, she watched Iain strolling along the sand, collecting shells; close behind him walked Anna, doing the same, following him like some beautiful, purple-bottomed monkey. Only minutes earlier, she'd witnessed her husband cradling Anna in the sea, his hands on her flat torso, across her abdomen, teaching her to swim. Her long legs had kicked and struggled like a baby gazelle's.

The sky made a grumbling noise. A few moments later it began to lash down and Nadia climbed out of the sea. Carlos continued to play football with his sons, whilst Uncle

Yugevny and her father huddled together under the tree, using their straw hats to keep out the rain. Across the way, she noticed Anna, Izabel and Iain squeezed together under the hawker's awning, eyes glistening.

Nadia took a breath and counted to ten.

Iain had his arms round both women as the water poured down the sides of the canopy. Both women were giggling out loud and shivering slightly. When Nadia looked at Anna, she thought she saw her wink at her. The veins ticked along her neck. Something across her shoulders knotted again.

Nadia exhaled. Thank God, she said to herself quietly, cupping her hands over her eyes to keep out the rain: thank God we're moving to Hong Kong.

Later, in bed, Nadia applied chamomile water and cucumber strips to Iain's sunburned forehead. "I told you to put on a hat," she said.

Iain closed his eyes and grunted. He was flat on his back, dressed in his underwear.

"It may blister up if you're not careful."

He slowly sat up, catching the cucumber fillets that slid off his face. "It's not that bad."

"You were showing off today, weren't you?" As she spoke, the pain tightened across her stomach. Her period had come early. It had started that evening; another month of fruitless hope gone by. "Prancing around like a teenager, racing up and down the beach."

"When?"

"I was watching you as you played football with the boys. You had your stomach sucked in all the time."

He shrugged, made a noise with his throat.

"You're thirty-nine years old, Iain. It's all right to act your age sometimes. You've nothing to prove."

"I'm not quite sure where this conversation is going," he said.

"She's pretty, isn't she?" Nadia said after a while.

"Who?"

"Anna."

"To be honest, I hadn't noticed."

"Hadn't noticed?" Nadia drew forward, examining his face. "Now I know you're lying."

"I'm not lying."

"In your line of work you're paid to lie and keep secrets."

Iain shook his head with irritation. "But I'm not at work now, am I. I'm at home trying to enjoy my weekend."

"You lied to me about Lazar all those years ago. How do I know you're not doing the same here?"

"Well, I'm not!"

Nadia looked over to her dresser for her pills. She hated this; hated feeling so vulnerable and insecure. "How can Anna have lived in Portugal all her life and not learned how to swim?"

"Maybe she's not from the coast."

"Barreiro's hardly up in the mountains, is it?"

"How should I know?"

Nadia experienced the cramps again. Her monthlies usually made her feel nauseous and tired, but now she felt as though she was being stabbed from within. "I'm surprised you haven't asked her. You seem very interested in what she does, writing little notes and . . ."

"Writing little notes? What are you on about?"

"You scribbled something on the dinner menu last week."

He shook his head. "What menu?"

"You like her, don't you?"

"Oh, for God's sake!"

Nadia got up and flipped open a jar of pills and swallowed an aspirin, washing it down with a glass of water. Her heart was pounding in her throat. The blood felt thick and fevered behind her eyes. She went over and pulled the shutters closed.

Locking his hands behind his head, Iain stared at the wall

for a few seconds. Then he switched off the light and turned on his side to sleep with his back to her. Usually, he liked to snuggle up beside her, his knees tucked in behind her buttocks. But tonight he slept facing the other way.

Neither of them said goodnight.

After a long silence, Nadia lay down and checked the towel-pad between her legs; she was beginning to ooze. Her breasts were tender, her insides continued to burn. She smoothed a dollop of wild yam ointment to her tummy and tried to rub the pain away. Surrendering to the darkness, she listened to the wind; the shutters rattled and sighed. The rain was still coming down. A minute later she felt an overriding urge to start cleaning things; she decided to go and scrub the kitchen floor.

6

The day of the ball arrived. The hardwood floors of the Bela Vista Hotel shone with polish and its crystal chandeliers shimmered with rich aqueous luxury. There were a dozen tables draped in linen and lace and set with Sheffield silverware and Baccarat glass. Surrounding each table were eight rosewood chairs, each with its own bright yellow damask cushion.

Nadia arrived early, dressed in a black silk evening gown with fitted waist and sleeves. Earlier, she had volunteered to oversee the seating plan, the flower arrangements, the party favours and the silent auction. She removed her new and rather uncomfortable shoes and set to work. First, she positioned a centerpiece of orchids on each table. Next she spread an assortment of paper masks and foil-wrapped chocolates amongst the tableware. And afterwards, having ensured that cigars from the Tabacaria were made available to guests, she set out the place cards according to the seating plan.

She put herself between a local hotelier and a man called Rodrigues, who was editor of one of the local newspapers. She sat Iain next to Izabel and the Governor's wife, Senhora de Sousa Barbossa on Table 1. And she sat Anna as far away from Iain as the ballroom allowed, on Table 12.

With this done, Nadia examined her face in one of the tall gilt mirrors and smoothed the front of her dress with her hands. She looked at her watch. It was time to lay out the auction catalogues, which she placed on every chair. She ran her eyes over the first six lots. There was a small watercolour by the artist George Chinnery, donated by the Governor; two tickets to see La Traviata at the Dom Pedro V Theatre; a pair of jade-and-onyx cufflinks; a hand-crafted 3-ft long replica of a Chinese Imperial junk made from Philippine mahogany; a complimentary dinner for four at Foo Lum Noodle Cafe; and – this one made Nadia smile – a set of Scottish dance lessons to be taught by Iain Sutherland Esq.

Nadia placed a phonograph record, a 10-inch seventy-eight by Jimmy Mackay, on top of Iain's bid sheet then went across the room to collect her shoes.

At six o'clock people started to filter in. They took their drinks from silver trays and stood on the breezy verandah overlooking the Praya, lit by the naked flames of garden torches. Women in stylish gowns brushed past each other; they emerged in and out of doorways exchanging hand-shakes and kisses, introductions quickly forgotten as they flitted from group to group like butterflies. Silk brushed against challis, batiste against tulle, flesh caressed flesh. Soon corks were pulled from bottles, wine swished and flowed and the bar was in full swing. At 6.45 the Jazz band started up.

The waiters ferried in a selection of canapés: oysters wrapped in bacon, fried baby squid, devilled quails eggs, miniature sausage rolls. And the room continued to swell with new arrivals.

Senhor Pinto spotted Nadia and thrust his short little arms high into the air. He pushed his way through a mesh of elbows and kissed her on the cheek. "How are you, my lovely?" he asked, needing to shout to be heard above the din.

"I am well, thank you."

"*Fantastico*," he said, clasping his hands together. "This is quite a turnout, eh?" He shot her a Stan Laurel smile, scratching the top of his head.

From the verandah whoops of laughter shot through the air, spilling over like a river bursting its banks.

"Perhaps we should go outside," said Pinto. "To get some fresh air and join the fun."

They squeezed outdoors. Nadia found Iain deep in conversation with a burly man known in Macao society as 'Grande Daddy' – they were talking about football and the upcoming World Cup to be held in France. Nadia excused herself to see how the silent auction was progressing. She trailed her eyes along the console tables. So far an offer of 200 patacas had been made for the Chinnery watercolour and there were a total of nine bids for the jade-and-onyx cufflinks. She had just turned to make her way back outside when she noticed a name scribbled on Iain's bid sheet. 'Goodness," she thought with a smile, "somebody's actually put in a bid for Scottish dance lessons."

She inclined her head to read the name and amount.

Anna Lopes - 15 patacas

She felt her shoulders knot beneath her gown. Hastily, she grabbed the pen and marked her name down for 18 patacas.

Moments later, she went in search of Iain and found him and Costa deep in conversation with the Consul General of Japan.

"I can assure you that Nippon hassa no indenshun to be aggor-essors towards China," said the Consul General.

"How can you say that?" Iain countered. "I have on good authority that the Japanese army has been conducting battle drills in Fengtai, near Peking. You're preparing for war, don't deny it."

"Are you trying to porovoke me?!" the diplomat cried angrily.

"No more than you're trying to provoke China?"

Nadia looked at Costa. "How are you?" she asked. "Busy at work?"

"*Deus!* I have never been so busy! With heem transferring to Hong Kong, Vermelho hash handed everything over to me. I have paperwork coming up to my eyeballsh!"

The gong was struck and people took their seats for

dinner. The appetizers were served within minutes. Rodrigues, the newspaper man to Nadia's right, tucked into his baked prawns and citrus fennel salad.

At 8.00pm Senhor Pinto spoke on behalf of the orphanage's board of governors, thanking everyone for their support and generosity. He urged the guests to enjoy themselves and called on them to reach deep into their pockets for the children.

When he sat down, Nadia heard a set of blunt footsteps echo across the dancefloor. She glanced round to see Anna, dressed in Katharine Hepburn inspired slacks and a crisp white blouse, making her way towards the console tables, heading for Iain's bid sheet.

After a few moments, Nadia excused herself from Senhor Rodrigues' conversation and rushed over to increase her bid to 26 patacas.

"Are you all right, senhora," asked Rodrigues when she returned to her seat, "you are looking a little flushed."

"I'm fine," she snapped.

"I see that the Japanese Consul General has just left the party early. Is that what has upset you?"

"Bawzhemoy!" Nadia shook her head. She looked across to Iain on Table 1. There was a self-congratulatory smile on his face.

Ten minutes later she heard Anna's brash, blunt stride sound across the dance floor once more.

Instinctively, Nadia picked up her dessert fork and started running the sharp tines along the back of her thumb.

"Mmmgoy," a voice announced behind her. *"Perdoe-me."* Nadia pulled her hand away. *"Galinha a Africana,"* the waiter said, placing a dish of grilled spiced chicken with buttered carrots in front of her.

Nadia took a sip of wine and played with her food, eating just the vegetables.

When the main courses were cleared away Nadia excused herself again. Despite her new and uncomfortable shoes, she glided across the stage with her head held high. This time her bid was for 34 patacas.

Iain shot her a funny look as she passed his table. He got up and approached her.

"Nadia, I can see quite clearly what is going on," he said. "You're playing a childish, and might I add costly, little game with Anna."

"I don't think it's childish."

"What are you trying to prove?"

"I'm not trying to prove anything. I want to learn the Highland fling."

"I can teach you at home."

"I don't know what sort of fees you charge. At least here I know the money is going to a good cause."

"Dear God, woman. You're my wife. Do you actually think I'd ask you to pay me for a few silly dance lessons?"

"Well, you are Scottish."

She arrived back at her table with a smile on her face.

The little charade continued for almost two hours, until Nadia was called away by Izabel to help present Senhora de Sousa Barbossa with a bouquet of flowers – a scrumptious collection of tiger lilies, sweet peas, honeysuckles and long-stemmed roses. The Governor had just announced a donation of 2500 patacas to the orphanage in the name of the de Soussa Barbossa Foundation, resulting in a spontaneous outbreak of applause.

When Nadia returned to the console tables, the silent auction had closed. The winning bidder for Iain's coveted dance lessons was listed as:

Anna Lopes - 100 patacas

She could have screamed out then and there.

7

A swarf of confetti fell from the sky, showering Hong Kong's colonnaded Victorian buildings and boulevarded streets. Lines and lines of soldiers were standing guard along Des Voeux Road and all around them the pennants and bunting and banners swayed: shimmering granite balustrades were draped with coloured lights, ionic columns and colonial turrets were garlanded with red and gold ribbons, and huge bamboo standards were slung with flowers and paper lanterns. It was a hot Wednesday in May, the day of the King's coronation.

A brass band in the uniform of the Middlesex Regiment played 'It's a Long Way to Tipperary'. There were flags and streamers and hundreds of people waving Union Jacks.

Amongst the clamour of firecrackers and car horns and the din of the crowd, Nadia and Iain stood on chairs at the back of the throng, waving at anyone and anything. Everywhere they looked, there was something to see. Dragon boats in the harbour let off Catherine wheels. Children banged on tin drums. People sang and laughed. Nadia heard the ding-dong bell of the trams as they passed, emblazoned with 'God Save the King' across their bonnets. By the clock Tower, acrobats travelled in troupes, tumbling and bouncing onto their hands. And by the pier, the silver dragon of the Fisherman's Guild came to life when the governor's wife, Lady Caldecott, dotted its eyes with black ink. Iain told Nadia that it was customary that a person of eminence should start the proceedings off by giving the beast its sight.

The dragon had an enormous head, the size of a wardrobe.

And the lead dancers, dressed in silk leggings, had to keep it elevated with crosspieces, like tent poles. Its body must have been eighty feet long, thought Nadia, and decorated throughout with silver braids, exotic yellows and royal-blue brocade. It made Nadia think of the lion-dance she and Izabel had gone to see ten years before. She craned her neck as the troupe wound their way through all the little alleys – there were thousands of people following it, crashing cymbals and banging gongs.

When the dragon disappeared from view altogether, Nadia looked up at the galleries of the Court House building; she saw ladies carried parasols in one hand and fans in the other, while the men wore topees or had their heads bound in white handkerchiefs. Piebald, rheumy-eyed, they sipped gunpowder tea on their Victorian verandahs, passing round silver trays of dainty, hand-cut sandwiches.

Soon afterwards, the Governor, His Excellency Andrew Caldecott, stood on a platform near the mouth of the pier, surrounded by military and naval personnel in full dress uniform. He was costumed entirely in cream linen with an ostrich-plumed hat. He was greeting everyone and welcoming them to the historic occasion when someone shouted out, 'What about the Japanese threat?' Nadia felt the mood change a little after that. She knew very well that Hong Kong was the headquarters of Britain's China Station Fleet. And even though the escalating tension between Japan and China was bringing prosperity to the colony, diverting shipping from Shanghai, and almost doubling the population in a matter of months as both poor and rich Chinese arrived from the mainland, everyone felt the tension.

Later, at a cocktail reception held at the military barracks, Nadia was introduced to several officers' wives, all of whom regarded her with tepid disinterest. Some were so cold to her that she could have sworn that frost had beaded their mouths. Others stared her down with pitying looks. She was presented to a Lady Hoarde.

"This your first posting, is it?" said Lady Hoarde, a large boned woman, of indefinable age, who looked like a pug in a floral dress. "Fresh off the banana boat, are you? Expect you must have sailed from Southampton."

"Well, I . . ." she began.

"Husband's name?"

"Sutherland," Nadia replied in her most pukka English accent. "He's a senior administrator with the passport control office."

Lady Hoarde sniffed the air as if his position was of no particular consequence. "Never heard of him. Not to worry, we'll have you settled in no time." She snagged a waiter and demanded a gin and lime. Turning back to Nadia she barked, "We have a ladies' tea party every Tuesday. Bridge night is Wednesday at the Golf Club. Of course you'll have to be vetted first."

Nadia looked at her blankly.

"Have you been allocated your household staff yet? We're breaking in a new cook-boy at the moment. What a trial! Beans on toast is all he can manage it seems. And you wouldn't believe his personal hygiene. Fingernails like a rotten old sailor's. Lord only knows why I let him in the kitchen at all!" She looked Nadia up and down. "Who was it that recommended your cook-boy? Daphne Soames? Mary Willis? Oh, you really ought to try Mary's sponge cake. Her little man Ah Wah's awfully talented. Used to be a pastry chef for the Jardine family yonks ago."

"We don't have a cook-boy," said Nadia, when Lady Hoarde finally stopped talking.

Lady pug widened her eyes with a sharp intake of breath. "Good Lord, why ever not? I suppose you're going to tell me that you do all the kitchen work in the house." She gave a nasty snigger.

"That's right, I do."

Lady Hoarde made a face. Her husband, a tall bearded man, came and stood beside her. He introduced himself as

Sir Peter Hoarde, said he was in the sugar trade, before looking over her shoulder to see if there was anyone more interesting to talk to.

"We've been given temporary housing in the Government quarters on Caine Road. My husband and I have recently arrived from Macao . . ." Nadia said, seeing Iain gravitate towards her. She reached out and took his arm.

"Macao? What a God forsaken place! People there have no notion of proper behaviour. I'd be surprised if they'd even heard of bridge. How *did* you keep from going mad?"

"Actually, I ran a cigar shop – "

"A *seee-gar* shop?" Sir Peter blurted.

"You mean you *worked* for a living?" said the pug, taking a long swig of her gin and lime.

Nadia couldn't recall ever meeting a more conceited old hag. "Lady Hoarde, some of us like to keep busy. There's more to life than cocktail party gossip and bridge. Perhaps you ought to try it sometime."

"Work in a shop . . . Why would any respectable English woman go and do something like that?"

"But your ladyship, I'm not English." She waited a beat, deliberately giving the words time to sink in. "I'm Rrrrrussian."

"Oh heavens," said the pug, wrinkling her nose. "Oh, heavens, heavens, heavens . . ." She turned her back, took her husband's arm and walked away.

Nadia glanced at Iain and shook her head. She rolled her eyes and made to leave.

"Wait," he said. Determined to have the last word, he took a step forward. "I say, Lady Hoarde," he cried, loud enough to be heard across the room.

The pug turned to look at him sharply. She cocked her head with disdain. "What is it?"

"I just want you to know that you'll be in good hands. That you're not to worry. There's no need to feel any embarrassment. People in the tropics catch intestinal worms all the time.

My doctor will send over the proper medication for you first thing tomorrow. You'll be cured of those writhing little parasites in no time. And if that fails he'll give you a warm-water enema for the flatulence. All right? Cheerio for now!"

The whole room seemed to pause in mid-sentence. All conversation stopped. Then a few people tittered as the lines of humiliation crept across Lady Hoarde's face.

Iain took Nadia's hand. "Okay, now that's done," he said to her. "How about we grab ourselves some supper?"

"Who are those dreadful people?" asked Nadia.

"He's a sugar trader who does a lot of business in Japan. He likes to think he has a special relationship with the Japanese because he sweetens their soy sauces and pickles."

They stepped into the steamy night. "Where are we going?" Nadia inquired.

"It's a surprise." They climbed into the back of a Foreign Office car and were driven through the western part of town, towards Sheung Wan district. Gradually, the architecture changed – gone was the colonial dignity of Victoria, instead a hive of low-rise, balconied shophouses mottled the streets packed tight with store-signs and decorations. There was the vibrant clatter of mah jong tiles, the undulating sound of Chinese opera, the loud cries of fruit vendors together with the throb of temple gongs and the clang of cooking utensils. Nadia saw the car approach a cul-de-sac lit by bulbous paper lanterns hung on poles, stopping close to the night market near Shek Tong Tsui.

Iain jumped out of the car and went round to open her door. "Here we are," he announced.

"Where is 'here'?" she said, seeing only a condiment shop and a tea house.

"It's where we'll be having dinner. And afterwards we've been invited to watch a Chinese ceremony."

"A ceremony?"

"It's called a Chinese bun ceremony, but more about that later. First we have to meet some friends."

They crossed Shek Tong Road and entered a brightly-lit Chinese restaurant with white ceramic-tiled floors. A sign said that they specialized in braised beef. In the centre of the room, scattered around a large round table, was Costa, Izabel and Carlos, as well as the two boys, Cristiano and Victor. They all stood to kiss her.

"Izabel!" Nadia yelled. The two friends embraced. "You never said you were coming!"

"You know how I love surprising you," beamed Izabel, wearing a stylish beret. "I tried to convince Mamuchka to come, but she decided to stay behind with your father and Uncle Yugevny."

"Is she still sulking because I left Macao?"

"Oh, just a little."

After greeting everyone affectionately, Nadia felt someone's hand on her shoulder. She looked around brightly. It was Anna. She wore a black Chinese mask over her eyes. Her hair was drawn back in a pony-tail and there was a pink linen scarf fastened round her neck, but it was still Anna. "*Recordar-me?* Remember me?" she said wearing a smirk on her face.

"How could I forget," said Nadia, her voice flat. She felt her joy suddenly stall, as if she'd been running happily along the beach, enjoying the sensation of soft sand under her feet, only to stub her toe on a rock. "What are you doing here?"

"I'm here to claim my prize, my Scottish dance lessons."

"Of course, you are. How good of you to come," she eventually said.

The highlight of the celebrations was a fifty-foot bun-tower; a bamboo pyramid draped in hundreds of sweet steamed buns. At the stroke of midnight teams of village men scrambled up the sides of the tower to snatch as many buns as possible, and the higher each man climbed, the better luck he brought to his family.

The crowd roared as a boy of fifteen reached the summit,

simultaneously enormous paper effigies of Di Zhang, the King of Ghosts, were set alight, with buns and incense sticks handed out to everyone in attendance.

Nadia had been waiting for an opportunity to take Izabel aside, judiciously, to talk to her about Anna.

"She's rude," said Nadia.

Izabel looked at her friend with an expression of incredulity. "I can believe Anna being unsubtle and mischievous and silly with her money, but rude? No, that's not like her."

"Well she is," said Nadia her slim frame throwing shadows in the downlight. "You should see the way she acts in front of me. She's just plain insolent."

Nonplussed, Izabel asked, "What exactly did she say?"

"She said my bathing costume was more suited for a younger woman."

Izabel looked confused. "She said this to you tonight?"

"No, of course not, it was at the picnic last month."

Izabel gave a little smile. "*Sim*, that does sound like something Anna would say. She can be brutally honest sometimes. She likes to speak her mind."

"I also think she's trying to steal my husband."

Izabel blinked, her thick eyebrows twisted. A few seconds passed as the words began to sink in. Then her smile broadened.

Nadia said, "I've seen the way she looks at him. I see it in her body language. Why are you grinning? I'm being serious!"

"I know you are being serious," she replied, covering her mouth to hide her grin.

It started to rain. A steaming rain. The water began to splash against their shoulders, plopping in thick errant drops. Nadia removed her low-heeled satin sandals and held a shoe in each hand.

"She's after my husband"

"*Isso e impossivel*," said Izabel.

"Why?"

"Because she wears her dress back to front."

"What on earth is that meant to mean?"

"It's a Portuguese expression. I'm trying to tell you that Anna is not what you think . . ."

"She's a shameless home wrecker."

"No, she's not."

"Stop defending her!"

"I am not defending her."

"Yes you are!"

"Anna cannot be a home wrecker and she cannot be after Iain because . . ."

"Because what?"

"*Porque e uma lesbica.* Because she is *lesbica.* All right, there, now I have told you."

"*Lesbica?*"

Izabel spoke slowly, as if addressing a child, "Lezzzz-beee-kaaa. She likes only women."

Nadia mouth grew big and round "No."

"*Sim.*"

"But . . ."

"There was a small scandal back home. She was involved with another nurse. The hospital she worked for in Barreira found out. There was much talk and, well, you know, it is a Catholic society. Too many people knew. She was asked to leave her job quietly, which is why she came to Macao, to get away from all the gossip. Fortunately for her the hospital gave her a good reference."

"But why is she so friendly with Iain?"

"Just because she likes girls doesn't mean she can't be friends with the opposite sex."

"You should have told me."

"It's not something one goes about telling, especially as she is family."

"Oh no."

"What?"

"Now I see why she responded the way she did when I

270

asked her about marriage. She said she wasn't interested in getting married nor was she interested in doctors. She must have thought I was teasing her."

"Oh, I think she enjoys it. She told me once that she liked sparring with you."

They were standing under the ornamented railings of the tea house, across the road from the Chinese restaurant. The rain spilled in billowing waves, dousing everyone and everything. "Maybe we should get back," said Nadia, feeling as if a twenty-pound load had been lifted from her shoulders.

"Yes, maybe we should."

"But first I have to do something." Nadia ran towards the night market, towards the bright red bulbs hanging in the flower stalls, her bare feet slipping on the wet ground. She returned a moment later with a blissful look on her face and a bouquet of peonies and blue delphinium in her arms.

They walked through the frenetic, clamouring throng. They saw a pageant of children dressed as godheads, some of them gliding above the crowd as though balanced on the tips of paper fans. After a few minutes Nadia found Iain and the others watching a Cantonese Punch and Judy show. Anna was standing with her young cousins under a canopy embossed with large red Chinese characters. Nadia approached her and draped an arm over her shoulder. She handed over the bouquet and Anna smiled, surprise and pleasure crinkling her eyes.

"What's this for?" she said, puzzled.

"I should have done this sooner," Nadia said. "It's an apology."

"An apology for what?"

"For everything. I should have been kinder to you when you first arrived."

Anna smiled and immediately something lightened between them.

"*Voce esta molhado.* You're wet," said Anna, unfastening

271

the linen scarf from her throat. "Dry your hair with this before you catch cold."

Nadia shook the water out from her hair and gathered her rain-drenched dress around her legs. A sensation of buoyancy entered her heart. The smell of the flowers grew sweet.

The days grew longer and hotter with the arrival of summer. The ceiling fan whirred overhead. Iain's shoulder buckled as he rolled off Nadia. Their skin was slippery and florid. Perspiration gathered in little pools across their belly-buttons and in the hollows of their throats, tickling as it trickled down onto the bedsheets.

Iain raised his body up so that Nadia could rest her head on his chest. His arm remained curled round her waist, his muscles slack and spent.

"Iain . . ."

"Hmmm?"

"I have to apologize to you about something."

"What?" he said, sleepily.

"I have to apologize about Anna. The whole thing was just a misunderstanding. It was silly of me. Very silly and I'm sorry." He kissed the top of her head as she spoke. "And I think I've finally come to accept something," she continued.

"Accept what?"

"That I'll never be able to have children."

Iain kissed her again. He had just cupped her face in his hand when the telephone rang. His eyes lifted over the pillows. Reaching through the narrow gap in the mosquito net, he stretched for the mouthpiece.

"Sutherland," he said in a voice still thick with coital froth. His face was hot from lovemaking, yet in spite of the July heat a chill ran up his back as soon as he heard the Oxford lilt on the other end.

"The Marco Polo Bridge? Yes, I understand," Iain said, sitting up, detaching his arm from Nadia's hip. "When did the Japanese issue the ultimatum? I see. So they started to bombard the town with artillery soon after midnight." Moments later he replaced the mouthpiece on its cradle and climbed out of bed. He took two steps towards the bedroom window and watched the deep blue shadow of cloud move against the moon.

"What is it?" Nadia asked, almost asleep. She flopped her legs across the counterpane.

His skin looked as pale as candle wax in the moonlight. "There's trouble southwest of Peking. Heavy fighting has broken out between the Chinese and Japanese Armies."

"Who was that on the phone?"

"Somebody from the office." He turned and looked at her. "He said this could be the start of something big. Nadia, if anything happens I want you to return to Macao, do you understand?"

"What do you mean *if anything happens*?"

"I mean if there's a war. If Britain gets embroiled in this war."

"Surely, I'll be safer in Hong Kong. The British China Fleet is based here."

"Look, don't argue with me on this." He came and sat on the edge of the bed, pushing the net aside as he approached. "Will you promise me you'll go back to Macao if I ask you to?"

She saw the determination in his eyes. Her throat trembled. The words welled up inside of her. "Yes, I promise." she said, clutching a pillow in her small fists.

"Good," he mouthed, wrapping his arms round her and holding her tight, feeling a fear catch in his stomach. He closed his ears to his own rushing heartbeat, which bumped in his chest as though he'd raced up a flight of stairs; instead he caught his image in the nightstand mirror. In the reflection the pallor of his face had turned bone-white, there was a cold gleam to his eyes; it was, he thought, as if he could suddenly see into the harsh, bloody future.

PART FOUR

1945

1

The man had been in solitary confinement for just under two weeks with his arms tied behind his back for eighteen hours a day. It was his punishment for being defiant to the Japanese sentries. During that period the guards had urinated on him and shoved glass shards into his mouth and nose. When, still, he refused to apologise for his show of disrespect, his tormentors tired of him and let him go.

As he staggered down the hill, away from the prison gates, a few fellow prisoners, stretching their shirtless bodies out of windows, shouted across and waved at him. He didn't wave back; instead his hands felt the dressing by his mouth with clumsy fingers – the searing pain had lasted almost ten days, but now his chin and gums felt scalded, as though they'd been stung by nettles. There was a metallic taste in his mouth as though he'd been sucking on a greasy spoon. Gingerly, he pulled the bandaging off as he teetered down the slope. His feet felt like they were weighed down with ballasts, but it was his face he was more worried about – there was something very wrong, as if the muscles that he had once used for smiling had been removed. He watched the dirty, ochreous gauze unravel and drop to the ground. He tried to work his jaws. There was no saliva left in his mouth and his lips felt like they'd been glued shut. At his feet lay scraps of cloth. It was then that he had a terrible thought: perhaps they'd cut off his tongue.

According to Sergeant-Major Hamuri, detainee 6177 was released from the Gendarmerie twenty-four hours early as a show of graciousness, a fitting act to commemorate Emperor Hirohito's 44th birthday, he'd said. To mark the occasion, members of the nearby garrison wore stiffly starched uniforms with high unyielding collars, and the camp commandant attached a chrysanthemum flower emblem to the rim of his cap. Field boots were buffed to a lush chocolate brown, bayonet frogs varnished, and Katana swords rubbed and cleaned with clove oil. Even the Sikh sentries, hoisting their laundry lines on the rocky points that looked onto Tai Tam Bay, decided it was high time to swap their soiled red turbans for fresh yellow ones.

During the morning an electric storm had rolled over Hong Kong, dropping lightning, cooling the baking earth with a *Tsssssss* of quenching rain. It had soaked the solid ground outside of B and C Block, turning it into mud. But three hours had passed since then and, with the day approaching noon, the April sun was out and the shorebirds and magpies were beginning to call again. It was the Emperor's birthday. It was also the day that the flour allowance was stopped.

Under the stippled shade of a cassia tree, inside the ration store by the kitchens, a tall man called Friendly, with a frizz of brown hair, stood with his shrunken chest bare, wearing nothing but shorts made from rice sacks. Friendly had once been an architect with Leigh & Orange. By his side, the Yorkshireman, Stepney, a former restaurant manager, bespectacled and stooping with hunger, watched with ravenous eyes. On his shoulder sat Mr. Yorkie, his pet mouse. Stepney was born with a defect to his limbs; his right leg curved outwards at the knee, and his left leg curved inwards, which made him look like a cartoon character swaying sideways in the wind. The two men were smiling – between them they'd found an unlikely source of meat.

The interior of the kitchen quarters was dark, lit by a halo of tiny battery lights, its air stagnant, and the dragging heat stifling. There was the smell of something dank, like mildewed fur, a feral stink which seemed to cling to the men's sweaty wrists. Friendly's hand sought the back of the cat's head, avoiding its teeth and raking claws. He gripped the animal firmly against the wooden block, pressing down with all his weight. Blunt shadows fell across the wall. Stepney was so hungry he brought a hand to his mouth, sucking his fingers with anticipation. The cat scratched and struggled as its hind legs were held firm. Mr. Yorkie shrank back from Stepney's shoulder and hid behind his neck.

Moisture came off the back of Friendly's neck as he thrust the cat's face to the cutting board. Temples dissolved with perspiration, eyes withdrew into their sockets. "God's sek, keep the bloodeh thing quiet!" hissed Stepney as the animal's shrieks rang round the stone-slabbed cookhouse and reverberated off the ceiling, soaring over the crumbling, cracked beams and across the wooden work benches and deep, stone sinks.

Another voice, male and impatient, said, "Fucking get on with it!" It was Hoarde, the former sugar merchant, who'd once done trade with Japan – little but skin over bony shoulders. His small beard glistened with sweat.

Friendly with the frizz of brown hair lifted his cleaver and brought it down with a gasp. For a moment nothing happened. Then the struggling ceased and the cat's head rolled away like a discarded trophy, a daydreamer's far off look in its eyes. "Hurry," said Stepney, his spectacles steaming up. "Fore anyone sees." Friendly nodded. He hacked off the tail and feet. Red smears pooled on the yellowed concrete floor. Next, Stepney's scraggy fingernails scratched at the loose fur by the neck stump. He pulled the skin away as he would the rind of an unripe grapefruit. There was a loud tear that sounded like tough fabric ripping, followed by a gurgling, bubbling sound which escaped from the animal's flooded lungs.

Having pulled out the innards, Friendly began sawing through the shoulders and ribs. "Looks like we've got ourselves an extra two pounds of meat today, eh Stepney?"

The Yorkshireman didn't reply. He was looking at the pearl-dead eyes of the cat. They stared at him from the floor, unflinching. He wondered whether he ought to shut them. Instead, he looked away out of the window. Mr. Yorkie made a squeaking noise and appeared from behind his neck.

In the near distance, the edge of the camp was fringed with skeletal men and women lining up for a drink, faces tweaking with thirst, lunging forward as if pulled by nose rings. They drank stale water from cups cut from tin cans, their collarbones exposed and vulnerable, all warped knees and lanky shadows. Further away, others sat with their heads in their hands, their mouths so stiff it was as though they were windows that had been painted shut. They were all looking out into the horizon, searching, backs bent out of shape, hoping to see American planes in the blue yonder.

The small peninsula where the internees resided was called *Chek Chue*. The British had named it Stanley after Lord Stanley, and it was, for a brief period in 1842, the administrative centre of Hong Kong. It sat on the southern fringes of the colony and had once been a haunt for Chinese bandits. The fishing village sat in a little gully with a steep funnel-shaped ridge on one side and the Maryknoll Mission on the other. The internment camp was made up from the dormitory bungalows of St. Stephens School and the outhouses of the former colonial gaol. It occupied an area approximately 1100 yards long and as broad as 650 yards across at some points. There were tall wire fences stretching to the throat of the bay and sentry boxes, manned by Sikhs and Formosans, along the perimeter. Yellow dust hung over it on most mornings like a cloud of gnats, raised by the troops of the 230th Regiment attached to the Japanese garrison a quarter mile to the south on Ma Kok Hill.

Stepney was still looking out through the window when he exclaimed, "Fuck a duck. Look who's just stepped out from between the prison gates." Friendly and Hoarde leaned forward and stooped to get a better view. They saw the man with the bandaged face blinking at the sharp midday sun, dazzled by the wind, the light, the glare coming off the sea. He'd been in solitary confinement for thirteen days. His pale red hair looked disheveled and his starved chest a little frailer. "I can't believe he's still bloodeh alive," said Stepney.

"Tough as buggery, that Sutherland," Hoarde said. "Tough as fucking buggery."

2

It was hot. Not a whisper of wind. Sunshine washed over Iain's profile, highlighting the deep splits of skin near his eyes, the gauntness of his cheeks, the dark florid crusts of coagulated blood. In front of him there was a mirror and an earthenware bowl containing freshly drawn water. He was in the small buttery that the internees had transformed into a washroom. The mirror, crazed and spotted, hung from the eaves, while the earthenware bowl balanced on wooden pilings salvaged from the sea. Iain soaked a piece of rag in the water, looked at himself, then dabbed his face with it. Once sinewy and athletic, his features now appeared stretched and withered. At the age of forty-six his rich red mane was turning white. It was the pale hair of an arctic fox. Forty-six! He couldn't believe he was that old. Would he see forty-seven, he wondered? He flexed his left shoulder. There was tenderness there, under the skin. Was that rheumatism he felt in the joint? Perhaps it was tendonitis affecting the ball-and-socket arrangement, some inflammation of the soft tissue by the clavicle. He winced as he flexed it once more.

His hand touched the scrawny rind of skin by his ribs. He hung back in startled surprise, incredulous that so much weight could fall off of him in two weeks. He raised his hands to the level of his lips. In the cracked mirror he saw how slowly his damaged face was healing, bold bruises over a terracotta complexion. There were snaking scars where the glass splinters had entered his mouth, white ulcers within; his gums were still bleeding, but his tongue was intact. He brought his hands down from his chin. His eyes, known for their sharpness, were sunless. His dazed senses heard noises around him, registered little. His arms felt as slack as tubular seaweed, his back stiff like a turtle shell. But no matter how bad he felt or how miserable he looked, he worried about Nadia more. If only he could see her. He'd received news from her that she and the family were surviving under deteriorating conditions in Macao, but that the Japanese had left Macao to its own devices. Yet, still, he couldn't help but worry.

Iain broke eye contact with the wasted man in the mirror. Behind him, in the receding shadows, he saw Friendly and Stepney squatting on their haunches, picking weevils out from a tiny sack of rice and crushing them between their fingers. Mr. Yorkie hopped onto Stepney's arm and clung to the black hair, his long tail trailing in the rice.

Food had become foremost in his thoughts now. Iain was housed with sixty others in a single building that used to be the prison mess hall. It was, he thought, ironic that there wasn't ever anything to eat in the former canteen. The two meals the internees were given, at noon and at 5 p.m., were never near adequate. Twice a day the brass bells rang and the endless crocodile queues formed, hundreds of mouths chewing on air even before the food hit their plates. They'd grown used to the smell of boiled rice, brown gruel that tasted of dirt, the sound of salvaged eggshells being ground down for calcium, the swarms of flies.

Hunger wound itself round his stomach like a constrictor, ever tightening. He hadn't taken in solids for over eight days and suddenly his head floated, as lightly as a cork on water. Beriberi, dysentery, suppurating sores, and other flesh infections were dragging him under. He thought about hot bowls of spiced noodle soup, buying *laap cheong faan* from street vendors on the Rua da Republica, plates and plates of fried eggs and chorizos piled high with crispy buttered toast, sipping a cold beer at sundown whilst gazing out from a bar on the Praya Grande – how he missed the sleepy rhythms of

Macao and the laughter of Nadia and her family and the kindness of Izabel and Mrs. Lo.

Iain stretched his arms over his head, executing a fluid, supple bend of the elbows. He brought his arms down and looked at his hands. His fingernails had stopped growing months ago. He stared down at his bare legs – his thighs were still thicker than his knees. With the economic blockade biting, the flour ration had stopped. Rice was now only 3 ounces per meal, potatoes 7 ounces. Meat had ceased completely, but they still received a forkful of fish twice a week, and one egg every ninth day. Neutrals were allowed to send internees parcels once a fortnight, but little of the provisions ever got further than the Sikh guards.

He did weekly health checks on himself – monitoring the increasing limpness of his limbs, testing his reflexes with a rubber ball, tracking the inflammations on his legs, the sharpness of his ribs and wristbones. And he'd long stopped scraping calendars on the walls, talked less and less about the future, and possible repatriation. Instead, he concerned himself with the here and now – the small victories over the trials of camp life. The growing of cabbages, potatoes, beets, the pilfering of goods from the Japanese garrison's ration store, the continued concealment of the radio and courier links, and the resulting weekly contact with the British Army Aid Group – BAAG – in Waichow, Free China. These became his bedrocks, the things he could set apart and control in a place of forever shifting dangers.

Iain looked once more at the mirror. Out of the tail of his eyes, in its reflection, he glimpsed a small figure behind his own face, a faint thread of black shadow. He experienced a sudden sense of foreboding.

"You are engaging in perilous pastimes. Very dangerous."

The voice, speaking in abbreviated sentences, cut into Iain's fatigued thoughts like a shark slicing through shallow waters. It brought him back with a jolt. He paused, steeled himself, and recognized at once who it was. He dropped his gaze and shivered, feeling an almost overwhelming impulse to flee.

He turned to see Sergeant-Major Hamuri at the door with Hoarde by his side. Hamuri's uniform, with the chrysanthemum flower emblem of the Gendarmerie embellished on its collar, was crisp and recently pressed. Iain and his compatriots saluted then bowed to the waist. Despite the heat, the Sergeant-Major wore his standard black field boots, studded with nails. Waddling like a constipated duck, he entered the room, looking eager for a skirmish.

Two Japanese sentries followed. One of them shouted, *"Atenshon!"* and stood rigidly to one side. The other turned and slapped the still genuflecting Friendly across the cheek, kicking him as he fell.

"Nononono," Friendly yelped, clasping his hands over his testicles, imploring them, "Stop, please stop." Mr. Yorkie jumped from Stepney's shoulder and hid in a hole in the wall.

"Ken'aku. Very perilous." Hamuri repeated. He spoke in English but broke into Japanese from time to time. "Radios are very unacceptable things to be hiding." He had a sculpted, mannequin-like appearance. There were no lines at all on his face or forehead. He was looking at Friendly and Stepney. The third man, Hoarde, had retreated to the far end of the room. "Don't you agree?" They were silent for a moment. Friendly began nodding vigorously. Stepney nodded even more vigorously. "I am aware of a radio being used in these quarters. Is this information true?" he asked.

His question met with silence again. He frowned, lit a cigarette, sucked at it greedily and turned to glare at Iain with frenzied anger.

"IS IT TRUE?" he shouted. The words sank into Iain like a skean-dhu.

"No," Friendly and Stepney answered in unison. They drew away from him. Hoarde continued to watch the proceedings silently.

The Sergeant-Major kept his gaze on Iain. "You enjoyed your stay in the *kangoku*?"

"I had a splendid time."

"I gather that my colleague forgot to question you about a radio." He sucked his teeth. "We can be very absent-minded. Tell me, have you been using a wireless?"

Iain made a face and shrugged.

"*Nisemono!* Perhaps you should spend another fortnight in the cells," he said in a threatening voice.

Iain ignored Hamuri's aggressive tone. Instead, he treated the Japanese officer casually, like he would a visitor stopping by to share in a pot of tea or a salesman offering a discounted set of encyclopedias. "No need to get all uppity, Hamuri. Yes, it's true," said Iain. "We *had* a radio. Up until last month, that is. When we heard that our former camp superintendent, Yamashita-san, was searching for one, we destroyed it with a hammer and threw the bits into the sea, over the fence near the Indian Quarters."

Hamuri seemed to hesitate and steady himself. The answer had caught him off-guard. He was expecting a flat denial. An expression of astonished doubt appeared in his eyes. He looked over at Hoarde then back at Iain. "Destroy?" he said, spluttering. "Why you destroy?"

"Because we would have been executed if you discovered it. Look, Hamuri, I've just spent two weeks getting my mouth torn open by you clowns, I don't fancy getting my head lopped off too. I've got enough to worry about here, what with starvation and unremitting boredom on my doorstep." Iain padded over to the window where a shirt was dangling on a hanger. He patted the breast pocket of the shirt and removed an empty carton of Lucky Strikes, crumpling it in his fist. "Listen, can I scrounge a cigarette, Hamuri, I've flat run out."

The Sergeant-Major stared hard at Iain, examining him. A penetrating look that was both smiling and critical at the same time crossed his face. "The splinter that sticks up from the wood will be shorn away," he said, his eyes bulging with resentment. "Search everything! Now!" he shrieked at the sentries, before sliding his black boots out the room.

When the guards eventually left, having found neither wireless nor any other contraband Iain said, "How the hell did they learn about the radio?"

Everyone shrugged.

"Good thing they didn't think about searching the attic."

"When did you move it to the attic?" asked Hoarde, his eyes sly.

"Last night," said Iain. "I found a small crawl space under the floorboards." He bent down and retrieved Hamuri's cigarette, giving the stub a few reviving puffs, smoking it down until it burned his fingertips. Iain looked at Hoarde. "You told them about the radio, didn't you? You led them here."

Hoarde shook his head. "What makes you say a thing like that?" His expression grew watchful.

"You could have gotten us killed. What did they promise you, more food and cigarettes?"

Hoarde froze. "I don't know what you mean," he mewled, nostrils splaying atop of his damp beard.

"You'll do anything to get ahead," Iain leaned his face into Hoarde. "Even betray your own people."

They squared up to each other.

"Get out!" said Iain.

"You'd best hop it," echoed Stepney.

Hoarde gave the air a sniff; he tilted his head to the left then spat onto the floor. They watched him leave. When he was out of earshot, Friendly said, "That bloody Hoarde. Ever since his wife died last Christmas, he's not been the same."

"Why'd you tell him it was in the crawl space?" asked Stepney. "He'll go running to Hamuri now."

"Because it's not in the crawl space, is it?" said Iain. "I moved the radio this morning. It's in D Block now, hidden under the floorboards of the shit-house."

"Crafty," said Stepney, stroking Mr. Yorkie's head.

"We bury the bloody thing tonight, though," said Iain. "Contact BAAG and tell them the wireless will be out of use for a month, then dismantle it, wrap the parts in blankets and bury it behind the old block of the Indian quarters. The soil's softer by the old block and won't look like it's been disturbed. Do it just after roll call. Don't breathe a word of this to anyone, especially Hoarde. Tomorrow the new camp commandant arrives. He may not be as lenient as Yamashita was."

Both Friendly and Stepney agreed.

Iain gave a tight, sour smile then walked over to sit on his bed, which was nothing more than a plank of wood resting on bricks. He was worried about Hoarde, knew he'd try to betray them again. Iain had to watch his step now. A bedbug scuttled across the mattress. Iain caught it and crushed it between his fingers, heard its abdomen pop. He held it up to his nostrils and smelled the perfume of its blood – a sour reek of coconuts and rusted nails. His hand dropped to his side.

The accumulated exhaustion of days without proper sleep overcame him. His eyes looked down and caught the tips of his bony fingers. He couldn't help but stare at the third finger of his left hand and remembered the day he was forced to hand in his wedding ring and other jewellery over to the Japanese. A painful despair stung him. His whole body bent forward and he held his head in his hands. He wanted so much to be with Nadia, to hold her close. He tried to picture her face, but his tired eyes kept closing. Where was Nadia now, he wondered. Where?

3

The late-afternoon sun danced on the water, sparkling like jadeite charms, angling in, still hot. The sea was no longer rising. The waves had softened. In the distance, to the east, dozens of fishing junks broke the horizon, the peaks of their ribbed sails snapping like hungry barracuda at the flaring sun. To the west, unstirred by the robust wind, a nest of orange-fringed clouds reddened with the twilight.

Under the cover of a withering sky, the junk entered Hong Kong waters from the south, skirting the Po Toi Islands. The sail hung, as it always did, on the starboard side of the mast. Nadia watched the land spread out before her, its colours contrasting against the blue of the sea. She saw mountainous terrain, bamboo forests, shanty towns caked to the lower valleys like ant nests, barren rock peaks and thin waterfalls that gleamed like streaks of bone. The junk entered a narrow stretch of channel. This must be the East Lamma Strait, Nadia said to herself, her heart beginning to thump. It was the first point marked on her map, beyond it, marked with a red circle, was the place she was to be dropped off – Aberdeen Bay. She folded the map carefully along the crease lines and slipped it within the lining of her tunic.

There were fewer buildings on this side of the territory, only a sprinkling of European-style houses, sword-blades of white that stood out against the green. Instead, she saw the dense shade of hills, the tropical foliage, the crowded settlement of sampan communities with their own floating boutiques and restaurants. Here the water gypsies lived, the *tang-kah*. The stern of their junks were the working and living quarters of their homes. Dressed in pajamas, the boatgirls did their house chores, grew vegetables in tubs of soil, bred chickens and pigs under the mizzens of their crafts.

Nadia was being smuggled into Hong Kong by the water people known as the Hoklo, sea gypsies who specialized in opium running and piracy. They had been paid a handsome sum for the privilege of getting her out of neutral Macao and into occupied Hong Kong. Only the Hoklo knew how to avoid the mines that plagued the waterways. They agreed on a delivery date – April 30th, the day following the Emperor's birthday, in the hope that the Japanese patrol boat captains would be nursing hangovers, or better still, be off-duty.

The sun sank into the horizon. Nadia stood under the foremast in the sun-dappled shadows, tight against the bow, invisible against the blackened scoop of deck. The floor under her feet was slick with ocean spray. She gripped the scummy ropes of the foremast as if her life depended on it. She wore a broad-brimmed straw hat and the dark, loose trousers of a fisherman made from coarse cloth. Her collarless tunic was fastened down the sides and a length of sash, like a Japanese obi, had been wrapped round her chest. Using hooks and eyes, she'd pulled it tight to flatten her breasts. She touched her compressed bosom fleetingly, nudging first the left breast, then the right, just to see if they were still there. Moments later, her ringless hands went to the back of her neck. Her elbow-length hair had been cropped short at the nape to resemble a boy; as short as it had been when she was in her late twenties; the feeling of bareness felt alien to her, yet comfortingly familiar. Using fabric scissors, she'd cut away the braid which she had been growing for six years, finding the sensation strangely liberating, as though she were Joan of Arc about to enter the battlefield.

Meanwhile, with great deftness, the Hoklo began to haul in their trawling nets, the drag of the trawl bridle showing the fishermen how good the catch was. Because of the mines their fishing was restricted to the six-mile horshoe between the twin Lamma Channels. *"Yut, yee, saam!"* they crowed in unison, arms straining, *"Yut, yee, samm!"* Within minutes the fishing holds were alive with pomfret, flowery grouper and humphead wrasse.

A strong breeze pushed against Nadia's body. The sails slapped against the wind, like the sound of a giant canvas bird flapping its wings. The sky grew greyer, closing on her like a hand, its colour darkening like a palm painted with henna. She was thinking about what lay ahead for her – it was as if her blood had turned cold and her lungs emptied of air. Her guts had been churning ever since they passed Lantau Island and a couple of times she had to lean forward and moan, the back of her throat sensing bile. She watched shadows dance on the rippling water and hated herself for feeling seasick.

Her hands seized the euphroe, a long wooden slat that secured the cord holding up the awnings of the sails. Her cotton sacks of belongings were tucked between her legs, her bare feet wet against the teak deck. She looked up into the night, beyond the elliptical curves of the masts, and her mouth moved in silent prayer. She crossed herself. Increasingly groggy and light-headed, she tasted the acid climb up and burn her throat once more. She dry-heaved and felt tears well in her eyes.

Costa grunted, scowled at her as if to say forty-three-year-old women weren't meant to get seasick. He bent his head forward and shook it. Nadia could see the olive sheen of his scalp where his hair had thinned. Wheezing and sweating, he emitted a snigger and scratched his belly though his shirt.

"What are you laughing at?" she said.

"I knew thees wash a bad idea."

"Shut up."

"You shut up."

Nadia felt her mouth fill with thick globs of saliva.

"Move!" she said.

"Why?"

"I said move, *Zasranec*!" She scrambled over Costa's massive frame and was sick over the side of the boat.

Shooting-stars fell from the sky, tails poppling like molten silver. Neither Costa nor Nadia had seen sleep for thirty hours. The anxious, animated thoughts racing through their heads defeated slumber. Beneath Costa's conical fishing hat, his face radiated anticipation. Looking though a spyglass, he could see the Japanese soldiers patrolling the avenues along the Aberdeen seafront, their rifles and bayonets catching the smattering of moonlight as the slope dipped into a rocky ridge. He shook his head no, paying no attention to the borborygmus of his whining stomach.

With careful deliberation Nadia pressed a pair of black coolie shoes to her feet and made a mental note of all the items she had in the two sacks by her ankles: thirty-two cartons of cigarettes, five tins of Pall Mall tobacco, a pocket-book full of Japanese Military Yen and false identification papers, a Swiss-made wristwatch with luminous hands and hour markers, four tangerines, a bottle of iodine sealed tight in newspaper, biscuits, wire cutter pliers, several beeswax candles, wrappings of preserved fruit, dried meats, two canteens of water, a much-used folding map of Hong Kong and a stack of European postcards depicting naked women in various breezy poses. There was also a single photograph concealed in a manila envelope, which she kept hidden from view.

"It ish too dangerous to get you ashore here," Costa said, shaking his head once more, his voice a dull rumble. He handed her the spyglass, which she placed in her bag.

"But it's the meeting point," Nadia protested. "Father Luke will be waiting."

Costa threw his head from side to side and his chin swung like that of a Bactrian camel. "No, I cannot allow it. We will try to get you onto one of the shmall beaches around Repulse Bay."

"How will we contact Father Luke?"

"Leave that to me. When we get you on land, head wesht, but shtay clear of the roads and Japanese patrols. We'll get word to Luke and egg-shplain that you'll meet in Deep Water Bay. There are three tall palm trees at the neck of the bay. It ish not hard to find."

Nadia nodded uncertainly. She knew nothing about Father Luke. All she'd been told was that since the occupation, the Catholic diocese had come under the control of the Portuguese Eurasians, and as one of their senior clerics, he'd expressed a willingness to help her.

"Are you nervish?"

"Yes."

"Don't be. You will be in good hands. Would you like to hear a *balada*? It will ease the tenshyn. My mother used to shing to me whenever I shuffered the calamities of conshtipation."

"No, please no. *Bawzhemoy*, I don't think I could tolerate your singing right now."

Regardless, Costa began to croon a quiet song. *"Oh, her nose was full of blackheads, and she was the belle of the ball . . ."*

Nadia shook her head and reproached him with her eyes. Despite herself, she smiled.

The junk moved slowly eastward. Somewhere along the coast Nadia saw stretches of overgrown lawn that might have been part of a golf course. Images of Iain practicing his swing welled up in her mind – the tilt of his shoulders, the graceful arc of his backswing, the pivot of his hips, the extension of his arms. The thought remained with her for some time. She stayed quiet, her right hand caressing the jade monkey pendent by her throat. She had not seen Iain since he was interned in January 1942, thirty-nine months ago. He was allowed to write to her once a month. During that time she had received twenty-six letters, each one written in a progressively faltering hand; she'd reread each one so often she knew them all by heart. In her left hand she clutched the last of the correspondence. There was just enough light for her to make out her name on the front. She looked at the flip side of the envelope where the words 'Prisoner of War Mail' and 'Passed by Censor 3287' were stamped in Chinese writing.

As usual, Iain had told her about his prickly heat, the awful meals, the continuous waiting, the never-knowing-what-day-it-was, how he'd had to make his own food receptacles out of old bully beef tins, and his imminent move to new billets. He mentioned that an anaemic baby had been born in Block F – three pounds, two ounces, a girl. She was not expected to survive. He also said that his address would remain as before until further notice: Block C, Room 11, Stanley Civilian Internment Camp. His message seemed mundane enough, yet, there had been other parts of the letter that had been picked up by the censors who'd drawn black ink over two paragraphs of text. Nadia tried to guess what it was that Iain had written. Was it something to do with BAAG, the resistance organization that helped prisoners escape? Was it a signal maybe, a tip-off? Or the failed escapes Costa had told her about? For a while she wondered what might have spurred them to run a black pen over his words. Had he been warning her of something? Was there something she needed to know? What had he said that made them so worried?

The junk approached a tiny bay.

"You know," Costa said, reverting to Portuguese, his eyebrows lifting with amusement. "Iain and I used to go into Coloane every month or so, whenever we could really, and play football against the teenage Macanese boys in the village. He ran fast down the right wing and had a mean cross. Your husband was *louco* about football and he was pretty good too. He was talented in the air as well, won many, many headers. Afterwards we would all go down to one of the *pousadas* on the beach and eat spicy prawns, salted codfish, suckling pig wrapped in hot bread. We never got home before sunrise. That was the year before he knew about you . . . 1927. I never thought he could be any happier. But I was wrong. Because then he met you and I never *ever* saw that big mouth of his smile and laugh so much." Their eyes met briefly. "You realize he is my best friend."

"I do."

"And you will find him for me?"

"Yes."

Costa's breath came in a turbulent rush. "You are shoor you are ready to do thees?" he said, speaking now in his deep mellifluous English. "Thees ees not an offee-cial mission. If BAAG finds out about thees, we'll all be in terrible trouble. You are an amateur. Naturally, I would go myself, but the Japanese probably have a file on me. If they catch me, they'll egzeecute me for shertain."

"This was my choice, Fernando. I have to do this, especially with the new camp commandant arriving any day. If he recognizes Iain, he'll shoot him. I have to get him out of there as soon as possible."

"You have four days. We will be waiting for you at the designated point on the map. You remember where that ish?"

"Yes," she replied. Though there was an undertone of anxiety in her voice, she held no fear in her heart. She felt that she was drawing ever nearer to Iain. Soon she would be able to help and comfort him. She looked into Costa's eyes once more and was surprised to see that they were pools of tenderness despite his blunt exterior. She realized with a flush of compassion that the big Macanese man was almost as close to Iain as she was.

"I owe it to *Vermelho* to get you here," he said. "And to get you back shafely."

She stretched forward and touched Costa's hand. "I know. Thank you," she said, looking now towards the land, determined to be with the man she loved, the man who had inhabited her thoughts, night and day, for seventeen years, forging an unbreakable emotional and spiritual connection.

"I'm going to find him, Fernando, and bring him home."

There was a pause, a fleeting moment of reverential silence. A whisper of hope that hung between them before it was whipped away in the wind. He nodded in assent. "I know you will, Senhora. May God go with you."

Costa let the cotton sacks fall into the sampan with a thump.

Nadia stood for a long time under the quartermast, her mind seething with thoughts. Her eyes were closed, her face tipped toward the sky. She fingered her father's lucky glass charm that hung on a thin necklace round her neck. Costa puckered his lips and made an indistinct whistling sound.

Nadia secured the buttons of her tunic.

She peered down at Costa, whose raised, clenched fist meant it was time to go. She adjusted the broad brim of her woven hat and lowered herself onto the sampan; the rope ladder creaking and clicking under her weight. The sea was getting rough again. The sampan woman was looking at her as if she was some kind of sea demon, as though she was the first Caucasian woman she'd ever set eyes on.

Nadia felt her legs lurch, her knees fighting to keep upright. The sampan bumped along the top of the surf. The water was jet black. She was aware of salt spray hitting her lips, gleaming wet on her face. She looked behind her and saw Costa's round-rumped bulk, his black-shadowed shape on the curved prow of the junk. She waved at him once, but he did not respond. His last words to her were to head west along the waterfront road and to look out for Father Luke the following morning by the beach with the three palm trees.

She was on her own now.

Over the side. Her legs hit the current and immediately she felt the rush of tidewater snatch at her thighs, pulling her to and fro, bending her knees. She fought her way through to the shore and slumped on all fours, cotton bags draped over each shoulder, hat falling off the back of her head. The only light came from the moon, temporarily hidden by a freckle of cloud. The tide was out so there was about eighty feet of sand between the shrubline and the sea.

She moved closer to the ragged row of trees, her shoes squishing water and sand, to within fifty feet of the road. Her head swivelled round. A mile from the junk now, and the slightest sound – the wind through the trees, the hiss of surf, made her flinch and look into the invisible frontier, straining to make things out in the darkness. Apart from a few frantic crabs, the beach appeared completely deserted. She stooped low and ran, feet catching in the contours of the sand, bags thumping against her spine. She ran as if propelled by a mighty, unseen hand. She could hear herself heaving for air. The drips of cool on her face felt like light rain.

She was about ten yards from the road when she fell. She'd caught her foot on something round, like a large coconut. With a powerful wrench, she pulled herself up and stared hard at the ground. What she thought were big, black stones lay scattered about the head of the beach. She bent down and reached forward with her fingers. The bit she touched felt like soft coir or straw. A streak of light appeared; the moon came out from behind the clouds, reflecting enough radiance to see by, throwing ghostly blue phosphorescence onto the sand. She pulled her arm away. Her blood turned thick and cold. Her hands bunched into fists and covered her mouth. A man was gazing up at her, a terrified, breathless, accusing expression on his face. His teeth looked brilliant, the darkish hair rigidly curled. The orbits of his eyes were full of fly larvae, writhing like syrupy grains of rice. A few feet away another man was gawping at the stars.

A hushed fragrance of death filled her nostrils. There were more decapitated heads to her left and right, one was still wearing spectacles. She saw, about five yards to the distant, a group of headless bodies lying on their backs, abdomens torn open, the sand around them sodden with blood and entrails. Their flesh was like slaughterhouse sullage where the pye-dogs had feasted upon the mutilated meat. In the stillness of the night she counted eleven cadavers in all.

The sand started blowing in gusts. Sparrows began to squabble over scraps of knotted muscle tissue. A chill came over Nadia's arms and neck. She narrowed her eyes. All of a sudden the trees appeared to light up in front of her. She heard the rumble of a lorry's engine bouncing and roaring, and wheels sizzling to a stop on the wet road. Another lorry loomed before her and pulled up. Headlight beams crossed in the darkness, branching out across the beach. She climbed hand over hand up a small ridge, and hid herself behind the scribed edges of thistles and spruces, her cloth shoes digging into the earth to get a hold. She made no movement, held her breath; the pulse points on her neck began to throb.

A steely, braying voice shouted, 'Sousou, sousou!' She caught the twisting glint of bayonets. A Japanese officer, the side vents of his tropical tunic open to the breezes, was shepherding a procession of shackled men towards an exposed area of tall grass. One of the captives struggled and was struck with the butt of a rifle. There was a shrill cry, a shriek for mercy. Nadia thought it sounded English. The lorry's headlights showed up a man's agonized face. She saw five figures, kneeling, their heads bowed as though for Sunday prayer. Dry-mouthed, she forced herself from delivering a shuddering sob. The officer secured the chin strap of his cap over his jaw, laid the black lacquered scabbard on the floor and lifted his long sword high above his head. He swung from the shoulders.

Amongst the shadows, her hands locked against her breasts, Nadia couldn't stop trembling. She wanted to look away, but her eyes were determined to see. She felt the blood grow cold beneath her bones. The world went still and mute.

4

Nadia halted twice during the night. The second time, she came across a European-style bungalow, shaded by Chinese pines and bauhinias, close to a bay with three tall palm trees by the foreshore. She spent what seemed like an eternity curled up in a dry watercourse, using dry leaves and twigs for a blanket, her sacks as pillows. For a long while she would not sleep. Horror-struck by images of men screaming their last breath, of a lorry's headlights slicing though the night, of defenceless victims lying in the sand, she felt as though her soul was under attack. The visions shone in her head brightly, refusing to fade. Worn out and paranoiac, she forced her eyes shut and repeated over and over that by morning everything would be fine, that the nightmares would have gone, that what she'd witnessed would be forgotten.

She lay in the dark, rousing herself eight or nine times so that she could stare into the blackness of the bauhinia grove, believing she'd heard whispers. She thought of the old stories told to her as a child. The stories of Baba Yaga – the evil hag who lived in the forest, in a house made out of chicken legs and human skulls, the witch that feasted on children.

She tossed and turned until exhaustion overcame her, sleeping fitfully with her hands squeezed tight between her knees. And when she dreamed, it was of headless soldiers walking backwards into the sea and swords falling like moonbeams.

She awoke at first light coughing, opening her eyes to see

sprinklings of early sunshine sifting through the branches and falling across her body. Somewhere, in the thicket, a rooster was crowing. Face emerging from the leaves, she tasted the ocean air on her lips and sat up. Dawn kissed the surf and the entire seafront was covered with a powdery haze. There were no Japanese light cruisers or patrol boats in sight.

Instinctively, she began to scratch herself. The carnivorous mosquitoes had been at her for hours and the bumps along her skin had swelled to the size of tiny boiled eggs. She congratulated herself for managing to sleep through the bites and monstrous, high-pitched whining, but now her clothes were damp and her entire body felt alive with stings. Her face was itching, her eyelids were itching, even her ankles and toes were itching. Nadia straightened up and removed a worm from her hair and a stink bug from her shoe. The last time she'd spent a night outdoors was in Tver, the night her home was razed. She massaged the base of her back which was stiff and sore. Mud was caked inside her trousers. There was sand in her eyes. Dreaming about calamine lotion, she rubbed her hands over her face. All she wanted to do was to free the obi sash from her chest and scratch herself until she bled.

Nadia fished into a bag and unfurled the map of Hong Kong which was old and slippery to the touch from overuse. She looked for Stanley and found it nestled in the south of the island. With her pulse points suddenly alive and throbbing, she worked out that she couldn't be more than four miles from Iain and the internment camp. Was she in Repulse Bay, she wondered, or Deep Water Bay? Unable to determine her exact position, she decided to do a little reconnaissance instead.

She walked through the long grass, noting that she was in a valley. There were two squatter huts by the foothills, made from driftwood, corrugated iron and packed dry earth. Apart from a solitary woman washing clothes and cabbages in a hillside stream some distance away, there was not a soul about. She did not like being alone. She came to a white-washed building. The bullet-scarred bungalow was deserted and the doors frayed, its windows blown-out. A wooden notice was nailed to an exterior wall, worn by the weather and the caprices of the seasons. Some of the words were washed away by rain. Black ink paled to white. It read:

British officers and soldiers! Surrender now! Why are you waiting for the Chungking army to save you? They will never come. The Malay Peninsula and the Philippine Islands are already under Japanese rule. Your comrades in Kowloon are in Shamchun and enjoying a happy, serene Christmas. Think of your families. This is your last chance to surrender.

Japanese Army. December 20, 1941

She found a brass plaque, mottled, muddy and scarred. Her thumb wiped away some of the dirt. Hanging on salt-rusted screws from a brick partition, near illegible from grime, it told her that she was in the grounds of the Deep Water Bay Golf Course. She looked over her shoulder and identified the three tall palm trees that Costa had mentioned.

The grass was as high as her knee. Whetted by hunger, Nadia walked around the fairway, which was lush and green and overgrown. She found herself a strip of shade under the Chinese pines and settled down in a spot where the road curved and began its climb up the hill. Here she sat and gazed at the sunlight on the water. She was still exhausted.

To keep her strength up she took a few swigs from her canteen of water and ate a biscuit and one of the tangerines. She wanted so much to jump into the sea and rinse away the previous night's terror, but the risk of being seen was too great. Instead, she closed her eyes and angled her face towards the sun. Spots of red and orange formed behind her eyelids. The breeze on the surf, the scent of rain in the air, the thin-sounding birdsong in the trees, contrasted with the sensations of fear and hope mushrooming violently within her.

Nadia emerged from her daydream, snatched from her stupor by the shrill, rasping calls of a black-winged kite. She watched the bird wheel away over the ocean above Deep Water Bay, its small, precise head angled earthward, scrutinizing the wrinkled waters for any fish that might be embroidering the surface of the sea.

The sky had grown overcast. A few scattered rays of sunshine shot through the clouds like drizzles of honey, pouring golden rivers through the grey. Specks of rain wetted her cheek. She sat bolt upright the moment she heard a motorcar approaching in the distance. Scrambling, she hid in the thicket, lying flat on her tummy. The downpour started just as an ancient-looking Morris Cowley pulled up to the palm trees. The wooden-spoked wheels ground to a skid. When Nadia heard the deep, violent *Ooogah* of a car horn, she sprang to her feet and ran through the deluge, tripping amongst the weeds and the stones. A black figure was staring though the windscreen. The thundering rain closed in on her.

5

The interior of the 1932 Morris Cowley was humid and cramped, choking with the florid smells of dead animals. The seats were sticky, the windows ochre-yellow and grainy, and the door panel was covered in tattered chicken feathers. A white hen scratched about in the back seat, looking for grubs. The smell made Nadia want to gag.

She looked at Father Luke Chow for a few moments, studying his balding head and protruding ears. "Hello," she said.

He did not reply and without so much as a nod began turning the car around, reversing the automobile so that its hind wheels bumped along the grassy verge. His was an ominous silence. Perhaps he was hard of hearing, she thought. Or perhaps he was shy and needed coaxing. She tried again, this time a little louder. "My name is – "

"I know who you are!"

The Morris lurched forward. Father Luke sat at the wheel with his back arched like a costumed monkey on an acrobat's trapeze. A poorly preserved Eurasian of fifty, with the salty, rumpled skin of a land turtle, he sat with his shoulder muscles tensed, his jaw clamped hard and his elbows set at right angles. He was brusque and tragedy-hardened, inured by the human cataclysm that surrounded him. "Number one thing," he said, speaking to Nadia as though she was a subordinate. "Take off your clothes." His hands, elongated and knobbly, appeared from out of his black cassock. "And put on this," he ordered, reaching back between the two seats and meting out a long, dark *sottana* with large brown buttons running all the way down its front.

"What? You mean now?"

"Yes! Now! There is a roadblock ahead. But do not worry, I have blessed it!"

"What, the roadblock?"

"Of course not!" Both of his hands left the steering wheel. "Take the wax out of your ears." He coughed, wincing and swallowing as if someone had run a scimitar through his lungs. "The cassock! I have blessed the cassock. Put it on!"

Nadia strained away from him, turning her back to the priest. She removed her fisherman's tunic, which was still damp from the wet grass she'd slept on, and slipped the double-breasted cassock over her head, buttoning it diagonally from the crest of her right shoulder to the point of her left shoe.

"*Pazhalsta*, where are we going?"

"To the prayer house dedicated to St. Nicholas the miracle worker." His voice bounced in tandem with the bumps in the road. "It is on Wing Lok Street in the Sheung Wan district. It will be your home for the next few days."

"But why aren't we going to the Cathedral on Caine Road, or St. Stephen's?"

"The Cathedral was badly damaged by bombs and St. Stephens," he gave a bitter laugh, his tone more cordial, "is now being used by the Japanese to keep their horses."

"I'm sorry, I didn't know."

Father Luke hunched his shoulders, made a gesture with his hands. The Morris Cowley clattered down the tar road, weaving one side and then the other to avoid the shell-craters. Nadia felt as though her insides were being rearranged as they thudded from one pothole into another.

"You are a good driver," she said, with a little sarcasm, gripping her seat with both hands. His elbows, still jutting out like wings, seemed to relax a little with her words. When

Nadia's knuckles returned from white back to pink she said, "Is this your car?"

"Yes, it is my car, but I am fortunate to keep it. The Japanese turned thousands of automobiles and trams into scrap and sent it to the Burmese and Bataan fronts. Because of my disability I managed to gain dispensation from Oda Takeo of the Foreign Affairs Department." Nadia caught a glimpse of the twisted instep of his club foot. He shot a look back at her. "Does the cassock fit?"

The sleeves fell down over her thumb joints, but that apart it fitted her fine. Nadia nodded.

"Put on this too," he said, handing her a black *biretta*, a stiff, square hat worn by the clergy. The *biretta* was too big for her head and fell over her eyes. "And jut your chin out! It will make you look more masculine."

Nadia pushed her lips out.

"No, you are pouting! Do like this!" He stuck his chin out like a deranged tortoise.

She tried again, wrinkling her nose in the process.

"Better!" He nodded. On his ridged face there appeared a hint of a smile. "Now, this is very important. Did Costa give you the new identification papers?"

"He did," she said.

"Have them at the ready. The Japanese remain suspicious of priests, so do not converse with the checkpoint guards. I'll talk with them if necessary. When we stop, get out slowly, stand up straight and bow to the waist. I'll do the same. Understood?"

"Yes," she nodded.

The rain had stopped and the sun was shining through the clouds, reflecting off the wet ground like sheets of stainless steel. They passed the bombed-out police station and the Western Brigade Headquarters. Above the low hill range that was Mount Nicholson, a rainbow of equatorial colours hung in the sky. They came to the first roadblock on Stubbs Road, a little more than three hundred yards from the

Catholic cemetery in Happy Valley. Nadia saw about half a dozen Japanese infantrymen milling around a machine gun nest that had sandbags stacked three feet high, as if against a flood. The soldiers were dressed in their distinctive khaki tunics and combat caps, their pantaloons fastened with puttees round the calf. One of them was slapping a Chinese man across the face for wearing sunglasses – his failure to remove them was deemed disparaging to the Army's integrity.

Father Luke fixed his stare in front of him with the resigned expression of a person sitting in a doctor's packed waiting room. An officer, with red *passants* indicating his rank, approached. He had the complexion of a taro that had been left out too long in the sun. When Father Luke nodded, Nadia climbed out of the car and stepped over the running board. She bowed as instructed, stuck out her chin and kept her eyes on the ground. The *biretta* fell over her ears. The officer studied the papers in Father Luke's hand, grunted and let them though without even glancing at Nadia.

As the motorcar drove off, Father Luke crossed himself. The chicken in the backseat made a low clucking noise. Nadia said, "That was lucky. You'd think they saw white faces every day of the week."

"They do. There are hundreds of us 'third nationals' living in Hong Kong – Portuguese, Eurasians, Russians. Germans and Italianos too."

"What do they all do?"

"Some like to trade." Father Luke stopped at a road junction and allowed an Imperial Army mini-tank to pass. As he waited, he pulled at his fingers in a nervous fashion until the joints cracked. His left leg was twitching and pumping up and down restlessly. "Some of them, together with the wealthy Chinese families, have formed close ties with the Japanese. Many of them . . ." He made a face, cringed, " . . . are just a bunch of swindlers. They have no scruples and will do anything to make money. They mix crushed sand to rice, add bleached dirt to milk powder, then they sell it to the starving masses. With children dying every day, these are sins I cannot forgive. Pffsst! No matter what confession and prayer they make, I cannot forgive them." He found his kindly, cleric's voice now. "You know, I do what I can to help. I grow eggplants, kale, broccoli and give them where I can to the families living near the mission. Also there is a group of Communist guerillas who come once a month and distribute rice. They live in Sai Kung and sneak in by boat under the cover of night."

The Morris skirted past the sprawling Victorian pile that was the Wellington Barracks, currently the Imperial Navy's administrative offices. Minutes later, the car circumnavigated the Murray Parade Ground. Indian troops were doing drills up and down the square. Apart from one army lorry, the streets were deserted of cars. Father Luke followed Nadia's gaze.

"You see over there?" he said. "These are former POWs from the Rajput and Punjabi regiments, they have switched sides. Now you'll se a lot of Indian soldiers patrolling the streets because the Japanese troops are being called back to active service in the Pacific."

"You mean they are traitors?"

"They prefer to see themselves as soldiers of the new Indian National Army."

Nadia exhaled and suddenly felt very tired again. She peered out of the grimy window at the general stagnation that blighted the city. Over three years had passed since the surrender of Hong Kong to the Japanese. During that time, Nadia would have expected some order to have been put in place, yet despite some haphazard cleaning-up of the colony's main commercial sectors, the aftermath of the fighting remained all around her. In parts of Western district, where rows of three and four-storey castellated buildings resided, she saw shells had crushed into walls, torn off doors and blown off roofs. In Sheung Wan, smashed bed frames and rickshaws poked through hillocks of rubble, on Pottinger Street the stairs leading to an underground public convenience appeared split in half like the backbone of an old book, while in Queen's Square the Imperial Army, with their insatiable appetite for scrap, had dismantled the bronze statues and transported them to Japan to be melted down.

Libraries, schools, restaurants, shops – most of these places remained closed. There were no cars or buses on the roads, only rickshaws and tricycles for transport. From out of an alley people pushed carts stacked with a strange assortment of merchandise – sacks of rice, wicker tables, cloth shoes, bales of wood, bicycle tyres, fur gloves, canned milk – all goods for barter. Along Shek Tong Tsui, the little restaurant she went to years before, the one specializing in braised beef was no more, replaced now with brothels, and she saw that all the road names had been changed. Everywhere Nadia looked there were the great red orbs of the Emperor's standards, the *Hinomaru*, hanging from buildings and flagpoles; like a bride's bed linen; discs of blood against a backdrop of virginal white.

"*Pazhalsta*, what has happened to the street signs? They used to be in English?"

"The old signs are now firewood. These ones, you see? All replaced with Chinese and Japanese lettering. The Japanese want pan-Asia harmony and democracy. They say that the Westerners were armed thieves, that it is their duty to rescue Asians from colonialism. There has been a big anti-colonial reprisal from the Indian communities. The rich Chinese, too, have embraced the Japanese."

Further down the road, she saw a group of coolies rounding up chows and mongrels, beating those that struggled with long bamboo poles.

"The locals believe the ones with black tongues are the most tasty," said the curate, his eyes swimming with disapproval.

The dogs had ropes tied round their throats; when they

reared up on their hind legs they were struck across the muzzle. Nadia blenched and hid her gaze. The dogs' ugly, nightmarish howls pursued the car all the way through to Wing Lok Street, where Father Luke parked the Morris in a lock-up near the Sheung Wan post office. They tumbled out of the car. As soon as they reached the open street they were besieged by children, asking for food or money. Threadbare, soot-faced boys and girls, their filthy feet stippled with ringworm hoops, jogged at their sides, scrambling on top of one another. Father Luke handed each one a currant from his pocket.

Everywhere Nadia looked, she saw the hungry, frightened features of the impoverished, appearing as mutilated and broken as the architecture that surrounded them. Their scrawny faces, grimed in dirt, made her think of Iain, made her pray that he was faring better than these poor destitute creatures.

Ragged men, mouths agape, scavenged the streets for combustible material for fuel – anything from dried grass, to leaves. Aged women, their filthy hair full of nits, picked at the wens on their cheeks and spied from the windows of the low, desolate shophouses. Sparrows, twitching their heads, pirouetted on the shorn electric wires, doing a dance of death. The wires trembled lightly under their weight. Were they the same birds that were picking at the corpses on the beach, she wondered. Up until then Nadia thought that sparrows ate bugs and worms and crumbs from discarded bread, not the stomachs and lungs of human beings.

They approached a railed-in enclosure. The courtyard to the mission was marked by a tall metal fence. "Come," Father Luke beckoned, undoing the security gate and re-moving the padlock from a heavy door.

They scaled a flight of tapering steps, Father Luke hobbling on his twisted shoe. Fat beads of perspiration were rolling down his balding head. "Sorry," he panted, "my heart . . ." The walls were sliding with damp, crawling with flies. Once inside he lit a candle. Nadia blinked as her eyes adjusted to the curdled gloom. She saw a bed and little else. "My home," he said, drawing his leathery lips back into a smile. He started pulling at the joints of his fingers again, waiting for each to crack.

Through the small window Nadia saw black clouds, with denser black clouds to come. Despite it being early in the day, the room was so dark it felt below ground. "The electric is kaput," the priest said. "Take this." In the rumpled light he reached for a carbide lamp. The lamp contained twin chambers, an upper and lower. The upper chamber was filled with water, while the lower one contained a square of carbide rock. Father Luke twisted a tiny valve that allowed droplets of water to fall into the lower chamber, onto the carbide. Soon the resulting acetylene gas was burning and adding colour to the room. "There is a bedroom upstairs," he said, his turtle face glowing with unearthly yellow fluorescence. "You will find a cot. I suggest you get some rest."

Nadia lingered a moment. She took the lamp, and with two cotton sacks slung over her shoulders, she climbed the stairs.

Her room was stark; cluttered with cobwebs. One cot stood in the centre, its four bed legs immersed in bowls of water to keep ants, millipedes and cockroaches away. She dropped her sacks and shut the door. A rancid staleness filled the high, open interior. It was the smell of sunshine and rain and dust trapped for years until it turned sour with mildew.

The trapped air was stifling, like that of a boiler room. She set the lamp down on the floor and removed her cassock and *biretta*. Lying on the bed, she turned away from the glare of the lamp and stared out of the tiny window. She didn't want to rest, didn't want to sleep. She wanted to go to Iain. She wanted to go now. The yearning to see him was almost unbearable. Despite herself, she yawned and experienced the slight sensation of sinking. Something loosened inside her muscles. Her eyes wilted. Colours faded far away, disappeared. Within minutes she was asleep. A dead sleep.

Nadia woke up panicked. The sound of a gunshot, dull yet jarring, rolled down one street and into the next. Still caught in the folds of half-sleep, she couldn't remember where she was. She felt slow and heavy, as if she'd been plunged under water, yet the blood was pounding in her head. In the near darkness she saw herself reflected in the underlip of the window – something white and silky and smudged, like a ghost. How long had she been out? She wondered. What had woken her? The carbide lamp had almost extinguished itself.

Another gunshot jolted her, punctuating the room with fits of shapeless noise. Its forceful report echoed like a thunderclap. She heard raised voices outside, and from somewhere below, in the torrent-gloom of the street, came the sound of running. Then a woman screamed. Two buildings down, a dog began to bark clamorously. Nadia went to her window, saw nothing but the rain. The woman screamed again and again, after which came an ominous hush.

Nadia opened the tiny window, pressing her head against the metal bars to peer out. Rust and paint chippings fell from the frame and spilled onto her hair. She averted her face. Then there came a new sound. At first she did not recognize it: the beating of gongs and saucepans, followed by more shrieks, this time so high-pitched they resembled the squeals of baby mice being dropped into woks of sizzling hot oil. The gongs and pan-beating grew louder and louder. Nadia stepped away from the widow. She heard banging coming from below, a deep, menacing thudding, as if a crowd was trying to smash through a wall. Then a crashing noise from the stairwell beyond her door shook her to the core. She paled from the noise. She heard someone call from behind the partition; the voice catarrhal and strained. She looked beyond the small bed and saw the doorknob twisting. She stared at the blackness, the way a blind person stares at the world.

"Nadia!" she heard again. Father Luke was standing straight in front of her. "You must come immediately!" he said. "The Japanese Military Police are downstairs."

6

Nadia's expression was wide. Sleep marks from the hard pillow scarred her cheek. The screams had made her think back to her childhood, to Svetlina, the servant-girl, being assaulted. "That horrible screaming, that yelling, what was it?" she asked in a slumberous voice.

"Two men were trying to steal a pig," replied Father Luke whose gaze cut to the floor to contemplate his twisted left shoe, as though suddenly aware he was in a woman's bedroom. "The people of the neighbourhood came out and beat their gongs and pans, making a big noise to scare off the criminals."

"What about the gunshot?"

"Military police. They shot one of the men. A coolie. He climbed over the fence and ran into our building." Father Luke began smirking, then laughing, which caused him to start coughing. "The bullet struck him in an unfortunate place, in his backside."

"And the *Kempeitai* are downstairs?"

"Three Military Policemen. Two officers. They want to know why he ran in here. They want to talk to everybody in the building. They are doing room-to-room search. You must come now!"

"Yes, of course" she said. "Wh-what time is it?"

"Afternoon, it is almost one o'clock. You were asleep for a long time. You really must come now!" He limped away down the staircase.

Moments later, having pulled the cassock over her head, Nadia reached into her bag and brought out one of the tangerines. It was soft, ripening quickly in the humidity. She stuffed it into the front of her trousers, under her cassock. She also pulled out a roll of money and stuffed it into her shoe before taking the stairs down.

In Father Luke's apartment the mood was tense. Nadia was confronted by a Japanese man seated at a desk, filling out a log with a Chinese brush rather than pen and ink. He was young, about twenty, and was wearing the standard M1938 field uniform. The other two men were older, dressed in cavalry uniform, sporting high leather boots and black chevrons on their sleeves. All three of them were soaked from the rain. The officers stood by the window; streaks of condensation ran down the glass. Nadia could tell they were both Junior NCOs as they carried *shinai* (bamboo Kendo swords) rather than the prestigious Samurai swords worn by their superiors. By their boots, she saw a Chinese coolie sitting on a low stool, like a child-sized seat, his head bowed. A small pool of blood gathered on the timber floor by the washstand. Stripped to his underwear, his clothes had been torn into swathes and wrapped tight around his left hip.

One of the officers began asking Father Luke a string of questions in Japanese. Father Luke cocked his eyebrows and spread his hands, suggesting bewilderment. The officer made a face, puckering his lips into a sphincter. Then, fixing Nadia a suspicious, querulous look, he marched up to her and said something incomprehensible. Nadia shook her head. He looked her up and down. "You," he said, falling into pidgin English. "You boy or geuul." His voice knelled like the jangling of bells.

"I am a boy," she said confidently.

The man puckered his lips again into the shape of a cat's arse-hole. "Boy?" he repeated. The air went still. He leant forward as if to share something in confidence. His hand reached out and grabbed her between the legs. She gave a stifled yelp. A moment later Nadia felt tangerine juice spill onto her inner thigh, trickling down to her knee.

"Boy," she said firmly, defiantly.

"*Ha, ha! Kono yaro*," he said in a gruff voice, flashing a gnarl of teeth. A minute later the *Kempeitai* frogmarched the coolie down the steps and out of the building.

Nadia and Father Luke listened to the sounds of their boots receding, for the front gate to clang shut.

"For stealing a pig, they will cut his head off," he said. "The *Kempeitai* are animals." Nadia remembered the beheadings she'd witnessed on the beach. "But how did you . . . the bump . . . how did you make . . . like a man?" the priest asked, scratching his bald scalp.

"It's a simple trick." She removed the tangerine and held it, noting the sureness of her own hand, surprised by its steadiness. With the Japanese officer staring her down, she had half expected her hand to be trembling, yet it wasn't at all. She was bolder than she realized. "I heard what happened in Nanking," she said, looking up, "with the thousands who were raped and the competitions that were held to see how many babies could be bayoneted in one day. I'm not taking any chances."

"You are resourceful."

Nadia shrugged. "What do we do now?"

"Now? Now we clean up the blood on the floor. There is a mop behind the door. Afterwards, we do rosary and share some food, then we go to Queen's Pier. The *Owa Maru* docked today right on schedule. We will pick up the Red Cross relief supplies and deliver them to camp."

"And I'll get to see Iain?"

"Yes, you will see your husband."

The *Owa Maru* was painted mint-lozenge green and had white Red Cross markings painted on its sides and funnels. Rusting, heavily veined, its belly crusted with barnacles, it was an 8000 tonne cargo ship that picked up relief parcels from the stockpile in Vladivostok, distributing them to camps from as far afield as Burma, Formosa and Japan.

Nadia and Father Luke stood by the docks, amongst the yammer of strained voices and the rickshaws lined up on the quay. Vendors of dried this-and-thats spread out their wares on soiled doilies. Nadia saw the lizards spreadeagled on sticks, the seahorses, the black mushrooms and salted bug-eyed squids. A middle-aged man unrolled a rattan mat onto which he scattered what looked like all that he had left in the world – an ancient turnip, a graveyard banana, a church candle and three sets of leering false teeth. *"Sun seen lor bak!"* shouted the middle-aged vendor. *"Ho sun seen!"*

Loiterers and skulkers joined them, together with a few fidgety cats, descending like famished seabirds, crowding around, filling the air with sour, conflicting smells. Women lined the landing stages, squatting on their haunches, shelling shrimps. Dry old men, their skin salted from the harbour breeze, watched the shirtless, cropped-haired labourers come off the small barges, lifting crates of milk powder and boxes full of tinned goods on their shoulders. They loaded the merchandise into the back of relief trucks, under the watchful gaze of the stevedores. Nadia saw other items being removed from the ship – great blocks of Manchurian ice, packed in saw dust, which were immediately transported to the cold storage depot on Ice House Street, together with aircraft parts, propellers, all kinds of munitions which were transferred separately onto military lorries.

"I thought it was a Red Cross ship," she said. "Are they allowed to transport weapons?"

"Pah! They cheat. Because of an agreement signed between the Japanese and American governments these ships are allowed safe passage. Of course, the Japanese load the ships with everything from guns to railway ties to crude oil. Any other ship would get torpedoed by submarines." He paused to hack his lungs out. "But the Japanese politicians have a history of cheating. They even cheat their own people, hiding the truth from them. They say they are winning every battle, which is plainly not true. What happened at Midway?" He started making lightning strikes with his hands. "Changsha? Guadalcanal? What about the American air raids we see here every other day? They do not tell their people at home about the losses, only the victories.

"And now, in Hong Kong, they come as an invading army, but tell the Chinese they are not colonialists, not an occupying force, but a liberating force; liberating the Chinese from Western oppression. Offering them pan-Asian harmony and democracy. It is all lies!

"Do you know that in Tokyo and Osaka, they say there is no food shortage? Yet they cannot feed their people. There is rice rationing, sake rationing, no eggs, no vegetables. Even Tokyo Zoo is affected. They cannot feed the elephants, the lions, the bears, so they have poisoned them." He washed his hands in the air. "All the animals dead. No food shortage? – Pah!"

In the middle distance, near the Kowloon wharves, fishermen slapped the water with their oars, driving fish into their nets, while their children, dressed in dark rags, waved and hollered at passing boats. Nadia saw a Japanese ship being towed back to port, its hull strafed with bullets, part of its main deck shelled with American bombs.

Behind Nadia, looking out from the Victoria seafront, the untidy roads shimmered with monsoon heat; spirals of yellow leaves dragged about by the gentle wind, leaving trawl marks along the muddied streets. Here, the fossilized Italianate exteriors of the Court House, the Post Office, the trading houses, long-ago ransacked, were now bulging with squatters and the indigent. Elsewhere, across the tramlines, buildings stood abandoned, their inlaid tiles torn up, baize-covered tables smashed, doorknobs and fixtures and other metal fittings ripped out. Even the rugged mountain behind, casting its huge afternoon shadow, was like a black cowl looming against the dusk.

It made Nadia think of the street procession she'd seen earlier, of a family, clad in white robes for grief, their heads hooded like Klu Klux Klansmen, walking behind a casket carriage being pulled by a man with hawsers. The air had been thick with incense to mask the dead man's rancid-rot smell. Whenever she saw a funeral cortege these days, she thought of Iain. She couldn't say why she thought this, but she did, and the imagery seared her soul; it turned her mind into a terrifying, claustrophobic room.

Not for the first time that day she felt overrun, bereft even, as if she was pitching helplessly into the unknown. More and more often now she experienced feelings of self-doubt. Was it because she stood on the edge of darkness, over the abyss, with her destiny shifting quickly beneath her feet? Was it because her gamble in coming here might get herself killed, or worse, her husband killed? She had lain awake every night for a month, thinking about how she was going to get to Hong Kong, how she was going to help Iain. It took weeks of planning. Now she was here, in this crestfallen land, she felt like a little girl bathing at the beach who had drifted out too far with the current and was now struggling to swim back to shore; it was a recurring daydream for her. One that refused to go away.

"Are you all right, senhora?"

Nadia steadied herself and glanced into the priest's eyes. On first meeting, he had been surly and bullying; now his attitude seemed to have moderated; his tone more benign. "Yes, of course," she said. "I'm fine." She was tempted to ask him how many people had died in the camps, but then quickly changed her mind. She wasn't going to let this feeling, nor the acid burn in her stomach, defeat her, she decided. She would not let it fester. She took a deep breath and looked up into the sky, felt her heart grow quiet. The cupreous sun was out again. Its fierce rays began to redden the flesh on Father Luke's bare scalp. "Do you believe in fate, Father?"

"As a man of the church, I trust in God's will."

"I believe in fate. Not in so much that our lives are entirely

318

preordained but that a map has been drawn for us to follow. How we read the map and what we decide when we come to a crossroad is up to us."

"You are, perhaps, thinking about your husband? Whether you are doing the right thing by coming here?"

"Yes."

"Are you a devout person?"

"I was brought up following the orthodox faith."

"What about the ways of the Catholic Church?"

"I save my soul by eating fish on Fridays, if that's what you mean?"

Father Luke's mouth curled into a smile. "The Lord will look after you, senhora. You have courage. You are brave."

"Me? Brave? I don't think so. Desperate maybe, terrified certainly, but not brave. Anyway I read that courage is the other half of fear. Without one you don't have the other."

"Trust that voice inside your head. You must follow your conscience, so long as your heart is selfless."

"I sometimes think I'm the complete opposite of selflessness. I couldn't live another day without seeing Iain. I've left my family behind to fend for themselves so that I can help the man I love – isn't that an act of selfishness? My greatest terror is that I will never see him again, that I cannot live without him. The truth is, I couldn't bear waiting, waiting for that one letter to arrive from a stranger saying, 'I regret to inform you that your husband . . .'

"I often fantasize about him coming home, carrying me up the flight of steps, filling the house with laughter and flowers. It seems that when I attach myself to someone I hold on for dear life."

Father Luke nodded and glanced up to the heavens. Crossing himself, he mentioned something about the book of Saint Mark, but Nadia wasn't listening. Her troubled mind was elsewhere. She was trying to work out what Iain would say when he saw her. Would she look different to him? Would she seem changed? How different was she now from the woman he'd last seen over three years before? And what about him, had the horrors of camp transformed him?

A few minutes later Father Luke tapped her on the shoulder. "Ration trucks are full," he said. "Time we go to your husband. But I must warn you, senhora, you may not like what you find."

7

The malodorous room was small and square, hidden behind the kitchen quarters of Block C, with a solitary window that looked onto the communal shithouse. The walls, once a light shade of cream, had darkened with mould, and parts of the ceiling were falling in from where the rain had poured through. Over the window, Stepney threw a scratchy cotton blanket to shield himself and his friends from prying eyes. "All set," he said. Mr. Yorkie, perched on his shoulder, bobbed his head in agreement.

Iain hunkered over the schoolmaster's chalk, using Stepney's eyeglasses as a surrogate magnifying lens. He looked up and fixed his gaze on the naked, spluttering bulb that dangled from the ceiling. It buzzed like a Zero with a shot engine.

"I can't see what I'm doing," he said.

Stepney hobbled over on his gammy legs and handed Friendly a long line of metal pipe. Friendly extended his arms to the ceiling and sheathed the light bulb in the piping. Almost immediately, Iain's hands were submerged in luminescence.

"Better?" asked Friendly, angling the beam over his shoulder.

"Better."

Using the edge of a specially-serrated razor blade, Iain peered through Stepney's eyeglasses and sliced into the schoolmaster's chalk, fashioning little white discs that resembled miniature ice hockey pucks. Next, with the aid of a metal ruler, he scored a line right across the centre of the pill, and carved the legend *M&B 693* above it.

As he laboured, he breathed in deeply, trying to clear his mind of the effulgent heat in the room, the tickles of perspiration dripping down his neck, the raw light that now stung his eyes. He had to press down hard with his thumb and forefinger, but not so hard that the chalk would split and crumble. Sweat dripped from his brow.

Twenty minutes later Iain had made a total of thirteen pills, despite his trembling hands. He rubbed the knuckle of his right thumb, the joints were tingling.

"What's the matter?" Stepney asked.

"My fingers are cramping up. Can you take over?"

"I don't think my hands are steady enough."

They were making tablets that were to be peddled to the Japanese as sulphapyridine, a medication produced by May & Baker Ltd in London as an antidote for the venereal disorders the soldiers caught from their caravans of *jugun ianfu*, the comfort women in their travelling brothels.

There had been no discussion of the American victory over the Japanese in the Bismark Sea, nor of the talk of a *Fuso* class battleship, armed with twin turret guns, patrolling the Hong Kong harbour, not even of the rumour that U.S. cipher breakers had cracked Admiral Yamamoto's five-digit number code. Instead, they worked in complete silence, with Iain's eyes, like his knife, cutting through the chalk.

A bead of perspiration flicked off his forehead and dropped onto the chalk. "Shit!" said Iain.

Iain pushed his hands away in frustration and the metal ruler clattered to the floor. He let out a staggered breath and kneaded the back of his neck. His face felt puffy and tense; there was a thick, gritty sensation in his mouth. He could feel it creeping up on him, brewing behind his eyelids. A migraine was coming. He scraped his chair back and plunged his arms between his legs, hunching his shoulders. He suddenly felt hopelessly exhausted. He pressed the pads of his hands to his temples and felt the muscles of his jaw tighten. Five days had passed since his release from the cooler; his strength was regenerating and his wounds heal-ing, albeit slowly. Seconds later the bell for afternoon roll-call sounded.

The internees fell in for roll-call in the dusty square. They formed a scraggly, irregular line, one misshapen body after the other, all elbows and knees. Iain stood in the front row, in a heat haze of dust, the afternoon sun stinging his eyes. His head was aching.

'*Hai!*' shouted one of the sentries. Everyone bowed deeply.

"The new camp commandant," somebody behind him whispered.

Out of curiosity, Iain rose on tiptoes and craned his neck for a better look. He saw Sergeant-Major Hamuri edge forward and salute. The camp commandant strutted along the line of internees, shoulders hunched. Iain watched the man approach. Since being interned he had developed a survivor's instinct for sensing danger. And something about the new Japanese officer told him that this man was dangerous.

Under the commandant's cap, Iain could make out a beak for a nose, skin as dark as loam soil. There was a dim glimpse of recognition. The ambiguous features seemed horrifically recognizable. He stopped close to where Iain was standing and peered about.

'I introduce your new superintendent," announced Ha-muri. "Colonel Takashi."

The name Takashi sounded familiar to Iain, but he couldn't quite work out why. Then suddenly he remem-bered and his face went white. It was as though he had woken next to a cobra.

The camp commandant stood on an upturned soapbox so that he could look down on everyone. He had humped shoulders, a beak nose and tapering eyebrows that curved like half-moons.

"Today," said Takashi, "being my first day, I wish to call on one of you to come forward. Internee number 6177."

Sergeant-Major Hamuri waved his hand, indicating Iain should step out and present himself.

Iain emerged from the line. He approached Takashi with caution, feeling as though his mouth was caked with dirt. He felt isolated. Colours were too sharp, sounds seemed strangled. His head ached more than ever.

"*Konichiwa*, Mr. Suzzerland." Takashi smiled blackly.

Iain did not respond. He bowed again.

"I remember you very well from our time in Macao," the commandant said with ominous menace. The vulture eyes from years before glared at him, measuring him. He saw that Takashi carried a leather crop in his hand which he raised with intent. This is it, thought, Iain, it's going to be a public flogging.

Iain braced himself, expecting a blow. Instead, Takashi clapped his hand on Iain's back.

"All of you listen," the commandant said, speaking to the crowd. "I want to formerly congratulate Iain Suzzerland for his work here. You should learn from zis man. He has proved that we can work side by side and come togezzer. He has supplied us wiss much information regarding the organization calling itself BAAG and on uzzer vital matters. His knowledge of possible escape routes into China has also been most enlightening. And please do not view his coop-eration as a betrayal to you, but see it more as a building of bridges between our two sides. Because of Mr. Suzzerland's collaboration, I will be rewarding you all wiss an extra portion of fish for tomorrow's meal." Takashi gave a sharp self-congratulatory sneer. "Dis is all."

The crowd, silent up to now, grew restless, breaking into disorderly mutterings – a muffled vitriolic hum. An Aus-tralian woman in the back of the roll call line, known only to Iain as Mrs. P., shouted out. "Sutherland," she howled. "You're a bloody traitor!"

"Shut your mouth, woman!" Friendly yelled, shouting her down.

Takashi made a face at the woman and wagged his finger like a pantomime baddie. After several seconds he stepped off the soapbox and, leaning in close, said to Iain in a shallow voice, "I am going to enjoy playing with you, Mr. Suzzerland. It will be like the cat and the mouse, no?" Then he squeezed Iain's arm and walked off towards the officer's mess as Iain was shunted back into line.

Later that afternoon, Iain was curled up in bed, knees drawn up like a folded child. The chalk dust swirled across the floor, over mice droppings, dancing like Gobi sand over desert dunes. Iain heard the spontaneous laughter of children coming from an adjoining room. There was also a faint sound of thumping. The shock of hearing giggles muddied his dream and shrank it, making it unseeable. The images of Manchurian snowstorms faded, whitening out into nothingness, as though a theatre curtain had come down, ending proceedings. Iain rose from the bed to see what was going on. He found Friendly making animal shadows on the wall using a hand torch. He was surrounded by a dozen skinny little boys and girls from the Married Quarters.

"How's the head?" asked Friendly, looking up from his bunny rabbit ears.

"Much better, thanks. Sleep did some good. Bloody ravenous though."

"Aren't we all? Listen, Sutherland, I just want you to know that none of us believe a word Takashi said out there. We know what kind of game he's trying to play. He wants us to turn on you. He obviously doesn't know us very well. And don't worry about Mrs. P making trouble. We've given her a stern talking-to."

"Thanks, I appreciate it."

Iain went to sit down on a bench. From an open window in B Block, he heard the thumping noise start up once more; a measured sound of dough being kneaded – the last of the flour before the ration supply ran out. He felt the hunger tighten round his stomach like a wire. His mouth wetted with the prospect of hot, baking bread. He tried to imagine the cushiony, spongy parcel of flour and yeast being gathered in someone's hands, being pulled apart, then flattened, and shaped. Would there be an egg to glaze it and give it that wonderful golden colour, he wondered? Just as his senses started to fantasize about bannocks and baps, buns and brioches, farmhouse loaves, sourdough, johnnycakes, crumpets with cream, slabs of thick butter, lashings of jam, Stepney came rushing into the room. He was panting and his shirt was sopping wet with perspiration. Mr. Yorkie, balanced on his shirt collar, was busy cleaning his whiskers.

"What is it?" said Iain. The children had stopped their giggling. Friendly got to his feet.

The Yorkshireman's spectacles were steaming up. "Red Cross parcels," he gasped for a fresh intake of breath, swallowing mouthfuls of air, "Father Luke's arrived with some parcels and he's got someone with'im."

"Who?"

"There's a woman, dressed as a priest. She made contact with one of the women in the Dutch Block, passed her this cigarette. Said it was urgent she find you." He removed his glasses to wipe his face.

"Show it to me."

Iain took the cigarette. He unraveled it, spilling tobacco like sparks. There was a message inside written in a small girly scrawl. Come now. Have plan. N. Iain read it through twice. The words made no sense to him. Who on earth was N? Why would BAAG send a girl and why had they not mentioned it in their last communiqué? Confused, he shredded the sliver of paper in his hands and headed out the door.

Under the long shadows of a setting sun, Iain and Stepney made their way from B Block, over a scrap of scrubland, past the row of bullet-scarred quarters that once housed St. Stephen's School, towards the godowns that overlooked the bay. Friendly had sprinted on ahead. It was here, at the base of the hillside that the ration lorry usually parked. Breathlessly, he wondered aloud why BAAG had sent a Chinese woman. Surely she was more vulnerable, more of a target for the Kempeitai.

They crossed the narrow strip of road, kicking up clouds of yellow dust that spattered their ankles like sun-dazzled gnats. In the distance a pair of Sikh guards completed a drill and marched behind some trees, disappearing from view; a little further on Iain spotted the green ration lorry.

He began to say something to Stepney when, all of a sudden, he felt his feet slide away from under him and his knees strike the dirt track. His eyes stared across the path as a wave of nausea washed over him. Gripped by a stomach-turning lightheadedness, Iain looked dumbly at the ground.

"Sutherland!" Stepney cried. It was only then that he realized he was on all fours and the muscles and tendons in his arms were quivering uncontrollably. "It's all right," whispered Iain, collecting himself, shaking his head. It was the days without proper food, he said, the migraines, the *Kempeitai* questioning, the injuries to his face; they had all taken their toll on him. Stifling the trembling and nausea, he lifted his head.

Stepney pointed to a nearby rock. "You ought to sit down."

"I don't want to sit down."

"What you need is a nice mug of beef tea," said Stepney. "D'you fancy that?"

Iain nodded. "I'm better now," he said.

"Well, then, let's see if we can grab a cube or two from the rations truck, ay?"

They stumbled along a few yards, their eyes on the horizon – the ocean was turning brilliantly pink with the setting sun, its waves cresting white. Iain's stride shortened to allow for Stepney's gammy legs.

"Is he drunk?"

Iain looked round to see the bearded sugar trader, Hoarde, leering at him. He had a tomcat in one arm and a tin of Peacock's peaches tucked under the other.

Hoarde's lips thinned into a thing of poison. "Like a pair of Glaswegian drunkards out on a Saturday night piss-up."

"He's not had proper food for days," said Stepney. Mr. Yorkie scrambled off his shoulder and hid in his shirt pocket.

"I don't need defending," Iain's eyes cut from Stepney to Hoarde.

"What're you going to do with the cat?" asked the Yorkshireman.

"I intend to have it for breakfast tomorrow. Pretty little thing, don't you think?"

"Better bloodline than its owner, that's for sure," Iain said.

"I'm worried about you, Sutherland. How're you going to manage your escape if you can't even stand up straight?"

"What makes you think I'm planning an escape?"

"Don't have to be a genius to know what you're up to. I'd watch your back, Sutherland. You've made a number of enemies in camp, especially, now that you've been exposed as a collaborator."

"We both know who the real collaborator is. Now bugger off or I'll – "

"Or you'll what?" Hoarde rubbed his beard and bared his teeth, delivered a dry laugh. He turned up the hill, swinging the can of peaches in his left hand like a trophy. "Oh," he called out. "When you see Takashi, tell him I said, hello. And ask him to send me some of that carnation milk he's got in his room to go with my peaches. See you by the India hut. *Sayanara!*"

"Nasty, treacherous little prick," said Stepney. "There's enuff moock between those ears to grow potatoes."

They shuffled their way down the slope to where a military relief truck was parked. There were about fifty people thronged around it, casting long, sharp shadows. Barebacked men were shifting crate after crate of condensed milk, tins upon tins of tapioca and bully beef. Friendly appeared from out of the shadows cast by the trees and stood outside the godown doors, waiting for them. Just behind him, Iain noticed about a dozen bamboo clotheslines strung with clothes and bed sheets, and a long line of galvanized tin pails where the washing was done.

It was when the sun glinted off the pails that he saw her through the crowd, standing at the far end of the laundry ropes, wearing a priest's gown and biretta, silhouetted against the backdrop of swaying grey-white linen. Bewildered, at first he refused to believe his eyes. Had he taken leave of his senses? Was he delirious? He blinked hard to erase the hallucination – but the more he blinked the clearer his vision became, etching out her form, her face, with increasing clarity. A cry of joy tumbled from his mouth.

His nausea gone, Iain threw himself into a run, made his legs move faster than they'd moved in months. A smile stretched the sides of her face; he saw her eyebrows rising in the middle; a look of happiness, relief, alleviation. With a lump in his chest, he saw her lips mouth his name; he longed for them, longed to hold the smooth softness of her flesh against his. He wanted to take her face in his hands, wrap his arms over her, kiss her, shout her name. The need to embrace her was overwhelming. He shortened his stride, began scraping his fingers through his hair, smoothing the front of his shorts. But then, six or seven steps from where she stood, he stopped abruptly. The flow of euphoria suddenly ceased. A shadow passed over him. A single tear ran down his face, which he quickly wiped away.

He realized he couldn't embrace her – the guards would be watching. He also realized she was in great danger. "How did you get here?" he asked. Paralysed by the thousands of conflicting questions in his head, he searched her face for answers. "What are you doing here?" he repeated. His anger was growing. "Nadia, for God's sake . . ."

He saw the lines grow around her mouth and her nose pinch with the injustice of his tone.

Her mouth went dry. "What do you think I'm doing here? I've come to see you," she said, keeping her voice low.

A mark of anger stained his cheeks. Sweat began to soak his neck, his back. He stormed off, found there was no place to go and came straight back. "Come to *see* me? Have you any idea what the hell you've gotten yourself into – "

"I'm here to help you. I've brought you some provisions – cigarettes and all sorts of things in my bag," said Nadia.

"No. You've got to get out of here. Now," he said, looking around.

Her voice climbed in protest. "Listen to me – "

"Turn around and leave."

"I said, listen to me! Will you just listen to me! We've been planning this for weeks," she said. "I'm going to get you out of here whether you like it or not. I don't know where this war is heading, I don't know which sides will win and lose, but I do know that I can't let you live like this. You're all I've got, Iain. I can't lose you. I'll be damned if I let you rot away in here!"

"Costa's to blame for this, isn't he? Did he put you up to this?"

"Nobody's to *blame*, Iain. I volunteered for this. It was my decision to come. And when we heard about Takashi, we knew we had to get you out."

Across the piece of ground, he heard his name being called. It was Friendly's voice; a call of warning. His eyes focused on the tall figure of a Sikh guard strutting towards them, truncheon in hand. He grew scared, not for himself, but for Nadia. He felt his shoulders stiffen, his insides boil and simmer with a new emotion now; one of dread. Panic gripped his throat, like jungle creepers tightening. Swamped by an instinctive, primitive urge to defend her, he tried to pull Nadia aside, shield her with his body, to push her into the shadows.

"You two!" the Sikh shouted. "What are the pair of you doing?"

"Leave this to me," said Nadia, muscling Iain to one side.

Iain's face drew taut. "Don't Nadia . . . they might . . ."

"What – take me in for questioning? I'll be a *yebanat vonuchii* if I let that stop me."

She took out her papers and showed them to the Punjabi. His skin was as dark as tea leaves.

He gave the documents a cursory glance. "I am watching the pair of you nattering." There was fire in his voice. "What is it you are plotting?"

"We were plotting nothing," said Nadia. "This man was asking whether we had any liniment for his face."

"Lini-munt?"

"Do you have any De Witt's Golden liniment in the ration store? Or any Chinese *Deet Da Jow*?"

"I do not understand?"

"Look at this man's face, look at his wounds. The bruises look like burnt toast. Shouldn't he be in the infirmary?"

"This is not my area of responsibility."

"Well, it is the Red Cross's responsibility to ensure that internees are treated humanely and it is the Catholic Church's responsibility to ensure that there is no mistreatment in this camp."

He was waggling his head. "I did not beat this fellow."

"Nobody said that you did. Now if you don't mind, please let us be." And here she motioned to Iain. "Kindly take a seat on that tin bucket and I'll see what medicines we have in the truck."

The Sikh grunted and went off in a huff, no longer swinging his truncheon.

Outside the double gates of the camp, by a screen of flowering blue hydrangea, Nadia told the driver to stop the lorry. She told him that she had to piss. Lifting the hem of her cassock she scuttled past the gendarme post, along the fence, towards the cliffs that commanded a view of Stanley Bay.

She took a deep breath, steadied herself, arguing that

Iain's belligerence was merely to protect her. Not even a smile or a how are you! *Svolotch! Sooksin!* She was glad to have left the camp when she did. She mulled this over for a few seconds then, quite suddenly and unexpectedly, her anger left her. She felt an unforeseen levity settle on her. And the more she wanted to suppress it, the worse it got. Tickled, her eyes melted and she almost began to giggle. Wondering where this lightheartedness sprang from – she quickly realized it was the result of finding Iain alive. Oh, but the expression on his face! Priceless! Like a pimple wanting to be squeezed – he looked like he was going to burst! His mouth, his nose, his ears turned tomato red, as if he'd sat on a thistle! The stupid ass! Anger jettisoned, she began smiling to herself with genuine pleasure. She had to bite her tongue to stop herself from laughing out loud, gloving it as best she could in her throat.

Glancing over her shoulder, Nadia noticed that the two Formosan guards at the gate were asking Father Luke about her – where was the boy priest going, what was he doing? He informed them that a man of God was not permitted to relieve himself in front of ordinary mortals.

Within a minute she'd passed the watchtower and reached the crag of shelly rock bordering the wired enclosure. With her back to the distant guard post, pretending to piss like a man, she studied the terrain in the dwindling light. She saw a long, snaking line of Burma reed; a thin, yellowing track on the outer seafront side of the fence; followed by a steep drop of 100 feet, at the bottom of which was a swirling suckhole of tidewater which caused the seas to erupt and crash against the rocks.

The skin of her cheeks tightened as she imagined herself negotiating the narrow trail in pitch-blackness. 'Opposite the flame tree,' Iain had said, his face as tight as she'd ever seen it, 'that's where I'll meet you. At 4 a.m. opposite the tall flame tree on the Stanley Bay side of the camp. And for goodness sake, be careful.'

She strained her eyes – it was only then that it occurred to her that she had no idea what a flame tree looked like. She looked down the twin lines of wire and crisscrossed metal, plucked at her sweaty collar. She saw two parallel railings running down the channel with curls of barbed wire in between. About a hundred yards away, the edge of a red-hued branch flopped against the bend in the fence. She made a mental note, tried to calculate the distances between the places offering visual cover, then she turned and made her way back to the waiting lorry.

8

Creepers and vines hung like giant cobwebs from the trees. Hidden like a trapdoor spider, Nadia counted off the hours, the minutes. Consulting the luminous hands of her wristwatch, she held off until 3.a.m., waiting for the whispers and isolated conversations to subside. Then, convinced that the Formosan sentries had dropped off to sleep, she inched forward.

Smoke from the guards' canteen drifted over the moonlight. The smell of boiled rice and dried fish hung in the air. A hot, stuttering breeze threaded through the stodgy trees, soundlessly. Leaves yielded. Bamboo thickets shuddered. The fogged air was stifling.

Couched in an opaque mist which folded itself over her, Nadia kept herself small and tight. She had to be alert and very careful. Avoiding the dry twigs and branches that laced the boundary floor, she edged into the damp darkness using quick elastic steps, holding on to the shadows. As she moved, she winced; the heavy cloth bags thumped lightly against her ribs; the shoulder straps were biting into her shoulder blades. The weight of the bags made her perspire and the salt sweat trickled into her eyes. She wiped it away – in the darkness she could see perhaps five yards ahead, no more. A leaf crackled as she placed her foot down. She froze, waited, waited some more. Her eyes raked the smothered landscape.

She became so preoccupied in trying to cushion the sound of her footfalls that she almost lost sight of the watchtower high above her, its brass and thick glass glinting weakly in the spotlight's shadow. Sitting alone, she saw the lookout engrossed in a book of sorts, his head bowed, preoccupied. A minute later, when she looked back, he was gone, swallowed by the mist and crushed shadows.

Heart trembling like a candleflame, she counted to ten and held her breath, then proceeded along the fence-line as quick as she dared. Not even a few moments had passed when she paused in mid-step, leg and knee suspended in the air, to listen to the surrounding night noise, the mulch of maple fronds fumbling underfoot, the scuffling of squirrels in the conifers. It took her about forty minutes to negotiate the hundred odd yards to the meeting point. By the time she got to the tree with the red branches and fringe-fingered leaves, she was exhausted and quivering from adrenaline. The waves came smashing into the rocks below.

She fingered the lucky glass charm around her neck. The ground was coated with fern pins, which pricked her arms and elbows, forming crisscross cross-hatch patterns on her flesh. *Chock, chock, chock,* went the song of the tree frogs. She lay behind a line of tall grass, a long drop of a hundred-feet lay behind her, her ears intercepting the voices of the patrolling guards, wise to the rustle of night animals, the *Ooo-oo-ooo* call of the horned owl, the sultry fizz of the whispered wind lifting off the trees, the crashing waters below. She concentrated on separating these sounds, compartmentalizing them, so that she might recognize the sounds of danger when they came.

She pressed her face against the grass; the heat wrapping her up like a fist. Surrounded by the smells of seawrack and damp earth, the sweat trickled down her back, down her neck. She listened to the sound of the night crickets and remembered that Uncle Yugevny had once taught her how to measure the air temperature by counting the chirrs. 'Count the number of cricket chirrs in 15 seconds then add 39,' he'd said. Within a minute she'd worked out that it was 86 degrees F.

Time passed slowly. A procession of dark-bodied ants shuffled past her nose, carrying a wasp in segments. She watched the black cortege make its way into a hole like shiny-hatted undertakers. Again, her skin crawled as her thoughts turned to death.

She peered into the night, lifting her eyes, not her head. Her mind waited, extracting the fugitive sounds from the natural. *Chock, chock, chock*, went the song of the tree frogs. Weren't there wild dogs here, she wondered? Silent hunters? Tigers even? A bat scraped overhead, filling the night with excited squeaks, its wrinkly wings thrumming the air. A branch tilted and yielded a clump of heavy, dry plumage. And then, suddenly some boots appeared before her. Two men, Formosans, were talking into the electric silence. They approached the wire and stopped. She could not tell whether they had seen her. Separated by twin fences, three feet apart, Nadia smelled their sweet tobacco burning, saw the red tips of their cigarettes, the sockets of their eyes, their gargoyle silhouettes.

The cigarettes were handed from black hand to black hand.

The guards cleared the phlegm from their throats and hawked, the sound of bones rattling in a sack.

"*Hoi!*" one of them shouted. He seemed to be staring straight at Nadia. She stiffened. Fear, dark and metastasized, came rushing down at her; it spread through her like ganglion roots. It ran up the bones of her back.

The guard picked up a stone and threw it so that the stone went crashing into the thicket to her left. There was a *thrump* of noise. A vast stretch of silence followed. As Nadia waited, muscles cocked, a disturbed lizard raced over her legs. Its claws caught on the underside of her knees, sharp tail snaking, shooting through the grass. Shrivelling, she remained death-like. Her crisscrossed flesh turned to goose pimples. She felt her fingers dig into the dirt, straining to get away. Seconds later, the guards were gone, dissolved in the great swells of darkness. *Chock, chock, chock*, went the song of the tree frogs.

She had watched him dance towards her, moving through the degrees of light and shadow, darting like a black crow through the curtain of stippled fog.

He crawled the last few metres to the fence.

Lying flat to the ground, they looked at each other. His shirt was ragged and unbuttoned to his chest. She noticed that his neck was long and skinny; his eyes huge against his face. "How do you feel?" she said in a whisper, her mouth shutting with a snap.

"Like a sucked lemon," said Iain, his face agleam with moisture. "Dry, wasted, and sour at the edges."

"I'm glad you still have a sense of humour." They were separated by over three feet of wire. "This is a Red Maple, by the way, not a flame tree."

"I'm from Sutherland. We don't have trees in Sutherland, only thistles." He smiled. It was a smile as welcome as an umbrella going up in the rain. He turned his face towards the sky and wrinkled his eyes. It began to drizzle. "Your hair looks nice," he said. There were no traces of his earlier resentment. "A little shorter than I remember it. Reminds me of your flapper days." For a moment he stared at her. Then, as if short of breath, he said, "You must have had quite a journey." Barely audible. "How are you?"

The past throbbed inside her like an engorged muscle. Nadia wanted to reach for his hand, run her fingers against his cheeks; a lightsome, delicate touch. Instead, she stretched her arm through the fencing and began to pass Iain cartons of cigarettes, parcels of dried meats and wrappings of preserved fruits. "I'm fine." Her eyes, a promise of softness, skimmed over his face. "Eat this now." It was a tangerine.

He put the tangerine to his mouth, bit into the skin, giving it a long suck. "What about Mamuchka, how is she?" he asked.

"She's well. She says why couldn't I be like Maria Carvalho

337

who lives next door. She married a doctor not a Scottish civil servant."

Iain grinned. "And Papashka?"

"Getting increasingly forgetful, but as good as can be expected given he'll be eighty this year. He spends most of the day playing chess or Chinese chequers with Yugevny. Poor Mamuchka can't find half the things in the house because he keeps hiding things."

"Hiding things?"

"In case the Japanese take over the Tabacaria." The corners of her mouth rose fractionally. She had a tin of Pall Mall in her hand. "These aren't for smoking, they're to be used as currency."

"Do you have a plan?"

"There's a boat that will take us to Macao."

"A boat? It'll be too dangerous escaping by boat. The shipping lanes must be littered with magnetic mines and the Japanese launches are fast and heavily armed. We'll never outrun them."

Nadia ignored his concerns. "It will be here in three days. You have to tell me where is the best place for me to cut through the wire and when?"

"You have a wire cutter?"

"Yes."

"Let me have it."

"No, Iain, if you're caught with it, they'll behead you."

He looked at her. "The problem with cutting through the wire is that it'll make a God forsaken racket. Listen to this." He flicked the fence with his wrist and the thin sound reverberated down the channel. "It's a big gamble . . ."

"I was always a good fan tan player."

"If you start snipping through it, the guards are bound to hear."

"In that case, someone will have to distract them. Give the guards the food and the tobacco. The same goes for the naughty postcards."

"Alright. Meet me here tomorrow night. Same time. We'll do it then." She nodded, handed him another carton of cigarettes, careful not to snag her arm on the barbed wire. His fingers crossed the threshold. He put his hand on her wrist and she stopped. She felt as though there was little air entering her lungs.

A lengthy moment passed; a long, damp, cocooned silence. Then Iain bundled his loot into a blanket and folded it over the goods, corner-to-corner, twisting the top into a knotted loop to form a handle. "Now go," he said, "before anyone sees you." He made to leave.

"Wait."

Her heart was surging like a pump.

Under a shudder of moonlight she passed him something more, a manila envelope.

He gave Nadia a look. "What's this?" he said, pushing his face against the fence, separating shadows from light. Inside was a rectangle of sheeny paper.

"It's a photograph," she said.

The black and white portrait was a close-up of a child. He squinted, bending the image towards the light. "Who's the little girl?"

A pleading look stretched across her face. Her cheeks turned hot. "Her name is Valentina. She will be 3 years old in September." A silence. "I named her after your mother. She's your daughter, Iain."

9

"But I thought you couldn't have children?" he spluttered. "I don't understand." His eyes were wide. "How . . . at your age . . . ?"

"I was forty when she was conceived."

"How . . . ?"

I don't know how, Iain. It just happened." She looked at her husband. It was hard to believe how much of his face she had forgotten – the shape of his mouth and lips, the freckles by his nose. "Do you remember that night in December? Three days before I left Hong Kong for Macao? Well, she was born on September 22nd."

He stared at her, stunned.

"Why didn't you tell me? Why didn't you say in your letters?"

"I was scared."

"Of what?"

"Scared you'd risk escape in order to be with us. Scared that you'd get caught trying . . ." She had to stop herself from sounding apologetic.

He remained silent for a long time.

"She looks like me, don't you think?" he eventually said, peering at the photograph.

"The spitting image. I used to cry all the time when I was breastfeeding her because she reminded me so much of you. It must have been my hormones or something." She had been – as Mamuchka had often pointed out – an unfailingly anxious first-time mother.

"You've got to go back!" he demanded.

"I'm not going anywhere without you," she hissed. "I'm going to get you out of her. You can't stay in camp with Takashi in charge. Do you want your daughter to grow up fatherless?"

"I don't want her to become an orphan!"

"Keep your voice down."

"Who on earth is taking care of her? How can you leave her by herself?"

"She's not by herself. She's with Mamuchka and Izabel, Anna, Mrs. Lo – she's surrounded by people I love and trust."

An image formed in Nadia's mind, burning into her: the rickshaw pulling away from the Tabacaria, seeing Valentina at the window, her head small and pig-tailed, the rickshaw continuing down the street as she watched, mouth crumpling. Seconds later she was gone.

"And if you think I wanted to leave her behind then you're mad. It kills me not to be with her."

"But – "

"No, buts Iain, you're going to do as I say. I have this under control. I'm going to get you out of here tomorrow night and afterwards we'll take refuge at Father Luke's. If you trust me and if you trust Costa then you must do as I say." She stared hard at his face; the taste of desperation in her mouth. She could see from his eyes that he was fighting with himself. "Takashi's going to hurt you if you stay. Are you listening to me? He will hurt you." Iain remained silent for a long time. He closed his eyes, as if he was making a wish. Nadia knew that in a few seconds he would either nod his head in assent or get up to leave. Holding her breath, she awaited his decision.

"How did you ever get so tough?" he finally said.

"By being a single mother for three years."

"Valentina," he repeated the name two, three, four times. "Tell me about her."

Nadia told him about Valentina's infectious laughter, her first words, how she'd learned to walk by holding onto Mamuchka's thumbs, the way she chewed on her comfort blanket before falling asleep, the way she ran around the house with Uncle Yugevny's drawers on her head and made doll houses out of cigar boxes.

Then turning serious, she said, "Tomorrow night at three o'clock, I want someone to distract the guards. It will take me about an hour to cut through this wire. I want you ready at four sharp. Don't bring anyone with you. We can't have anything slow us down. Father Luke will be waiting a half-mile up the road, at the Tai Tam junction. I'll get you to the bottom of the hill and into his car. And stop looking at me like that. Your eyes might pop out."

Iain nodded, gave a quiet chuckle. He slid the photograph carefully back into the manila envelope and gave it a little pat. He levered himself up, rose to his knees, then up to a half-crouch. He looked at her. She watched him edge backwards towards the enfolding darkness and retreat into the shadows.

Nadia waited ten minutes. Waited for the luminous hands of her watch to reach the four thirty mark. Then she started walking, silently, in the direction from which she came, past the creepers and vines. Dead leaves and fern pins yielded beneath her tread. She moved cautiously. In the near distance she spied the guards' canteen – the smell of boiled rice was less strong now. Her mind should have been more focused and alert, but it wasn't; she was thinking about Iain.

And then she saw something. A dark shadow, half-concealed, was leaning against the long, pale walls of the watchtower. A figure of a man, dirty and broken, was watching her from behind the fence like a pie-dog. He was regarding her without emotion. She noted that he had a beard, that he had Caucasian features. She froze. They eyed each other for several seconds before the man stepped backwards and out of the dim light.

When she blinked again, he was gone.

When Iain returned to his small dormitory, he immediately noticed that Hoarde's bunk was empty. Stepney was on his back snoring, with Mr. Yorkie curled on his shoulder, and Friendly lay asleep on his side. But where was Hoarde? Had he been in bed when he left to meet Nadia, he wondered? He couldn't recall. Iain sat on his cot; in his chest a mixture of curiosity and trepidation brewed. He stepped out into the night once more and looked about. When he saw no sign of Hoarde he went back to bed.

After much tossing and turning, Iain concluded that he wasn't going to get any sleep. He waved the flies away from his mouth and lay in bed thinking about everything Nadia had told him. For long moments, in the darkness, he stared at the photograph of his daughter, making out the shape of her mouth, her eyes. Nadia had said they were going to escape by boat to Macao. That wasn't going to be easy, he decided, especially with the Imperial Navy policing the harbour and military patrols guarding the southern shores of the island. That was how the Japanese had caught him in the first place.

He was struck by a sudden image of being at sea. It was the day after Christmas 1941; he was in a police launch commandeered from the naval dockyard. Days before, the British had offered him an escape route out of Hong Kong, together with members of the Indian Intelligence Bureau. He declined. Instead, Iain piloted the launch himself and dropped the men off in Mirs Bay where they could flee on foot into Free China. He calculated that he had enough petrol to take him as far as Macao, but on the way back from Mirs Bay, three Japanese Military Torpedo Boats intercepted him, opening fire with their guns. He had no choice but to surrender.

Three days later the Japanese held their victory parade. Two thousand Imperial Army soldiers, led by Lt. Gen. Sakai on a white horse, marched through the streets from Victoria to Happy Valley. On January 3rd, Iain together with 2800 other British, American and Dutch nationals were ordered to gather themselves at the Murray Road parade ground. From here, they marched the eight long miles to Stanley peninsula.

Iain's thoughts were interrupted by the sudden sound of loud voices. Six guards burst into the room. Stepney tried to scramble out of bed but lost his balance and fell. One of the Formosans held Stepney to the floor as another brought the butt of his rifle down on Mr. Yorkie, crushing its little head.

Iain sat up and held his arms out in self-defence, but the guards grabbed him by the hair and pulled him through the door. He felt a boot thud into his ribs. He tried to work out what was happening, why he was being dragged away, and then he realized that they were taking him towards the Indian quarters. Suddenly, he remembered Hoarde's words *see you by the India hut* and with a wave of anger he knew how he'd been betrayed.

Seconds later, he stood before a mound of freshly excavated earth. The radio that they'd buried was in pieces and sitting on the top soil. In the shadows he saw a man with a beard hovering, a look of triumph flashing in his eyes. "Hoarde, what the hell have you done?" he yelled. "Hoarde!"

10

Nadia spent a miserable night in the hills. She was expecting Father Luke to pick her up at eight o'clock, but that was still two hours away. At daybreak the storm clouds shook the trees with thunder. Under a steady downpour, American B25s and P-40s flew in off the coast heading towards Victoria harbour. Within minutes the barrage from the anti-aircraft guns could be heard in the distance, followed by the flattening *whoomp* and *budung* of exploding bombs.

Cheeks wet from the rain, Nadia, with the mountains as her backdrop, watched the internees from a treetop perch. She looked though her spyglass. The men and women were marching in a line, queuing for their breakfast, mostly barefoot, wearing old vests and scarves as headgear to keep out the rain. Some sagged, unable to get their breath; a few squatted down to rinse their utensils in the rain puddles or in billycans; the rest remained erect, like flimsy saplings, dull-eyed yet resilient as the weather washed over them. Instinctively, a few ducked each time an Allied pilot flew overhead. Once in a while a Formosan guard fired a potshot into the sky.

With the American air raids concentrating on the Wanchai district, Nadia began to wonder what prevented the B25s from dropping bombs onto Stanley itself. After all, it was positioned next to a military barracks. Shouldn't the internees have painted white crosses on their roofs? And why, she looked on in sudden horror, were there machine gun platforms on top of the old colonial gaol? Didn't international law forbid the use of anti-aircraft fire from within internment camps?

Nadia put the spyglass away and stood up.

Her mind scampered. The *whoomp* and *budung* in the distance carried on unabated. She pursed her lips. Her eyes locked on a black finger of billowing smoke across the water. A terrifying premonition struck her like the haunting splinters of a dream. The bombs were falling like raindrops.

Some of the internees placed bets on how long Sutherland would last this time; one Dutchman offered 2-to-1 odds that he might survive the week; some wagered whole tins of creamed corn that he'd be dead by the morning. It was rumoured that Hoarde had been offered his freedom by the new commandant; sanctuary for revealing the whereabouts of the all-important wireless. The internees had yet to learn that Hoarde's head had been removed from his shoulders an hour after first light – punishment for being an *uragiminomo*, a snitch – and his body thrown off the cliff.

Up in the sky the crows cawed and flew in predatory circles. Bits of Hoarde's stringy guts were dangling from their crimson beaks.

The door was sealed with a wooden latch. On the narrow altar table, Iain made out a set of scalpels and rubber tubes. The light from the oil lamp licked the darkness.

Using a pulley, they hung him by his hands from the ceiling. Arms tethered above his head with binder twine, they hoisted him aloft. His dangling feet were bound, coated up to the ankles with molasses; in the recesses behind his knees they attached sharpened chopsticks, preventing him from drawing up his legs.

Below him, a metal oil drum, where inside, a knot of ravenous, busy rats threw themselves against the slippery-steel inner-lining.

The pulley block creaked as they relaxed the rope and began to lower him into the oil drum. He began to grunt and struggle.

"Save your strength," said Takashi, seated in a Meiji dragon chair. "You are going to need it." He was smiling. "Many years ago, you remember? You found a man in the sewers wiss his foot eaten away?"

"You can't do this. The Geneva Convention states – "

"You are a spy, Mr. Suzzerland. We found you wiss a radio. Yamashita-san, my predecessor, naturally had no knowledge of dis, but I've kept files on you for some time now. I can do anysing I want to you."

The rats became a jumbled gnarl of black matted hair. They sprang like leaping fish, yellow teeth gnashing. The vibrations made by their clawed toes passed over the room.

"I also know," Takashi continued, "about you having an ally outside of the camp. A girl dressed as a priest, no less."

"That's pure nonsense."

"I can assure you she will be dealt wiss too. But first maybe I will let my guards have some fun wiss her, no?"

Iain lowered his eyes, saw his toes begin to creep down towards the rim of the barrel. Now, he could see their shiny black marbles staring up at him. The rats could smell the molasses and climbed onto their hind legs, baring their razor blade fangs. The rope groaned. He tried to sway his body, tried to dislodge the knot that bound his wrists together, but the twine held; the fastening was too secure.

The rats jumped, snapping wildly at the air. They clawed at him but his toes were still just a few inches out of reach. He watched a rat's mouth quickly open and close. Seconds later it leapt again.

Iain's body tensed.

His ankles crashed loudly against the sides of the drum.

Nadia flinched at the sound of bombs falling and to the *shboom* of artillery fire to the east, angry and muffled. Once in a while the sky juddered and popped with a powder-cloud of black smoke. Not convinced she could see everything from her perch, she climbed off the tree and crawled under the palm fronds to see the reddening dawn and an American P-40, its tiger shark mouth aglint, spraying ships with tracer fire. Higher up, a B25 was dropping 500-lbers onto the Japanese Naval Headquarters across the harbour.

Flattening herself against the tall grass, Nadia grabbed her spyglass and watched the fighter twist and spin from its ground attackers, its single engine howling as it made dive after dive. Within moments, the P-40 was joined by a twin and the pair of fighter planes, dancing and swerving, peppered the ships with their payload.

Nadia watched, transfixed, a lump of fear in her throat. This is not good, she said to herself, not good. She looked down towards the camp and saw the internee children being ushered into F Block, while the Sikh guards fired their rifles into the mackerel sky.

Suddenly, there was a new and terrible noise, much closer than the others. Nadia lowered the spyglass and saw a number of Japanese soldiers gathered at the machine gun platform at the top of the prison roof. They were firing at the planes.

It took the P-40 pilots some seconds to realize they were under attack from a fresh position. They pivoted, flew low, and poured a stream of 7.9mm shells into the prison walls.

The machine-gun battery on the roof kept firing.

"*Bawzhemoy*," said Nadia. "They don't know it's an internee camp."

She watched in horror as the P-40s climbed and lifted into the red skies.

Seconds later, a team of soldiers were pulling an anti-aircraft gun into the garrison forecourt.

"*Bawzhemoy*," Nadia repeated, shaking her head.

The soldiers hoisted the type 88 75mm AA Gun into position.

Before she could stop herself, Nadia was on her feet, running down the hill.

She was seventy yards from the camp. Fifty. Twenty yards now. The P-40s wheeled round, ready for another flyby.

Fingers outstretched, she began gesticulating at the planes, swatting at them to stop. Her hands grasped at air.

She could see the P-40s coming in low, off the Tai Tam Bay, a hundred and fifty feet above the trees, flying through a cloud of flak.

The AA Gun opened fire.

Its blasts shook the earth beneath her feet.

The P-40s loomed, shark-teeth snarling, coming in quick and shallow. Nose-mounted machine guns rattled off, shuddering the air. Nadia saw the fitted bombs detach themselves from the underwing racks. The bombs spiralled, spinning out of the cloudless blue like ospreys diving for eels. There was a low, inhaled whistle. Triple plumes of smoke.

The bombs smashed into the camp and its prison buildings. The explosions rocked the ground. Nadia's stomach, chest, soul emptied. The world broke apart before her eyes.

Lumps of earth and airborne dirt rained from the sky. The force of the explosion lifted Nadia off her feet and threw her to the ground, ripping through her like a thermal surge of solid air. She wanted to get up quickly, but found that her head was spinning and the breath had been snatched from her chest. She blinked, blinked again, suddenly realizing that everything had gone horribly quiet. No machine-gun fire, no crump of bombs, nothing at all. Instead there was a sharp restless hissing in her ears, a thick white noise cutting off sound.

Neck and shoulder muscles rigid, she tried to stand again but toppled over from the rippling shockwaves. Frantic, she got herself upright and as her ringing ears began to clear she heard again the *whoomp* and *budung* of the 500lb bombs and the stuttered pounding of the AA Gun. The image of the prison building breaking apart, shooting up smoke and dust and debris, followed by the fireball and the razor-sharp blanket of heat came flooding back to her.

She shook her head to get rid of the paralysis cottonwooling her brain and within seconds was running down the hill again. Sprinting with her eyes down against the sun's glare, she crossed the road, passing the screen of blue hydrangea. At the camp gates one of the gate sentries was sitting, his back to her. His head was blown off. The other guard was nowhere to be seen. She rattled the double gates but they wouldn't budge. The barriers were drawn shut.

"Open up!" she shouted and began struggling with the barrier again, hoping it would yield. It wouldn't budge. She tried to bypass the lock and crawl underneath the metal frame, but got stuck halfway and had to pull herself back out again. "Come on, you bloody thing, open!" she cried, kicking at the fence with her heel.

Slowly, Nadia realized there was no way through. But then, seconds after, she began to make out a ring-ding-dang noise coming from behind the trees. It was the clanging bells of the garrison fire truck making its way up the hill. She went and hid in the undergrowth.

Moments later she followed the fire truck through the double gates and into the camp, circling the forecourt. Trees were on fire. Bodies lay burning. The heat was unbearable; it felt as though the sun had opened its mouth.

Sheets of white ash covered everything. Her eyes began to sting from the saltpeter. She ran her sleeve over her face, puffing. It was hard to breathe.

Down the slope, a quarter mile to the south, Nadia saw the soldiers from the Japanese garrison pouring out from their digs. Some were in their uniforms, others were half-naked, dressed in their *fundoshi* – sparse little loin cloths. They were shooting blindly into the sky.

A man raced past her, arms raised to protect his head. She chased after him. "Iain Sutherland," she shouted into his ear. "Where is he?"

"This way," the man replied, squinting as aircraft bullets peppered the building opposite. The man didn't stop running. He stretched out his hand and she took it. They arrived in C and D Block.

Nadia looked up towards the second-floor of C Block. There was no sign of people being inside and the windows had been blown out. "Iain!" she cried. She wiped the sweat off her face with the back of her hand. She tried again, "Iain!" She pushed through the door regardless. In the darkness she could make out that the staircase had fallen in, battering a crater in the floorboards big enough to fit a lorry. She cupped her fingers and called through them "Iain!" she shouted, but nothing stirred. She groped about in the darkness for a while but found nothing. There could have been trapped bodies in there, but she had no way of telling. Nadia retreated outside, unsure where else to look.

Nadia began to despair. She knew Iain was hurt, she could sense it, feel it in her bones. "Iain Sutherland!" she cried. "I'm looking for Iain Sutherland!" She pummelled the wall with the flat of her hand in frustration.

"They all got out," said someone to her left. A group of people were helping to console a few of the survivors of B Block, kneeling on the muddied ground wrapping wounds.

"I'm looking for Iain Sutherland," she said again.

"Have you tried the prison?" A voice replied from behind. It was one of the female internees helping with the wounded. "I heard he was taken by the guards this morning." Nadia felt a wave of hope replace her exhaustion and fear. "You'd better prepare yourself," the woman continued. "A bomb hit it a few minutes ago." Nadia's hope dissolved.

Her pulse rate rocketing, she reached the prison enclosure. An inferno was still blazing two buildings away; bodies were being dragged through windows and down ladders, most of them lifeless, asphyxiated from smoke. She heard the fires spit and pop. A horrid fear gripped the base of Nadia's throat. "Let me through!" She yelled, pushing hard, getting nowhere. "My husband is inside! LET ME THROUGH!"

A few people breached the shattered building, racing through the gap. Nadia shoved past the melee and clambered over the rubble. Masonry broke off in her hands. She feared the building might collapse around her. The east and north walls of the jail had crumpled, its square roof erased. As Nadia took in the wreckage she saw prison cells blown open by bombs, blackened limbs sprawled all over the place, a man dangling from a telephone wire.

A metallic voice came through what sounded like a tannoy system. It was a Japanese guard speaking in English through a funnel-shaped loudhailer. He was giving orders, urging people to stay out of the prison compound, warning of the dangers of exposed gas lines and falling debris. She was fighting back tears now, desperate.

She peered through countless ironwork windows. A pall of smoke and brick-dust shrouded everything. Water gushed over the floor from a splintered main. It was hard to breathe. He'll be fine, she told herself, he'll be a little bruised, but fine. She pushed aside scorched brick and stone, searching from room to room, trusting her instincts, all the time reaching, stumbling, sweeping the dirt from her eyes. From somewhere she heard a cry of pain. It came to her with a far-away thinness. Then a distraught voice was screaming, "I'm coming, darling! I'm coming!" Only later did she realize these were her own frantic cries.

Inside a cubicle at the end of a long corridor, she found a metal oil drum, a few mangled rats, some burning embers. And in a puddle of black blood, like an upturned water-spider, there lay a severed hand. She shrank back.

She was standing at the edge of the bomb rubble, peering into the darkness of the smoke-filled room. Papers and documents lay scattered, flying about with every gust of wind. Nadia turned slowly and saw a body covered in ash. His limbs were drawn across at odd angles, like a dead dog on the side of the road. Cautiously, she rolled the body onto its front and saw the face of a Japanese guard. She let out her breath.

A moment later a shadow twitched in the corner of the

room and she thought saw something move. A foot, followed by a knee and a darkly stained thigh, slipped in and out of the gloom. It was a man.

He was lying motionless on the floor, his blackened face facing away from her. There were glossy pools of debris all around him, red as printer's dye.

Drawing the cassock above her shins, she knelt down, wiped her hands on her front and pulled at the man carefully. His back was sticky and slick with blood. She tried to turn him over. His left arm was missing, blown off just below the shoulder. She shuddered. A swirl of wind nudged his hair. She caught her breath.

It was Iain.

Where her fingers touched, his body was as warm as her hand; he was still breathing. Nadia removed her cassock and began to tear the fabric into long strips. She drew the sleeve of his shirt back. When she saw the exposed bone, she pressed the cloth to the stub of his arm. The purple flesh was mutilated and ripped above the elbow.

Despite the pressing she'd made he continued to bleed profusely. With the cassock now soaking, Nadia began removing the obi sash which was wrapped round her breasts. Soon her hands were drenched to the wrist-bones. Hastily, she made a tourniquet and folded swathe after swathe over the wound, six layers thick, coiling it tight. Then she found a short stick and tied it to the tourniquet with a square knot; she twisted the stick until the bleeding subsided. In the darkness Iain's face looked gaunt and his skin pale, as thin and fragile as volcanic ash. Fastening the stick securely in place, she rolled him very cautiously onto his front and turned his head towards her. "Iain," she pleaded, "Iain, look at me. You have to wake up." His breath came in small bursts. "Iain!" she repeated.

Eyelids fluttering, he began to stir. He emitted a long gurgle of pain then began to cough. When he finally opened his eyes, the corners of his mouth lifted in a grimace.

"My feet," he said with a rush of panic. "The rats were at my feet."

"Your feet and legs look fine," she replied, calming him. "There're some cuts by your ankles, but nothing serious. Your toes are all intact." She found a scalpel lying across the floor and used it to slice the rope around his ankles. "Iain," she said. "You've lost an arm."

"Lost an arm?" he said in baffled, faltering voice.

"You're also losing a great deal of blood. I have to get you out of here. Can you walk?"

"I can walk," were the only three words he could manage.

He winced when he tried to move. Nadia rocked him to his left side and then to his right side, next with one arm around his waist and the other under his right armpit, she hauled him upright. He swore to himself then gave a stifled howl. Getting him to his feet was like lifting a heavy sack of rice; a deadweight.

"You have to keep your left arm elevated above the heart. Can you do that for me?"

He nodded.

Nadia looked at him. He was panting. The veins on his throat bulged. She gripped him possessively.

"Christ, you're strong for a wee lass," he said, trying to make light of the pain that was racking his body.

"My ancestors must have been *muzhiks*. Good peasant stock."

From outside, they heard the shouts of the Japanese guards. "How am I going to get you out of the camp?" she asked. "And how am I going to get past the sentries? I'm practically naked."

"Over there," he said, jutting his chin towards the fallen rubble. "I was in this room with Takashi and a guard when the roof fell in. He should be over there."

She propped Iain against one of the standing walls. Perspiration salted the corners of his mouth. As he rested there, bathed in sweat and blood, Nadia began to push and kick the fallen debris to one side. She came to a body and without hesitating, removed Takashi's tunic, trousers and boots. Her hands fumbled with the buttons, ignoring the large blood-stained patch by his heart; she climbed into his clothes. The shoulders sagged on her and the shirt-tails fell to mid-thigh. She tucked the tunic into the trousers.

"You need his hat to hide your face," Iain said, his voice thinning.

Nadia disentangled the visor cap from Takashi's head and pulled it over her eyes.

There was nobody in the corridor. The air was thick with insect-thrumming heat. Gripped with exquisite pain, Iain stumbled outside, leaning his weight on Nadia's shoulder. Walking out into the open was like walking into a tropical maelstrom – they saw a hazy patchwork of destruction, a shallow trough of smoke and scorched dirt. "We don't stop for anything," she said. "Do you understand me? No matter how much pain you feel we don't stop." The dull thudding booms had ceased, the sputtering gunfire had stopped. Nadia waited for a pair of mustard-khaki uniforms to hurry past carrying buckets of sand. "Come on, come on," she heard herself say.

Trembling from blood loss, Iain's limbs felt soggy and weak. A pang shot up and down his left arm with every step. He lifted his face towards the sun, gasping air, wanting to howl out senselessly. The pain made him clumsy. He tripped, recovered. His vision blurred as dazzling white spots danced before his eyes. She held him close.

The chaos worked to their advantage; nobody stopped or looked at them. It took them a full twelve minutes to reach the entrance to the camp, but the time moved swiftly for them, shooting past like fast-moving images of a cine camera.

At the double gates, Nadia eyed the slouched heap that lay by the post. The dead Japanese sentry hadn't been moved. She saw the gates ajar, left open by the fire-trucks. Both breathless now, they hurried through the opening and made their way down the road.

Moments later she spotted the Morris Cowley with Father Luke sitting anxiously at the wheel.

"Is that your husband?'

"Yes."

"What's happened to him?"

"An American bomb," was all Nadia said as she eased Iain into and across the back seats.

"What do you expect me to do with him?"

"Get him to a hospital, of course. He needs medical attention."

"If you take him to a hospital, the Japanese will be onto us within hours."

"Well, send for a doctor then! He's going to die if we don't – "

"It is too risky!" He cut her off. He was playing with the joints of his fingers. "How can I bring a one-armed *gweilo* and a woman impersonating a Japanese officer into my house? There are neighbourhood watches who report anything out of the ordinary to the military police."

Nadia banged the bonnet of the car with her hand. She fixed him a ferocious look. "He will bleed to death if he's not treated!"

"Get into the car," he ordered. "I will think of something as we drive." He paused and touched his chest as if in pain.

"What is wrong? Are you hurt?"

"Just a twinge. Hurry we must go."

The Morris headed towards Repulse Bay. They travelled in a tense, inhospitable silence. From time to time, Nadia looked behind her, studying Iain's condition. He looked drawn and pale with his teeth clenched between his lips. After several minutes she said, "What if we're stopped at a checkpoint?"

Father Luke did not reply. He was taking the long route around the island, heading towards Aberdeen. "Even if I took him back to my house, I wouldn't be able to find a doctor. I have some medicines of my own, but I don't know what I can really do to help him. He may not make it."

Nadia did not like the priest talking about Iain as if was not there.

"And even if he does survive," he went on, slightly out of breath now, "I can only shield him from the Japanese for a short while. They'll be doing house-to-house searches. They'll know by tonight that internees have gone missing." His eyes were on the road. "When is your rendezvous with Costa?"

"In two days."

"Too long."

"We have to do something!" She tried to rein in her accelerating thoughts, her flying panic.

They came to Deep Water Bay, passing the derelict golf club. Father Luke's shoulders stiffened, as if suddenly galvanized by an enlightening thought. "I have an idea," he said.

"What?"

Father Luke said something that Nadia did not understand. "What did you say?"

"I said I will take you to Sai Kung by boat."

"Where or what is Sai Kung?"

"It is across the water, in the New Territories. There's a group of about a hundred Communist guerillas that have been camped out in the Sai Kung mountains for years. They claim to be part of the East River Column. They have an understanding with the Japanese in so much that they leave each other alone. Their leader was a former barman at the Peninsula Hotel. His name is Pang. We went to primary school together. Two of his men used to be surgeons at the Tung Wah Hospital."

"How do you know?"

"How do I know what?"

"How do you know the surgeons are still there? If you're wrong and the doctors have gone, Iain will die."

"I know they are still there because some of the guerillas were in my district last week. Once or twice a month Pang orders them to come at night and hand out what they can to the poor. When I asked them about Chung, the surgeon, they said he was still living with them."

"Are you sure you can get hold of a boat?"

"I can in Aberdeen harbour. A local junk maybe, but we will have to pay."

Nadia pulled off a shoe and extracted a roll of cash. "I have Japanese Military Yen." She brightened. "But why must we go to Sai Kung? Why can't the junk take us to Macao?"

"No, Nadia, these people in Aberdeen are fishermen. They will not risk leaving Hong Kong waters."

"Then we have no choice but sail to Sai Kung."

11

The two Hakka women heaved and rocked on their long oar, steering through the narrow harbour. As they swayed to the knocking of the current, the sampan made its way silently through the blanket of morning haze. Below, underneath their bare feet, beneath some removable deck planks, Nadia, Iain and Father Luke lay flat on their backs, knees and arms folded across their bodies like unborn infants. Nadia knew they were entirely sealed off from prying Japanese eyes, yet still she felt more afraid than ever before.

"How are you, Iain?" she whispered, mere inches from her husband's face.

Iain nodded, his jaw set.

Nadia could feel his head resting on her chest; his breathing had grown protracted. She squeezed his right hand in encouragement. They were both drenched in perspiration.

The only noises she could make out were from bow waves as they slapped against the hull and the creaking of the oar on its rowlock fitting. Even through the wide planks of wood, Nadia could feel the winds begin to escalate. Little eddies of salt air whirled through the tiniest of cracks. She imagined they were leaving the outer harbour now, gliding into the choppy waters of the East Lamma Channel. Everything was black; there was no colour in anything.

Up above, the Hakka women's loose trousers flapped erratically in the wind. Through the tiny opening Nadia saw their knees bending, straightening, bending again, heard the occasional splash of water. She could see the wrinkled leathery undersides of their bare feet.

The early summer currents carried the sampan out to sea, causing the stern to bob.

Tirelessly, the Hakka women guided the little craft onwards, arms pumping.

Somewhere in the remote distance, she heard a buoy's bell toll and then there it was: she could see it clearly now – the six-sailed outline, the mastheads with the red pennants, even the bamboo battens. It was a small ocean-going junk.

The junk captain was a florid man with a pirate's smile. Nadia followed Father Luke down into the galley by way of a series of rickety ladders where the air smelled of scorched tin and chaulmoogra oil. Everything creaked. She could hear a grinding of metal chains and assumed the anchors were being raised. High above, broad canvases flapped noiselessly in the shifting breeze. "This way," Father Luke said to the two crewmen who were carrying Iain in their arms. The men found Iain hard to lift and harder yet to transport down the rope ladders. They descended, ferrying him on their shoulders, one hand under the other. Iain sucked air through his teeth as they placed him on a bunk.

"How far are we from Sai Kung? How many hours of sailing?" Nadia inquired. Father Luke lit a candle, looking around at the bunks, at the tins of food, the sacks of sorghum and bladders of drinking water.

"About three hours," he replied. "I will make contact with the guerillas and leave you in their care. You have nothing to fear from them. They are good people."

Nadia thanked him. She was changing into a set of coolie clothes supplied by the captain Woo. "I feel like I'm backstage in a pantomime, tearing off this dress, pulling on that dress, pulling on trousers, tearing them off again." She secured the string around her waist and went to boil some water. There was a wooden crate to sit on, beside it was a portable kerosene stove with a single hob.

The junk began quivering now just a little bit as it set sail. The canvases grew noisier, rustling like tall palms. Nadia caressed Iain's forehead with her hand.

"Will he make it?" asked Father Luke, who sat clutching the left side of his chest.

Nadia gave her husband a kiss on the cheek. Iain responded by raising his eyebrows, keeping his eyes shut. His breathing was slow, his voice leaden. "Of course he will," she said. "He has to. His daughter is waiting for him."

Father Luke followed, falling behind with every step, growing more and more out of breath, until finally he had to stop.

Using a stretcher made out of sail-cloth and bamboo, the crewmen carried Iain through the countryside, across a stream, up a steep gradient dotted with trees which eventually thickened into a wood. A deep chasm separated the narrow path from the stream below. Small bedraggled huts formed from bamboo and wattle snaked along the side of the hill like a row of slumbering mice. When the dogs began to bark, the villagers came out and stared at them, curious to the identity of these peculiar strangers. They lay Iain down in the shade and then, later, transferred him into something that resembled a field hospital. After a while the crowd of people thinned.

"Where is Father Luke?" Nadia asked. But nobody seemed to know. Unfazed, she sought out the surgeons and explained what had happened to Iain.

The surgeons, a man called Chung and a woman named Lee-Phua, did what they could for him. From a tiny medical supply they broke open vials of morphine and sulphur satchels. Suppressing the subclavian artery, they cleaned and redressed the wound, stitched up what they could. When they were sure that they had stemmed the bleeding, Chung pushed a long double-sided knife, through the muscle near the shoulder joint and cut away some flesh to make a flap. Once completed, they turned the flap onto itself and covered the exposed bone, sewing it tight, applying tea-tree and iodine to stave off infection. Finally, Lee-Phua padded and bound the stump with gauze and bandages soaked in garlic. He was transferred to a darkened hut.

The very next evening, the same evening that Father Luke's body was discovered in the chasm by the footpath, Iain developed a high fever.

Being in the camp so long, Chung told Nadia, with the malnutrition, the privation, Iain's body resistance was very weak.

He was given broth made of roots and certain grasses. But the fever grew worse. He shivered and sweated and when he opened his eyes, his look was far, far away.

They drained the arm of pus and made him drink a tea made from elder flower, opium and chamomile. They gave him lemon balm to help him perspire. His shivering lasted for hours making him delusional. Nadia sponged him with lukewarm water and forced him to take in liquid. Then in the middle of the night something terrible happened. He suffered a kind of febrile seizure. His legs began kicking uncontrollably, his throat cried out. Both Chung and Lee-Phua held him down. "Is he going to die?" Nadia heard herself scream. "Please don't let him die!" They strapped his legs to the bed with twine. There was froth spilling from the corners of his mouth.

Nadia fell to her knees. The candlelight was a fragile glow. She prayed to Jesus. She prayed to Saint Nikolai Chudotvorets and to the Holy Mother of God. She prayed until the wick burnt down to the stub and guttered and the room turned black with her tears.

He grew deathly still.

Earlier that week Mamuchka, convinced that her daughter was in terrible danger, went to see the Governor of Macao. It was a mother's instinct, she said. He had no news to tell her.

As far as he knew there hadn't been any fresh reports of Macanese citizens being harmed in Hong Kong or held as prisoners.

"But she was due back yesterday. The plan was that she was to be back yesterday!"

The Governor, mouth downturned and sympathetic, merely shrugged his shoulders.

After a further three days of agonized waiting, a letter arrived addressed to Mrs Nadia Sutherland. It was a Prisoner of War envelope, inscribed 'Stanley Internee Camp' on the reverse and franked with Japanese Occupation 2s stamps. Across the front, the words 'Passed by Censor 3472' were punched in black ink.

Mamuchka, hungry for any information concerning her daughter or son-in-law, left Valentina with her grandfather and went into the bedroom to be alone. The colour had already drained from her lips. She took a few deep breaths, steadied herself and opened the envelope.

Dear Mrs. Sutherland, she read aloud in her faltering voice. *It troubles me greatly to have to inform you that your husband, Iain Sutherland, internee number 6177, has been reported missing, feared dead. This follows a series of USAAF air raids on Hong Kong resulting in bombs landing and exploding within Stanley peninsula. Up until now, a thorough investigation into the list of wounded in Tweed Bay hospital have been for naught. Please accept my deepest sympathies and may God walk by your side during these long dark hours.*

The Reverend John Anderson
Chaplain, Stanley Internment Camp

Mamuchka stared at the words for several moments. Her first thoughts were for her daughter, and then a sudden cold stab to the heart told her that Nadia too was nowhere to be found – missing, dead . . . she did not know. Caged nightmares of every shape and size entered her soul. Something sharp and high-pitched escaped from her chest. Deliberately, she folded the letter back in half and returned it to its sleeve.

Seconds later she pressed the envelope to her forehead and began to weep.

Nadia walked down the hill towards the set of Chinese tombstones. She knelt by the newly erected wooden cross. The yellow wildflowers clutched in her hand seemed to her so inadequate. She placed them on the soil. The sky had turned grey.

She trailed her fingertips across the name, so roughly and inexpertly carved into the wood, and felt a tear run down her face.

Behind her, one of the village children stared out across the valley. The little boy was watching a water buffalo as it pulled a plough through the rice fields; he had a small wooden boat in his hands. After a while Nadia took the path down to the hillside creek. The little boy handed her the small wooden boat and with a match she lit the incense stick.

"Incense to purify souls," she whispered, caressing the lucky glass charm around her neck. She lowered the boat into the water and let it go, watching it drift away, getting smaller and smaller. She closed her eyes and wrapped her arms around herself.

It began to rain in the middle of the night. A dispassionate drizzle that thrummed against the wattle roof like falling blister bugs.

Iain's fever broke in the early morning, just as the hillside trees became tinged with the colours of dawn. He drank some water. Afterwards, he slept for three days and nights. A nurturing, curative sleep. When he woke he thought he still possessed an arm because he reached out to touch Nadia's face. She beamed him her brightest smile. It took him a moment to remember that there was nothing at the end of his elbow, that his hand had disappeared.

In the ensuing hours, they bathed him in the hillside creek, sponging him, leaving the stump of his arm dry. Once in a while his forearm would itch but when he went to scratch it, it wasn't there. "My fingers tingle," he said to Chung, bewildered, "as if a hundred ants are running about on my missing hand."

A week passed, then two. The pattern of life rarely changed. While Nadia held vigil over Iain, the guerillas went about their lives as per usual. They scythed grass for fuel, harvested rice and root vegetables for sustenance, collected jungle vines and bamboo and palm fronds for shelter construction.

The June rains came and went and all the while Nadia watched Iain age before her eyes; the trauma of the last weeks had weathered him; there were deep creases on his brow and his eyes were sunken. It almost seemed to Nadia that the bones of his face were now visible through his skin. He did, nevertheless, seem to enjoy the fuss that Nadia made over him. She wiped his forehead, soaked his bandages in watered-down disinfectant, fanned him when he was hot, shooed away flies, told him stories about Valentina, offered him handfuls of wild sage to chew to restore his appetite and generally gave him back his self-belief.

Because of the late planting the rice harvest was not ready in July, nor was it by August when a small typhoon swept across the peninsula. Yet, slowly, Iain grew in strength. With his one arm, everything seemed to him strange yet familiar. He found that his relationship with his body had changed. What used to be instinctive – tying a shoe lace, buttoning a shirt, cutting up food – now had to be thought through and planned out.

In time, he learned to do things with one hand, so that by the end of the summer months, he was almost himself again. And as he regained mobility, adjusting to his handicap, he found there was plenty to keep him busy. He contributed to the summer planting in the paddy fields, hoeing and seed-ing; he fed the long-legged village chickens; he even helped the guerillas restore a Japanese military motorcycle they'd found abandoned in a gully. It had a Kurogane sidecar with a pentagonal body, seating capacity for two, and a mounted 50 calibre machine gun. Listening to the distant sounds of Japanese artillery, Iain would eye the rusting weapon, hoping he would never have to fire it in anger.

Meanwhile Nadia befriended several of the local women, especially Lee-Phua and her sister Lee-Ping. Each morning, having placed fresh wild flower on Father Luke's grave, with the mist clinging lazily to their clothing, they went digging for water chestnuts in the swollen marshlands at the base of the hills. Often they talked about their own children – their first words, what they liked to eat. But Nadia's mind was constantly elsewhere. Time and again she thought about Father Luke – had he died as a result of saving Iain? Had it been too much of a strain on his heart? Would he be alive today if she had looked over her shoulder and seen him struggling up the path? Up that steep gradient? Had she pushed him too hard? The guilt gnawed at her. But another type of guilt ate away at her too: Valentina.

Every day she dreamed of her beloved daughter, her parents and returning home, but there was no way of knowing what was happening in the exterior. Occasionally, the guerillas came back with pockets of communication, and once in a while Pang, their leader, would talk of the Japanese laying down their arms. But with hardly any solid intelligence, there was no way of really knowing.

Often, late at night Nadia spoke at length to Iain about Valentina, who was going to turn three in September. They lay beside each other, listening to the cicadas, to the dark, distracting themselves with thoughts of home. She desperately wanted to be with her daughter and each time she thought of Valentina a sweet anguish filled her heart. She talked of feeling helpless, frustrated, stagnant even, like an idle kite left indoors on a windy day. "Is there any way of making it over the mainland to Macao?" she asked, but Iain said no, it was too dangerous. He told her they would have to wait for an armistice or at best Japan's surrender. But the idea of travelling overland played in Nadia's mind incessantly. As if a tick had crawled under her skin it itched at her constantly. Yet each time she brought it up Iain hushed her, telling her to be patient.

So, with no distractions from the outside world, they continued to live their day-to-day existence, waiting for the endgame. They slept rough, on lumpy sacks bagged with weeds and sedges and beard grass. They took their water from the stream and from a nearby well. With mud around their ankles, they performed their ablutions amongst the trees and bushes, exposed to the casual glances of their neighbours. Sheltering indoors during the heat of the day, they ate whatever Pang's villagers offered them and sometimes sat around a table and played fan tan with the Lee-Phua and Lee-Ping.

And all the time Nadia's frustrations grew like a spate river rising after week-long rains. It seemed to her that the spell of monotony would never be broken. That she would never return home. At length she fell into long periods of introspective silence. But then one morning in August, with the weather cooling, all the guerillas suddenly disappeared. Nadia woke to find the village quiet, deserted but for a few women and their toddlers and a squawking chicken shedding feathers and droppings along the footpaths.

What's happened, asked Nadia. The old *por-pors* clacked their tongues. The guerillas had gone to fight, she was told. Rumours flew that with the Japanese on the verge of capitulation, the East River resistance had seized Yuen Long, Tai Po and some of the outlying islands. Nadia also found a note pinned to the door of her hut. It was from Lee-Phua. It wished her much happiness and luck for the future.

The following day a farmer arrived from a nearby village wearing a broad smile and a self-congratulatory air. He had the red flag of the Chinese Communist Party, with its yellow star and black hammer and sickle, draped over his shoulders. "Hirohito's turnip heads have surrendered," he cried, his feet stuttering excitedly across the ground. "The war is over."

Twenty-four hours later, after a tiring journey across land and sea, Iain and Nadia stood on the wharf of Queen's Pier. Behind them, the bombed-out Victoria Harbour was deserted, hardly a junk or Walla Walla in sight, only a lone sampan bobbed on the water. They tried to find a hotel room, but instead, discovered that the city was gripped with widespread lawlessness and that most of the guest rooms were billeted with drunken Japanese soldiers. The war might have been over but the place was in a state of bedlam; bandits roamed the streets; infrastructure was non-existent; and instead of seeing victorious Union Jacks flying from window brackets, the roofs and sills were lined with Chinese Nationalist flags. There was a perilous sensation of insurgence in the air.

After questioning a pair of military policemen, Iain led Nadia to the former French Mission building where a provisional government was being setting up. The MPs, seeing them dressed in coolie clothes, gave them funny looks but allowed them through. Up on the first floor Iain found a few of his old comrades, recently released from Stanley camp, and asked them what was going on. They informed him that Hong Kong's fate hung in the balance.

"We don't know who will receive Japan's formal surrender," Friendly told him. "It might be China, America or Britain. The airwaves are full of political jostling. The Chinese Nationalists are looking to claim Hong Kong for their own, but the Yanks won't allow it. Truman wants the colony received by an American or British officer, you see, but Chiang Kai-shek's standing his ground. Nationalist troops will be gathering at the border soon.

"But knowing the Yank top brass, they'll get their way. General Wedemeyer's dead-set on getting here first. I just hope to God that Harcourt arrives here before him. Yes, we're in America's hands now all right, at MacArthur's beck and call. Hell, we're not even allowed to hoist the Union Jack unless we get Truman's prior consent, at the same time the bloody Nationalists are flying their white sun flags all over the place. It's mindless, I tell you, mindless."

Later he came across Lieutenant-Colonel Richard Hughes, the most senior Army officer left in the colony. Iain briefed him about his past and his relationship with BAAG and British SIS.

"I just got out of Shamshuipo POW camp so forgive me, old boy, if I'm still trying to find my bearings," said Hughes. "All I can tell you is that we're desperately trying to set up a British civilian government. At the same time we're scrambling to ensure that gas, electricity and water services are maintained. Bloody hellish, I tell you. Trying to restore order is nigh impossible. Even though the Japs have surrendered, their troops are still meant to be responsible for keeping public order, but some of the buggers've gone to seed. Kanazawa, their police commissioner, has promised to bring discipline back into the ranks, but in the meantime we're forced to call on the local Triad outfits to act as auxiliary police units. 'Course we've got nothing to pay the buggers with but that'll change once the Treasury is up and running. Then there's the problem of foodstuffs and supplies of course . . ." he trailed off. "If you're going to hang around, we could use your help."

But Iain declined. He said he needed to find a boat to take them to Macao.

"Careful. The waterways are thick with mines."

"May I have your permission to requisition a Japanese coastal defense vessel? I can engage it in mine-sweeping duty along the Hong Kong-Macao sea passage and help clear the way for Harcourt's arrival."

"With your credentials, old boy, you certainly don't need my permission. But what I can do is give you an authorization letter to employ the vessel and a crew of five beyond Hong Kong waters. You'll need to gain Kanazawa's signature too. Meantime, I'll wire the British Consulate in Macao." Hughes looked at Iain levelly, whilst taking in, as though for the first time, that he was missing an arm. "We've all been through hell, haven't we?"

"Some more than others."

"Tell me, why are you so determined to get to Macao?"

"My daughter will be three years old soon. I've never seen her. She's waiting for me."

Hughes nodded. "Meantime I'll arrange for you to meet the quartermaster and we'll see if we can find you a billet and some proper clothes. We can't have you meet your daughter dressed like a rice farmer, can we?"

"Thank you, I'd appreciate that."

He gave Iain a clap on the shoulder. "Just make sure you send the bloody ship back, old boy."

EPILOGUE

Everyone was running.

They rushed out of the house, hearts trembling: Mamuchka, Valentina, Uncle Yugevny, Izabel, and Mrs. Lo. Even Papashka, still in his cotton pajamas, was walking as briskly as his frail body allowed, plunging his twin sticks before him, as if some miraculous springtime agility had reinvigorated his eighty-year-old limbs.

Valentina was shouting, "Mammy, Mammy."

Nadia's eyes were streaming with joy, alive with love.

When they reached Nadia they fell on her, engulfed her. Their voices leapt with laughter. Everyone apart from Papashka ended up in a heap, rolling about on the Largo da Sien, giggling wildly through passionate tears.

After several minutes they straightened up.

"Iain," Nadia said, laughing through her tears, smoothing the front of her dress. "This is Valentina."

Iain, dressed in a plaid shirt that was too small for him, looked at the little brown-haired girl and smiled. Her face was slender, slightly frowning. She had big blue Slavic eyes. Blue the colour of the sea. So blue they could have been cut from the sky.

Valentina stared at the man before her, wondering why his droopy left sleeve was pinned behind his back.

"Hello," he said.

Valentina wrapped her arms around her mother's leg, hiding her face, shy at being confronted by this stranger; this stranger, her father.

Iain sat back down on the floor so that his daughter didn't

have to stare up at him. He noticed a little storybook tucked into the crook of her elbow.

"What's that book in your hand?" he asked.

"Beeter Baan," she said, quietly.

"I like Peter Pan. He's one of my favourite heroes. I like Wendy too."

"What happen to y'arm?"

"My arm? Oh, a naughty alligator ate it."

"Just like Capin Hook," she beamed.

"Yes, just like Captain Hook." He stroked her cheek. "What about showing me your house and the room where you play, can you do that for me?"

She nodded and smiled. Her smile melted Iain's heart like chocolate warming on a stove.

Iain got to his feet and offered Valentina his good hand which she took a little shyly. Together they walked back towards the Tabacaria.

Three weeks after their return, it was Valentina's birthday.

"Come on now," Iain said, "I want you all to smile." He and Papashka were dressed up in pink-and-blue clown outfits. Uncle Yugevny sported purple robes and a crown cut out of paper. Valentina wore a thin muslin costume that made her look like a fairy, whilst Nadia and Mamuchka donned dunce caps with big cardboard ears. "This photograph is going out to all our friends."

The flash gun went pop and everybody jumped.

That evening, sitting at the bay seat and looking out into the dusk, Nadia felt a calm descend over her. Out on the Largo da Sien a few children were playing a game of hopscotch as the church bells rang in the distance. With the fragrance of cooking lingering in the air, she placed three candles on the dining table and moments later paused to count the number of guests on her fingers. She set out eleven crystal wineglasses.

Down the hall, Mamuchka and Mrs. Lo were in the

kitchen, making sure to prepare everyone's favourite things. Mamuchka had earlier pawned a gold ring to get her hands on the ingredients that she required. Despite the relative food shortage, there was a roasted duck served with pickled berries for Papashka, Iain and Nadia, cold chicken garnished with tinned apples for Valentina, dried codfish, pumpkin fritters and boiled potatoes for Izabel and her boys, and dark chocolate pudding (made from chocolate powder) for Costa.

"What's next?" Mamuchka asked, sliding the pumpkin fritters out from the oven and wiping her hands and face with her calico apron.

"*Bolo Rei*," said Mrs. Lo. "The birfday cake. It's your specialty."

They worked the dough with their hands, forcing flour through a sieve. Carefully, Mamuchka formed a trough in the pastry and enhanced it with an egg, then she kneaded together butter, lemon zest, pine nuts and raisins, moulding it into a large pie shaped like a wheel. She drizzled warm butter over the top and sprinkled it with sugar, brushing off the excess into a cupped bowl. Finally, she inserted small coins into the sides of the dough before transferring it into the oven.

An hour later the Pereras came through the door bearing gifts, followed not long after by Mrs. Lo, Costa, Senhor Pinto and Anna Rodrigues.

"Who ish a big girl now, eh?" said Costa, almost crushing his god-daughter with the force of his embrace.

"*Parabens!*" Anna cried, giving Valentina a gentle hug.

Valentina tore open her presents as laughter swelled the house. After a few drinks, Nadia stood up and sang the opening verse of a Russian folk song she'd learned as a child. Singing was something she rarely did and when she finished, everyone applauded and Iain planted a kiss on her cheek. A few seconds later he excused himself and said he needed to take in some fresh air. She watched him slip out through the front door.

"Where is he going?" asked Izabel.

Mamuchka and Nadia exchanged glances. "I'll be back in a moment,' said Nadia.

Nadia grabbed her coat and raced down the steps. She followed him through the old town along the cobbled streets. She cut through the back alleyways towards the mouth of the bay.

When she caught up with him they were both a little out of breath.

"It's through here, I'm sure," said Iain. "Mrs. Lee used to live somewhere along here."

As Iain approached the place where he had come so often after Peter Lee's death, he found that only a wasteground and a skeleton of rubble stood at the far end of the street. The ramshackle building behind the Praya Grande was gone, bulldozed to make way for a Red Cross refugee shelter. In its place was a wash of grease slicks and foul-smelling water leading to a black stone wall. All along the wall were sagging lean-tos, rusted metal drums and wooden shanties populated by roaches and weeds. By day the place was deserted, but at night it was seething, lined with hundreds of recumbent bodies crammed under the metal sheeting running over the shelter, covering every available inch.

Nadia turned to look at Iain.

"I'm so sorry," she said. Her voice was quiet.

"I wonder where she's gone," he said, mystified. "I was hoping to bring her back to the party. I wanted her to meet everybody."

A moment later Nadia took his elbow and led him home.

"Strange isn't it," said Iain. "The Lee family's completely gone but here we are united at last."

When they returned home Senhor Pinto broke into a delirious song and Uncle Yugevny filled everyone's glasses to the brim, Cossack-style. Shrieks of laughter and shouts of 'slainte mhath!' and 'na zdorovje!' echoed across the square. Costa raced outside and let off a firecracker, while Papashka

374

entertained Anna with a little jig on his sticks. And when Mamuchka brought in the birthday cake with three candles burning at its centre, Valentina drew in a big breath and blew out the candles in one go.

After dinner, with the plates cleared away and her daughter dozing on the sofa, Nadia went over to stand by the living room doorway. She turned into the corridor to fetch another bottle of Sandeman for Costa then stopped – something pulled her back, made her pause and look round.

The house had gone suddenly quiet and everyone was watching Valentina, asleep like an angel with a blanket draped over her tiny shoulders. Nadia looked at each and every person then remembered her father's words from years before: *The problem with us Russians is that we spend all our time reminiscing and forget about the present. We must love what we have now before it has vanished forever.*

Nadia's eyes grew misty. She felt happy. She felt blessed. The smells of cooking still filled the house. She lingered by the doorway for a long moment, surrounded by the people she loved, looking at her family, at her friends.

The Gods were awake once more and they were smiling.